Brydus, The Mark

The Dark Days Chronicles Vol. 1

Norma Lopez-Stewart

Table of Contents

Dedication

I would like to dedicate this novel to my wonderful husband, Gregory Stewart, who saw my dream and worked endless hours on this project.

To my family and friends who encouraged, supported, and believed in my vision.

Acknowledgments

To my husband Gregory Stewart, who encouraged me every day, pushing me forward and believing in my dreams…I love you, baby!

My children, who make me proud every single day with their love and support when I needed them the most. The best gift God ever gave me…I love you forever.

Special thanks to family, my daughter Melissa Marshall Lopez, brother Roy Lopez, great friends Leroy Reber, Raulston & Tamara, and Lesley Kelly, who helped make this possible.

To all the wonderful family and friends who prayed for me…thank you, I love you.

I would further like to acknowledge:

Joann Lentz – final draft editor

Caroline Ortiz – draft editor

Gregory Stewart – cover illustrator & book trailer

Danae Savignon – book cover model

Photography by: Mai Edwards of Mai Memories Photograph

About the Author

Norma Lopez-Stewart was born in New York City but spent most of her life in Reading, PA, and now resides in Tampa, FL. She's an author with a great passion for storytelling. She has worked on a series of strong female leads, entitled, *The Dark Days Chronicles*, in which she uses her Latin heritage to bring her characters to life.

Prologue

It looked like just yesterday, when the world was alive, and our future goals were within our grasp, and there was nothing we could not accomplish if we put our minds to it.

I remember the laugher coming from the children as they played in the lush green parks without a care in the world. I remember watching budding romances, young love in bloom. Couples dreaming of retiring and traveling to far-off lands, with just a simple train ride, across the great spans of the world. All were living for the moment.

Imagine a world filled with beauty and tranquility. Man was in harmony with nature and with each other. There were no wars, and only a few third-world countries still suffered from famine. No threats from neighboring countries, and no conspiracies to one-up each other. The world was finally at peace.

Drilling for fossil fuel was no longer allowed. Food was in great abundance in many of the major countries, however, some of the third-world countries still struggled. The borders of all nations were open to all that wished to travel. Technology was so far advanced that everything was at our fingertips. Oceans and space were constantly monitored for natural threats such as tsunamis or asteroids. It was as if the universe itself knew that man was tranquil at last. We felt safe and believed the best that life had to offer on this planet was yet to come.

However, some radical groups argued that we had gone too far with science and technology and did not heed the warnings of ancient writings, like the Bible and other religious books.

Discrimination and prejudice had been eradicated using technology and enhanced cosmetic procedures that erased color from the ethnic population. Fetuses were used as blank canvases, born as the parents designed them. We had balanced the races.

The air, rivers, and our oceans were clean. Most of the broadcast's news had brighter and more pleasant stories to report, such as human-interest stories, the latest advances in cosmetology and technology, and how to make your life more exciting.

Diseases and sickness were at an all-time low, as science had made great strides in ridding us of abnormalities in an individual's genetics and DNA.

People were ignorant of what was happening elsewhere. As long as it did not interrupt their everyday lives, it did not matter.

I, Nylaya, witnessed firsthand the carefree lifestyle of those days. It was a time that I will not soon forget. Yes, some might say those were times of vanity, abundance, and excess.

I once read an old scripture that quoted that God himself was sorrowful that he had created man. His reasoning was the wickedness of man's heart. Seeing all that we have accomplished over the years, I often wondered if God had changed his mind about us.

We had forgotten the Great Depression, slavery, and the Holocaust. The heartbreaking truth of what humanity does in the name of God. Those hiding behind the walls of secrecy and deceptive teachings, lest we forget that pride cometh before the fall. Boasting that we do not need anything or anyone, that we are invincible. Boasting that nothing can touch us! That we are too big to fall! That was until the tiniest enemies spiraled us into what we now call…

"The Dark Days"

Chapter 1: State of the World

World Holocaust – The Dark Days
August 7, 2242- Agua Blanca –South America

There was such a significant difference between the 22nd and 23rd centuries. Technology was something people took for granted. Ninety percent of the world's households were connected in one way or another. It was a great time to be alive, and for most of the world's populations, the gap between countries was narrower than ever.

North America was finally completely energy-sufficient, with major solar grids that powered the United States. This provided more than enough power to exceed the nation's demands. Therefore, the surplus was sold to countries with money or had something to barter.

Most major illnesses were under control with childhood vaccinations or simple remedies. The economy was growing at such a remarkable rate that nothing could stand in the way of its progress. The coast-to-coast speedways allowed passengers to ride with ease and arrive at their destinations in a timely fashion, to and from most of the major cities in the United States. This opened the job market and travel for those with high-powered jobs or important meetings.

The creation of **The International Transporters** was an underground super nuclear train system that would permit the populace to ride from the United States to anywhere in

Europe or Asia in less than six hours or from Canada to Florida in two hours. It was the fastest system ever built. People could work in almost any part of the country and commute easily daily. Your typical car or local transportation systems made it easy to run errands, go to malls, shopping trips, and take the children back and forth to school. They were best used for short trips. The new cars were solar-powered and affordable. They were sturdy and easy to maintain, as were the buses, trucks, and other transports.

The Human Cell Cosmetics Corporation

A breakthrough in beauty

On September 10, 2058, the Human Cell Cosmetics Corporation discovered they could safely change the human eye color – a breakthrough using a new procedure called *The Gene Molecule Formula*. Five years later, they were able to change human skin color using the same type of genome. It was costly, however, those that could afford these procedures plunged into them as if they were just another cosmetic enhancement.

Nevertheless, capitalism has its downsides. In order to make this mind-blowing and revolutionary breakthrough available and affordable to everyone, they began experimentations on the poor third-world countries looking for extra income.

This craze interested other companies in joining the cause, racing to create a product that would beat the competition. So, in the name of beauty on-demand, you were now able to decide not only the sex of your child but what hair color, eye color, and skin color a couple's unborn child would have. The Human Cell Cosmetics Corporation made trillions of dollars by giving the people what they wanted.

These highly aggressive experiments were performed on people of color to show the results from a darker skin pigment to lighter shades. The transformation was remarkable. Children were born absent of the rich melanin that gave them the beautiful pigment of their skin. Millions of people of color lost what made them who they were. These huge corporations preyed on the poor who volunteered to put food on their tables.

Because of the income from the experimental trials, they had more money and opportunities than ever to give their children a better life and educate them for a better future.

The company's representatives held huge seminars showing the advantages of being part of these experiments, and the poor, naively, took this opportunity as godsent. The idea of having the means to take care of their families took on a new perspective. These corporations exploited uneducated people who did not see anything wrong with having lighter skin or different colored eyes. As children were born without color, people did not realize they were selling their culture. When people became lighter, color began to fade, and future generations lost their uniqueness. It was gradual at first, and in the beginning, it was just another crazy trend.

There were trendsetters who agreed it was the most incredible breakthrough ever. Others fought to keep their legacy alive, but it was too late. The process could not be reversed, and those who tried, failed and were left to live with horrible consequences. These corporations were uncontrollable and took over people's lives, controlling them. The new products they developed were extraordinary, and people ran to get the latest craze.

GLOBAL SCIENCE INTERNATIONAL
The Institution of Abnormal and Deadly Diseases

AGUA BLANCA, SOUTH AMERICA

This highly sponsored organization was known to the outside world as the **Institute of Abnormal and Deadly Diseases**. Billions of dollars came pouring into this fake institution. Millions of people raised money under the banner of research with the hopes of ending the misery of strange, devastating diseases that still plagued the people of this century.

The commercials were so heartbreaking even those with small incomes felt it was their duty to help find a cure for these illnesses to protect future generations. Educated professionals with great hope held huge fundraisers. The stockholders in GSI knew they had the biggest cash cow of the century.

From the air, the three-story structure lay beautifully among acres of lush land. It had a fortified electric fence and a landing pad for aircrafts. Sharpshooters guarded the only road that led to and from this facility.

When investors visited the facility, a sympathetic host guided them up the marble steps, which opened into a spectacular lobby. These investors spoke to actors posing as patients who were supposed to be receiving treatment. These fake patients urged investors to help them, pleading for a cure for the disease. These actors told their stories on cue, claiming a cure was close, but more money was needed to accomplish this goal. They provided fake tears to make it more believable. The more tears they could muster, the bigger the paycheck.

These rich visitors were wined and dined to help loosen their wallets. They were beguiled into believing the charade about all the new medical breakthroughs that would benefit people worldwide. Investors were blinded by the institutions' good intentions. However, they were unaware that the real dangers lay ten floors below. Right under their feet in high-tech laboratories.

GSI was the headquarters and residence for the most famous scientists from all over the world. Each country of power had its representatives working toward the same goal: creating weapons more lethal than the other, with the purpose of controlling populations and societies.

Ninety-eight percent of the scientists lived in exclusive, massive complexes. They were afforded a beautiful living space with all the comforts of a home. The ten-story underground structure was equipped with stores of all kinds, including barbershops, beauty salons, movie theaters, bars, and even golf courses.

One of the biggest benefits for the scientists was that they could bring their families to live with them. So, schools, internet teaching, and homeschooling kept the families together. The GSI provided warmth and wealth to its employed scientists.

Other assistance workers were compensated with high wages and were kept in the dark about the truth. They were not privy to what was going on in restricted areas. If anyone began to get nosey, they would disappear from their apartments, never to be seen again.

The villagers' livelihood also came from GSI, under the banner of the greatest research facility in the world. They were proud to work for GSI, even if they were underpaid and overworked. They believed in what the institution stood for. They had no idea how dangerous it truly was. To keep them pacified, GSI built free health clinics, schools and dug wells for clean drinking water. Even when strange tales and conspiracy theories began to spread, the villagers were still dependent on the resources GSI provided and paid no heed to them. There were rumors of whole villages disappearing, leaving behind only traces that it was a populated area at one time. GSI reassured those who questioned the whereabouts of these missing villagers that they were relocated to a better place and the gullible villagers accepted any explanation the GSI community organizers gave them.

After a while, no one noticed when people disappeared in the middle of the night. These were populations out of the loop; they could not be traced or missed. Native outsiders, they called them. Expendable subjects who gave very little to modern society.

GSI had giant incinerators to dispose of dangerous materials and cremate animals. The organization was not held accountable for what they were doing. Employees kept quiet for fear of losing their jobs or, worse, going missing.

People lived carefree lives, going about their daily routine. It was a time of peace all over the world since oil was not in demand. The world welcomed the belief that peace could be achieved, but the peace agreements were only for outward appearances. The quest for world dominance was fought on an intellectual level. The question was who truly had the strongest and deadliest weapons that would not only destroy the delicate balance of the earth's natural resources but could kill hundreds of thousands with just a small vial. This was done under great secrecy on the tenth level of GSI's state-of-the-art super laboratory. For all purposes, as long as the stockholders were making money, they did not care about the destruction left in its wake.

An unnatural imbalance was created, and no one or nothing could bring these giants down; the stockholders were rich, and they felt invincible… or so they thought.

On *August 07, 2242,* something happened that shattered the world. In the remote jungle of Agua Blanca in South America, an earthquake shook the foundations of GSI's underground facility, which carried the real name:

<u>The Development of Germ and Viral Warfare</u>
<u>Experimentations</u>

Even with all the precautions taken against any assault from the outside, they had underestimated the destruction that came from a natural source. GSI never considered the obvious; they had not contemplated nature's fury that came from beneath. There were no records of an earthquake in that area for more than two hundred years. Because of its seclusion, the company concluded it was the safest place to operate in secrecy. Far away from any kind of investigation, keeping the rest of the world thinking it was fighting strange and deadly diseases.

Headlines: Major Earthquakes Ravages Central America; August 07, 2242

The sirens and flashing red lights shrieked throughout every floor of the underground compound. None of their drills prepared them for the earth's shifting, caused by a major earthquake that shook the foundation of the underground city. The first wave knocked equipment from walls and tables. Scientists scurried to make sure what they were working on did not escape the safety precautions in place. They looked at each other and smiled, hopeful that the damage was not severe. Engineers hurried to assess the damage and announced confidently that the damage was minimal. However, they were not prepared for the subsequent impact, which took them by surprise. It was too late when seismologists saw the massive wave coming; they could do nothing to deter the destruction.

Like a dragon on the prowl, the earthquake seemed to grow stronger as it came close to the structure. There were no more warnings except a loud booming sound as the floors began to collapse, initiating massive explosions. Workers tried to claw their way up the stairs while doors were automatically locked down as a precaution to prevent any dangerous contaminants from escaping topside.

The first tremor shook the foundation, but the second wave cracked the underground city into thousands of pieces. The massive explosions killed countless people who lived and worked there. The few that escaped died shortly after. The safety measures left hundreds of people crawling towards the massive doors supposed to keep them safe from their research and experiments.

The tremors continued shaking the earth for eight days, bringing destruction to everything in its path. Any safety measures they had put in place were hopeless against this vicious foe.

For days, smoke and pestilence spouted into the atmosphere. Nothing could stop the release of powerful, deadly germs, viruses, and airborne contaminants that escaped into the atmosphere, mutating as they took flight.

News reporters tried to calm the pandemonium that had erupted around the world, stating that no one particular deadly virus could possibly live outside in the elements. Nevertheless, they were mutating and changing at an extraordinary rate.

The media gave so many false reports that people did not know what to believe, considering their own governments did not know what they were up against. The only people who knew anything were dead.

Everyone on earth saw the dark cloud of death coming and could not stop the impending doom. People were ordered to stay home and seal their doors and windows as if duct tape could keep death away. Millions died in the first twenty-four hours. Like in horror movies, there was nowhere to go or hide from the destruction. All over the world, people dropped dead in the middle of the streets or while they were helping others. The lucky ones just died in their sleep, a much humane end of their lives.

Even those that lived within the Luna Space Station's population decided to come back to earth and join their families. Scientists on the Luna Space Station worked around the clock to develop a solution. The task was overwhelming, and after a while of watching the world crumble beneath them, they abandoned their stations and returned to earth. They wanted to see if they could help the suffering, as whole families were lost to this monster or to the paranoia of people who went overboard about the catastrophe around them.

The elderly and young children were hit the hardest. Powerful governments all over the world collapsed as people tried to protect their loved ones. Scientists fought with everything they could to come up with something, anything, that would allow them to fight the beast, but without knowing what they were fighting, they also fell victim to the darkness.

End of the world purist fanatics and religious groups sprung up everywhere, adding more confusion to the chaos. They destroyed whole communities, stating they were sent by God to purify the land, once again killing millions in the process. One of the last news releases showed thousands of people running wild in the streets, setting fires and explosives to all they could, screaming, *"It's the end of the world. God's wrath is upon us for the vanity of the world!"* which worsened the paranoia.

Lesser populated islands did not know what to do with their dead. They had to load boats with dead bodies and push them out to sea to be incinerated on the mainland in an attempt to stop the disease-ridden corpses from spreading to the rest of the population. It was the same scenario all over the planet.

The world was in chaos. Once the darkness lifted, a true picture of the aftermath that ruled the earth for three months was finally seen. Skyscrapers, massive buildings, and bridges crumbled under the massive fires. With so many people dying, bodies contaminated some of the drinking water, and others died without knowledge from diseases that could have been prevented. Billions of people perished.

Whether it was China, Europe, or Russia, whether their population was small or large, not one part of the world was spared. The beast demolished communities and destroyed metropolitan areas. The earth was melting down without a savior to come and rescue it from destruction.

Headlines: Billions Die As Whole Cities Collapse

Headlines: These Are the Dark Days – The World Apocalypse and the End of Times

Humankind scrambled to make sense of what was left and what was needed to survive to begin picking up the pieces of humanity. Humanity continued even in the midst of chaos and uncertainties. Small communities banded together to create a sense of normalcy in their lives and for protection. They tried to use their skills and few resources to start over again.

They created colonies and tribal communities, and once again, the tribes of the New America were formed to survive. Very few of the modern technologies functioned. The Inter-Atlantic transits were rendered useless because of radiation. Most of the technology that had made people's lives easier was lost. Anything that remained was bombed or torched by fanatic groups because they deemed it against their religion. So much was lost, and the world went dark and silent. All that was good died with the bad. People used paper money to keep warm, since now it was now considered worthless.

Out of the seed of men and women, another empire would spring. An empire that would not repeat the sins of the past. They would rebuild a better nation and a better class of people.

This is where our story begins, twenty-five years after everything ended in disaster. People rose from the ashes to create a better world, but to do so, they had to go back to a more primitive way of living.

Chapter 2: Before the Dark Days

Valley of God

Who are the people of the Valley of God? After years of trying to make changes in a country where the working class was misunderstood, a group of families decided they had had enough. An influential committee came together to form the National Committee of Advanced Living (NCAL). This committee was made up of ordinary working-class people. Two hundred families banded together financially and began to buy land in the area of the Tiadaghton State Park in Pennsylvania. The park, once a jewel for vacationers, was now abandoned for lack of funds. It lay in ruins with its abandoned buildings and campgrounds that once held so much promise. The 215,500 acres were bought over the span of ten years.

By the time the land was secured, the movement had grown to over 20,000 families. They ranged from doctors to mechanics, scientists, and gardeners. The families were put through rigorous background checks. They had lawyers that created and wrote their own charters, and special laws were put in place to keep the integrity of their new way of life.

Another ten years went by before NCAL could clear enough land to build homes, hospitals, and schools. The committee members were people who stayed within the perimeter of the law. They were determined to make a better life and future for the children born into the new society they were developing.

They worked toward a life without the influence of a giant organization that controlled every aspect of their lives. They had children, without being forced to choose gender or color. The NCAL stayed away from the insurance companies that wanted to get a kickback from organizations that forced consumers to pick and choose what their child would look like and how many children a couple could have.

They wanted to grow their own food without being fined every time they failed to use the pesticides that the large corporations controlled.

However, life was becoming more unbearable for NCAL; they were getting opposition from all sides. The new settlers were determined to break away, to be free at last, and the only way to do this was to control who came into their new communities.

Homes were built that used the resources surrounding them to generate their own power sources. They had a goal that they would be self-sufficient in every way within twenty years. They manufactured their own clothing, grew their own food, and had everything a community needed to prosper and educate their children. In twenty years, they not only became a growing threat to the giant corporations, but they also became a closed society. A hundred years later, after fighting back and forth, the people renamed their home The Valley of God, and they settled into an exciting way of life for themselves.

The families came from all cultures. They were encouraged to embrace who they were and share it with others. The children of the Valley were taught how to value the sacrifices their ancestors made to have the kind of life that gave them the freedoms they now enjoyed.

They were free from outside influences, but the world around them was changing, and as the years went by, disturbing news from the outside continued to filter into the communities through their guarded borders. Many went looking for the Valley of God but would become disoriented with the density of the forest and usually turned back before they encountered the armed guards.

During the Dark Days, they were prepared for what was coming, but they were unaware of the world's devastation beyond their walls. They thanked God that they suffered very few casualties and were relieved the Valley was spared from what the rest of the world was experiencing. The Valley communities embraced their neighbors who lost loved ones to help them heal. The scouts returned with the news that gave horrendous accounts of the aftermath. Their mission was to bring back whatever they could find to preserve what was lost; books, pictures, and anything they could salvage.

On one of the missions, one of the men stumbled upon an Iron Safeguard Storage Facility. They were overjoyed and celebrated the precious discovery. After securing the site from thieves, they were happy that a part of the past would be secured for the future.

The people of the Valley of God continued on and refused to be part of the world, but those born with "The Mark" were taught to survive and sent into the same world that The Valley of God's people fought hard to escape. It was the law.

Chapter 3: The Mark

January 22, 2251

Despite ten hours of labor, poor Christina struggled to bring a new life into the world. After two miscarriages, she prayed that God let this baby live. Reina's hands shook as she continued to keep a cold compress on her daughter's forehead. Beads of perspiration ran down her face as the hours ticked by, and the baby took its time progressing down the birth canal.

Reina closed the bedroom curtains, keeping out the light and making the room as calm as possible. She had delivered other babies, but this was her grandchild, and it terrified her with each contraction her daughter had. She always had encouraging words for the many mothers she serviced. But for her own child, all she could think of was the pain that she was in. Trying to feel useful, she continued pressing the cold cloth down her daughter's face.

Christina tried her best not to overreact to the pain because she had refused any relief. "Take something for the pain, baby," Alfonso whispered in her ear.

She smiled at him between contractions, "I've got to do this my way; it will be worth it," she whimpered as another contraction shook her.

Alfonso turned his face away, "Mama Reina, maybe you can talk some sense into your stubborn daughter," he said, frustrated and scared.

Reina smiled nervously, "I have to let her do it her way, don't worry, it will soon be over."

Christina smiled, "I promised that I would give you a perfect child, my love. Just bear with me." He kissed her with saddened eyes as he tried to be strong for her sake. Her mother knelt by her bedside, crying as she started to pray. Reina knew how much her daughter suffered trying to hold on to the other two pregnancies. Lying in bed for weeks and then losing them. It took her months to bring Christina out of the overwhelming depression and pain of possibly not having any children of her own.

Reina remembered how Alfonso pleaded with her to help with his wife's grief. "I can't lose her, too," he said, crying into his mother-in-law's shoulder. Reina's strength kept him sane as days turned into months, and Christina refused to let him touch her. She wanted to divorce him so he could marry someone who could give him children. Alfonso would get angry and storm out of the house. He knew that Christina would eventually pull herself together again, and she was also thankful that he always came back. After all, she loved him. With each pregnancy, she became stronger and determined to have a child to complete their family.

All Christina ever wanted was to be a mother. When she and Alfonso got married, they wanted to start a family right away. However, month after month, when her monthly visitor appeared, she grew fearful that she would not be able to give him a child. Alfonso tried to be supportive, but he was hurting. After the two miscarriages, he tried to assure Christina that he loved her, and if a child was not in the cards for them, they could always adopt. However, no matter how hard he tried, there was no comfort for her until she tried again.

This pregnancy seemed different. The baby was growing perfectly, and there was no bleeding or strange, unexpected pain like the others. Christina prayed every day until the doctor said the baby would survive after passing the 35-week mark. She became a different person, and her happiness began to show on her face. All her friends and family gave her an exceptional baby shower. She was glowing. Alfonso took pictures of her and her belly to show the baby when he or she was older.

The next few weeks were like a dream for Christina. The doctor said the baby was in position and she would be able to deliver naturally. Her mother and mother-in-law were going to help deliver the baby because of their previous experiences with deliveries.

Christina wanted to have her baby at home, but the labor was worse than she had anticipated. Reina held her daughter's hands and prayed as she had never prayed before in her life. "Holy God, please let this child live, let your grace and mercy be on my daughter and son-in-law who want a child to complete their family," Christina let out another excruciating moan.

"How much longer will you let her suffer, my Lord?" Reina begged.

Alfonso put another pot of tea on the stove and said a silent prayer. He could hear his wife's cries from downstairs, where family and friends waited patiently. They looked at him with great concern, and he tried to smile to let them know he was all right.

"How is she doing, son?" His father, Alfonso Sr., asked.

Alfonso shrugged his shoulders, "They keep on saying soon… but that was two hours ago."

His father gave him a much-needed embrace. "Everything's going to be fine, son… it's a boy; they are always harder," he smiled.

"I guess you're right. I remember Mama saying I was no picnic."

"Go to your wife. Help her push my grandson into the world."

His mother, Mitra, hugged him as she ran past him to get more towels. "Honey, I'm going to need you to help her push."

He grabbed his mother's hand gently, "I'll be right up, Mama," trying to assure her he was on board. Alfonso took the stairs slowly, pausing at the door before he entered. Christina was sitting in the birthing position. He started to panic when he saw the blood, and tears sprung to his eyes. Exhausted, Christina fell onto the bed, so Reina helped her back into the birthing position.

"Help me, Al. She's weak, but it's time."

Alfonso gathered his strength and sat behind her to help her sit in position. "It's time to push, baby," he whispered in her ear.

"The baby is crowning," Reina cried, "That's it. Help your wife as she pushes your child into the world."

Mitra took her place on the other side of Christina, "Give me some big pushes honey ready… push!" Mitra urged. Christina took a deep breath and pushed with all she had as Mitra massaged her belly.

"I don't have any more strength," she cried out of breath.

"One more big push, honey," her mother urged again, "I can see the top of his head, one more big push. Come on, sweetheart." Christina took one more deep breath and pushed with all she had, sending the baby into her mother's arms. Everyone laughed hearing the baby's cry.

"It's a girl, new papa..." Reina exclaimed excitedly. Alfonso cried when Reina put the tiny baby into his waiting arms. The baby continued to wail at the top of her lungs. Christina laughed, exhausted but thrilled to hear the cries from the baby she so desperately wanted.

"You did it, baby," he said, kissing Christina's face.

"Thank you for believing in me, sweetheart. Mama... where's my gift from God?" Christina asked, overwrought but smiling for the first time in months.

"Let me clean her up a little for you, sweetie," Mitra answered, taking the screaming baby to the dressing table to weigh and clean her up, "7lbs 14oz. twenty-one inches, what a girl." Reina continued to help Christina with the afterbirth, getting her comfortable so she could put her baby to her breast.

Alfonso kissed her, still fighting back his tears, "She's a beautiful baby, like her mama," he said, still very emotional.

"I want to see my angel... I want to count every finger and toes," Christina smiled.

"Son, can you come over here and help me, please..." He did not like the tone of her voice.

"Mama, what's wrong?" He whispered, trying not to alarm the already exhausted Christina.

"Look," she murmured. Reina pointed to the purple mark on her lower back, "She has the mark." Every hair on his body stood on end. His mouth dropped as he looked back at his wife, who was waiting patiently for her baby. The baby cooed as he wrapped her in a pretty yellow blanket and gently put her into her mother's arms. Christina's smile faded as she held her baby.

"Mama… what's wrong with my baby… why is she so dark? Is she breathing alright?"

"She's perfect, love," Reina said as she took the baby, holding her in the light, then realized why the other two were so quiet. She held her breath, "She is a blessing, Christina, a true blessing from God," she placed her into her mother's arms again.

Christina cried and kissed her baby's tiny fist. "Oh, my God," she cried out, shocked as tears flooded her eyes. She knew right away the future of her child.

Reina tried to comfort her daughter, "It's a blessing, sweetheart, God sent you a special angel," she began to cry as their tears mingled. "You are honored among many women."

Christina let out a heart-wrenching scream, "All I wanted was a baby, a part of Alfonso! I didn't ask for a special child!" Reina hurried to her medical kit. "All I wanted was a baby! Why, Mama? Why?" Reina sedated her own child as she continued to sob uncontrollably.

Alfonso could only watch his hysterical wife, "Mi amor, it's our child, she's beautiful, absolutely perfect," he kissed Christina over and over. Tears escaped his sorrowful eyes as he kissed his beautiful daughter. How could this happen? He thought. They had waited so long for a child, and now the one that lived, they would have to give up.

"She will love her baby. Now take your child downstairs to meet her family," his mother urged. Christina fell asleep. Reina was still in shock. *Everyone would treat them differently*, she thought. The child will be favored above all the rest. She will be raised and supported by the community. There will be a great celebration throughout the communities of the Valley tonight, but not for the parents or families of the child with the mark.

Alfonso and Mitra carried the baby downstairs, where the others were patiently waiting. They were so happy when they heard the baby's cries that they cheered. Everyone had been waiting in the living room. When Alfonso appeared at the entrance, their excitement mounted. However, when they saw Alfonso's face, they knew something was wrong with the baby.

"Son, what's wrong?" His father asked, concerned.

Alfonso shook his head and forced a smile. "Nothing, nothing, Papa… she's absolutely perfect." When he uncovered her, they all realized why he was upset.

"She has the mark," they whispered as he held his beautiful newborn to his chest, a full head of dark black hair, skin reddish-brown, and the purple mark on her tailbone, the indicator. Everyone was shocked. The family surrounded him and prayed for the future of the gifted child. A child that would be theirs for a few years, and when the time came, would be sent into the outside world.

It was the law, written over two hundred years before she was born. She would go into a world of chaos and unknown dangers. The community would have to prepare her to fight for her life outside the safety and sanctity of their world.

The Law

Thus, was written into law: in the year of our Lord, January 21, 2175, by the first honorable settlers of 'The Valley of God'.

It is written that those born with The Mark are chosen by God. Therefore, they must be sent into the world. They carry the true identity of a lost people, a people who were stripped of their true color. They must learn, by any means necessary, how to survive on the outside. The community of The Valley of God must

provide all educational methods to create an environment of confidence and self-reliance.

It is written that by the age of eighteen, this individual must be prepared to seek their own destiny and shall not return to, or have contact with the Valley, for a period of two years. If it is found that the individual is still not fit to assimilate into the outside world, the elders of the community and committee members will make the determination. Whereby this individual must have the ability to survive and enrich the outside world.

As a community, we cannot allow the world to forget us. We were the people of color, and our children will restore our identity. Therefore, as we send our children into the same world we fought to escape from, it is not a punishment, but a sin to keep such treasures to ourselves and deprive the world of their beauty.

Moreover, as our community grieves for the absence of our children, we know they were meant for greatness, and therefore we give this gift to the world.

Written and signed in pain of blood and tears into law by the following members:

Manuel Lopez, Ricardo Bonilla, Christian Brown, George Sanders, Millie Rosario, Tamika Johnson, Leroy Harris, Ebonique Stewart, Gail Wilson, Janet Ford, Andrew Cornish, Silvia Jackson, Ana Marie Rodriguez, Ming Lee, Namit Gupta, Joseph Lombardi,

Haku Mossman, Lola Smith, Roberto Nunez, Richard Wynn, Kazim Husain, Sami Balasubramanium, Maria Greco, Tabitha Kihike, Dalaja Mehta, Suyapa Altmirano, Beba Sanchez, Jayan Narayanan, Riana Tebaldi, Jun Zhou, Pia Gambimo, Lakshya Dutta, Susan Chong,

Signed into law - January 21, 2175

It had begun with Nylaya Roman Leroy. She was the first daughter of Epifania Cruz and Jerome Leroy Roman. She was born before the Dark Days, so she knew the world before the great fall. She was the first to leave The Valley of God and set the tone for the others to come

Chapter 4: The Journey

Christina collapsed against the closed door, clutching the letter to her chest. From deep in her soul, an agonizing cry escaped her lips. She slid to the floor, cursing between sobs. From the other room, Alfonso watched her briefly, dreading to go near her, knowing the content of the letter. Nothing could prepare them for this day. There would be no words to soothe her pain and anger. Slowly, he made his way towards his lovely wife as she sat on the floor. Gently picked her up, then kissed her teary face. "Baby, you knew it was coming," he whispered.

The knot in her throat made it hard to speak, "Why our child?" She said in a voice just above a whisper, "Why does it have to be our baby?" She cried. Christina clung to him, wanting to feel his strong arms around her. As tears streamed down her face, she buried her face in Alfonso's chest. "Oh God… help me, please," she sobbed. Alfonso carried her to the sofa, sitting her in his lap, so she had someone to hold.

"Christina, it's time to talk. For weeks you have avoided this subject… it's not going away," she hung her head. "Sweetheart," he lifted her chin to face him, "You knew this was coming for months. The council was very diplomatic about the whole decision."

"She's my baby… she's still a baby. How can I let her go?" She argued, trying to come to terms with her daughter's future.

"Hey… look at me… she will always be our baby. I knew this was not going to be easy for us. Nicole is also having a difficult time understanding why her sister has to be sent out into the world," Alfonso tried hard to keep it together. On the outside, he was calm as a rock, but he was falling apart inside.

"Al, is she ready to face the outside? Please, tell me the truth," she asked, begging him to be honest, clinging to his shirt.

Alfonso rubbed her shoulders as he pondered the question, "I tried to find a reason for her to stay, but the truth is that she is more than ready. Even Master Lu Jung and Mistress Chong are impressed with her ability to protect herself. She is highly skilled."

Christina's head was starting to throb. She rested her head against his chest. "You know when she was a baby, I would keep her out of the sun to see if her skin would lighten," she sniffled, "And maybe her eyes would begin to turn green, then I could yell into the street that my child is normal, she is just like everyone else."

Alfonso tried not to laugh as he kissed her neck, "Look, when she was born, I cried. All I wanted was to hold my child and be the best parent I could be. I read the law and the reason why our child was so special. Though it does not seem like it now, we were blessed, and I try to see things from our elder's perspective. When Nylaya was sent forth, the world was a different place, and she helped mold so many people's lives. The elder's question; do we have the right to deprive the world of what used to be? People of color were the dominant people of the world. Sometimes, I think keeping her here in the Valley would be a mistake. As much as I hate the idea, I know it's the right thing to do… to let her go," Alfonso started to get emotional, "And that is why… I have busted my ass to make sure she had the best instructors and teachers I can get to train her." Tears ran down his cheeks. He tried hard not to let his wife see how much it affected him. Christina had never thought about Al's feelings. She only considered her own heartbreak.

She caressed his face, "I'm sorry… I know how much you adore her, and I know how much you will miss her."

"Sweetheart, since she was old enough to walk, we've done everything together. Thank God we have Nicole. I can give her the time she needs to develop her gift."

"Nicole is a handful, but I wouldn't have it any other way," Christina said, relieved.

"I know one thing. We have to control our emotions in front of her. Brydus is already nervous. If she sees how upset we are, it's going to be harder for her when it's time for her departure."

She hugged his neck, thanking God for Alfonso and his support, "I know you're right, and I promise I will do my best to hold back the waterfalls," she agreed.

Alfonso squeezed her tight, kissing her neck. "Mmm...I know I talk a lot, but I'm going to trust God with my daughter's future."

"I have to believe that God will protect her, but it is hard to let go."

They held each other for a long time, letting reality soak in. A few weeks from now, Brydus would start her journey into the unknown.

During supper that evening, Brydus was unusually quiet and preoccupied. Nicole dominated the whole evening from the moment they sat down to eat. With her fiery red, out-of-control hair, Nicole bounced around the kitchen, looking at the clock, hoping her father would finish eating.

"Papi, I don't mean to rush you, but the clock is ticking," she pouted.

"Oh really, the clock is going to keep on ticking if I make you stay home," he teased, winking at his wife.

"Okay, Papi, I'm sorry," she took a deep breath, "Take your time. I'll be over here by the door when you're finished," she replied sweetly. This was a big deal for

Nicole. She had finally convinced her father to allow her to go with her best friend for a sleepover party. Her energy level was through the roof.

Christina watched Brydus play with her food all evening, "Brydus, honey, are you not feeling well? After dinner, I need you to try on your winter cape. I have to make some last-minute alterations before I pack it," Christina said, not letting Brydus' demeanor bother her.

Brydus tried to force a smile. "I just have a lot on my mind. I have to meet Derrick later."

Christina exchanged a concerned look with Alfonso who rolled his eyes at the sound of Derrick's name.

Nicole sat across from her father with a huge smile, watching him take his last bite of food. "Papi, please... I don't want to miss a thing," Nicole repeated, throwing some apples and oranges into her bag. "In case I get hungry," she giggled.

"Calm down, princess. I'll get you there in plenty of time." She rushed from her mother to her sister, kissing them repeatedly.

"You behave yourself, young lady," her mother warned ahead of time. Nicole could sometimes hurt someone's feelings if they did not understand her.

"Don't I always, Mami? I'll be on my best behavior and make you proud of me," she saluted them, hugging her mother again. "Papi, I'll be outside," she escaped, letting the door slam behind her before he could tell her to stop.

"That girl is going to drive me crazy," he said. "I'm going to drop her off and then stop by Dee Parker's place. She's having trouble with one of the animals," he said, kissing them before he left.

Christina was hoping that Brydus would open up on her own. After pinning up the hem of her cape, she could tell Brydus' mind was far away. "So, sweetheart, is there anything you want to talk about? You were so quiet during dinner… is it about your trip?" Brydus sat at the edge of the bed. She ran her hand over the beautiful gray fur cape her mother had spent so many weeks sewing for her.

"It's lovely, Mami, so simple yet so beautiful. I wish the rest of my life were as simple… I do have something very important to…" she hesitated, "To talk to you about," she looked down at her hands. "Derrick has asked me to marry him… he said it would keep me from having to leave."

Christina tried not to overreact to the news. She turned away from Brydus, not wanting her to notice how much his name alone bothered her, "Wow… this is sudden. How long have you two been talking about marriage?"

Brydus looked at her mother, meeting her gaze. Confusion shadowed her face, and eyes pleaded for understanding. "Not long," she shrugged her shoulders,

"He's been bummed out about me leaving. Derrick said this would be the answer for us to be together."

Christina sat down next to Brydus and caressed her hair. *She is so young,* Christina thought to herself, wanting to spare her daughter much pain and heartache. She wanted to shelter Brydus from all the evils she would face. However, marriage to Derrick would be one of the biggest mistakes she could make. Christina was relieved that she spoke to her first before bringing up the matter with her father. He would not be as tactful delivering his response.

Christina knew how to handle Brydus. She had to approach the problem in a way to make her see what kind of life she would have with Derrick. The only way she knew how was to try to understand her reasoning and let her come up with her own conclusion.

"Brydus, sweetie, marriage is a serious step. This is not something you just jump into in a few weeks. Let me ask you, do you love him?" Christina fished for a truthful answer. Brydus could only stare at her wide-eyed and confused, a question she asked herself a million times.

"Brydus, my beloved daughter, don't make this mistake because of fear. Search your heart and tell me… do you love him? Do you love him so much that you can't wait to see him when you're apart?" Brydus turned her face so her mother could not read her expression. "What do you feel when he kisses you? These are very important questions, my love."

"I don't know, Mami. I like him a lot, but... I do not know if I love him, not as you and Papi love each other. I watch the way you two look at and touch each other. I think I'm missing that in our relationship, but Derrick said that love will grow."

"Honey," she held her face tenderly in her hand, making Brydus look at her. "When your Papi and I married, we were madly in love. When he touched me, my knees grew weak, and when we kissed, sometimes we would have to hold back our passion, especially when children came into the picture," she giggled.

Brydus' chin started to quiver as she tried to hold back her tears. "Sweetie, sometimes love can grow out of a loveless marriage, but sometimes... resentment takes over, and the marriage can become unbearable. You and Derrick are young. I understand the reasons... but marriage is not always the answer, not now. This is an emotional time, and it's not good to make such impulsive decisions at a time like this."

"Mami, I want love and passion just like in those romance novels. Is that possible? Is that kind of love and passion possible? I want to feel that... that heat and fire, I want to feel like I can't live another moment without him."

Christina tried not to laugh, "Brydus, you are truly my daughter in every way." Brydus put her head on Christina's lap, allowing her mother to play with her hair.

"Hey, did I ever tell you my love story? The tale of your father and me? It's wonderful."

"I know it has to be like a storybook. My Papi is so handsome."

"Your father, yes, he is, but before he was my husband or even my boyfriend, he was your Uncle Julian's best friend. They did everything together, like brothers. Whenever you saw Julian, you knew Alfonso was not far behind."

"I, on the other hand, was wild and crazy. A tomboy, like Nicole, which is where she gets her craziness. I wanted to be like my big brother and your father. Alfonso Moreno and I fought all the time because I always wanted to tag along. Your Uncle Julian… well… he was the best brother anyone could have. He was kind, loving. Sometimes they would let me come with them when they went fishing or hunting. Your father would always complain, calling me a brat. I remember one time your father even picked me up and threw me into the lake." They giggled, "However, I got back at him. When they went swimming, I put mud in his shoes. Boy, did he cuss me out. I stayed away from him for a week until he cooled down."

"When Julian died, your father stopped coming around. He took my brother's death very hard. It was a very sad time for our family. Julian was so young, so handsome. Your grandfather never recovered from that tragedy. Soon after that, Al went away to school. He was studying to become a veterinarian and was sent to school outside the Valley."

"I was only thirteen, a budding teenager when I last saw him. I helped your grandmother with the pharmacy. Doing whatever I could to assist her with taking care of my papa. He was depressed, and not getting any better. I was eighteen when Papa died. Then it was just Mama, Abuelita, and I. 'The girls' we called ourselves."

"I concentrated on finishing my degree, pharmaceutical, so I could help Mama. It allowed me very little time for dating. Not that I lacked suitors. I dated James Whitmore for a while. He was very sweet, but something was missing. We had great times, and I thought for a while that love would grow between us. He asked me to marry him, but I turned him down very gently. I could not see my life with him as man and wife. We would kiss, and it felt just all right. Afterward, we continued to just be friends."

"It was during the fall harvest that your father walked back into my life. Cousin Alma insisted I go with her to the festival. Your grandmother was behind this. I thought she needed me, but it was the other way around. I guess I was afraid to leave her alone for one minute, afraid I would lose her too and be left alone.

"There was music and dancing, hayrides and food. Love was in the air. I remember that day as if it were yesterday. It was a warm evening, so I wore this lovely red dress with spaghetti straps that molded my breasts and womanly curves. I put my hair up, Alma applied my makeup, and we walked to the square in high heels. I was smoking hot, and many single young men were giving me a lot of attention. We danced and laughed a lot that night. I had forgotten how to have fun. Alma flirted with every single male there. She was a mess, but you know Alma, it was hard not to love her. She was beautiful and wild, and I envied her spirit.

"Alma loved to dance as much as I did, and the two of us were burning holes in that dance floor. I remember walking to the table for something cool to drink… that's when I saw him… my heart skipped a few beats when I realized it was Alfonso. He was more handsome than I remembered. Only my diary and I knew what a mean crush I had on him. Your father wore a green shirt that matched his eyes, and black pants. He was taller than I remembered. He was truly stunning that night, clean-shaven… his long hair pulled back into a ponytail. Well, he was something else, your father. However, he was not alone… it was so disappointing because Ellen Rogers was hanging on his arm. She was really pretty, and a nice girl, too. It was hard for me to dislike her. The buzz around the dance hall was that they were engaged."

"I wanted to go say hello, but he was surrounded by so many other girls, so I stayed back and just watched him from afar. I felt this rush of excitement when I caught him looking at me and smiling. However, I made no attempt to go and speak to him. I remember him looking at me again and nodding in my direction. I wasn't sure if he knew who I was. It was a magical night, but my feet were starting to hurt from all the dancing. It was getting late, and I knew I should be heading home.

"I found myself alone when Alma left with a boy and didn't tell me. Therefore, after a while, I took my heels off and started to walk the long way home. In truth, I did not want the night to end. I was caught up in the beautiful evening. The moon was huge and bright. I didn't feel like going home, so I went to drop some coins in the wishing well and made a wish. Thinking of your father, I closed my eyes, turned around, and threw a coin over my shoulder. *I wish I may, I wish I might, have the wish I wish tonight...* let me find my true love. I wished. Then I heard his voice, I could never forget his voice. It is ingrained in my memory forever.

"'A penny for your thoughts, Christina?' Your father said. I was stunned. There he was, looking like a mirage.

"'I've been waiting all evening for you to be alone. You have grown-up, brat,' he said, smiling. I almost passed out. I tried to talk, but nothing came out at first.

"'So have you,' I replied, not knowing what to say. I was hoping he did not see I was turning a few shades of red. We exchanged pleasantries, and he walked me home. We talked as if all these years apart did not matter. He made me feel different. I knew at that moment I loved your father. When he kissed me that first time it was electrifying! I felt that kiss from my head to my toes."

"Was Papi engaged? Or was it a rumor?" Brydus asked, engrossed in the story.

"According to him, he never gave her a ring or made any promises. Ellen was heartbroken and led everyone to believe that they were engaged. I felt really awful, not wanting to be responsible for her pain. I didn't want to believe he was engaged, but when Ellen came to my house crying, begging me to give him back, I wondered if he was playing us both. I stopped receiving his calls, and when he came over, I refused to see him."

"Mami, what did Abuelita say to you?"

"Well… she had a lot to say. She told me I was a fool and told me to stop acting stupid. Nevertheless, you know. I had my pride, and as much as I wanted to run into his arms, I stayed away. I knew that if he came close to me… I would lose my mind, and that's what happened. He came into the pharmacy with another girl, and I wanted to die. He was cold and stern when he asked for his mother's medicine. When I handed him his change, he held on to my hand tight. He said, 'I'll be at your house tonight at 7:00 PM, and you better be outside to receive me,' then he turned around and left just like that.

"Well, I wasn't going to let him have the last word. *Who did he think he was?* I said to myself. That night, I dressed carefully, showing a little cleavage to see if he was still interested, and I waited on the porch. Just like clockwork, he came around that corner in a white shirt looking all clean-shaven and better than anything I had ever imagined. He pinned me against the door, then told me that we were getting married… and your father was very persuasive," they giggled. "Your abuelita yelled from the window, 'It's about damn time. I thought I'd never have grandchildren!' We all laughed. He told me that Ellen confessed to him that she came to me and begged me to stop seeing him.

"We loved each other with a deep passion. Just like now, when we catch ourselves staring at one another, something stirs inside of me. Do you feel that way… does Derrick make you feel tingly inside? Derrick is a very nice boy, but I don't think he's the man for you."

"Mami, that's the most beautiful story I have ever heard. I want my love story. I want to hold my son or daughter and tell them how I fell in love with their father. But how will I know Mami? How will I know when it's love and not just lust, or if it's just because a person doesn't want to be alone?"

"You'll know it, sweetheart, don't sell yourself short. You're still young, with so much to experience. Who knows, maybe things will change when you come back, and maybe you will feel differently."

Brydus laughed, "Yeah, and do you think time would change my papi's feelings towards Derrick? I know Papi never liked him. I see the look on his face when he comes around."

"Sweetheart, the man you pick will have to be a special one for your father to like him. Al is truly an overprotective father, so do not count on it. Brydus, your father adores you. He wants a strong and stable man, not some boy who still depends on his family for everything. Now tell your mother, what's the real reason, why marriage?"

Brydus put her head on her mother's shoulder. Christina loved the sweet moments they spent together. "Mami, I'm afraid… I know that I was isolated for weeks during my wilderness training. But I always knew in the back of my mind that when I returned home, you would be there with a hot meal, a hug, and a kiss, waiting for me. Even when I went away with my trainers, I knew that I had a home that I was returning to, but when I leave here this time, I will be on my own."

Christina tried hard to hold back the tears, "Yes, I know you're scared, my darling, but your father is right. We cannot deprive the world of someone so special and beautiful. Do you realize that there are people that have never laid eyes on someone like you? The Valley has been blessed with four, Nylaya, you, and now the twins that came to us from nowhere."

"I don't feel special, I feel like a freak at times, and I wonder, why me?"

"I'm sure Nylaya felt the same way, but she went out there and created a great name for herself. She married and had a family. Her son Jesse is a major force in the Inner Cities. Had she stayed home, she would have denied the new America a great mind."

"Mami, I hope people are not expecting great things from me. She was the first, and she was extraordinary."

"Yes, she was, but so are you, and you will always wonder what you could have achieved if you stayed here. I know your fears. The world is young again, and who knows what kind of dangers lurk behind every tree. That is why your training was so severe. Your father and all your teachers wanted to make sure you were prepared for this journey. Sweetheart, this is not forever. After the time that the law states, you can always come home. Your destiny may be here with us," She kissed her daughter's forehead.

"Mami, I love you so much, I couldn't ask for better parents." Christina held Brydus tight, not wanting to let her go. "I sometimes wonder about Derrick. Is it me he wants, or is it what I am, that he must have? He has all these beautiful girls at his feet that only have eyes for him, and yet he chose me."

Christina was surprised at her statement, "Are you kidding? Do you think you're not good enough for him?" She pulled her in front of a full-length mirror, "Look at this exquisite creature in the mirror."

Brydus looked at herself differently for the first time. She was 5" 7, with long, muscular legs and arms. Her eyes were large, the color of almonds. She could stop anyone in their tracks with just one look. Her dark, beautifully shaped eyebrows and thick lashes enhanced her beautiful oval face, along with her perfectly formed and well-defined lips. The only other mark on her face was a small dark mole by the right side of her upper lip. Her breasts were proportioned perfectly to her hard well-sculpted shapely frame.

"Women kill for natural black hair and a body like this. He should be kissing your feet." Brydus kept her hair long, thick and wavy to shelter herself from the cold winters.

"Mami, you're so funny. You always make me feel good… hmm, I think I look like you."

"I think you have the best of both of us. So, what's it going to be?"

She shook her head, not seeing a future at all with Derrick, "I don't want to get married. I think you're right. We are too young, and I don't want to get married for the wrong reasons. Now I have to convince Derrick, hoping he understands my reasoning. He can be so childish at times."

"That's my girl. As much as I would love for you to stay, you will regret marrying him right now. So, let's not tell your father about our conversation."

"I think you're right. I'm meeting with Derrick and some of my friends at Tech's. I hope he understands."

"Sweetheart, he's a man. He'll get over it, don't worry."

Christina walked Brydus to the front gate. She waved at her beloved daughter as she rode her horse, Blackie, into the moonlight, like she had so many times before. Her heart was breaking, but deep inside, she knew they were doing the right thing, letting her go to find her destiny. Marriage would be a disaster for Brydus right now, especially with Derrick. She shuddered at the thought but was proud of herself for handling the situation the way she did.

The house was quiet as she returned to her room, where she laid out the fur cape she had made for Brydus. "God, keep my baby safe and warm," she held it against her cheek, knowing her daughter would be wearing it. It wasn't going to be easy for Christina, but she promised her husband that she would try to keep from upsetting Brydus and making her anxious about her departure.

She pondered the thought in her mind. Brydus was highly skilled and very smart but didn't realize the effect she had on men. Christina sat by the window, waiting for Alfonso to come home. Right now, she had to be strong for her daughter and her family. Nicole needed her. For so long, the focus had been on Brydus.

Poor Nicole. She had the most difficult time understanding why her sister was leaving. They were so close and had a special connection that no one else understood, like their own language. They sometimes conversed with merely looks. It was only when Brydus promised to come back that Nicole could let go.

Tech's Game House

Brydus could hear the music coming from Tech's. It was her favorite place, where young and old came together to indulge in fast food and games. They had holographic pool tables, all sorts of video games, and bowling lanes. The bright neon lights illuminated the stables and the parking lots where some parked their bikes. The picnic tables were full of teenagers singing and dancing to their own tune, their laughter infectious. She handed her horse, Blackie, to the stable attendant.

James, a dear friend, met her at the stable doors. He was two years younger than her but admired her greatly and often spoke from his heart. "Brydus, my Nubian Princess, I offer myself to you. If you wish, I shall go with you on your journey." Brydus laughed. He spoke like an old person, very formal.

"James, you handsome devil. I shall miss you terribly, but I can't allow you to sacrifice yourself for me. I will be fine. Remember all the preparation and training I went through for my journey."

"I would give my life for you… I hope you know that."

She was touched by his sweetness and knew it was from his heart. "That's the sweetest thing I've heard. James, don't make me kiss you."

His eyes flashed open, "That would be the greatest thing that ever happened to me," he sounded like a little boy with a crush. When she kissed him lightly on the lips, he took a deep breath. "Wow… can I have another," he asked jokingly.

"It was my pleasure, my friend," she needed to change the conversation, "I hear your father has returned from the outside with some books and artifacts for our libraries."

"Yes, some fascinating black history books. It must have been something to walk the streets and see people of color everywhere you looked. People of every shade of brown, from the lighter to the deep dark pigment."

"I know what you mean, people like me, like your people and culture. You never know, James. There may be others like me. Maybe someday, color will come back to our people, and this time we will embrace who we are instead of being dissatisfied with our appearance. People altered themselves for vanity, and in turn, lost their identity." James smiled. He always loved speaking about his ancestry and the way things were. "Well, my friend, I have to find my boyfriend. It is going to be a stormy night. Have you seen him?"

His happy face became serious, "Just follow the line of girls… Brydus, you can do better. He doesn't deserve someone as wonderful as you."

"James, I've never heard you talk like that about Derrick. I thought you two were friends."

"Never friends, I just tolerate him. He's a jerk. Everyone knows it, except the females… I don't understand why they can't see how fake he truly is." Brydus didn't know what to say. "I'm so sorry Brydus, please forgive me for my over-opinionated outburst."

"It's alright. You're not the first who has said something negative about him… he is not the easiest person to get to know. There are many layers to Derrick."

"Thank you for not hating me. So, we will see each other before you leave, won't we?"

"I'm counting on it." They hugged before she left.

James was right. Tech's was packed, and in the middle of the crowd of girls was Derrick, with Brenda holding on to his arm. Brydus could hear him flirting with the girls and laughing aloud. Derrick was an extremely handsome young man. He never left his house without every strand of hair in place. His clothes were always specially tailored to his taste with great care. When he smiled, it lit up the room.

His family had money to spoil their two children. They always said they wanted to make sure their children had the best of everything. Being the oldest and so attractive, Derrick put on airs in the community, not caring about anything except his own popularity.

Valley society was based on how you contributed to their communities. Every person, young and old, had a role. Derrick didn't have to contribute. His family gave the community enough for him to frolic around and just look pretty. He wanted to become a lawyer but did not want to do the work, so school was not in his future. What was important right now was how much he could shine in the midst of all the pretty girls.

Though he had many girls ready and willing to be with him, it was important for him to be seen with the right one. He had always been interested in Brydus. She was someone special, and the fact that every single male her age in the Valley had the hots for her, made Brydus even more appealing to him. She was exciting, beautiful, and made him work for her attention, unlike the other girls who threw themselves at him willingly. It was always a challenge with her, but Derrick knew it would be worth it when he finally made her his wife. That was his plan from the beginning, which would make him even more superior in the eyes of others.

Brydus was unhappy when she spotted Brenda hanging on Derrick, rubbing her breast against him. The two girls were once friends until Derrick asked Brydus out, and they became a couple. Brenda turned cold towards her, and on some occasions, they even had shouting matches. Derrick enjoyed the attention. However, Brydus refused to go down that road with her anymore; that was two years ago. Now she just stared her down.

Brenda moved away reluctantly when she saw Brydus approaching. Brenda was a petite girl with blond curly hair, electric blue eyes, and dimples. Derrick pulled further away from Brenda when he realized Brydus was watching them.

"Hey there, my princess," he kissed her, "I got our favorite table, come on, let's make plans." Brydus followed him to the table near the bowling lanes. He was smiling, making her feel a twinge of guilt, knowing he would not be happy with her decision.

"So… how did it go with your parents? When is our big day?" He asked excitedly.

"Derrick, we're not getting married, at least not yet."

Derrick's attitude changed quickly. "What are you talking about? We've done nothing but talk about this… and did you forget you only have three weeks before they shove your ass out the gate?"

"I know, but I don't want to get married for the wrong reasons. You're starting school soon. I've trained for this all my life… what am I going to do with myself?"

"God, what are you talking about? Your place is here with us and with me as your husband. I thought you loved me," he was starting to whine like a spoiled child.

"It has nothing to do with how much I love you. You know what you're going to do with your life, I don't," again, the guilt of not loving him enough was killing her. They argued back and forth, becoming so loud that her good friend Ciara thought it would be an appropriate time to come to Brydus' rescue.

"Calm down, you guys… people are putting bets on who is going to win this argument. Everyone here knows your business," she slipped into the seat next to Brydus.

"Ciara, I asked Brydus to marry me so she doesn't have to leave. She turned me down. Can you believe it?"

Ciara looked at Brydus and then towards the bowling lanes, where her twin girls played with their friends. She reached out to hold her hand, "I will miss you deeply, my sister. I know the pain you must be going through about your great journey. I tell you this, when it's my girls' turn to go… I shall leave with them." Ciara was not much older than Brydus, but she was the mother of two beautiful twin girls that bore the mark just like Brydus, or natural-born as they are called.

"Oh, hell no… you're not helping. But what do you know, you're just an outsider," he said sarcastically, not caring about her feelings.

"So, you're going to throw that up in my face? That I am an outsider. Please, Derrick, I don't know what strange powers brought me here. When I look at my girls, I know it was fate. Your parents are on the council. Go speak to them about this matter."

"My family still believes in this voodoo crap. She belongs here, with me, as my wife," he banged on the table then turned to speak to Brydus. "Look, Brydus, you have until the end of the week to change your mind. I'm going home where people make sense. Call me."

Brydus felt empty and abandoned when he left. She tried to feel something besides anger towards him. Could she marry someone who doesn't rock her boat? Someone who doesn't make her weak in her knees? She searched her heart for an answer.

Ciara smiled at her, trying to be supportive. "I'm so sorry. I guess I should have stayed out of it," her heart went out to her dear friend, knowing what was ahead for her. "Honey, don't worry about him. When you're gone, he'll have plenty of support. The girls are lining up."

"Believe me, I know. Derrick just doesn't understand. If things don't go his way, he throws a fit," they burst into laughter, "Men," Brydus said, shaking her head.

"They are strange creatures," Ciara said, ordering a pizza for them.

"What about you, anyone special? Are you still seeing the doctor about your memory loss?"

"I still see the doctor for the headaches and the dreams… they are very disturbing. Sometimes I dream that I'm in this beautiful field of wildflowers. I'm wearing this long green dress and a crown of flowers on my head. The place seems familiar to me, and I feel like I belong there. In the distance, I see this rider coming towards me, and I'm happy to see him. He lifts me up in his arms and keeps on riding fast, holding me tight. I feel so safe in his arms. I could feel his heartbeat against my face. He smells so damn good, and then all of a sudden… we both fall off the horse. I am screaming and pulling at him to get up. When I look at my hands… they are full of blood, and I keep on screaming until I wake up in a panic."

"Wow, they are strange dreams. Do you see his face? Is it someone you know?"

"No, I can't remember what he looks like… but sometimes I think… what if I killed someone. What if I was raped? And killed the father of my daughters. How can I start a life with someone when I don't even know who I am?"

"That's bizarre. Does the doctor give you any hope that you will remember who you are, or anything from your past?"

"He says that something traumatic happened to me, and it may take something traumatic to bring my memory back.

I don't even know how old I am. The doctors think I'm between nineteen and twenty-two."

"I remember when I first met you, Ciara. You were very young, and I thought you were maybe fifteen at the most."

"Well, that was seven years ago, and I'm still no closer to remembering anything now than I was when I was bought here."

"I don't think you killed anyone. You're too sweet-natured for that. Sometimes the mind works in strange ways. I hope that by the time I return, you will have regained your memory and have moved on."

"It would be nice. I'm trying really hard for the girls' sake. I know I have a family out there somewhere, and my girls deserve to know who they are. Don't you think?"

"Yes, and so do you. You're much too pretty and kindhearted to spend your life alone."

Ciara always wondered how it would be to find the special person as she watched couples together. Sighing, she said, "I do want to fall in love and maybe have more children. Huh, here I am going on and on about me, and you're the one who needs someone to talk to. Brydus, I'm sorry for hogging up your time."

"That's alright. It keeps my mind off of Derrick and how I wish he would grow up and really support me."

"Brydus, the truth is… I hope you find happiness. Derrick does not deserve you. He is good to look at, but you're too much of a woman for him. I will be sad to see you go, and the girls are having a hard time knowing you are leaving soon. I have a feeling you will have many challenges ahead of you, but I'm sure you will be just fine."

"Well, I'm glad someone has faith in me. I will miss you and the girls, and I will pray for your memory to return soon. I wouldn't know what to do if I didn't have my family pushing me, loving me, and supporting me."

"I love you, Brydus. You're like a sister to me, and although my heart is going to be hurting when you leave, I pray you to have a safe and fruitful journey."

"Thanks, Ciara. I can use all the well wishes and prayers I can get."

"You got it, and don't worry about Derrick. If he decides to go to school, he'll be swamped."

Chapter 5: Childhood

Brydus grew up with loving and caring parents and grandparents as well. Though her mother was very protective, she still wanted her to be educated like the other Valley children. Brydus' looks sometimes kept her isolated. The children didn't understand why she looked different, so they would tease her, call her dirty and hurtful names and gang up on her. However, Christina and the grandmothers would not tolerate such hateful treatment towards their precious girl. Christina fought for her daughter to be treated like an equal. Which caused stress among some of the other mothers because Brydus was special to the communities and was guarded by the elders.

"No one is going to treat my angel like shit!" Reina yelled, distraught, recalling the time when she held Brydus in her arms, wiping tears from her sweet face. After that, she spent an hour assuring her she was perfect, and that the little girl teasing her didn't know any better.

Reina remembered her daughter complaining. "Mama, this happens all the time," Christina argued. "Lydia Benitez knows better, for heaven's sake. We used to play together when we were children. How could she allow this to go on?"

"That little bitch is jealous of our angel. I will not have it, Christina!" Reina said, grinding her teeth, "If I have to wipe another tear from Brydus' eyes because some snotty-nosed brats call her names, there will be hell to pay!" Christina was surprised by her mother's outburst, as she was usually the calm one.

"I'm going to the council and speak to the committee members. These children need to be educated. They have to be taught that Brydus isn't a freak, but instead… a beautiful child, and her feelings run deep."

"I'm going with you, and I'm sure Mitra feels the same way. She spoke to me yesterday about how disgusted she was that some of these parents allowed their children to tease Brydus about her skin color and her eyes. When Mitra brought it to Lydia's attention, all Lydia would say was that they are children and smiled."

When they arrived at the meeting, Christina stood up and spoke directly to the council, "These excuses are not going to fly with me anymore. Children mimic what they hear." Christina stated, very upset. The council had promised to support and protect her child but had failed. Soon Brydus would be starting school, and Christina worried that she would be coming home upset every day.

The council was very concerned that this was going on. Brydus was an exceptional child, a natural-born. Just as they embraced Nylaya, the first, they would embrace Brydus. The committee rallied around the family, and soon every child knew Brydus was not a target for teasing and harassment.

Brydus developed a hard shell. She decided early on that she would not be a victim. One of her trainers, Mistress Chong, instructed Brydus not to use what she had learned on her peers, but sometimes things would get out of hand, and she would bang up some boys pretty bad.

Brydus was determined to excel in everything she did. Math and science came easily to her. She could do difficult calculations in her head better than anyone else her age. The others laughed at Brydus because she would be daydreaming when the teacher called on her. Her mind would be elsewhere, but she always managed to give the right answer.

"Earth to Brydus," her favorite teacher, Phil Murray, would say. "It's time to land back on this planet." She would laugh. Her mind did wander more than it should.

Brydus knew she was different. As a young girl, she could not play like the normal children of the Valley. While the others played with their best friends, her best friends were her fighting instructors. They started her training when she was old enough to walk, and they were brutal. Mistress Chong worked poor Brydus to the bone. "You must listen, butterfly, the world is hard and dark out there, and you must be ready for anything." Mistress Chong would say, narrowing her eyes at Brydus in her broken English, then blow smoke in the air. Mistress Chong loved smoking her cigars, but she always warned her students about the evils of tobacco.

At times, the workouts would be so severe that Brydus would go home crying to one of her grandmothers for comfort, and they would always say the same thing. "What doesn't kill you will make you stronger, my angel." They would say, hugging her tightly. They didn't want to tell her the truth. That she would need to learn as much as she could, both physically and mentally, to survive what lay outside the protection of the Valley's walls.

When Brydus turned seven, her instructors took her on a ship to Asia, where they introduced her to different fighting styles to give her a well-rounded education. So, every summer for ten years, Brydus prepared herself for the worst two months of her life. Her mother dreaded those days when she had to say goodbye to her princess. Christina would get into arguments with Alfonso, protesting that they were taking time away from her. However, deep inside, she knew it was just as hard for him as it was for her.

Brydus never cried about going away, because if she did, it would only be worse. Mistress Chong was a hard teacher, but she was also loving and kind. She would say the nicest things to Brydus to make her feel better about herself, even when she made mistakes.

Mistress Chong's husband taught Brydus discipline. How to use whatever she can get her hands on as a weapon. "Your environment is your weapon," he'd say, "Look around you, and prepare yourself for the fight of your life."

Getting used to new customs and languages was hard for her. Everyone had a different set of rules. So, when it was time to come home, she was grateful that she had made it through another two months of hell. When she returned home from training, her family would give her a grand party every year. Some of her mother's friends would bring their children to celebrate her homecoming.

It was at one of her welcome home celebrations when she met Ciara. She was not from the Valley and was very shy. Henry, a close family friend, found her half-drowned and pulled her out of the water in the woods. Brydus had just turned thirteen, and everyone assumed that Ciara may have been about fifteen. The girls bonded right away and became the best of friends.

Ciara was pregnant when they met and had no memory of who she was. So, in a way, they both felt like outsiders. The connection between them grew stronger, and they both had a great understanding of how the other felt. Brydus was ecstatic when her sister Nicole was born and ran around the house, driving her parents crazy. It took the focus off her, so her mother would not be too sad whenever she went away.

As she became older, the intensity of her lessons became more severe.

Every day she came home with new cuts and bruises and a lot of pain. Mistress Chong was proud of her student, she pushed her hard, but after a while, Brydus started pushing back.

Mistress Chong and her husband Lu Jung had set their sights on Brydus as soon as they found out about her birth. They knew she would need the best training to prepare for her time to leave the security of the Valley. A second blessing came to the Valley when Ciara gave birth to twin girls, who looked like Brydus. The girls were beautiful. They were curious, identical twins ready to get into anything. Ciara's new parents couldn't be happier. They never thought their home would ever be filled with the pitter-patter of tiny feet, and now they had two girls to love and spoil.

Alfonso wanted the best for his daughter. When she was a preteen, he would drop her off in the wilderness, both summer and winter. He knew she would have to learn to survive in all weather conditions. Brydus remembered how scared she was during her first outing. She was only thirteen and unsure of herself. But after the first night, her instincts kicked in. She was able to remember the things her father and other instructors taught her.

Her father had an instructor for everything he wanted her to learn. Things she needed to know to help her make it through any situation that presented itself during her journey. She was taught how to hunt and handle different weapons. Also, how to trap, skin, and prepare her to catch. Her father taught her to filter water, so she would always have fresh water to drink.

Brydus grandmother Reina taught her how to use different plants to cure simple ailments. From her other grandmother, Mitra, she learned how to use wild herbs to make tasty food. Mitra was one of the best cooks in the Valley and would force Brydus to memorize recipes. It seemed like everyone in her family was a teacher and wanted to prepare her.

Mistress Chong challenged her at every turn, "Butterfly," she would call her; "You must anticipate the other person's moves. There may be more than one attacker, and you must be able to defend yourself from all who come to hurt you. Now move when you're fighting!" She would yell. Sometimes Mistress Chong's husband would jump in during her matches – and unforeseen additional attack.

When Brydus was seventeen, during a marathon fight with Mistress Chong, she accidentally hit Mistress Chong, knocking her down. Brydus kicked her in the mouth, making her bleed. Brydus was immediately respectful and went down on her knees, taking her position on the mat. When Mistress Chong got up from the floor, she looked at Brydus and said, "Now that's the way you kick ass. Never hold back when it comes to your enemies. You will have plenty of them coming at you. So, you must be alert like you have eyes at the back of your head."

They made her fight against most of the men in the classes, and her instructor's son often tried to challenge her. They laughed at each other, then they would fall down exhausted after sparring back and forth for hours. Sometimes he would just give up when Brydus became too aggressive. "You're a vicious bitch," he'd say, "Girl, you need to find a man and get laid."

"And you need to stop acting like a little puss every time you get hit," she replied as they laughed and teased each other.

Tan Jung loved Brydus. She was his companion during their travels, and always covered for him when he would sneak out to see some girl he met on the road.

When the twins joined the classes, Brydus became their junior instructor, treating them how her instructors had schooled her. They were a pair and would both sometimes gang up on her during a sparring session. She enjoyed watching them excel, grow, and fight without fear. It was easier for the twins. They had each other and didn't feel so isolated. By the time the twins came around, the Valley children had gotten used to why they were different, so the girls had many friends and were very popular.

Things were beginning to change by the time Brydus reached sixteen. The boys started coming around, and her father dusted off his shotgun. He was not letting anyone come near his oldest daughter. When she mentioned that she wanted to date Derrick, they bickered constantly. Alfonso didn't like Derrick. He called him an opportunist and a lazy mama's boy. Nevertheless, Christina wanted Brydus to have normal experiences before her life changed.

"Al," Christina called him, "Let her have a boyfriend. She is a beautiful young woman. How is she ever going to get sick of him if you fight so hard to keep them apart?" she tried to reason with him.

Alfonso turned to his wife. He stared at Christina standing in front of him with her hands on her hips. "You didn't get tired of me when we were dating," he replied, smiling.

She laughed, "That's because I knew you when I was younger. You were my brother's best friend, and I always had a big crush on you."

"So, I ask you again, what's the difference? We grew more in love with each other; at least I knew I loved you when you finally grew up."

"There is a difference, my love. Derrick and Brydus are so different. She is all natural and sporty, and he is… well, he will not get his hands dirty. I want her to experience a normal relationship. She's young and beautiful, can't you see that?"

He rolled his eyes, knowing Christina was making sense. "Alright, I get what you're saying, but… and…yes, there is a 'but' somewhere in this equation. He will come to the house like a decent person and ask for her."

"Good, I think that's something she can live with. Now was that so hard?" she teased.

"It's killing me, sweetheart. However, maybe you're right. She may see him for what he is and grow disgustingly sick of him… I can only pray. Just make sure you talk to her about the birds and the bees… you know…that stuff mothers talk to their daughters about. I don't want to… but I will break that boy's neck. I've already schooled her on what boys are thinking when they're with a young woman."

"Really, Alfonso, you forget you were once his age, don't embarrass the boy."

"Hello, that's what I'm talking about. I remember how I was at his age, hormones raging through my body, and I'm speaking from experience. I will break his freakin' neck," he made a gesture with his finger crossing his neck.

"Honey, we've had many talks about sex before."

"And make sure you tell her the truth, not that romantic stuff you women come up with."

"Alfonso, if you don't stop, I will hurt you," she said as he laughed, pulling her into his arms, kissing her sweetly. "You know what I mean. I don't like this boy much either, but I think if he is around her more, she will get tired of his ass. And you will not have to threaten him. She is a wonderful young woman, and things have not been easy for her. She's not stupid, and I trust her. I'm glad that she comes to me and expresses her feelings."

"Well, I'm going to express my feelings to him by putting my foot up his ass if he tries something with her. I'll deal with his parents if I have to."

"God help us when it's Nicole's time to date."

"Sweetheart… I can only deal with one boyfriend at a time."

Derrick was not happy with the arrangement, but he went along with her father's wishes. He knew that Alfonso didn't care for him, but it did not matter. What Derrick wanted, he got, and he wanted Brydus ever since they were in grade school together.

When Derrick came to visit, he was always on his best behavior, but when he was alone with Brydus, he tried to pressure her into going all the way. Brydus would hear her father's voice in her head every time Derrick tried to plan a quick getaway. "I will put my foot up his ass so far he will need surgery to remove it, do you understand me?" He would say, and Brydus would try not to laugh at him, knowing he was serious. Brydus tried to make Derrick understand that her father was only trying to protect her. When she was scheduled to leave, Derrick nagged her until she accepted his ring, and promised to speak to her parents about the marriage.

His parents were not happy with his plans to marry Brydus, knowing she was scheduled to leave. They knew Derrick was not ready to marry anyone. With pain in their heart, they decided to not interfere in it. Derrick would get into shouting matches full of rage with his parents whenever they tried to reason with him and make him understand. He would call them names and tell them how stupid their rules were. He blamed them for his unhappiness, trying to make them feel guilty. However, his family stood firm with the elders. Derrick had to learn that this was out of their hands.

Chapter 6: The New America

Christina spent most of the morning preparing food for Brydus' last days with the family. It wasn't easy for her, but deep down inside, she was coming to terms with the decision.

Alfonso pulled her into his arms and kissed her, "Everything is beautiful. How are you holding up?'

"You know I have to believe that she will return to us. Last night, Nicole and I had this meeting of the minds. We sat down by one of the picnic tables to have one of our mother and daughter talks. Nicole said something that made me feel better."

Alfonso held her hand, "I know Nicole has that second sight like my mother. Sometimes she scares me. So, what did she say?"

Her eyes began to well up with tears, "She dreamt that Brydus had a baby in her arms, and she was happy. It gave me comfort. You know… I think I'm going to be alright."

"Well… somehow that gives me peace," he said, comforted. "If there's one thing I want for both my girls… it is for them to find the same kind of happiness I have with you." He kissed her hand. "I love you so much… I'm so proud of you, my love."

"You make it easy. At least I know we have each other to lean on. I only wish… my mother was still alive to see what kind of young woman she helped raise."

The celebration went on for two days. Everyone came to wish Brydus a safe journey. The elders said special prayers for protection and great success for their special Valley child. Brydus' greatest disappointment was the scene Derrick put on in front of her parents, family, and some of the council members. He rushed through the door, insisting they go outside to talk. All week they had fought about everything, and when he tried to force himself on her, she took it defensively, fighting off his advances. She was surprised when he showed up at her door uninvited. This was supposed to be a special time for her parents, family, and close friends.

Derrick only thought about himself. He was going to ruin her last day together with her family. "What are you doing here?" She could see the anger on her father's face.

"I can't believe you'd rather leave than marry me… you never loved me," Derrick exclaimed.

"I'm sorry; I wish you would understand that I'm not ready to marry anyone. It has nothing to do with you."

"It has everything to do with me! You and I were meant to be together… this crazy law that some scared fools made up a long time ago means nothing… all you have to say is "No!"

Her father angrily watched as he heard Derrick rant about her decision not to marry him. Christina joined Alfonso by the door, hoping to stop him from going outside and beating Derrick up for upsetting Brydus right before her departure.

"Honey, let them work it out. Stay out of it," Christina urged. However, no words could console Alfonso. His daughter was leaving, and all Derrick could think about was his own selfish feelings.

He kissed Christina's hand, "Not today, sweetheart, he can throw a tantrum somewhere else, but not in my house, and not today." He was hurt and angry. A lump formed in his throat as he made his way towards them.

"That's enough," he said, keeping his distance. "My daughter is leaving in twenty-four hours," he said in a low and controlled voice, "and you're making her feel like shit because she doesn't want to marry you."

"Sir, with all due respect, this is between Brydus and me," he replied sarcastically. Alfonso closed the distance between them.

"Papi, please don't," Brydus pleaded.

"No, I've stayed quiet long enough, and to be honest, I never liked this relationship. You're a spoiled brat that has never done an honest day's work in your life. You have the nerve to come into my house and make my daughter feel guilty because she doesn't want to marry your sorry ass! Boohoo."

"Sir, the problem is that nobody's good enough for Brydus. You won't let her make up her own mind. You're letting these clowns talk you into sending her away."

"You're right… she's too good for you. She deserves better than some mama's boy who doesn't know how to wipe his own ass. Now I'm asking you as nicely as I can. Please leave. You are ruining this night for us." Brydus was afraid her father would swing at Derrick.

"I would think that you would want her to stay. I'm offering her a way to stay here in The Valley and be my wife. You should be grateful."

Alfonso gave him a side-glance. Brydus could see the tension on her father's face as he tried to hold back.

"Grateful…boy, who the hell do you think you're talking to? I'm not one of your piss-ass friends. Do not get it twisted. I'm not afraid of you or your parents. I am asking you as nicely as I possibly can again. Please leave my house before it gets physical."

"Well, I guess I'm leaving…" he turned to speak to Brydus. "I'll give you the two years… if you don't come back, then I'll know you never really loved me." He made his way through the house, mumbling along the way and slamming the door on his way out. It took all the self-control Alfonso had not to go after him and pound him into the ground as he wanted.

"Papi, I'm sorry, this isn't how I wanted my last day at home to be." Alfonso held her tightly in his arms.

"I'm sorry, sweetie, I… just couldn't stand by and let him rip into you… not in my house."

"Don't worry, Papi. He just doesn't know how to lose."

Some of the council members commented about Derrick's behavior and how inappropriate it was. Derrick always felt superior to everyone else because his parents were involved in just about every committee in the Valley.

The topic for the rest of the night was Derrick and his family. Everyone had nice things to say about the family. However, the two Cádiz brothers were spoiled rotten. The Cádiz were a very powerful family, and they had a lot of influence in the community. They loved Brydus, but they also knew the law and stood by the law that was written as part of their charter years ago, even if it broke their son's heart.

Nicole didn't want her sister to leave. She knew just how worried her family was, but like always, she had comforting words for Brydus.

"Don't worry, Brydus. He won't be alone for too long."

"And how do you know this, baby sister?"

Nicole gazed at her as if looking through her, "I just have this feeling… I had a dream last night, Brydus."

"You and your dreams," She said, hugging her.

"In my dream, you were crying about something, but then you looked up, and you smiled at this really tall man. He had dimples and a great smile. You took his hand, and the tears were gone. I was happy because you were happy." Brydus could not help but embrace the little red-headed spitfire. Tears came to her eyes as she realized that she would miss Nicole's strange way of telling the future.

Nicole was such a free spirit, and the way she commanded attention made her unique. For a long time, they took the ten-year-old's strange predictions as made-up stories. Last year when a young boy went missing, she woke up screaming. She knew where he was. However, no one believed her. Alfonso had just gotten home from searching for the boy all day and almost dismissed Nicole's dream. However, she insisted and cried so strongly that he notified the others, and within a few hours, the boy was found in the very place she described. From that day on, whenever she spoke of a feeling, they never took it for granted.

Once everyone left, the family huddled together to cherish their last few hours together. They laughed and cried together about sentimental events in their lives, remembering her grandmother, who passed away last year. Brydus drew strength from her family and her little sister, who told her the most strange and profound things. "Have courage, Brydus. Your angels are watching over you," Nicole said, kissing her cheek.

The next morning after breakfast, the family gathered together. Christina did as she promised and held it together, at least until the family rode to the outer border to bid their farewells. Nicole made Brydus promise to come for her once she was settled. James' father gave her a simple map of routes to travel to help her find some safe areas to rest along the way.

As Brydus turned to wave goodbye to her family, it finally hit her. She was alone. There was no one to run to when she had a problem. She had to figure things out on her own. All her young life, she had prepared for this moment. Now all Brydus could think about was turning around and going back home to the comfort of her family.

It took her several minutes to gather enough courage to move forward. This would be a test of her will, a test to see if she would remember all the things she was taught. Fear gripped her again as she pointed her horse south.

Brydus traveled the Blue Ridge Mountains. It was breathtaking, and there was plenty of food and water, thanks to a phenomenal fishing spot. She covered her black hair, braiding it and tucking it under a hat, and wore dark glasses to shield her eyes. Along the way, she met strangers that would look at her, wondering what a young woman was doing traveling alone. Sometimes she would ride with a group of people traveling in the same direction. However, as per her training, she always stayed wary of whose company she kept. She had yellow-colored glasses to wear at night, to hide her eyes from strangers that wondered who she was. They watched this strange and mysterious woman who spoke very little but commanded respect. The secrecy was hard to maintain. Some people did not take to Brydus, an unknown girl who wore strange clothes, a hoody, and glasses at all times.

The New America, as they liked to call it, was still a disaster. The roads were badly damaged, and old rusted cars and trucks littered the side of the roads. They were stripped of anything that could bring value to a hungry family. In some areas, the brush was overgrown, and parts of the roads were missing. Brydus traveled through the small towns and cities. The smell of burnt buildings was in the air. It made her sad to know the breakdown in society had allowed this to happen. There were boarded-up stores, dirt, and litter everywhere. She witnessed small children digging through the piles of trash, looking for things to sell so their families could eat.

Some of the larger towns and cities were beginning to rebuild and take control of their economy. Schools were open, children played in the streets, and the market places sold their labor fruits.

It was strange to see how some people lived. Brydus still tried to understand how brutal and cruel people were to one another, even after all that had happened. The personal boundaries some people set were mind-blowing. Family units encouraged their young daughters to sell themselves without care, just like a regular job. It was expected of them. The young boys were often the solicitors of clients for their sisters, or in some cases, their mother. At times, it was so heartbreaking for Brydus that she chose to leave in order to not see the perversity. Some of these acts were not done in private, but as entertainment without considering who was looking on.

Time was rushing by as Brydus realized that two months had gone by, and still she had no clear direction. All she did was drift from town to city, meeting nice people with who she enjoyed spending time. On occasions, she had to become physical with men and women in order to get them to leave her alone, thinking she was an easy target. It was getting harder to keep her identity undercover. Her sunglasses shielded her eyes, and during the summer's scorching sun, everyone tanned, so she felt safer. Sometimes, she could rent a room for the night and pay to shelter her horse.

She soon realized just how dangerous the streets were, having to fight her way out of a few rough spots. In the city of Reading, PA, she ran into a band of young teenagers who tried to ambush her and steal her horse. She confronted them, kicked their asses, and tossed them around a little with the hope they would get the hint and leave her alone. When she took off her hat and glasses, they ran away, calling her El Diablo, making the sign of the cross when they saw her long black hair blowing in the wind and her brown eyes glaring at them. She laughed at them, watching as they tripped over things and bumped into each other, trying to get away.

With each passing day, she grew a thicker skin, not trusting easily and staying alert at every moment, knowing danger hid on every corner.

Brydus watched as people traveled at their own pace, searching for a better life, towing all they owned with them. They carried their hurt and hardship on their faces, but their spirits would not let them believe there wasn't a better life for them somewhere. Others just wanted to survive, scratching out a living wherever they could. However, there were those who continued to follow the path to civilization. With the hope that they could find a place where they could live in peace. A place to start all over again, restoring this once great nation to what it used to be, as an example to the rest of the world that was still in turmoil.

Brydus learned a lot about life after the Dark Days when the smallest killers destroyed the world. She realized how isolated life was living in The Valley of God and how God must have sheltered them from this cruelty.

The determination of these people gave her hope and made her stronger.

There were good and bad settlements developing all along the East coast. These settlements were under the rule of overlords and tribal settlements, and they kept order in their districts. Tribal communities were very popular with their close community environment. These communities used their skills to develop their lands, build housing, and resurrect a dying society. The dreams of the inner cities were being realized, so young people took on the struggle of rebuilding a better place where people could find hope.

Nevertheless, the shadows of winter nearing made Brydus uneasy. The winds were changing, and the trees were turning colors. Brydus was more confused than ever about her place in this new world. She found it threatening and exciting at the same time. *Where does my destiny lay*, she thought each day. Tonight, she pulled the blanket tightly around her shoulders as the cool winds blew through the campground. She wished that her grandmother Reina were still alive. She could always talk to her and let her know what was in her heart. She threw more sticks into the fire, keeping the flames burning.

When she was younger, Brydus would sit with her grandmother by a raging fire, and she would tell Brydus stories. Stories passed down by Reina's great-grandmother of days when people of color walked the earth in abundance, always making her feel special.

Her other grandmother, Mitra, would make the tastiest meals, teaching Brydus old recipes only using a few wild ingredients. *God, how I miss them*, she thought to herself.

When the Valley children made fun of her, grandmother Reina came to her rescue, holding her, making her feel better. Brydus cried as she remembered the last day she and Derrick were together. He was so cruel, yelling and screaming at her, calling her a chicken for not loving him enough to go against her parents. She grew more perplexed, feeling a sense of loss. *Maybe I don't really love him*, she thought. Maybe it was merely the thought of being wanted by the most popular guy in the Valley that made her stay with him.

She let her mind drift, wondering what her parents would be doing at this very moment, thus making her homesick. Tomorrow she would have to find a safe place to spend the frigid winter months. Without her horse Blackie, she would be in severe danger. Brydus said a special prayer that night before falling asleep, "God, you know what I need. Please show me the way."

The next morning ushered in a beautiful Indian summer day. She traveled along the river, wondering if somewhere there were cabins and homes abandoned long ago. "This area was too beautiful not to have caught the eyes of many people," she said out loud, talking to Blackie as if he understood her. The water glimmered like pearls reflecting in the sun, and the trees were adorned with the finest dresses of yellow, orange, and golden shades. The water was inviting as she led Blackie for a drink.

It is cool, and a nice swim would sharpen my senses, she thought.

She was used to swimming in the cool waters of the Valley. Brydus kept a close eye on Blackie, who waited patiently for her at the bank's edge. After drying off, she noticed that Blackie was fidgeting nervously. Something was bothering him. "What's wrong Blackie? Come on, boy, what's making you crazy?" She looked around and found a nest of snakes nearby. Carefully she picked up a wooden board lying a few feet away to cover the nest, only to discover that it belonged to a large sign. After brushing off the dirt caked on the carved letters, she read "Wonderland Cabins by the Lake." Smiling, she knew her prayers had been answered, "Okay, Blackie, now we're cooking. There are cabins around here somewhere." She walked him back to the road and began to follow it around the curve until she found what she was looking for. It was the overgrown road entrance. About a quarter of a mile through the brush, she found a beautiful log cabin nestled between some lovely oak trees. In front of the cabin was a small pond with six rowboats resting on their side. Although they were faded, she could tell that they used to be painted in bright colors of blue, red, and green.

There was a barn and two other sheds along with a stable that could board six horses. Brydus was excited. The cabin had its own power source, as many of the homes did this far out. After making Blackie comfortable, she headed towards the cabin to see if she could get in without breaking the solar frames on the windows. It was a well-built log cabin with a side porch. She walked up the three steps to the cabin and looked through the small window in the door.

Brydus pulled some of the boards off the window easily and tried to open it, but the thick dust and dirt changed her mind. She then tried the front door, but it was shut tight. Frustrated, she went around the side entrance with a screened porch and patio furniture. She pushed twice on the door, and the key went flying off the edge of the frame.

When she opened the door, it was dark, with streams of light filtering through the cracks of the boarded-up windows.

There was dust and cobwebs everywhere. She coughed as she entered the dark kitchen, feeling around for a switch. All the homes were solar-powered, and she hoped the generator was still operational. Brydus opened the kitchen window to let in enough light to see her way around. "Finally," she said, exploring the first floor. Next to the kitchen was a small hallway with hooks where the family used to hang their clothes. She pulled open the narrow door and found the power source. Searching for the switches, she flipped them on and off until she heard the buzzing sound of the generator. "Thank you, Jesus!" she cried.

The cabin was beautifully laid out with a massive fireplace that divided the living room from the dining area. *Rich hardwood floors, excellent décor,* she noticed. The fireplace mantel held dear memories and pictures. The pictures told a story of a wonderful family that enjoyed memorable summers there. Pictures of the children when they were just babies and photos of the same toothless children throughout adolescence were scattered around the house. The parents' photos went from having beautiful hair to receding hairlines and gray. Brydus couldn't help getting sentimental as she remembered her own family pictures she had begged her mother to hide during her awkward years.

She opened all the windows and doors to let air into the place. Exploring the up and downstairs of the four-bedroom, three-bathroom cabin. She spent the next few weeks dusting and cleaning her new winter home. A great find was discovering a root cellar full of preserved fruits, vegetables, sweet and regular potatoes preserved perfectly. There were also herbs and spices neatly labeled, bagged and preserved. She had everything she needed to get through the long winter months. Nevertheless, after six weeks of no human contact, she was beginning to become melancholy.

The cellar was filled with all kinds of fruit wines. Sometimes she would set the table and place family pictures on the empty seats to pretend she was having dinner with the family. Brydus would watch the old occupant's home movies repeatedly just so she could hear the sound of human voices speaking, laughing, and singing. When she felt the walls closing in on her, she would go fishing, welcoming the frigid cold just to keep her sanity.

Every night she prayed to God to keep her from going crazy. She read a lot, which she enjoyed greatly. Novels about love, mysteries, and history intrigued her. Brydus read about things of the past, when airplanes and spaceships dotted the sky with people flying to the moon and mars. She read about all of man's achievements before the Dark Days, before the world was turned upside down. When billions of people died. She saw pictures of people like her, with dark skin, even darker skin than she could imagine, including some famous people. She smiled and danced around, shouting legendary quotes that went down in history. Brydus also understood why people of color faded from sight and why everyone stared at her when they saw her without her covering.

She looked up at the sky and saw the clouds rolling in, "It's going to be a long, cold, lonely winter," she mumbled. It was frigid outside. After feeding Blackie, she skinned the rabbit that she had caught, chopped it up, and added it to the boiling broth. Then she heard a strange sound coming from the driveway, but she ignored it, remembering the many times she heard peculiar sounds before that had turned out to be nothing. She chalked it up to being stir crazy and wanting someone to talk with. After adding the carrots and potatoes to her stew, she walked over to the large cross that hung in the living-room hallway.

"Okay, I'm going to make this easy on you," she said with her hands folded in prayer. "Please don't let me go crazy, I'm too young, and I have to find my destiny out here, somewhere." A loud noise like a gunshot interrupted her prayer, startling her. "Now this is getting weird. Please, God, send me salvation."

Chapter 7: Jake

Brydus was thankful it was early spring. Had she stayed on the mountain a day longer, she would have surely lost her mind. With great sadness, she gathered her things for her journey down the mountain to be among people.

Before she left, she picked fresh wildflowers. "Widow's Tears," her voice was strained with emotions, "You would like them, Jake, the pink ones match your cheeks in the cold, and the blue ones are the color of your eyes, and the purple…because you were the King of Jazz in my eyes." She laid them gently on the grave, and her eyes began to swell with tears again. "Jake, you were a godsend; you saved my life." She patted on the freshly dug earth and placed some large rocks to indicate a grave. Brydus had buried him under a large oak tree that would give plenty of shade from the sun in the summer. She pushed his rusted motorcycle under the same tree. "I love you, Jake," she would always remember him fondly as the Jazz Man of New Orleans.

Three Months Earlier

Brydus could still remember the startling sounds that interrupted the quiet seclusion of that cold winter's night. It was a week before Thanksgiving, and she was already a bit stir-crazy when she heard a buzz and a backfire coming from the driveway. Brydus immediately feared the worst. She pulled out the old shotgun she had found in the cabin and had cleaned it so it would be in good working condition for situations just like this. Slowly she moved to the living room window and watched closely as this odd figure moved closer. The noise alone was disturbing, sounding like explosions coming closer. He stopped right in front of the cabin but was puzzled to see the floodlights come on. Brydus ran through the kitchen, throwing on her fur cape. Jake turned and found himself facing a person pointing a weapon at him from the side porch. His mouth went dry. Looking around, his mind immediately raced with a million thoughts of how he would talk his way out of this predicament. Brydus could smell the exhaust fumes coming from the old motorcycle. Perplexed but excited at the same time. She met him with the shotgun fully loaded at the door and pointed it at his head. Instantly both of his hands went up in the air.

"Whoa, there now, it's me, Jake, just coming to visit," he smiled, hoping Brydus was just one of the family members that didn't recognize him.

"State your business here!" she shouted. Then he realized it wasn't a family member and that he may be in trouble.

"Miss, I mean you no harm. I swear I did not mean to intrude. I know the family that used to live here. Our families used to vacation together a long time ago."

"Oh really, then you must know their names. What is the families' last name?" Brydus ask suspiciously, with the shotgun still pointing at him.

"Well, the family name is Archie, the mother is Esther Archie, and then there is my best friend Richard Archie and their children, Edwin, Patricia, and Ebony. Oh, and they had two dogs, Chichi and Howard." Brydus lowered the shotgun. She knew the family from all the photos and videos around the cabin. Jake looked more like Santa Claus with his full white beard, long white hair, and rosy cheeks from the cold.

"Miss, I didn't mean to intrude. If I can just warm up a little, and if you can spare something warm to eat, I will be on my way in the early morning. I promise." Brydus waved him in. It was the first human voice she had heard in seven weeks. Jake parked his motorcycle on the side of the house.

When he entered the kitchen, Brydus started to laugh, "I prayed for a friend, and I get Santa Claus," Jake shook his head, joining in her laughter. The kitchen was warm and inviting. He just wanted to warm up, he said. When Brydus took off her hooded cape, his jaw dropped, surprised to meet someone like her.

Brydus was used to people staring at her, but she hoped that he wasn't some sort of freak, "My name is Brydus. All I can offer you is some rabbit stew. I wasn't expecting company." Jake was still stunned at the beautiful woman he saw before him.

His fascination mounted, "Ah, may I touch your arm? I just want to make sure you're real." Brydus looked at him, puzzled, but realized she was not at home where everyone knew her.

"Don't be silly. Why would you say that?" she snapped. Jake took his helmet off and placed it in the closet where he used to keep it whenever he came to visit.

His face turned bright red, feeling awkward and foolish. "I know I must look like an idiot, but I haven't seen one of your kind. Do my eyes truly behold such beauty?" Brydus sighed. *Here is the only human in miles, and God sent me a kook*, she thought.

"Well, mister, if you want to stay here, you're going to have to stop acting so weird."

Jake started to laugh, "I'm sorry, my name is Jake Armstrong. They call me the Jazzman of New Orleans."

"Well, Mr. Jake Armstrong, welcome. I guess you know where everything is around here. There are clean towels in the bathroom if you want to wash up. I'll set the table for two."

"Well, thank you for your hospitality. I'm not going to lie. I am cold and as hungry as a bear."

Brydus began to jump up and down with joy when Jake disappeared into the back bathroom. Even if it were only for a little while, she would at least get to hear another human voice. She danced around the dining room, "Thank you, God, I love you," she whispered.

During supper, Jake dominated the evening's conversation with stories about the family that had once occupied the cabin. Brydus didn't care; she just wanted to hear another person's voice beside her own. She let him talk all he wanted, and he sure had a lot to say. Brydus enjoyed every minute of it. At times, she thought maybe he was making up some of the wild stories he told, but it didn't matter to her; he was engaging and funny. He was here, and for now, the walls didn't seem to close in on her.

Brydus was surprised to hear that some of the children and grandchildren in the photos were still alive. Most of them were doing well, according to Jake, and that made her happy. After weeks of looking through old photo albums, she had grown fond of the Archie family.

Jake was a creature larger than life. He was intelligent, poetic, and always had the greatest adventure stories to tell. Brydus could not help but be captivated by his humor. A major blizzard blew in that evening, snowing them in for the winter.

It snowed continuously for a week. Brydus thanked God every day for Jake and his wonderful company. Every day they would go out to see what they could hunt for supper. There was so much small game they did not have to go far for food. To top things off, Jake loved to cook, and with the cellar well-stocked, he made some delicious, savory meals. The wine cellar was also filled with great fruit wines.

"I used to cook for the family, that is, my wife, Susan and me. She was the one who taught Esther how to make wine and how to make preserves. Esther was very eager to learn, and as you can see, she took what she learned to the extreme. I guess it was a good thing for our sake. It was Richard's idea to build the cellar. Esther and he fought about that for months, but he won. They were a pair, loving, sweet, and great with those kids. You would have liked them, really down-to-earth folk. They were really great people."

They roasted a wild turkey for Thanksgiving and had a fabulous dinner. Afterward, Jake sang and played the piano. His soulful voice made the evening perfect. Brydus listened to him for hours, enjoying his music and sipping wine.

"Tell me about your wife, Jake. Did you love her?"

He smiled at her with his sad eyes. He had not spoken at length about his wife since she passed away two years ago.

"Susan Hightower, she was from the deep south. My wife came from a long line of wonderful African American families. Her father taught me how to play the piano. If there was a man of soul, it was Five Finger Curtis. He was the smoothest piano man in New Orleans. His wife and my godmother, Silvia, were good friends. Silvia would pick me up from school and take me to old man Curtis' house. Little Curtis Junior and I would play together. They called him Cutie for short, a name he came to hate as he grew older. Mr. Curtis heard me playing his piano one day. Just mimicking what he did. So, he made Silvia, my godmother and babysitter, bring me around more often so Mr. Curtis could teach me. That's how I got started. He would give me lessons every afternoon. It was great! He told me to feel the music. Ah, what a wonderful time it was when I used to jam with Mr. Curtis. He was a true man of soul."

"Susan was this skinny, rat-looking girl at the time. She was shy and would hide every time I came around. I watched that skinny girl grow into a beautiful woman. Susan played hard to get," he laughed, "But when I put on the charm, she melted in my arms." They laughed.

"It's not hard to believe that you were a sweet talker, Jake Armstrong," Brydus teased.

"I was something else back then, Brydus. Susan was seventeen when we married. We were so much in love and had many good times together. We bought our very first home right across the street from the Archie family. That is how we met and formed a great friendship. Susan taught Esther how to cook. That poor woman could not even boil water before. Esther was young and inexperienced, coming from a well-to-do family. I do have to hand it to her, though; Esther wanted to do things independently. Richard inherited the cabin from his grandparents, and they really put their heart and soul into this place. Towards the end of each summer, they would ask us to come spend a few days with them."

He paused, remembering those fun times, shaking his head, "Yeah, we would go fishing and hunting. The girls cooked whatever we caught. It was great, that is, until the Dark Days. That's when everything changed. My son… he did not make it. Some of Susan's family had succumbed to the beast, the destroyer we did not see coming. We did all we could by burying them as they fell beneath the horror of the time." It was hard for Jake to recall; he had lost so many of his family members during those times.

Jake lost his wife of forty-nine years just two years ago. He stayed in New Orleans playing and singing in some of the more popular clubs, but he knew his health was failing. He wanted to visit the one place where he and his wife had created fond memories and where his son, little Jake, was conceived. He knew the cabin would be empty, so he started out but didn't realize how quickly the weather would change and how cold it would get. He was surprised to see that someone was keeping the place warm for him. *A very pleasant surprise*, he thought.

Jake was very sensitive to Brydus' moods. When depression tried to overcome her, Jake was the one to pull her out of the funk. "No time to be a sad girl. It's the best time to be alive for you." He would say and play his harmonica, urging her to dance.

Brydus saw him not as an old man but as an equal, "Love you, Jake, you're my soulmate," she would say.

Brydus sometimes would drink too much, missing her family. She would whine like a child, wanting her parents. He would hold her and allow her to cry on his shoulder. Jake would listen to Brydus talk about the people in The Valley of God and its history. To her surprise, Jake knew a little about The Valley of God settlement and why there was so much controversy when people began to buy land.

Jake was fascinated with Brydus. Her laughter and sense of humor were infectious, and her wit was uncanny. She made him forget how old he was when she challenged him. Slowly without knowing it, he fell in love with the dark beauty.

What I wouldn't do to be forty years younger, he thought, watching her practice her fighting skills and dancing to some of the soft music the Archie family had left behind. When she asked him questions about sex and love, he would blush.

She was so innocent in so many ways and filled his emptiness, and for once in the two years since he lost his lovely wife, he felt alive again.

They entertained each other during the long, cold winter months, playing cards or word games. "Jake, my man, you now owe me two million dollars," and they would laugh as they signed IOUs, which they promised to pay as soon as they left the mountain. Jake was concerned about Brydus. He schooled her about the New America and cautioned her about going too far south. The roads are treacherous, and an element of danger lurked in every corner.

Jake informed her that they were having a lot of trouble with human trafficking in some of the southern states. Brydus was frightened when he said that someone like her could sell millions on the black market. She listened intensely as he advised her where not to go. He also gave her tips as to where the best settlements were if she needed to settle somewhere for a while until she decided what to do with her life. "Stick with me, girl. I'll take you to some settlements and tribal communities that will take your breath away. I passed some on my way up here. I was most intrigued with some of the communities that were prospering. That's where you need to be, a place that has life, nice folks that are trying really hard to pick up the pieces, you know what I mean."

"These settlements, are they safe? I've been to some really rough places."

"You can tell a good settlement when you see the town's folk, and the sheriffs patrolling the area are always visible. Women and children are comfortable walking the streets, and businesses aren't afraid of displaying their wares outdoors; you can tell by the progress."

"It sounds like a dream come true. I've seen some areas that are really trying to achieve that kind of progress."

"Many of the tribal communities are working hard towards a better society. I was very impressed by their gains. Our country is moving in the direction of recovery. It's coming slowly, but it's surely on its way, and you, my dear, will enjoy the benefits."

"What about you, Jake? We'll stay together so you can enjoy the benefits too."

He smiled, wishing it were true, "I'm old, sweetie, my bones ache, and my heart... well, it's not working as it should."

"Jake, you old goat, you're going to live until you're a hundred." They laughed.

They made plans to travel together for a while, and Brydus was surely looking forward to having a grand adventure with him. He even drew a map showing where they could stop and enjoy some communities. Brydus was thrilled, and every now and then, she would trace the routes with her finger.

For Christmas, Jake made Brydus a small backpack out of animal skins. She cried when she opened it. "Jake, it's so beautiful and detailed. You're so gifted. Here's your gift. I hope you like it." She made him some warm knitted slippers from yarn that she found in baskets around the cabin. It was a very emotional time for both of them, they missed their families dearly, and this was the very first time that Brydus would spend Christmas away from her family.

Brydus would urge Jake to read aloud to her. Listening to his soothing voice calmed her anxiety. If there was something she didn't understand, he took his time to explain it to her, always in a colorful way. Jake saw a beautiful spirit in Brydus. He loved her, but he was born too early. She breathed life into his old bones. There were times he would stare at her when she fell asleep reading. He felt privileged to have met her and wished that things were different between them. *I see a beautiful, desirable woman, and she sees a tired old jazzman,* he thought. He would cover her up at night and whisper under his breath, "I love you, sweet Brydus."

Spring was in the air, and Brydus was excited about leaving the mountain. Jake continued to educate her about men and relationships, where to go, and what places to avoid, but she didn't care. All she knew was that Jake would be with her, and she was ready for new exploits with him.

The earth was ripe with activity. The small creatures were out looking for something to eat, and the world was bright and new for Brydus. But once again, someone dear to her was taken away. Two weeks before they were to leave the mountain, Jake died in his sleep. She begged him to wake up and talk to her. Her heart was breaking into millions of pieces as she knelt down next to him with tears streaming down her face, "Wake up, you old fart! Please don't leave me like this, Jake… I love you. You promised me that you would show me how to play the harmonica and cook jambalaya… you promised me. Jake, Jake, please wake up," she sobbed over him. For hours, she sat next to him, trying to will him back to life, "Jake, how could you leave me like this?"

It took Brydus hours to break ground to bury her dear friend. In between her tears, anger, and pain, Brydus dug a place for her friend, the jazzman who came to rescue her from her madness.

Present

Brydus arranged the flowers on Jake's grave before saying goodbye to the mountain. "I will always remember you, Jake. L love you." Quietly she pointed her horse south to escape the mountain that had kept them prisoner for the last four months.

The pain of losing Jake left a deep hole in Brydus' heart. She knew it would take time to heal from this terrible loss. Depressed and sad, her first thought was to go home and not travel any farther. However, she felt there was more beyond the walls of the Valley to explore. Listening to Jake's stories made her want her own adventures. She had rested for four months, and now it was time to move forward.

The trees were budding, and the wildflowers adorned many pastures. The chirping sounds of the many birds gave Brydus hope. Suddenly she didn't feel like she was the only living thing around. She sang some of the songs that Jake had sung to pass the time and tried to play his harmonica.

The warm rays from the sun felt good against her face as she traveled by the river's edge, watching the geese making their way back north safely. She looked at life differently now, enjoying the interactions with the ducks and other animals.

Brydus fed Blackie carrots, his favorite treat, when she heard a strange sound. A low humming sound. Blackie's ears stood up, letting her know that he heard it too. Slowly and cautiously, she continued down the river, following the humming. As she continued walking, the sounds turned into moans. Low, painful, moaning cries. Brydus crept closer toward a small opening beyond the bushes, aghast at what she saw. Women and children were lying around an ill-burning fire, dirty and lethargic. She sat back behind some bushes to think. She felt her heart beating a mile a minute, wondering what to do next. They seemed confused, and she wondered why they were without a guide or male companion.

Brydus mounted her horse and wandered slowly towards the camp, not wanting to scare them. Nevertheless, there was no reaction to her presence until she spotted an older woman – dressed in a tattered black dress which dragged on the ground – walking slowly toward her. Her clothes were worn out and dirty as if she were dragged by the mud. The woman smiled. It almost seemed as if she had been waiting for her. The woman stopped and started to pray. "Thank you, Lord Jesus, for you have sent us an angel." As the woman raised her arms to the sky, a strange chill went up Brydus' spine. "Thank you for coming. I've been expecting you," the woman announced.

Brydus felt her heart racing again. She backed up, "I don't know what you're talking about."

The woman came closer, her eyes pleading with Brydus. "I had a dream, and in it, the Lord said to me that he would send a dark angel that would save our lives… and here you are! Just as the Lord described you." She started to cry, praising God for sending her the dark angel.

The children walked towards her, moving slowly like in a trance. Brydus was frozen in her saddle, controlling Blackie, who was starting to sense her bewilderment. The poor, filthy children surrounded her horse, begging for food and whining about how hungry they were. A lump formed in Brydus' throat as she tried to get away from the children, but they cried louder, begging her for food. She wanted to cover her ears and run away. Finally, she tossed the woman a large bag of dates and nuts she had packed for her long trip. "Make sure they all get some," she said in a whisper, rearing her horse and galloped out of the grim campsite.

She stopped at the river to throw up and cry. She couldn't get those hungry faces out of her mind. "Now, what would Jake do?" she asked herself. "He would go back and help those people," she said, coming to her senses. "Jake, you owe me," she said as she looked up at the sky. "I will collect when I get to heaven."

The other women sat around waiting to die. All they did was moan, not doing anything to help their situation. The children were getting their fill of the dates and nuts she had left, laughing and giggling as they tried to speak with their mouths full.

Everyone watched this strange dark woman carrying some wild hens. They looked at each other, wondering if they had died. After building a proper campfire, Brydus began to cook some stew, using the spices she brought from the cabin. The aromas awakened their senses, and the smell engulfed the camp. One by one, they sat by the fire, waiting to eat. Brydus noticed dark circles under their eyes, revealing a sign of starvation.

They followed Brydus' every move, "First of all, everyone who wants to eat must wash up. If you don't wash up, you don't eat." She instructed. Two teenage girls started to fuss but quickly changed their minds the minute Brydus glared at them. They were afraid of her brown eyes, and Brydus had a way of intimidating people by just looking at them. It was dark when everyone finished the first hot meal they had in a month.

As they slept, Brydus surveyed the condition of the group. There were three grown women, three teenagers, five children, and the older woman who spoke to her. They were malnourished, but still in good shape. She slept far from the rest, not wanting to get close to anyone, not wanting to feel the pain of losing them as she did with Jake. The sorrow was still raw, and every time she thought about him, the pain struck her hard. Maybe this was her destiny, she thought, to bring these people to a good settlement. Then she wished once again that she could go back home, feeling homesick and confused.

Brydus was ever so grateful to her father and teachers, who taught her how to survive in the wild. She knew how to look for food in places that a normal person wouldn't think about twice. By the time the others awakened, Brydus had built a big fire and had already made some tea and coffee. They fussed at her angrily when she would not let them eat until they had washed up. One by one, she tossed the children into the river. They screamed as they hit the cold water. Afterward, it turned into a game as they began to get used to the cool water. The teenage girls took another approach using a washcloth to scrub their faces and hands, and by the time they were done, it satisfied Brydus, and they were allowed to eat.

They all stared at the beautiful woman who didn't speak much. However, she yelled at them at every turn. They wondered where she came from, since they had never seen anyone like her before. They began to believe that she was an angel of God.

Brydus made them wash their clothes and showed them where to look for food. She made a game of it for the children, who happily followed her directions. Brydus knew she had to get them somewhere safe, hoping to find a settlement that would take them in, so they could start over. Looking at the map that Jake had drawn, she realized they were not very far from a good settlement, but walking was going to take much longer. She spoke to the older woman, who smiled and nodded a lot, urging her to speak to the others to do exactly as she instructed.

Chapter 8: The Settlement

Within four days, the women and children returned to life. They could walk faster, and the children had enough energy to skip, run, and play games. Brydus was happy with the progress and gathered them together to let them know about her plans.

The girls looked about the same age, fifteen to sixteen. They were thin and wore their hair up, matted to their heads, except for Tenisha, who wore a dirty blue bandana over her hair. Amy was the petite one of the three teenagers. Her tiny features made her look younger than she was, but she was loud and always had something negative to say.

Helen was in her early fifties with a round face, gorgeous blue eyes, and wide hips. She was a pretty woman who walked with a limp and colored her hair reddish-brown. She loved dark colors. However, now the gray roots made her look older, like it hadn't been colored in a very long time. Emma was a tiny woman, around the same age as Helen, with her silver blond hair blended in with the gray. She was sweet and hardworking. Maryann was tall and younger. She was the one who disciplined the children and made them listen. Maryann liked to keep her hair short. A mixture of red and graying hair adorned her round face. She had a sweet disposition when it came to following rules. Then there was the leader, Rev. Wilson. She kept them moving, kept their hopes up. Rev. Wilson was older. She wore her short, coarse hair in a tight natural curly hairdo.

Rev. Wilson bore the pain of the world in her eyes. Brydus felt a connection to her right away, remembering her own grandmothers, who were also strong women. The women and children had been through hell and back, and they wore their struggle like a badge of honor.

The children sat quietly, wide-eyed, wondering what came next. When Brydus spoke, they stood at attention. However, the teenage girls gave her the most grief. Every time she opened her mouth to speak, one of the teen girls complained about something, which annoyed her. They grumbled under their breath, but Brydus stood her ground. "Look, I'm trying to help, and I can only help you if you do as I say. I am not a miracle worker, but I have a map, and it has a list of good settlements. I can take you to one, but that's all I can do. The rest is up to you. However, I assure you that you will die if you continue to be lazy," she said, scolding them.

She cut her eyes over at the girls, who continued to fuss every time she asked them to do some work or help with the children. "Everyone needs to get off their asses and pull their own weight. Nobody gets a free ride. Now, the first settlement is not far from here, and I think there may be some farmhouses a few hours away where we can rest. So, let's stop all the damn bitching, and get it together. I know how to survive out here, but you have to trust me."

The roads were very hard to travel on foot, so many of the main throughways were damaged during the Dark Days, after the collapse of humanity. However, they moved onward as quickly as they could.

Brydus stopped to pick apples from some trees, finding berries of all kinds. She had the children gather as much as they could. Amy laughed as she tried to climb one of the apple trees, which turned out to be difficult for her. So, she pushed some of the boys up the trees to shake the limbs. It began raining apples everywhere. They gathered them to eat as they traveled along. Brydus let them enjoy their moment. They needed to laugh and lighten the mood before they moved on. It made her uneasy knowing they had no protection, no weapons except her own. They could not even fight back if they were attacked on the road.

They walked a few miles, and as she predicted, she found a crossroad called Chancy Road, which led to a small farm. It was a quarter-mile off the road, hidden behind overgrown bushes. The girls and children were excited as they raced ahead. Everything looked bare and desolate, but to Brydus, it was a gold mine.

The abandoned farmhouse had a barn, a few storage units, and a chicken coop. The house was in poor shape, but the four-bedroom farmhouse had everything they needed. It looked like someone had just got up and walked away, leaving the door open. The children ran to explore the barn and storage units. But the three teenage girls just sat on the porch, pouting and making remarks under their breath. Amy was the first to complain, then Jessica and Tenisha chimed in.

"I'm hungry and tired, and it's so hot," Tenisha whined.

Brydus wanted to knock her out, knowing all the work that still needed to be finished before they could settle in for the night. She searched for the power source throughout the house, hoping it was still operational. From the back of the room, she could hear Helen fussing at the girls. They argued with her when she asked them to help. They were refusing to help clean up the kitchen, so Helen could start cooking.

Brydus could not stand it anymore. When Helen broke down into tears, frustrated with their attitude, she stepped in, not in a friendly way. She would not tolerate laziness. "Alright, you three, it's time to fall off the monkey tree. If you want to eat, you all must help. I told you before; to survive, we must be a team."

"But why is everyone stressing out? We do not have to do everything in one day. We can stay here. I'm tired, and my feet hurt," Jessica whined, crossing her arms in defiance.

Brydus was now furious, but she understood that they were young girls who had been through a horrible experience.

"Look. I understand you people have been through a lot. I do not know the whole story, but I get it. I recognize you have had many disappointments, but this is not the place to settle down. First of all, you have no way of protecting yourselves. The place is unsafe. Don't you want to be someplace where there are people your own age… you know, boys and stores to buy pretty clothes and shoes?" This made the girls sit up straighter. They looked at each other, and their faces lit up.

"Can that be possible again? I would like to get married someday and have my own children," Tenisha said, almost in tears.

"It is possible, but you need to pitch in and help as much as you can and work hard to make it happen. I promise you; we are only a few days away from some good settlements that are alive with people. Therefore, this is what's going to happen. Jessica, you help Helen in the kitchen and wherever else she needs you. Tenisha, I need you to get the bathrooms cleaned and in order. Everyone has to take a bath and wash with these plants that will get rid of the lice and bugs in your hair, before they travel to…" she pointed to her crotch. The girls were grossed out.

"Can that really happen?" Amy asked, surprised, touching her own hair.

"Yes, so tonight, everyone takes a nice hot bath. The hot water heater is solar, and it's fully charged."

She turned to Helen, who listened carefully while she was talking to the girls. "Helen, I'm going to bring you some plants to boil. We need a lot of it. I'm going to create a concoction for everyone to use. Now girls, let's get to cleaning. We have a lot to do before tomorrow." The girls gladly started their chores. Amy cleaned up the dining room and living room area without a fuss.

"Thank you, Miss Brydus, they are good girls, just… hurt and confused," Helen explained.

"I know, it's not easy losing everything. Sometimes it is hard to see the bigger picture, but once they're around others their age and feel secure, their attitudes will improve."

"I'm sure you're right. I'll be waiting for the plants. I found some big pots we can use."

Brydus took Maryann and Emma out into the fields not too far from the house. They stepped over some broken fences. Maryann and Emma watched Brydus with amazement as she crouched down and pulled something up from a leafy area.

"Look at this. There is food all over this field. You just have to know what to look for," she said as she pulled more from the leafy patch, "Parsnips are a great source of sugar."

"Oh my God, it's growing wild," Maryann said, surprised.

"There are carrots, beets, bean sprouts, and over there, we have onions, snap peas, snow peas, and I'm sure if we look closer, there's cabbage somewhere. Let's get the children out here and get some of this picked and packed for our trip." Rev. Wilson started to weep as she tagged along to learn what to do.

"I didn't realize how unprepared we were. How many abandoned fields did we pass, and we were dying of hunger," Rev. Wilson said, feeling beaten down.

"Don't blame yourself. You didn't know what you were looking for. Now come over here, see this plant. It is bitter, but it will help kill anything growing in your hair. We need to pick as much as we can and get it to Helen." The field was full of that plant and other herbs.

"Miss Brydus, Miss Brydus, come quick," Jason waved at her, "come quickly, we found something." He ran towards the large storage house and followed him inside. The other children were pulling the box out into the open. "It's a tent. Can we use it?" Jason yelled, excited that he had found something important.

Brydus gave him a broad smile, "This is a great find indeed. It's big enough for all of us to sleep in." The tent was still in its box, never used. "Great job, Jason. We have shelter now."

The girls helped bathe the children and comb their hair. They were starting to feel good about themselves. They even found some clothes that fit; one would have thought they had hit the lottery the way they were carrying on.

That evening, after everyone had eaten and was clean, they sat around the living room, listening to Emma play the piano. The girls sang, and the children danced along with them. Brydus was caught up in the moment. She was happy that she could help, but she still had an irksome feeling in her belly. The girls dedicated a song to Brydus, while the other children made a ring around her, dancing and laughing. It was very different from the condition she had found them in.

"You have done so much for us in just a little over a week, Brydus. Is there anything you want from us? How can we ever repay you?" Rev. Wilson asked lovingly.

"There is one thing. I want you all to promise me, even you little ones. When we get to the settlement, and people begin to ask questions about me, tell them nothing. Please promise me."

"But why Miss Brydus?" Amy asked, confused.

"I won't be staying, and the fewer people know about me, the better. Plus, I prefer it that way, alright?" Everyone agreed. The girls helped put the children to bed, but Brydus sat outside on the porch, looking out over the landscape, thinking how it must have looked long ago. Rev. Wilson sat down next to her.

"It's a beautiful night," she said, sitting in one of the old rockers.

"Yes, it is. It is nights like this that make me homesick. So, tell me, Rev. Wilson, why would someone like you take a chance and start out into the wilderness without knowing what you're doing?"

Rev. Wilson lowered her head, trying to hide her tears, "I buried my husband on our journey," she said quietly. Brydus could see the pain on her face. There was great sadness in her eyes. "He was such a great man... with so many plans for our community," she tried to smile. "We weren't always this pitiful," she sighed and continued. "After the Dark Days, we stuck it out," she took an agonizing breath, "We buried so many... it was the worst thing anyone could ever imagine. It was a mystery to us. I didn't understand why some died and others survived. We just took it as a sign from God, that those who survived were chosen to rebuild and move forward.

It was not easy…yes; it was tough to see the beauty of our town destroyed. We were helpless, fighting the invisible demon that invaded the air and trying to comfort those who had lost their loved ones. On top of that, outside evil fanatics made things worse, putting the Lord's name to all the terror they inflicted. However, our community stood strong and rebuilt what these groups had burned down. Families opened their doors and took in those that could not fend for themselves. It was lovely; the way people came together. My son petitioned the Inner Cities for funds and supplies. I was amazed at how they stepped up to the plate. Every month for a year, they would send us seeds for growing our own food, medicine, timber, and cement to rebuild our clinics and schools. We wanted to do things on our own. Families would move in, and some would move out. It didn't seem as if we had a care in the world for a while. However, we did not heed the warnings from the Inner-City council. They said we needed to establish a military unit. They urged us to have one in place to keep our town safe. There were so many heated debates over it, and after so many meetings, it was voted down." She looked down at her hands, then looked back up at Brydus. Her voice was strained as she spoke about what had happened.

"We lived to regret that decision," Rev. Wilson continued. One Sunday afternoon, it all went up in smoke. Yes…it did. All of it. My husband gave such a beautiful sermon that morning. Rev. Martin Wilson was on fire that day. After church, we practiced with the choir, learning a new song. Once the adults left, the children's choir started practicing. Then all of a sudden, we heard loud shooting sounds."

"Those beasts swept through our town like locusts destroying everything in their path. They came in on their noisy motorbikes. Those hums, I still can't get the sound of those things out of my head," she covered her ears, remembering the sound the bikes made. "They drove around in circles… just kicking up dust and shouting obscenities. The women were half-naked with bright colored hair and painted faces. The men were even worse, those dirty savages. They ran over anyone who got in the way of their bikes, driving them in and out of stores. Busting windows, killing everyone they saw. Our church sat on a small hill looking over the town so we could see everything that was going on. All we could do was cry in horror."

"My husband's name was Martin, you know, named after the great Martin Luther King of the 20th century. He fell to his knees and cried out to God as we hid the others. That afternoon will stay embedded in my mind forever. They killed men, women, and children indiscriminately. Breaking down doors, pulling poor helpless people into the middle of the street, and just shooting them. It was like a game for them, and they laughed as the people begged for mercy.

Those barbarian women held down our town's women and laughed as their men raped them. Young girls, it didn't matter what age they were."

"Emma was coming to play piano for our rehearsal. She rushed in, screaming, 'they are going to kill us all!' That poor woman was scared to death.

"We helplessly watched as they dragged our men behind their bikes, especially those that opposed them. The girls and children were hysterical. Martin's heart was breaking… I could see it on his face. For a full day and night, we were too paralyzed by fear to move. Before they left, they set fire to everything. Two men busted into the church, and I held my breath, trying not to alert them about us. My Martin knelt at the altar, praying, asking the Lord to receive our souls, tears running down his face. It was like a miracle, I tell you…a miracle. They just turned around and left. They left Martin and the church alone.

"When we were finally able to go outside and see the horror…everyone was dead, hundreds… we buried our dear friends and families with heavy hearts, wondering why such calamity had befallen us. What had we done to deserve it?

The children lost their parents and siblings. Martin knew we could not stay unprotected. However, to be honest, who would want to stay in a place with so many horrid memories? Therefore, we packed up what we could in the only operational bus left and followed my husband into the wilderness. He said he had a dream that the Lord would lead us to a promised land. That God would take care of his flock. The bus broke down twice. It was just too damaged. After going only 105 miles, it could not be fixed, and we were stranded. My beloved Martin died in his sleep a week after we set out. The strain was too much for his heart. He did not tell me he was sick. I didn't even have time to grieve his death," Rev. Wilson looked at Brydus with eyes full of sorrow.

"God does work in mysterious ways. I guess you wonder why God allowed this to happen," Brydus asked, trying to understand.

"It was our own fault. We were warned this could happen. The Inner Cities advised us to put some kind of military unit in place. However, money became the issue, and most did not think we needed extra security."

"I'm so sorry; you must miss your Martin terribly. I know how it feels to lose someone special," Brydus said, relating to her own pain. The grief of losing Jake helped make that human and compassionate connection.

Rev. Wilson tried hard to push back the tears welling in her eyes, "Everyone began to shut down. Our food was gone in a week. We must have wandered around in circles for days. Most of us just laid down to die, but in my spirit…I knew that place was not going to be our grave. I got up that morning, and I prayed as I had never prayed before. I begged God to send someone who would lead us out of the wilderness, and into the promised land that my Martin had spoken to us about. That night I had a strange dream… no, I remember it was more like a vision… someone came and sat down next to me where I lay. I was too afraid to open my eyes and look. The sweetest voice I have ever heard in my life said, "I have sent you a dark angel who will deliver everyone from despair," and as I opened my eyes… there, you were, with your black hair on your black horse. With your beautiful brown eyes full of love and compassion for us. My heart leaped with joy! So here we are, the dark, beautiful angel teaching us, feeding us, and giving us hope. We are alive and getting stronger every day because of you… God Bless you, Brydus."

Brydus reached for her hand and squeezed it, "We've saved each other. You have no idea how much meeting you women has helped me. Look, I want to show you something." She pulled out a map, "Here is a great settlement," she pointed. "Jake said it was booming with activity. You can find work and housing there. However, we have to ask the overlord for permission to settle. I'm pretty sure he won't turn you away once he sees your needs, and according to this map, it's only a few days away, depending on how fast we can walk."

"Brydus, I have great hope. To see the girls happy and my friends full of hope. We can see the light at the end of the tunnel now," Rev. Wilson said, taking a deep breath, relieved. Feeling sure in her heart that God was leading them on the right path under the leadership of this beautiful young woman.

"Good, hope is a good thing to have," Brydus wanted to assure her. "Now go get some sleep. We have a lot to do tomorrow."

Rev. Wilson got up from her chair, lifting hands reaching towards the beautiful night sky, "I am ready, yes, Lord, ready for this part of my life to be over. The best is yet to come," she smiled.

Brydus clapped her hands and smiled with approval.

Chapter 9: Demi

The glow from the crackling fires illuminated the sky as they fought to put it out before it spread to some of the other buildings. Demi and his men fought for hours to put out the raging blaze. Finally, by midnight, the weary men collected themselves at the main camp house to assess the damages. He was exhausted as he washed the soot from his face and arms in the workers' bathroom. The air smelled like smoke and sweat. All his men had the same raccoon eyes from the masks they wore. They were filthy from fighting the fire that took longer to get under control than anyone could have imagined. Demi was happy that no one was injured during the blaze. The thought made him feel at peace.

Cisco approached him with the damage assessment, "Let me have it," he groaned, "What are we looking at?" Demi asked, disgusted with the whole situation.

"It could have been worse, boss. Luckily, they hit the small warehouse that didn't have much in it," Cisco answered, reading his notes.

"Great," Demi replied agitated, "get all the foremen to meet me at the mess hall for a few minutes so we can decide what we're going to do next." Demi wiped his face and hands, ruining another towel. "Those sonsofbitches!" he cried. He was very distraught about the whole fire and burglary incident. The fact that outsiders were able to sneak into their restricted area under his watch didn't sit well with him. It wouldn't sit well with his older brother, who was away at a conference.

"Boss, we have to be more careful. If they did it once, they will try it again," Cisco expressed.

"Yeah, let them try this shit again, and they'll be in for a big surprise. I'll meet you in the mess hall." Demi said as he stared into the mirror. It was his responsibility to keep the estate safe. Thank God, it was a wet spring, and the fire was contained to one area. Had the fire spread, they would have lost valuable seeds and equipment needed for the next harvest.

He took a deep breath, trying to clear his mind. It would smell like burnt wood for a while, and he was unhappy with the constant reminder. Across the street from the men's barracks was the mess hall. He could hear his men talking and raising their voices in anger.

Demi laughed at his foremen. The soot on their faces was so thick that all he could see was their bloodshot eyes and teeth when they smiled. "Alright, guys, I'll make this brief. We all know that this fire was just a distraction from what they really wanted. I have a list of items that were stolen from the warehouse. They took whiskey and rum, some wine, beef jerky, and some other odds and ends. Normally I would have said, "Okay, they were hungry and let it go, but… they pissed me off by setting it on fire… this is too close to home. These assholes came on our property and took what they wanted. I'm disturbed that they actually out-smarted our guards and got away."

Troy sprung from his chair, "Isn't it funny how they knew which one of the warehouses to target. They attacked Manny at the guard shed. This was planned. They've been watching us," Troy bellowed, extremely upset with the whole situation.

"That's what I'm getting at, Troy. They didn't have enough balls to attack us here, where we have weapons and guards. What kind of terror do you think they are inflicting on others that don't have any defenses? We promised to take care and protect our people. If they attack them, it's the same as attacking us directly. This is our land, dammit, and our people! We vowed to uphold the law and protect our way of life. It's time to whip some ass and show others they can't just come into our home and take what they want."

Troy stood up again, "That's the shit, boss, and who better to stop them from coming back again and hurting the people we stand to protect. It's ass-kicking time!" Troy shouted as the others chimed in, getting excited. People worked too hard to build what they had just so some assholes could come in and take what belonged to them. They had to be stopped now.

"So, Demi, they shouldn't be too hard to track down. Let's go after those bastards," Big Willie yelled, who was ready for action.

"Big Willie is right! We cannot let them get away with this shit. I say we go after them and put them out of commission," Troy chimed in.

Demi calmed down his overly exhausted and angry crew, "Alright... I understand we're all tired and pissed off. I'm going home to take a shower and try to get some rest. I suggest you all do the same. I'm asking for volunteers to go with me tomorrow. To track down these assholes and send them to Prison Island, where they belong so they can't hurt anyone else. I need at least ten good men at seven, bright and early. We don't know how many or how heavily armed they are, so let's be prepared."

"Alright, it's about time," Big Willie shouted, "I've been waiting for some action! Let's take this to the next level and send a clear message that we kick ass first and sort out the bodies later!"

"So, we're straight, tomorrow at seven. Don't feel bad if you can't make it."

The house was quiet as Demi dragged his tired body up the stairs to his room. After a long hot shower, he lay in bed looking at the ceiling, hating the fact that his brother had left him in charge, and this had happened. Every bone in his body screamed with pain. It wasn't easy holding on to those hoses as they doused the fire, keeping it from spreading to other warehouses.

Demi looked at Audrey's picture as he did every night. She teased him with her bright green eyes and smile that lit up his world every time he looked at it. It took Demi a long time to realize that Audrey was lost to him forever. All these years and not one sighting or trace of her… it was as if she had disappeared into thin air.

The pain of losing her was still affecting him deeply, and sometimes, around her birthday, he would spiral into depression and go on a drinking binge. His brother Joaquin was always there for him to keep his head from falling into the toilet and drag him back home. Joaquin never judged him and never tried to preach to him. Demi appreciated that about his brother. Now he felt like he was letting Joaquin down again. *After all, how patient can a person be*, he thought. "Good night, my sweet angel," he said, blowing a kiss in the direction of Audrey's picture, "I'll love you forever."

Demi usually had a hard time sleeping, but he was so tired tonight he slept like a baby until he heard the alarm blasting in his ears. "Oh God," he grumbled as he awoke. "Audrey, my love, if you were here, you would be waking me up with hugs and kisses and maybe… some happy time." He had the habit of talking to Audrey's picture. "Duty calls, my love… shit, what a way to start the day," he said out loud. He dragged himself out of bed and down the stairs near the back entrance. He could smell the fresh coffee brewing in the kitchen. "Mattie, my love, what would I do without my number one girl taking care of me?" he kissed her chubby cheek.

She always had a cheerful smile for Demi, "I have to take care of my boys," she laughed, "you sweet-talking devil."

Mattie ensured all the men had coffee and toast before they headed out to track down the criminals who had invaded their peaceful home. She always worried about Demi. He was a soulful young man who was quick to anger but had a heart of gold. When his older brother was away, she always looked after him, making sure he ate and didn't go off the deep end.

By morning, Demi had a plan in his head and was surprised to see all the volunteers waiting for him by the stables. "Thanks for coming, guys. I was thinking about it last night, and I figure they probably didn't get too far from here. I'm sure those idiots stopped and had themselves a party last night with all the booze they took. But let us not underestimate these fools. They may be stupid, but they have weapons."

"Yeah!" Big Willie shouted, "Let's show these assholes what we're made of! Shit, I'm ready to bust some heads."

The rest of the men cheered, ready to go. Big Willie was an oversized kid. They teased him, saying he had a beard by the time he was ten years old. He was six feet four and all muscle, a steel wall on the outside, but inside he loved children and greatly respected women. Raised by his grandmother, she instilled great pride in Big Willie about his history. She would remind him that he came from a long line of African kings, making him feel special.

Cisco was part American-Indian and grew up on one of the reservations. He was only five years old when the Dark Days devastated their home, and most of his family members died. His older sister and her husband fled east, carrying Cisco with them. After wandering around the different parts of the country for a while, they found the Quintanilla settlement. Cisco was loyal to the overlord ever since he settled in the territory. He never forgot where he came from and used his skills to help his bosses. Remembering all the days he went hungry and slept on the ground, wondering if he would ever find a place where he would feel safe. He would defend the land that embraced him with his life.

Cisco rode ahead to scout the area. He was smart, and his Indian instincts kicked in as he surveyed the road looking for any sign that would help track them down, "Demi, they left a trail a mile long. I don't think we'll have any trouble tracking them down," Cisco said, pointing to the debris left behind by the thieves. Cisco was the bloodhound of the group, and when he hunted, he never came back empty-handed. He loved being part of the Quintanilla Ranch team. They were growing in territory, and prospering. He was excited when Joaquin gave him a chance to prove that he was not a screw-up, and Cisco impressed him with his tracking abilities and loyalty.

Demi and Joaquin depended on their men to keep order. Joaquin especially needed them to be vigilant when he traveled to the Inner Cities for conferences and meetings, leaving his men in charge of the communities and safety of the estate. Demi and his men laughed aloud as they passed the debris the thieves had left behind – empty bottles, wrappers, even clothes.

"What the hell? Are these fools running around naked? Look at the clothes they left behind," Louis said, laughing at the pair of underwear hanging from a tree.

"They probably needed to make room for all the booze. You know it can get heavy carrying around all that wine and rum. Heaven forbid they leave that behind," Demi argued, shaking his head.

Demi hoped his brother didn't get home before they returned. This was the first time in years that Joaquin had asked him for help in managing the daily operations of their territory. Demi realized this was his chance to make amends and was happy to take charge. Joaquin had enough stress dealing with the ranch business, patrolling the boarders, and the meetings that he had to attend took him away for weeks.

It was his turn to sober up and turn his life around. For the last year, he had been committed to gaining his brother's trust. It made Joaquin happy to have his brother back. However, this was a setback in Demi's eyes and could not have happened at a worse time. He had to prove himself not only to his brother, but also to the others. To be the leader he wanted to become. Now he needed to concentrate on getting the criminals that dared trespass on their territory and steal their property.

Cisco led the men through another side of the countryside where most farmers lived. Troy looked for any signs of disturbance in case one of the farmers had encountered the thieves as they traveled through the farmland. However, as far as he could tell, all was fine. The only sounds they heard were dogs barking in the distance, possibly warning their masters that strangers were lurking around. Farmer Peter Richardson greeted Demi and his men at his back gate. "Master Demi, I heard there was trouble by the ranch last night. Do you require any assistance?"

"We are tracking some criminals that escaped in this direction. Did anyone hear or see anything last night?" Demi asked.

"The dogs were mighty upset last night. We did hear some noisy travelers passing by around midnight or so. All of us went on alert, but they just passed us by. It gets awfully dark out this way at night. You know we are always ready to assist if you need help. Hell, if it hadn't been for the generosity of the Quintanilla family, we'd all be eating dirt. So, anything we can do, we are ready and willing."

"Thanks, I appreciate the offer. I think we can handle this, but keep your eyes open. You know what to do in case of trouble."

"We sure do. Don't worry about us. We know the drill," Peter Richardson said, smiling.

"Good, we were worried they might try something out here. We'll catch you on the way back."

They traveled for a few hours when they started to see some more debris, "Looks like this is where they stopped to rest," Troy said, looking at the litter that the criminals left everywhere as they moved on. Wine bottles and wrappings were scattered all over the place. Cisco felt the campfire ashes then looked at Demi.

"I don't think they're too far. These ashes are still warm," Cisco announced with a devilish grin.

"Yeah, it looks like they had quite a party last night," Big Willie added.

"I hope they had fun because it's going to be the last one they'll have for a long time," Troy commented.

"Good, that means they won't put up much of a fight when we catch them," Demi said, still worried and wanting to apprehend them before they did damage elsewhere. Cisco counted at least nine distinct sets of footprints.

Farmhouse

Meanwhile, at the farmhouse, Brydus lay awake looking at the map that Jake had drawn for her. Jake said this was one of the best settlements he had visited. She remembered how excited he was as she pointed to a circle on the crude map. The town was thriving, he had mentioned more than once. "It was a lovely place, compared to some of the others. That's where you need to be," Jake had said, drawing a circle to mark the area. Brydus thought about getting a job there and feeling the place out for a while. Now being out in the world, she felt there was so much more to see. The Valley was such a closed society, and now the world seemed vast. She understood why Nylaya left and seldom came back to visit. There were new things to see and conquer. At first, the grief of losing Jake made Brydus homesick. However, meeting these people gave her a new perspective on life. She was going to explore her options.

They stayed for a few days to regain their strength. Afterward, they gathered food and washed their clothes for travel with the hope of starting a new life. They had a new determination and a positive attitude towards life. Nevertheless, travel was slow as the sun beat down on them. Brydus could see the small clan struggling with the heat.

That irksome feeling in her stomach was back again. After traveling through some rough terrain, she decided to break for camp and give the group time to rest and recover. "I spotted some wild turkeys a quarter mile back. Let's break for the night," Brydus shouted. "I'll see if I can find something to eat."

The girls came together and set up the large tent where they would all sleep. They gathered wood and went down to the lake for fresh water. A fire was built to cook the vegetables they carried. Brydus jumped on Blackie and rode back to where she had spotted the wild turkeys and tracked them a little while. She started to get that nagging feeling in her stomach again. It wasn't the first time she felt this way, sensing danger.

Demi and his men followed the gang's path, over the broken roads, through the dense wilderness. Every time they stopped, they found evidence of stolen food left behind. Cisco knew they were getting close, and it was getting dark.

Brydus felt something was wrong back at camp, Blackie's ears were pointed, so she decided to give up tracking the turkeys and hurried back. She heard two of the girls screaming from a distance and Rev. Wilson begging some strange men to let her go. The leader had Tenisha by her fragile arm, twisting it behind her and pulling up her dress. The other men laughed as they witnessed their leader torturing poor Tenisha.

"Where are your men?" he bellowed, lifting poor Tenisha off the ground. The frightened girl screamed hysterically. Brydus snuck closer to the camp as quietly as she could and came up behind one of the men standing watch – a short skinny man who looked more like a young boy than a man, did not see her coming. She silenced him with one twist of his neck. She crawled over to a second man and tapped him on the shoulder. He didn't make a sound as she strangled him then hid his body under bushes.

However, Brydus knew she could not take them on alone while they still had her friends. The intruders held the women and children as hostages, and they were hungry for flesh. The leader laughed at the discomfort of the women. Brydus' anxiety grew more every moment, hearing every agonizing scream coming from the girls. She couldn't risk them getting hurt. She did not want to fail them after she promised her protection. If she could take out the leader, she thought, maybe the others would not put up much of a fight.

The strangers were thin and extremely dirty. They looked like they survived by bushwhacking easy targets, taking what they wanted, then moving on.

Brydus had to take the chance. She rode into camp to distract them from the girls until she could take them on one at a time. Quietly and peacefully, Brydus rode into the camp as if nothing was going on. When the leader saw her, he let go of Tenisha. Another man had Amy by the neck, laughing as tears streamed down her delicate face.

"I have died and gone to heaven," the leader said, walking towards Brydus. She winked at the frightened women.

"So, what do we have here," she asked as she pushed him away with her foot. "I'll make you a deal, you leave these girls alone, and I won't kill you." They all started to laugh aloud, making rude remarks, as she scanned them for weapons.

"I don't think you're in any position to demand anything, young lady," the leader replied, laughing at her once again. One of the men still had Amy by the neck. Brydus could see the stream of tears rolling down her cheeks.

"Let her go," she said sternly, and the man let her go. Amy crawled away, back to Maryann's waiting arms.

Brydus smiled, teasing the assumed leader, "So you must be the big bad man in charge of this pack?"

"That would be me, baby," he laughed loudly, showing his yellow teeth. Brydus didn't exhibit any fear, knowing she could defend herself, but the others were at their mercy. One of the men tried to take her horse, but Blackie reared up on his hind legs and kicked him in the head. He ran screaming behind his boss.

"Don't mess with my horse. He doesn't take well to strangers. If you do it again, I'll have to kill you."

"Now, now, sweetheart, we can work something out. I am a reasonable man, and a woman like you…well, she can change the mind of any man… if you know what I mean." This time when he smiled, she could see that his teeth were yellow and rotting at the gums.

"I'll tell you what… you leave the girls alone, and I'll take care of each of you…one at a time," she pointed to the tent, "We're going to need some privacy. You know how things can get, big boy. There are children present."

He started to tug on his crotch. "Why don't I just take what I want and then some, you little bitch?"

"Like I said, I will kill you." Now it was her turn to smile. "I don't think you really want to mess with me. So just leave the girls alone, and I'll take care of you… one at a time, like I said. That is, if you can handle what I have to give you. What do you say, big boy?"

He couldn't take his eyes off her, "Oh…I can handle it, baby. I can handle everything you've got," he was drooling.

"Alright then, I want you to promise that you won't molest these young girls and lovely ladies, or else the deal is off."

"Leave these bitches alone," he yelled to his crew. The women huddled together, holding each other and covering the crying children.

"Well, that's not fair," one protested, "why should we get sloppy seconds?"

"Just do as I say. We'll have some real women later. There's a town not far from here, we can sell some of this rum, and you can get all the tail you want," the leader argued.

Brydus winked at Rev. Wilson. Then she walked over to her and slipped her a gun, "If anyone of them comes near you, blast them in the balls, you got it?" she whispered in Rev. Wilson's ear, who was as pale as a ghost. She nodded back slowly. Brydus could see the paralyzing fear in her eyes. "Everything will be alright, trust me," she winked at her again.

He pulled Brydus towards him and turned her around. "First, I have to tie you up, sweetheart. I hope you like it rough because I do… if you know what I mean," laughing boisterously as the others joined in, knowing it would soon be their turn.

"Not a problem, big daddy, whatever you want. I'll give it to you nice and hard. Trust me, you'll never forget it."

"Now that's what I'm talking about, whoopee," he shouted as Brydus led him into the tent.

The others were angry, but they knew Boyett would hurt them if they ruined his chances with this strange and beautiful woman, who promised to take care of all of them. Rev. Wilson hid the gun under her wrap and told the girls to be really quiet.

Boyett was the leader of the crude gang, pushing Brydus playfully from behind as they entered the huge tent. She played along. He pinned her against the tent's center pole and tried to kiss her. But Brydus moved her face to avoid the kiss. She tried to hold her breath, not wanting to inhale the foulness coming from his mouth. Boyett laughed, ripping open her shirt and exposing her undergarment. He looked at her, wild and hungry, and then breathed heavily, looking at her beautiful full breasts. "God, I must have done something right in my rotten lifetime. This is as close to heaven as I'm ever going to get."

Meanwhile, Demi and his men heard the women crying and pleading not to hurt the children. Demi's crew hid when hearing the men's loud voices, shouting indignities and profanities at the women. Cisco motioned to the men that it was the thieves. They were on their game doing what they did best, stealing and terrorizing the weak. Cisco circled around the back, looking for a safe place to position himself, when he came across a body. It looked like someone had strangled him from behind. The deceased was dressed the same as the others, smelling like stale booze and dirt.

Demi motioned to each of his men where to go and wait for his signal. When everyone was in place, he commanded to sweep the area.

Inside, Brydus smiled at Boyett, unaware of what was going on outside, "Oh… you'll be closer to heaven than you think by the time I'm done with you," she licked her lips seductively.

Boyett clumsily unbuttoned his pants, "Little lady, you will not be disappointed. They don't call me Big Daddy Boyett for nothing," he tugged on himself.

"Well, let's see what you've got, big daddy," she smiled, taunting him. Boyett went for her breast, kissing then squeezing them viciously. She waited until he positioned himself just right and then jammed her knee into his groin as hard as possible. She watched as his eyes crossed and rolled back in his head. Boyett felt the searing pain and fell to his knees, holding himself, unable to utter a sound. He looked at Brydus, dazed and confused, trying to recover. She kicked him on the bridge of his nose, and blood spattered everywhere. "You should have listened to me when I told you to leave us alone," she snarled. He cursed at her as he lay on the ground, bawling in pain.

Brydus could hear a commotion coming from the girls. She jumped over the ties on her hands so that they were at her front. Then found a big rock and hit Boyett over the head, knocking him unconscious.

One of Boyett's men had decided he wouldn't wait for him to finish with Brydus. He wanted relief right now. He picked up Helen by the hair and ripped open her shirt. "Yeah…I like them with some meat on, he said." The other men laughed as Helen fought to free herself from his grip.

Brydus struggled to free herself, listening to cries of panic coming from outside.

Rev. Wilson begged them on bended knees to leave Helen alone. "Have mercy, sir, please, please have mercy. God is watching your every move."

The men thought it was funny, laughing and mocking her, "There, take that, you stinking bitch." One of the men struck her in the head, sending her to the ground, shouting, "There is no God."

Helen's attacker struggled to pull off her pants. She was so scared; it made her sick, puking all over him. He was so angry; he raised his fist to strike Helen. Just then, she heard an explosion in her ears, and the filthy thug fell to the ground. Another one of Boyett's men grabbed one of the children, using him as a human shield. Cisco took aim, shooting him between the eyes. The others surrendered without much protest. Louis covered the hysterical Helen with his shirt and tried to calm her down. The campsite was a mess. The women didn't know who was who anymore.

Rev. Wilson and the rest of the girls didn't know what was happening. Men were coming from everywhere, screaming and yelling. Weapons were drawn, and the bandits were not resisting. Cisco had the pillagers on their knees with their hands behind their heads.

Rev. Wilson grabbed Big Willie by the arm, "He has her in there. Please help her," she urgently said as she pointed to the tent. Big Willie nodded to her and motioned for Louis to follow him.

The women and children huddled together, afraid of the new men who invaded their camp with guns and rifles drawn. When Big Willie opened the flap to the tent, all he saw was a wild woman standing over a body on the ground. Big Willie looked at Louis, who was standing right behind him. Brydus panicked, listening to the screams coming from her friends. When Big Willie started to approach her, she kicked him so hard in the chest it knocked him backward, taking Louis down with him. When Demi rushed in, he found both of his men on the ground.

"What the hell's wrong with you two," they pointed at Brydus, who still had her hands tied. She was confused and did not know who these new men were. "She's just a female," Demi said, wondering who she was, rushing toward Brydus, scaring her. However, before his men could get the word stop out of their mouths, they saw Demi go down in slow motion holding his crotch. Louis went to help him, but Demi grabbed him by the shirt, "Get the net," he grunted between bouts of shooting pain. Louis helped Demi to his feet with difficulty. When Big Willie came back with the net, he and Louis cornered Brydus to bring her down. She collapsed under the weight of the net, still fighting fiercely to get away. Big Willie had a hold of her arms, and Louis held her legs. "Let go of me, asshole!" She yelled as they dragged her outside into the open. It was getting darker, making it hard to see.

"I swear to God I'm going to kill this bitch," Demi yelled, still trying to recover.

Rev. Wilson ran to him, "Please don't hurt her. She was only defending herself."

Demi looked at her as if she had three heads. "Are you kidding me? This bitch just kicked me in the nuts! I'll be lucky if I can function as a man again."

Brydus continued kicking and wrestling with Big Willie, who was trying to get her free from the net.

"Please, Madam, we're not going to hurt you," Big Willie said, trying to calm her down. Nevertheless, Demi was enraged. He was not going to take any chances with her.

"I will knock your damn lights out, bitch, if you don't stop!" He shouted, pulling on the net. Brydus stopped struggling long enough to allow Big Willie and Louis to free her. When they finally pulled the net away, Demi came face to face with a pair of angry brown eyes. They were all shocked, "Oh shit!" Demi cried.

"Let go of me, you prick, unless you want the same thing the others got!" Brydus yelled, eyes blazing with anger.

Demi's jaw dropped. He took a few steps backward, shaking his head. "God help us."

"Please don't hurt her. She was just trying to protect us," Helen pleaded with Demi.

"No offense, lady, but you can't hurt the devil," Demi said, staring at Brydus, still holding his crotch.

"Let them go and take me instead," Brydus offered.

Demi wanted to laugh, "Oh, and what am I supposed to do with you?" he questioned.

Brydus stared him up and down, "Untie me, and I will show you. You're a big boy. Let's see who falls first."

Demi realized her hands were still tied, "Don't tempt me, woman, I'm not in the mood. Big Willie!" He yelled,

"Remove this beast from my sight. Before I forget she's a woman and beat her like a man."

"Release me, and I'll show you how hard this beast can hit," she replied with sarcasm.

Demi stood face to face with her, "I said, don't temp me, woman, there's a first time for everything."

Louis and Big Willie moved Brydus to the other side of the camp. They were afraid to untie her hands. Demi gathered everyone in the middle of the camp. The women and children still huddled together, afraid, not knowing what would happen to them next. "You!" He pointed to Rev. Wilson, "Come here." She moved slowly toward Demi, who was still very upset.

"Yes, sir," Rev. Wilson answered, still afraid of this new group of men.

"What's going on here?"

"Well, our town was burnt down, my husband died on the journey to a new settlement, we were dying when Brydus came along… she saved us," she said, pleading he would understand.

"So, who is this woman? Where does she come from?"

"I don't know… she is very private, but she's smart and knows what's she's doing. Brydus told us she wanted to help us find a good settlement… a place where we can start over," she explained almost in tears.

Demi felt sorry for the woman. He looked at the rest of them and realized how scared they must be, having lost everything and being attacked again. "Alright, get back over there with the others and make yourselves comfortable. We're here for the night. You can sleep peacefully. We were hunting for these assholes." Demi walked over to his men, who were tying up the prisoners. "Alright… um, I kind of got a little information about these people… not much on her though," he said, looking at Brydus. "They are actually looking for a place to settle down and start a new life… so I guess we're stuck with them too."

"What about that one… with the brown eyes and wicked black hair? She's terrifying, but damn, damn, damn, is she fine," Louis said, staring at her from across the camp.

"Yeah, she has the look and body of a goddess, but she is dangerous," Demi said. It had not escaped his eyes just how strong and beautiful Brydus was. He would try to get more information out of her. Demi also wanted to see if they could let her join the others untied.

Brydus did not exhibit any fear on the outside, but she remembered Jake's warnings about human traffickers inside. His words of caution screamed loud and clear in her mind recalling him speaking about people who would pretend to care. However, instead would sell you to the highest bidder. She would not sleep well or any other time until she determined what the men intended to do with her and her friends.

Demi took a deep breath to get into a different frame of mind before he went to speak to Brydus. Big Willie could only stare. He was fascinated with her.

"Take a picture, freak. It will last longer," she yelled at him. Big Willie turned red and looked away.

"I'm sorry, miss, I don't mean to stare… please forgive me."

She tried not to laugh at him, "Untie me, big boy, or are you chicken," she said, provoking him.

"Um," he was puzzled, unable to get his words together, "No, miss, I mean…I can't untie you, and yes, I am a chicken," still feeling the effect of the kick on his chest, he rubbed the sore spot.

Demi was tired but needed to find out who killed the two thieves in case there were others around beside them. Brydus watched Demi come toward her again. She stood straight and unwavering, arching her left eyebrow to unnerve him. "Alright, tell me who killed those two men," he tried to sound hard and stern.

She couldn't help but look at the handsome man with dimples and smiled, "I killed them, and I would have killed every one of these assholes had you and your goons not shown up."

"Somehow, that doesn't surprise me," Demi said. "Well, at least you're honest about that. I hope you can also be honest about the rest of what I'm about to ask you. Are you dangerous?"

She smiled again, looking at him with her eyebrow arched seductively. "Are you really asking me that question? I can whip your ass… and his," she pointed to Big Willie.

"Well, isn't that special? Looks like you're going to sleep with your hands and feet tied. I don't trust you."

She stepped closer. "And I don't trust you! Look, I don't care what you think about me. I only care about what happens to them. They have been through enough shit, and I promised to take care of them. Nothing else matters to me, not you or the rest of your clowns."

Demi closed his eyes in frustration, "You're one angry bitch… now tell me, am I going to have trouble with you? I want to know."

"I think you can answer your own question. If you think I'm going to submit to you or anyone else, you'd better think again."

"So, what you're saying is…"

She interrupted him. "What I'm saying is that if anyone of you comes near me, I will beat the living shit out of you, hands tied or not, and that's a promise!" She yelled at him, "Are we clear?"

"Loud and clear, woman, but I can assure you, none of my men will harm you. However, for the safety of my men and myself, you will remain bound and under guard."

"Whatever," Brydus said as she looked away.

Demi was angry. He did not anticipate so much drama. He thought he would just gather up some drunken thieves, send them on their way to Prison Island, and be done with it. Now he had a bunch of women and children to care for. In addition, a beautiful, sexy woman who would drive any man crazy with lust. Demi joined the rest of the men who had built a larger campfire and were feeding the children. He sat down, pouring himself a cup of coffee, "God, what a mess," he said, looking into the fire.

"Yeah, those poor fools didn't know what hit them?" Cisco said, sitting down next to him.

"Who's talking about those fools," Demi stated. I'm talking about… her, man. Look at that freakin rack and those damn brown eyes… I wonder if we could be related," he had a second thought.

"Are you serious? What if you are, and you've been treating her like shit?" Cisco laughed.

"Hey… I'm not the bad guy here. Remember where she kicked me?"

"Yeah, and she gave it to you good, one kick, bam, and you went down to your knees holding your nuts," Cisco teased. His men could not keep from laughing at Demi's situation.

"Ah, you know what? All you assholes can go straight to hell. But don't come crying to me when she kicks you in the nuts and your boys run and hide in your stomach," Demi bellowed as they continued to torment him. He could only laugh along with them.

After stabilizing the tent, the women and children settled down to sleep. Rev. Wilson tried to comfort Brydus. Big Willie and Louie had handcuffed and shackled her to the tree. The anger rose in her, wanting to lash out, protesting loudly at Demi, who laughed at her predicament.

"They seem pretty nice, Miss Brydus. What do you think?" Rev. Wilson asked.

Brydus didn't want to scare her with horror stories Jake had shared with her. "We'll see. Now go and get some rest. Let me worry about these clowns. Tomorrow will tell us more about who they really are."

"Brydus, you know it's alright to trust people. Not everyone is bad," Rev. Wilson smiled at her. She really wanted to believe that she was right.

Demi was dead tired, but he could not help thinking about the sexy woman who stirred his blood. *Who was she, and where did she come from,* he thought. Dealing with Brydus brought back memories of his grandmother, who was just like her. She was sweet and kind to the family and those who knew her. But he had seen his grandmother in action. He recalled an incident that he would never forget. He and his mother were accompanying Nylaya, his grandmother, to a farm close to where they lived. All of a sudden, they were ambushed by four men. Demi remembered being scared to death. They looked like giants to him. He sat on his mother's lap as he watched his grandmother whip those men from one side of the road to the other. He heard bones cracking as the men begged for mercy. When Nylaya was finished with them, they were a bloody mess. Demi remembered his grandmother holding him, trying to comfort him, "Don't worry, my sweet little man. Your grandmother will never let anyone hurt her boy." That was the first time he had seen the other side of her. Her pretty black hair was streaked with gray now, but those brown eyes were sharp, and she was deadly.

Demi finished the rest of his coffee, making himself comfortable for the night but keeping one eye open. *What a day,* he thought as he drifted off. "My brother is never going to believe this. Boy, do I have a story to tell Joaquin, and he will probably be amused," he said to himself.

Chapter 10: Quintanilla Estate

Morning came, and it took the camp forever to prepare for the long trip ahead. The children were still confused. They did not know whether to trust or fear these new men. Demi knew his beautiful captive would be trouble. She was very defiant and refused to answer any of his questions. He wanted to make peace with her, but Brydus was making things very difficult. Demi cornered her by a tree. "So, is it safe to assume that you will try to escape if I untie your hands?" Demi asked as he took the handcuffs off and replaced them with a cowhide strip to give her wrist some relief.

Brydus didn't want to make any waves. The girls were still very afraid. They looked to her for support and guidance. "I won't cause any problems unless you do something stupid to make me angry. I am here to take care of these women and children, understand?" she warned.

Demi pulled her roughly toward him by her bound hands and laughed sarcastically. "You are one cocky bitch, aren't you?" he smiled at her as she pulled away.

"Bitch is my middle name," she sneered as he pulled her back.

"Fair enough, but just so you know, these men here," he pointed to Cisco and Troy, who sat with the women drinking coffee. "They are the best trackers in the area, and if you run, we will find you."

Brydus laughed, "Oh my, and is that supposed to scare me? I eat men like them for breakfast," she exclaimed, showing that she was not afraid of his threats. Demi's eyebrow rose as he laughed a little. He didn't know what to think, so he just shook his head and turned away from the beautiful young woman.

Demi remembered her favorite target on a man's anatomy and grabbed his crotch. He thought about what his grandmother used to say, and she was right. Another fight would not solve anything. Besides, they needed to get moving.

Brydus still didn't know what to think of these men, although they seemed nice enough. They made sure that the children were fed, giving them treats and playing games with them along the way. However, she had heard so much about human trafficking from Jake that she was afraid to let her guard down. The horrific stories Jake told her still haunted her and made her cautious. As it was the nice people who pretended to care. But their motives were far from friendly or genuine.

She kept her eye on Demi. He was a very handsome and strong man, even with his animosity towards her. Rev. Wilson was full of hope. "Here, eat some fruit, my dear."

She handed Brydus an apple, then looked towards Big Willie, who carried one of the boys on his back. "They are really good with the children. Maybe they are what they seem, decent folk."

Brydus wanted so much for her to be right. It would break her heart if they turned out to be scum, so she continued to keep her suspicions to herself. She wanted for them what she promised, to find a settlement where they could start over and not have to be afraid anymore. A place where the girls could go to school and learn how to trust, love, be normal teenagers. For them to someday find a nice man to marry and have a family of their own.

"They are really nice people. Brydus, you should try to be kinder towards the really good-looking one," Rev. Wilson said, teasing her about how her behavior was making Demi crazy. "He's trying to find a way to be nice to you… and he's very handsome, don't you think?"

Brydus tried not to laugh, "Cute doesn't mean we'll get along." Brydus laughed. "We would probably kill each other. Besides, you know what they say if he's handsome; he's either married or gay."

Rev. Wilson almost choked on the apple she was eating, "Oh no, my dear, he's not married, and he's definitely not gay. He looks at you as if he has never seen a woman in his life. He told Amy he wasn't married, and she looked at him with stars in her eyes." Rev. Wilson added, advising Brydus.

"She's at that age where young girls think of boyfriends, dating, and a man who will swoop down to save her. You know, like a knight in shining armor… so why wouldn't he be the target of her first crush?" Brydus said, smiling.

"What about you, Brydus? Who holds that special place in your heart?" Rev. Wilson asked.

Brydus paused a few moments to think about that question. "There is no one. I thought I was in love with my boyfriend once, but my mother was right. It was just puppy love. I think I was more in love with the idea of being in a relationship."

"That happens. You will know it when it is love, as I did with my husband. God in heaven do I miss him," she said sadly.

"I have always compared what I felt for my boyfriend to what my parents have. The way they looked at each other. I remember how they treated each other with respect and compassion. I guess that's what I was expecting from my boyfriend when we dated, but it didn't manifest itself that way. My mother told me that the heat and passion she felt for my father were there from the beginning. Even though she didn't know it at first. It was there since they met when she was very young."

"Ah, I know what she's talking about. It was the same way with Martin and me." Rev. Wilson thought of her recently deceased husband. It always made her melancholy. "He was one of those men, people considered larger than life, strong, and full of ideas. He loved the Lord with a passion. That's what drew me to him. He had been married before but had no children together. She divorced him when he found God. Yes, I remember as if it was yesterday when I heard him preach and sing… Lord. I knew that he was the man I was destined to marry. We clicked instantly. We dated for a few months before we were married," she laughed. "I know that wasn't an ideal time frame, but when you know, something is right. I could not resist his charm and strong personality. We were married forty-six wonderful years and had two beautiful children."

"Your children, are they still alive?" Brydus asked, surprised.

"Yes, our children survived the Dark Days. Roianna fell sick for a while, but the Lord restored her. They both married missionaries. Roianna lives in Haiti, and James and his wife live in Santo Domingo. We also have six wonderful grandchildren. When we are settled, I hope to send them word of their father's passing. They will be devastated, but they know he's not suffering and is with the Lord."

"It's a scary time we live in, Rev. Wilson. These women are lucky they had you and your husband to lead them and share your faith."

"The faith comes from good people like you, who could have easily walked away and allowed us to die in the wilderness. I believe God has special plans for you, Miss Brydus, and as for love… well, I think it's just God's way of saying thank you, my child, for doing what is right." She looked down at Brydus' tied hands and laughed.

"I don't know, but I'm starting to feel like Joseph in the Bible right now," Brydus said, laughing too.

"Ah… but remember, Joseph became second in command of an empire." The Reverend added as she winked at Brydus. "Everything is going to be alright, sweetie."

"I'm sure you're right." Brydus smiled. She always felt good when she spoke with Rev. Wilson. Like Jake, she was full of knowledge and great stories. Just like her Abuelita Reina, who always reminded her of why they chose to move to the Valley of God and leave everything else behind for a quiet, simple life.

Brydus did not make things easy for Demi. It didn't matter how good-looking she thought he was. Every time he tried to talk to her, she would turn her back on him. She did not want to make friends with him or his crew. Being friends meant that she had to feel something, and she didn't want to go through the pain of losing someone again.

Demi never slept well when he had prisoners underhand, and on top of it, 'that woman', as he called her, was driving him crazy. Not sleeping made him cranky and worried about everything even more. He hoped that his brother would not see this as a failure since it happened on his watch. Joaquin worked so hard, and now it was his turn to step up to the plate and take his place. "That damn woman is driving me to drink," he whispered to himself.

The next morning, Demi was in a foul mood, and it didn't help that one of the children fell out of a tree and hurt his arm. Cisco attended to his needs after making sure he would be all right. Demi couldn't wait until they were back at the estate. Travel was prolonged, and the heat was not making things any easier. Spring was upon them, but it felt more like a steamy August morning. Some of the kids whined and complained about having to walk. To make things more troubling, Brydus had shut down and still would not speak to him except for short one-word answers.

Demi prayed that God help him make it through this trip. The next night brought more stress for him. The prisoners were starting to speak among themselves more. His men were getting restless and couldn't wait until they had their prisoners in a proper jail. It was Demi's turn to keep watch over the prisoners. He threw more wood in the fire to keep it alive. As he crouched down by the fire, he felt an odd movement behind him. One of the prisoners had gotten loose and was about to jump him from behind, trying to take his weapon. The prisoner knocked him off balance. By the time he had regained his footing, Brydus had the criminal on the ground. She used the ties that bound her to strangle him and pull him off Demi.

The man struggled to get free from her grip, but Demi knocked him out with one blow before she had a chance to kill him. The ruckus woke up everyone in the camp, and the prisoners were put under a tighter watch. Demi had to admit, he was glad that Brydus was also a light sleeper. He started to believe she wasn't really a danger to them after all. He went over to thank her and take the ties off her hands as she lay back down.

"Hey, listen, thanks for… for what you did. You did not have any reason to help me, but I'm glad you did. It would have been bad if they had gotten free."

"I didn't do it for you! I did it for them," Brydus said as she pointed at her friends. "They've been through enough shit in the last month. They need to feel safe, even out here." She growled.

Demi, stunned by her verbal attack, struck back, "You know I came here to thank you and tell you I'm sorry for how I've treated you. Why do you have to be such a bitch?"

"Because I don't want to be yours or anybody's friend. I will be on my way as soon as you get me before a judge for killing those jerks. All I want is for you to please do your job and protect these women and children," she whispered, trying not to let the whole camp hear her.

Demi came closer, pinning her against a tree so that only she could hear him. "Let it be known to you, miss, that I tried to be nice to you, but you are impossible to please. I pity the man who takes you as a wife. Because you would want to wear the pants all the time and keep his balls in a jar. You are not going before a judge. What you did was justified. I'm taking you before my brother because I have this strange feeling that we are kin."

She was puzzled by his remark. "What do you mean, kin?"

"You'll find out tomorrow when you meet my brother."

"Kin or not, if you come at me again like that, we will fight, and I won't go easy on you this time," she threatened.

Demi's jaw dropped as he stood up and questioned her, "Are you sure you're a woman, or do you have a pair of balls hiding in your panties? You know, you sure have a lot of mouth for someone your size."

"Don't let my size fool you, Demi," she said, addressing him by his name. "I'm one of the meanest bitches on this planet, and I don't need to have a set of balls to prove it."

He was amused, "I'll tell you what? When we get back to my place, we'll duke it out hombre to hombre, no pulling punches. I don't have a problem knocking a woman on her ass."

"I welcome the challenge, tough guy. Oh, and make sure you bring some backup. You're going to need it," she sneered. Demi walked away, shaking his head once again at the crazy woman. The problem was she probably could beat him, as he thought about the two dead men they left behind. Demi laughed at himself as he wondered what his brother would say when he met the wildcat.

The men took turns watching the prisoners, making sure their hands remained securely tied. Early the following day, they were all up and ready. It was only five more miles to their estate. The roads began to get better as they progressed slowly closer to their home. People along the way waved at the men as they passed by. Some actually came out and brought them water. They addressed him as Master Demi and smiled as if glad to see him and his men.

The prisoners feared for their lives as they realized how loyal the locals were to their overseer and would do anything to protect him.

Brydus began to relax as she watched the smiles on the people's faces. Even in their work clothes, they were well dressed and looked very healthy and strong. Some of the farmers offered lodging in their homes when they found out that the women and children were homeless. Brydus was overwhelmed with relief that they had finally made it. This is a place where they could put down roots and start over. Brydus didn't care what happened to her at this point. She could easily take care of herself. Demi had not bothered her all morning, and she rather liked it that way.

Chapter 11: Monet

If you were to describe her, the word flawless would come to mind, and an image of Monet would appear next to the word in the dictionary. She was an unblemished beauty with long pale blond hair, porcelain skin, and a figure that had been described as perfect. Beautiful blue eyes and rose bud lips. Monet was a masterpiece to be admired, and many men found themselves captivated by her beauty and sexuality. However, Monet had other plans. She was not going to be just another pretty face on a poor man's arm. She set her eyes on a prize that would keep her in the comfort she wanted. Joaquin Quintanilla was the perfect catch for her. It took her a while to develop the perfect scheme to get into his inner circle, and now that she had arrived, nobody was going to doubt. This was where she belonged.

Monet had her own style, living and surrounding herself with beauty. Her room was decorated just like her, in rich blends of pink and gold everywhere. Beautiful rose-colored curtains trimmed in gold lace with matching comforters and sheets. An oversized full-length mirror hung against one of the walls so that she could admire herself clearly from every angle.

Everything she surrounded herself with was of high quality and over the top. She chose to stay in smaller quarters to be close to Joaquin's suite. Insisting on making her smaller suite as elegant as possible. A place where she would feel like a queen.

Monet knew this was the life that she was meant to live. A life with a rich and handsome husband who was powerful and well connected. Joaquin was that man.

She loved to look at her naked body in the mirror and admire her loveliness. She thought she could conquer the world with this face and body. After all, Joaquin was just a man, and men think with their penises. "Tonight, my lover," Monet said as she admired herself. "When you come home, I will take care of all your needs and then some. How can you resist this body?" She touched herself seductively, closing her eyes, feeling the heat rising inside her, a throbbing sensation that begged to be quenched. "After all, my lover… how can you resist all this," she laughed aloud.

One of the housemaids, Jenny, paused outside Monet's door before entering her room. "God help me," she whispered, mentally and physically preparing herself while dealing with Monet's outbursts and tantrums. Monet's verbal abuse started the minute Jenny opened the door.

"Well, it's about time! How many times do I have to call for you?" Monet whined. "Are you deaf, stupid, or both?"

Jenny shrugged her shoulders, "I was downstairs, where you sent me to look for your blue dress…" Jenny replied timidly.

"Oh, never mind, you useless piece of shit. I swear, sometimes I think Joaquin punishes me with your lazy ass. I love that man, but he has no clue who he hires, and you people take advantage of his good nature." Jenny struggled to keep silent. She carried scars from Monet's anger, making her dread serving her. Every demand came with a tantrum, and Monet threw them in abundance.

"Help me find that damn dress, or you're in deep shit!" Monet threatened. Jenny rolled her eyes behind Monet's back. "I know your kind, stealing everything that isn't nailed down. Don't think I haven't noticed how you look at my jewelry." she fussed, pulling things out of her dresser drawer and throwing them on the floor.

Jenny checked all the closets again. "I found it!" She yelled happily. "It's in the bathroom closet right where you put it. Remember, you put it in that plastic zipper bag?" Monet snatched the dress from Jenny's hands. "You put it there, Miss Monet, so no one would touch it," Jenny added, holding back her laughter.

"Maybe I did it, so someone with sticky fingers wouldn't touch it – not that you could fit your fat ass into it. However, it would bring a hefty price on the black market. Now, come over here and zip me up, and don't even think about pinching my skin," she hollered as Jenny made faces behind her back.

The dress fit her like a tight glove. It outlined every single curve, hugging her in all the right places. Monet loved the way it looked on her.

"Now, don't I look fabulous? I cannot wait until my darling hunk of a man sees me today. He better be ready for some hot freaky sex." She laughed at her own words, "Jenny, don't you wish you were me? I have all of this." She touched her body seductively. Jenny rolled her eyes once again. "I have a very hot man, and I can do whatever I want," she loved to tease Jenny and the other staff. "I know you bitches are envious of me, though I don't blame you, when you look as good as I do."

Jenny was anxious to get away from Monet before she became obnoxiously abusive, "Do you still need me? I have some things to finish downstairs."

"That can wait. I'm more important than anything else you have to do," she said conceitedly, facing Jenny. "Don't think I don't know what you piss heads say behind my back. All of you are just jealous of my beauty because you are all fat and ugly. You couldn't even get a man if you paid him." Monet turned her back to Jenny brushing her long silvery, silky hair. "Hm… I guess I would be jealous of myself, too, if I were you. I feel nothing but pity for fat, ugly girls that can't get a man to look at them twice."

Jenny tried to ignore her stupid and hurtful remarks. With Hurricane Monet, this was an everyday occurrence. Jenny would mimic Monet when she wasn't looking. She hated her with a passion. Her beauty masked her mean and malicious demeanor. Monet treated all the servants with contempt and disregard. She never had a kind word to say to anyone. Whenever Joaquin was around, she would use her silly fake way of talking and pretend to be nice to everyone.

The only reason Jenny tolerated her was because of Joaquin. He saved her and the only family member she had left, her father. They saved her from a band of raiders that terrorized their small town, leaving many dead or injured, critically wounding them.

Luck was on their side. Joaquin and his men were on their way to the Inner Cities and had to make a detour that led them through Jenny's hometown. They discovered the small town on fire and dozens of people fighting for their lives. Children were screaming and crying in the middle of the street while the fires raged on. Joaquin shot the two men trying to rape Jenny after running her down and beating her senseless. Gently, Dan and Joaquin put their jackets around her badly beaten body to cover her nakedness.

She thought she had died and gone to heaven when she could finally open her swollen eyes. At first, she thought Dan was St. Peter, putting a wet cloth to her brow, assuring her that everything would be all right. The next thing she remembered was waking up in a clean and warm bed and her father recovering in the very next room.

"Where…am I?" she struggled to say while not being able to open her mouth. Jenny remembered the first time she laid eyes on Mrs. Grayson. She tried to smile because, at that moment, she knew they were safe.

"Now, now, dear, try not to speak. Your jaw is wired shut. I have some nice warm tea and some chicken broth to help make you strong and healthy again." Mrs. Grayson said, helping Jenny sit up in bed so that she could drink some of the warm nourishment. Jenny was overwhelmed and could not stop crying. Every inch of her body hurt, and she didn't know how badly her father was injured.

Dr. Ayala gave her something for the pain, and she finally calmed down enough to drink something. That's when she met him, her savior. Joaquin smiled at her, and she lost the few senses she still had that functioned.

"Are you alright?" he asked in his low baritone voice. She slowly nodded yes.

"Good, I know you have many questions…your father is here and doing well. He suffered a broken leg, but Dr. Ayala says he should heal nicely. Doctor Ayala will take care of you until you recover. We have a home for you and the others who survived the attacks. When you and your father are well enough, if you want, you can stay here as long as you like. I would like to offer you employment at the main house, or maybe we can help you find something else. Whatever you decide. Right now, I just want you to get well and relax. You're in great hands." Tears escaped her eyes; silently, she thanked God. Later she found out that the gang that terrorized her town were captured, and some had died in a shootout.

Life was good at the estate until Monet came to visit, worming her way into Joaquin's bed. Now Jenny felt like a prisoner in this beautiful home serving the meanest woman that ever walked the earth.

Jenny didn't know what to do, growing tired of the abuse, which sometimes turned physical. Monet looked at herself in the full-length mirror. After she applied her makeup and brushed her beautiful hair, letting it fall softly down her back.

"I have great plans for my man," Monet said. "Yes, great plans…you know what I mean, don't you. Oh… I forgot you can't get a man." She laughed. "I'm sorry, I didn't mean to be so insensitive. I know how you homely people get. Now, I want this room clean, and I mean really clean. So, get started." Jenny looked at the mess in the room. She made a bigger mess every day, and Monet wanted her room cleaned up quickly.

"I'll get Mrs. Lawrence to help me," Jenny suggested.

Monet pushed her into the door, "No, I don't want that old hag to touch my things! It's your job," Monet replied, poking her in her chest.

"But it will take me all day! I have to help in the kitchen because Maggie is out sick…"

"I don't care…make it happen, or you know what will happen to you." Monet came menacingly close to Jenny, whispering and threatening her. Jenny just stood still, quietly blocking her out mentally. The last time Jenny let it get to her, she ended up with a black eye. Monet was always full of anger, and she always took it out on Jenny.

"Now that we have an understanding, get to it," Monet snapped. Jenny took a step back, and Monet grabbed Jenny by her dress and pushed her over a stool onto the floor. Before she could recover, Monet had taken her brush and began to strike Jenny on her arm and shoulder. Jenny covered her face, then managed to get to her feet and fled the room. "You better get back here and clean up this mess! Wait until Joaquin gets home! Your ass is out of here!" Monet shouted at the top of her lungs, slamming the door, and began to rage uncontrollably. She stopped when she looked in the mirror and saw how twisted her features were from anger. *I cannot continue to let myself lose control like this,* she thought. She touched her beautiful face tenderly, touching the lines that formed on the side of her face near her eyes. "No, no, I can't have lines around my eyes and mouth."

She was letting things get to her. The last time she spoke to Joaquin, he wanted her out and was willing to give her anything she needed to get her to move. However, this was not in her plans. He was not going to push her away as the others did. All she ever dreamed of was being the estate's mistress that represented a castle to her. This would help her make it to the top of society's ladder. In Monet's mind, this would erase all the ugliness she experienced and give her all the things that she felt she was entitled to, all of her life.

Monet knew the kind of effect she had on men. When she finally found out who her real father was, she turned against her stepfather, Ramon. Her real father was rich and lived in a beautiful luxurious home. He knew how to govern with authority. Monet's real father was a cruel businessman and treated his family the same way. His new wife, Gigi, was thirty-seven years younger than him. However, she feared him and jumped every time she heard his voice.

Gigi had been pregnant three times and lost the babies. Now pregnant again, she didn't need the stress of having her around. When Monet came to visit, they instantly hated each other. Gigi looked a lot like her, very curvy and extremely blond. Nevertheless, she felt that Monet was trying to push her around by making demands on her staff. So, after a few weeks of arguments, Monet's father was getting irritated with both of them. Gigi could always get what she wanted after a few moments of sex. "Larson dear, has Monet said anything about how long she will be staying with us? She's a sweet girl, but I don't want her to overstay her welcome."

Larson sighed deeply, "Frankly, I can't stand to look at her, but she is my child."

"Are you sure? Her mother was with someone else at the time."

"Hey, she's my brat. She and Larson Jr. could be twins. She may look like her damn mother, but she has my temperament. To be honest, I could care less if she stays or leaves." Gigi smiled at his remarks.

Monet liked what she saw and was more determined than ever to break into the social circles her father enjoyed rubbing elbows with wealthy people. She desperately wanted to prove to her father that she belonged.

However, Gigi had a different agenda. She wandered into the dining room where Monet was having breakfast. Gigi stared at Monet, provoking an argument. She smiled wickedly, "You don't think he will choose you over me, do you? So… when are you leaving?" Gigi asked with an attitude. "You know two bitches can't live together, little girl."

"I'm staying as long as my father wants me to stay," Monet challenged.

Gigi stepped closer to ensure that Monet was the only one to hear her, "Look, you little bitch. I put my time in with your father. He's an asshole, but I have to put up with his shit to live. I will never again have to worry about where I will live or how I will survive."

"So, it's safe to say you don't love my father," Monet asked, smiling.

"What's to love, honey? He's a cruel and evil man. But I know how to handle him. So let me set you straight. If you think that you are going to get anything out of him by being here, you're sadly mistaken. He has no love for you. You remind him of your mother. You have the same features. However, she was a nice person, but you're just a cold-blooded bitch. I knew your mother, yeah. She was a fine woman, but you, you're a filthy skank whore… you may have her looks, but you have his soul. The only person he truly loves is his son, your brother, Larson Jr. He adores his son, but Larson couldn't care less about his father. Larson Jr. will inherit everything except for one of his homes and a nice amount of cash that he has set aside for me. Unless I give him a child, well… then that changes everything."

"I don't understand you. Why are you here putting up with his shit if you're not getting all his money?" Monet asked, perplexed.

"I just want the same thing you want… to live in a nice house, and not worry about anything… like food or clothing. He gives me money every month to do whatever I want. My mother used to clean this house," Gigi said. "That's how I knew your mother. I saw how your father beat that poor woman and raped her whenever he wanted. However, he's slower now and not so aggressive. He's afraid of being alone, so he doesn't beat me. It's just verbal abuse, and I can deal with that."

"Well, you're going to have to move aside, sister; this is my daddy."

Gigi started to laugh, "Like I said, there isn't room for two bitches. We'll see who he chooses."

Two weeks later, after another huge argument, Monet was asked to leave. Her anger began to build as she traveled back home. After that, she and her mother fought all the time, and poor Ramon was caught right in the middle. When Monet was out of control, Ramon tried to keep his wife safe. She would say the most awful things to her mother, accusing her of leaving everything behind to live in squalor with Ramon.

Monet's mother tried her best to give her the things she wanted. Her younger sister always went without. Emily was such a wonderful child. She always made way for Monet. They were close as children, but Monet shunned her as Emily grew and blossomed into a beautiful woman. Then when Emily fell in love and married a wonderful country boy, Monet yelled at her, calling her a fool.

Monet knew she was destined for something greater, which meant she had to leave her family behind. So that's what she did. She cut all communication and ties to her mother and family, wanting to forget where she was born and how she grew up. She made up her own past and history, not including any of them. Monet acted as if they were dirt beneath her feet, except when she needed something from them or was in trouble. Even then, her family helped her as much as they could, trying to give her the love and support they thought she needed. She would betray them and always guilt them into doing what she wanted.

Chapter 12: The Overlord

Joaquin was glad to come home early. He loved the serene atmosphere as he entered his home. The house had an eerie silence to it. Usually, there were always people running him down trying to get a meeting with him, but it was nice not having to think about anything the minute he walked through the door.

He went straight to his study to attack the mountain of paperwork and charts left on his desk during his absence. After a short briefing with Rudy, he sat back and stretched his tired bones. He welcomed the solitude, but by mid-morning, Mattie poked her head into his room with her shiny smile.

"Master Joaquin, I thought you may want something to eat. I made you something special. Come on in, Cassia." She motioned to the other cook. Cassia carried a tray with rice soup, bread, and fruit juice, placing it on a small table by the window. Joaquin put his arm around Mattie as she removed the lids from his food and folded his napkin.

"You know, I'm going to marry you, right?" he kissed Mattie on the cheek. As always, she blushed.

"Oh, Master Joaquin, what would you do with an old fool like me?"

"I love you..." he winked, "look at how you take care of me."

"I would walk on broken glass for you, Master Joaquin. My greatest joy would be to see you happy." Mattie was a full-figured woman with pretty green eyes and a rosy round face. She lived to mother anyone that would let her, and she loved to cater to 'her boys', as she called them.

"I know you would," Joaquin said smiling, "that's why I love you." The two women giggled as Mattie covered her face with her apron.

"You and your brother are a pair. However," she paused for a minute, knowing he didn't want to hear what she had to say. "Master Joaquin, that lady is looking for you…should I inform her that you are home?"

Joaquin took a deep breath before he answered. He made a face that let her know what he wanted. "I don't want to deal with Monet right now. I just want to enjoy my food and wait until my brother gets home. Can you have him come and see me when he arrives?"

"Certainly, sir, I understand. I won't let anybody mess with my boys."

"Thank you…you're the best," he winked at both of them, "that's what I like."

Joaquin savored the soup Mattie, and Cassia brought him. He could see Demi and a caravan of people from the window behind him. He smiled to himself and shook his head. His brother was truly back, he thought… after many years of grieving for his lost love. He was now coming to terms with her death. Joaquin felt a pinch of guilt when he thought about Demi and Audrey. That kind of love they had for one another, even as young children. He wondered if he would ever feel that kind of love and passion. But Joaquin hadn't any time to think about anything aside from what he would do next – how he was going to get his providence and his people to the next level. He had been thinking about his life, and sometimes it saddened him.

Joaquin picked up a picture of his family and wished they lived closer. He tried to touch them through the frame. The picture of his mother and father holding each other and smiling made him long for them even more. His grandfather was holding his grandmother from behind, kissing her cheek. He could see the love on their faces. He missed them terribly. When his family came to visit last year, he was angry, having the suspicion they left suddenly because of Monet.

His mother had an instant dislike towards her. This bothered him because his mother was always so caring and sweet to everyone. Nylaya, his grandmother, was not impressed with Monet. After a week, they packed up and went to stay at his Aunt Alexandra's home. He remembered how upsetting it was that they left without giving him an explanation. He was miserable. He followed them to his Aunt Alexandra to spend more time with them before returning to Africa. He felt like a little boy all over again. The feeling of abandonment crept back into his heart.

Nylaya kissed him and held him so tight that he wished she would never let go. She told him something he would never forget, "She's not the girl for you, my son." She held his face tenderly between her hands, "but the one who will fill your heart is out there…you will see. Wait for love, and love will find you."

Those words have haunted him ever since. It was as if she could see into his soul. The loneliness he was experiencing, wanting something to fill the void. When Nylaya spoke to Demi, it really touched him. He can still hear the sweet sound of her voice comforting Demi as he sobbed uncontrollably in her arms. "Everything will be alright, my son, you'll see." She held him until he was weak, and when he left that room, he was a different person. He emerged like a new man and apologized for being mentally and emotionally absent for the last few years.

Joaquin tried so hard to love Monet. She was good to him at first and was very attractive. But she was also clingy, and that drove him crazy. He hated clingy women, and Monet was the queen of whining and complaining. The only time he enjoyed being with her was in bed, and even that was lacking. He knew she had other lovers, and normally it wouldn't have bothered him, but she wanted to get married. Monet had become a nag, and it turned him off.

The last time Joaquin left for the Inner Cities, he tried to end this unhealthy relationship by promising her a house of luxury, jewelry. Anything she wanted, if she would just leave his house. They fought for hours; she cried and acted like a small child, displaying a high degree of drama.

Demi did not get along with Monet either. Something happened between them that caused Demi to hate her. She would cry and say that Demi was jealous of their relationship, but Joaquin knew there was more to it than she let on.

He knew that Monet was one of the most desirable women in the area. She could turn any man's head. However, there was a coldness in her heart. Lack of emotions towards others he could not warm up to. He didn't know what it was, but his mother sensed it, and his family didn't like being around her. Joaquin knew he would never consider a wife that his parents disapproved of, and Monet didn't understand how important family was to Joaquin.

When Joaquin's family left, he was determined to find out why. He questioned Monet to see if anything happened between her and his mother, but she assured him that words never crossed between them. However, he always knew when Monet was lying.

Joaquin was his brother's keeper. As the elder of the two, all the responsibility fell on his shoulders, and he didn't mind, most of the time. When Demi fell apart after losing Audrey, Joaquin took care of him, dragging him out of the taverns so drunk that he could hardly walk. Sometimes even pulling him out of brothels after days of being missing. It was only when their family came to visit that Demi realized what he was doing to himself, and it felt great to have him back.

Joaquin was a little taller than his brother Demi, standing at six feet three inches. Slim build with curly blond hair hanging to his shoulders, he wore a goatee and had striking gray eyes. He had full lips and beautiful teeth like his grandmother, Nylaya. Joaquin was very handsome but had little time to socialize with the women who flocked to him. Demi, on the other hand, was a little shorter, six feet one, with broad shoulders and dimples when he smiled. He also wore a light beard, which he claimed made him look sexier and older.

The brothers were devoted to each other, always trying to keep a sense of family ties within their relationship. Joaquin always looked after his brother and knew he was still grieving for Audrey. Sometimes he would catch him talking to her picture, making him sad. He wondered if he'd ever find love in someone else's arms.

Joaquin stared out of the large picture window. He could see the land was finally taking on a rich green color. All the hard work they put into it was now beginning to show its beauty and worth. Nevertheless, if only he could get a grip on his social life, he would be happy. He thought it wasn't going to be easy getting Monet out of his house and into her own place, but he had to try.

Meanwhile, Brydus noticed that the estate was absolutely breathtaking as they approached the main mansion. The rolling landscape was maintained to perfection, and everyone addressed Demi in a respectful manner. It made her change her mind about Demi and his crew.

She could tell he was still angry with her for what she had said to him. He led the women and children to one side of the building, and she was led to a filthy basement. It was dark and damp. They went through a few rooms, dragging the prisoners into another part of the basement with cells big enough to house the men. Demi pulled her into one of the cells, cuffing her against a cold wall. She pulled on the cuffs, "Is this necessary, or are you just being an ass?" she asked sarcastically.

"Oh, excuse me…now you want me to talk to you after cussing me out every chance you got?" He was inches away from her face. "Let's see how you feel after being down here a few days. Maybe you'll be nicer to me."

"Look, I know you don't like me, and I can't stand you either, so take me to your brother so we can get this over with," she argued.

"Still being the bitch of the ball, I see," Demi said as he looked down her shirt.

"You're a pig!" She glared at him.

"I won't deny the fact that you're super hot… and have a great rack… and the rest of you, well, it speaks for itself. But someone needs to put you in your place. So be a good girl, and maybe in a few days we can talk again."

"Are you serious? Don't cross my path, Demi. I will kick your ass!"

"Save it," he laughed aloud, slamming the cell door behind him.

"Demi, you dickless shithead! I want to go before your brother so I can get the hell away from you and all these crazy ass people." She could hear him arguing with Big Willie about his treatment of her. Brydus was tired, and she longed for a hot soothing bath and a warm bed. Now she had to wait until his brother decided to send for her, which could take days.

Demi startled Cassia when he pulled open the back door that led into the kitchen.

"Master Demi, you'll be the death of me yet!"

"I'm so sorry, Cassia, and how is the love of my life?" He smiled at her as he washed the dirt from his hands in the sink.

"You and your brother, always promising a girl a good time," she giggled, "your brother is expecting you in his office."

"Good, I have much to tell him. Cassia, can you please tell Mattie that I have fifteen people who are in terrible need of her assistance? They are women and children, homeless, hungry, and tired. Can you take control of this situation, get them cleaned up, fed, and find them a place to sleep for the night?"

"Why didn't you say so, oh my dear," she ran to the window, "they look dreadful."

"Big Willie is helping settle the prisoners in the basement."

"Prisoners too, oh my," she said with a frightened look on her face.

"Very dangerous people, so don't go near them until you hear from me, got it?"

"Oh, I got it alright…prisoners… hm, mercy."

Demi laughed at Cassia's expressions. The estate had the best kitchen staff, and they were always willing to help others. He took the stairs up to Joaquin's office two by two.

Even though he was tired, he had a lot of energy, or maybe it was because he was home. He was never happier to see the mansion's roof in the distance as they approached, relieved that his mission was now over. His attitude changed, and he enjoyed seeing all of his people along the way, greeting them. As he turned the corner, he ran right into Monet, almost knocking her over.

"Well! So, you're home. Where the hell have you been? You smell like roadkill." Monet said, blocking his way.

"Move it, wench, I have business to attend to," he rolled his eyes.

"Umm, I'm sure you do…but what's your hurry?"

"None of your damn business," Demi said, not hiding his dislike for her.

"Hm, still playing the evil, hurtful brother denying his attraction to me. You never did get over the fact that I picked your brother over you," she said seductively.

"I know where to get a whore if I want one." Monet slapped him across the face, but he managed to grab her wrist when Monet tried to slap him again. "Don't you ever do that again – you are no lady in my eyes. I will knock you on your ass and enjoy it." Demi noticed that she was getting aroused and quickly let go of her hand. "You're disgusting," he said under his breath. She blocked his path again, leaning in towards him.

"Why deny that you have strong feelings for me?" Monet rubbed her body against him. "We can make this work… your brother doesn't have to know a thing." Demi felt the heat rise inside of him. He pushed her hard against the wall, but it only made her moan.

"Freak – I wouldn't touch you with someone else's dick."

Monet came closer, pressing her breasts against him, "We can have a great time together. I'm woman enough for both of you," she laughed.

"One day… one day… whore… Joaquin is going to see what you really are, a lousy no-good bitch in heat."

Monet wanted to hurt Demi. He was the only male for miles who didn't succumb to her beauty or charms. "Watch it, Mr. Demetrius," she called Demi by his full name. "I will tell Joaquin how you tried to force yourself on me."

"In your dreams, bitch, he won't believe you. He knows how much I loathe you. So, why don't you go polish something and leave me alone? You're wasting my time."

Monet grabbed Demi's arm. He looked her in the eyes, "You are not that important… your time around here is very limited, so don't get too comfortable. You're only a piece of ass to my brother. You will never be his wife." He pulled his arm away abruptly and then walked towards Joaquin's office.

Monet had to take a moment to compose her thoughts. There was something about Demi that she found sexy as she watched him walk down the hall. He always woke up such desires in her. Then she remembered her original mission, harassing the kitchen help for lunch.

Joaquin was just finishing up with Big Willie when Demi walked in. "Big Willie, how'd you get up here so fast?"

"I saw you were detained, so I came up the back way," Big Willie knew there was trouble between Demi and Monet, judging by the scene he had just witnessed. Big Willie turned toward Joaquin, "OK, I will get on that right away, boss," he said before walking out.

"How is my brother?" Joaquin asked, turning his attention toward Demi. "I would hug you, but you stink… no offense.

"None taken. I wouldn't hug me either."

I heard you had some trouble while I was away. What are the damages?"

"One of the small warehouses was burned down to distract us, while the other losers broke into one of the storage sheds. They took two barrels of whiskey, some wine, a few cans of meat, and some other small stuff, so we went after them. We couldn't let them get away with it. That would send a message to others that we are weak. Afterward,

I learned that they were the same gang going around terrorizing the other settlements on this route."

"Really, any casualties," Joaquin asked curiously.

"Very few… two men… but we didn't kill them."

"What happened? Did they kill each other? That doesn't make any sense."

"When we found them, they were in the middle of terrorizing a camp of women and children. Those men were already dead when we got there."

"Ok…" Joaquin said, perplexed. "Whoever killed them may need to see a doctor. These things can be very traumatic for women and young children."

"Mmm… somehow I doubt that. I think she rather enjoyed the kill. She's a beast!" Demi got comfortable in a big armchair. "Sit down, brother. You're going to love this. This chick is a she-devil, but I think we found a cousin."

"Are you serious? How can you be so sure?"

"Well, I'm not sure. I just have this feeling. She is the meanest, black-haired, brown-eyed bitch I've ever met. I've never seen anything like her, and the only reason I didn't kill her myself is because… she may be kin."

"So… you're saying she's like our grandmother?" Joaquin asked, interested.

"No doubt… however, she is very dangerous. I know she killed those men without a weapon."

"Oh really, how did she kill them? With bad language or does she have magic powers?" he scoffed.

"It's not funny. She's a trained killer," Demi replied.

"So was our grandmother; you've seen her in action."

"Yeah…my guess is that she was defending herself and the others. And brother… she hurt me bad… really bad… so bad that the family jewels may never be the same."

"Ouch! That bad, huh?" Joaquin grimaced. "Did you ever think that maybe she was scared and was trying to protect herself. You guys are scary looking."

"Protect… what, who… brother; we're the ones who need protection. She's pure evil, evil," Demi repeated.

Joaquin was amused. He laughed heartily. "Damn it, I wish I was with you guys," he laughed. I want to meet this woman that brought my brother to his knees. Bring her to me." Joaquin smiled, but the look on his brother's face said it all.

"That shit wasn't funny, bro. I don't know if I'll be able to function as a man again." He shook his head and huffed. "The worse thing about it was. She had her hands tied, and… I… kind of walked into it."

Joaquin laughed again. "I know, I heard."

"This is too much… does everyone know?" Demi mumbled, covering his privates.

"Oh… only the whole camp. I feel for you, little brother."

Demi sprang out of his seat, "Hey, it wasn't just me. Remember, there were two bodies and some other poor slob on the ground. She knocked down both Willie and Louis… at the same time."

"Really…interesting. I believe they left that part out. Surely she must be a big, strong woman…and you think she's kin?"

"Actually," Demi paused, remembering her beauty, "she is one of the most beautiful women I have seen, well, you know, besides Audrey," Demi said. "She's about this tall," he raised his hand; "five-eight feet tall, powerful legs, and those breasts… her eyes alone will set your loins on fire. I tell you what, brother. I had to remind myself that she may be kin and come back to reality on how much she hurt me. That helped put out the flames."

"What an experience! So, where is she now? I want to meet this woman…with; ah, shall we say assets, and who is most likely traumatized about having to kill two men?"

"Oh, she's not traumatized. I told you she's evil, mean and… and has no fear. I put her in a cell downstairs."

"You can't do that; she didn't commit a crime. She was defending herself. Bring her to me. I'll deal with her," Joaquin argued.

"She's dangerous, and a bitch, no matter how beautiful. She called me out a few times, saying she can whip my ass."

"I'm sure that she just doesn't trust you or any of us. Let me handle her, alright?"

"You got it, bro… but I'll tell you what. If she comes at me. I'm going to knock her on her sexy ass. That one is no lady."

Joaquin chuckled, "I understand…thanks, Demi. Hey, you did well. I'm proud of you. Those people probably would have died if you hadn't come along and brought them here."

"I don't think so; wait until you meet this witch."

"We will take care of them anyway."

Demi ran into Monet standing at the office door on his way out. She pretended to ignore him as she turned all her attention to Joaquin, "You naughty man…you've been here for hours. Why didn't you let me know?"

Joaquin took a deep breath, "I was busy, and I needed some peace and quiet." She grabbed him and started kissing him repeatedly. Joaquin pushed her arms away. "Monet, I have a lot of work to do. We have to find lodging for the people Demi just brought, and I have a meeting with some division heads."

"You work too much, honey. Why don't you let Demi handle that?"

"Because it's not his job...plus he's tired," Joaquin admonished.

She pouted and sat on his lap, "I'm sorry; I didn't mean to get you angry with me. I've missed you and want to spend some time with you, that's all, honey."

"I'm sorry; I didn't mean to sound cross," he sighed, "I wondered if you had time to think about our last conversation just before I left," he questioned.

"Darling, why are you bringing up such an unpleasant subject? I like it here with you, my love." Joaquin pushed her gently off his lap and pulled his chair in, trying to put distance between them. She knew how to push his buttons. For a few months, Joaquin had tried to get her to commit to moving into her own place, but it had not worked.

"You need to think about it. Wouldn't it be great to be the queen of your own household, having everyone at your command?"

"Sweetie, this is my palace! Why do I have to move?" Monet hugged him from behind, running her hands down his chest to his groin." Joaquin stopped her hand from going any further.

"Why do I have to repeat myself every time we have this conversation? This was never supposed to be permanent; you knew that. Besides, you need more than I am willing to give you."

Monet started to talk like a wounded little girl, "Sweetheart, please don't be mean to me. All I want to do is pleasure you, just say you will come to me. I promise we'll talk about anything you want, I swear," she kissed his neck.

"Alright, but I have things to do right now," he said, hoping she would take the hint and leave.

"Anything for you, my love," she kissed him and glided away, believing she had him right where she wanted him, "I'm going to make you feel like a king," she said, looking out of the window.

Meanwhile, Brydus wondered how long she would have to stay in the dim, dusty basement. She could hear the other men pissing and moaning about how things had gone down. When they started to yell back and forth, she began to get annoyed. The wall she rested against was cold, damp, and she cursed Demi for leaving her down there. She closed her eyes and prayed that his brother would see her soon. She was tired, hungry, and just wanted to leave this place, never to return. Now that the women and children had found a settlement, she could move on. A few minutes later, she heard other voices; it was Louis, accompanied by Demi. He peeked into the cell where Brydus was kept shackled to the wall.

"Hey, crazy lady, we're coming in, so don't do anything stupid," Demi shouted as he searched to find the right key to open the door. Brydus really wanted to hurt Demi, but she had no idea where she was. Every bone in her body ached, and her attitude went from bad to worse. Without warning, Demi pinned her wrists to the wall and leaned up against her in an attempt to intimidate her with his closeness.

"I'm going to take you up to my brother now. I swear, if you do anything stupid, like trying to attack me again, I will drop-kick your ass. I don't care if you are a woman or related to us." She didn't understand what he meant, but the wall was cold, and she was drained. Brydus walked upstairs peacefully between the two men. People throughout the household stopped in their tracks to stare at her, making her feel uncomfortable. However, she could understand their fears looking the way she did. To them, she did resemble a wild woman.

When she entered Joaquin's office, she wished she hadn't let herself go as she did. She couldn't help but stare at the handsome man with the exquisite woman sitting by the window. She was stunned when she saw Joaquin, and in comparison, she looked filthy. Her face and hair were covered in dried mud.

Monet made it known that Joaquin was taken as she wrapped her arms around his neck, and would not let go, even as he tried to dislodge her.

"I'm scared, Joaquin. What is it?" she said, pointing at Brydus, who paid her no attention. Monet purred like a cat hanging around Joaquin's shoulders.

"Stop it, Monet, get out. I have business to attend to now," Joaquin said sternly.

"Demi, how could you bring this…thing here? She's disturbing," Monet whined.

"Monet, get out!" Joaquin yelled, getting annoyed with her usual drama.

"But honey, it's not safe. I'm afraid to have this… this thing under the same roof."

"I'm not going to tell you again. Leave, or I'll have Louis physically remove you."

"Okay, darling, I'll talk to you later…kiss, kiss," she said before grabbing and kissing him. Joaquin wiped his mouth, hating her behavior. Whenever a woman was around, Monet would put on a scene. She flashed Brydus a dirty look but didn't get as much as a glance from Brydus, who would not be intimidated by her.

"Take her chains off," ordered Joaquin, feeling terrible they had her in chains.

"Okay, it's your funeral, my brother," Demi replied.

"Alright, I'll handle it from here. Can you tell Jenny to come here, please? Thanks." Joaquin turned his attention to Brydus.

"First, allow me to welcome you to our home. Please, sit down." Brydus just stared at him and stood where she was. She was filthy and didn't want to ruin his nice furniture. She looked around the exquisitely decorated room, which had family pictures displayed on some walls. The office furniture was rich dark brown leather, with green and black accents.

Joaquin couldn't help but stare at the beautiful dark-haired beauty before him. Even the dirt couldn't cover the beauty and power that encompassed her. For the first time in his life, Joaquin felt like an awkward schoolboy, fumbling for something to say. Her dark eyes were hypnotic and extremely provocative.

"Alright, you can stand, if that is what you prefer. I want to apologize for my brother's behavior. He meant no harm. You'll be a guest in our home until we figure out how to deal with this situation. Unfortunately, we have laws, and we need to make sure that these laws are followed." Jenny knocked before she entered. Joaquin's face turned red with anger when he saw Jenny's eye starting to turn black and blue. "What happened to you? And don't tell me you walked into a door?"

Jenny turned her face away, "It's nothing, sir, an accident, that's all."

"It is something, Jenny. I won't allow abuse in my house. You will no longer assist Monet. I don't want you anywhere near her. I want you to promise me that you will come to me if something like this happens again.”

“Yes, sir.” Jenny smiled shyly.

“Jenny, this young lady is our guest. I want you to treat her like one. Put her in one of our best suites.” Joaquin turned his attention back toward Brydus, who had not flinched.

“Please be aware that if you decide to leave, I have guards all over the estate that will hunt you down and bring you back,” he informed her. “This is not a threat. I just need you to understand that I have to follow the law, and until things are taken care of legally, you need to remain here. In addition, you are expected to join us for dinner tonight. Jenny will assist you with whatever you need.”

Brydus followed Jenny down the beautiful hallways, noticing that each room was more elegant and more beautiful than the next. On the second floor, Jenny stopped in front of double doors. When Jenny opened the doors to let her in, Brydus was overwhelmed by the size and beauty of the suite. It was decorated in black and white, with splashes of corals and greens to accent the room. The bathroom was adorned in the same way. There was also a beautiful black claw feet tub in front of a huge, frosted window. The room was filled with candles, flower arrangements, towels, and pictures.

Jenny started to fill the tub with scented water as Brydus took the delicate brush and brushed all the tangles and dry leaves from her hair. Jenny hummed to herself cheerfully, enjoying the new change in her status. She busied herself laying out a navy-blue robe with matching slippers, two huge towels, shampoos, and conditioners. She smiled at Brydus and hoped she was just as nice as she was beautiful.

"Miss," Jenny said, "let me help you into the tub." When Brydus took off her clothes, Jenny stared at her strong, well-built body. Unlike Monet's, which was soft and delicate. Brydus welcomed the hot steaming water. She let out a few moans as she lowered herself into the steamy bath. She hadn't realized just how tired she was, falling under Jenny's pampering spell. Gently Jenny massaged her head and shoulders and shampooed her hair. Brydus was so relaxed, nearly falling asleep in the heavenly water.

"Let me help you out…" Like a helpless child, Jenny led Brydus to a massage table and began to rub scented oils all over her body. Then came the waxing and the plucking. Brydus was enjoying every minute of her beauty treatment. She wondered what kind of people would lock her in a cold dark cell and then set her up in a beautiful room like this. *Only time would tell*, she thought. She was leaving as soon as she could, maybe heading home, where at least she knew who her enemies were.

Monet jumped on Joaquin's back playfully, "Stay in bed, love, stay and play with me," she teased.

"Monet, I don't have time to stay in bed all day. I have things to do, and people to see," he said, putting on his shirt. "You promised me that you would consider moving. I don't want to resent you, so please think about what I said. We want different things in life, and marriage to you is not my agenda."

"Don't be cruel, lover. Why would you say that? We want the same things, love, sex, and marriage?"

"Really, I want a woman who doesn't screw other men. I don't trust you, and I also want children," he reminded her.

Monet acted stunned, "Who has been lying to you?" She started to cry. "Why does everyone hate me… is it because I'm beautiful? You have no idea how much that hurts."

"Stop crying. You always start this shit when I bring up the subject of marriage or moving you into your own place."

"Joaquin, I love you. I wouldn't dream of being with anyone else, and I want a child someday… too."

Joaquin stared at her pretty face. She sounded like a suffering child. "Look, I'm tired, and we are just beating a dead horse. I have too much work to do, and I don't have time for any more of your drama."

"Why can't you get someone else to do those things?" she asked, pouting like a child.

"Stop complaining. It isn't becoming on you," Joaquin said as he rolled his eyes at her.

"You were gone for two weeks. I missed you. I can't stand it when you are so busy because you never have time for me," she whined.

"I really have a hard time believing that." He tried to put his pants on, but Monet grabbed them first and hid them behind her.

"Come and get them, lover," she teased.

"Don't play…I'm not in the mood."

She threw his pants at him, "You're so crabby, but I still love you." She grabbed him from behind. "Why don't you ever tell me you love me?" She asked, pressing her face against his back.

"Look, Monet, we've talked about this before…so why are you bringing this up now?"

"Because a woman wants to know if her man loves her and how much," she argued playfully.

Joaquin sighed, "Monet, I told you before, I am not your man…and I don't love you like you want me to. I don't like hurting your feelings, but you don't seem to hear anything I say."

"Oh…I hear you loud and clear, lover. Your actions speak louder than words."

"My actions only say that I'm horny, and I want sex. That isn't love," Joaquin explained for the hundredth time.

"So… if you make me your wife, I can please you day and night. Let's get married."

"I guess our little talk just went out the window… look you can believe what you want, but that will never happen. I am leaving now. I have important things to do."

"Where are you going? You're going to see that ugly woman, aren't you?" Monet questioned.

He turned around slowly to look at Monet, "By the way, that young lady you so rudely insulted in my office is probably related to me. Therefore, I want you to listen to me very carefully. Do not show off at dinner tonight; she is my guest, and she'll be staying for a while."

"You're kidding…but why? She's dreadful! Look at that black hair and horrible brown eyes," Monet didn't let go of any chance to let go of people.

He turned to face her, "Did you forget my grandmother has black hair and brown eyes?"

Monet tried to recover, "But your grandmother is different…she's regal and beautiful. However, this girl, heaven knows where she's from. She's probably some whore that your brother picked up along the way and is passing her off as kin. So, what is it that she really wants from you?"

"Just try to conduct yourself like a lady. Do you think you could do that? If not, then don't bother coming to dinner; I'm fine with it either way," Joaquin clenched his teeth.

"Oh, I promise," Monet pulled him towards her again. "I'll be a good girl…so are we on for tonight?"

"You need therapy," he answered, shaking his head.

"No, my love, all I need is you, hard and ready."

Four Weeks Later

Weeks went by, and Brydus still refused to eat dinner with the house. When Joaquin tried to engage her in conversation, she answered him in short and direct sentences. She was so uncomfortable being around him that she got butterflies in her stomach every time he came near. One time, her nerves got the best of her, and she threw up.

Brydus was angry that Joaquin refused to speak to her about the two men she had killed. She wondered how long she would have to stay in this house of torture with a handsome man that drove her crazy whenever he spoke or came close to her.

She avoided everyone. She tried to stay out of sight when she went on walks or sat down outside to read a book. The only exception was sweet Jenny, who would always bring her news of what was happening at the ranch or in the main house. Sometimes late at night, Brydus would hear arguments between Joaquin and Monet, which always ended with screaming and crying.

Brydus was happy to hear that the women and children were doing well. Now they could start over, but she still couldn't bring herself to open up to Joaquin. When they passed each other in the hallway, she would nod her head to avoid making eye contact. The hurt and pain she suffered from losing Jake were still heart-wrenching for her. But this man, this beautiful man, with his boyish smile, and body that made her blush, was slowly breaking her down. He haunted her dreams, wondering how it would feel to have him touch or kiss her. Even if it was only once, she could die happy.

On the other hand, Monet was relentless. She was determined to get him to propose, chasing him down in front of people without any sense of pride. "How can you be so cruel, Joaquin? We've been together for two years. I'm embarrassed when I visit my friends, and they see I don't have a ring on my finger," she whined.

"You really don't hear me when I talk to you, do you? I told you a long time ago that we're not getting married. Monet, I don't want to go round and round with this damn subject again. I want you to find a place of your own. I will pay for it, but I'm done with you and your craziness."

"It's her, isn't it?!" Monet screamed at him. "Don't think I haven't noticed how you look at her, and how hard you are when you come from her room. You're screwing her, aren't you! Well, I don't care if you are, just as long as I am Mrs. Quintanilla. You can have all the bitches you want. All I want is some respect from everyone."

Joaquin was stunned. How had he not realized that all she wanted was the title and prestige of his last name?

"That's all you ever wanted, isn't it? My last name and everything you will get being the wife of a rich man, isn't that right?" he asked, questioning her further.

She threw herself at his feet. "No, no, Joaquin, you have it all wrong. I love you, and I want to be your wife. I want to have your children. I love you enough to share you with other women. If that is what you want, that's true love, Joaquin. What other woman would put up with a man having more than one mistress? I would do that for you because I love you, baby."

"Monet, you surprise me at every turn. I know you don't love me. There is no question that I get excited when I see Brydus. I can't help it, and I will not deny it. However, she has hardly said two words to me in the weeks she's been here. Nevertheless, that doesn't change what is happening to us. This relationship has been over a long time, even before my family visited. I just wasn't around enough to see that things went sour. Now I'm asking you to make a clean break. So please leave my room. I want to take a shower and get ready for dinner. Oh, and like I warned you before, if Brydus happens to join us for dinner, please don't embarrass me with your childish antics."

"One day, you will see her true colors. She's evil, and you're too damned horny for her to realize it. Why can't you see how evil and dangerous she is."

Monet slammed the door on the way out and headed to her room. This wasn't the first discussion they have had about her leaving and getting her own place. When his parents came and went, they had a terrible fight. However, Monet managed to stay put. All she had to do was allow him to calm down and want sex, she thought, smiling. Monet knew how to put the moves on him so that he couldn't resist her advances and touch.

Brydus had fallen into a deep slumber. She dreamed of being home with her family, enjoying a nice hot meal, and happy together. When there was a knock at the door, Brydus ran to answer it and was surprised to see Derrick. He had been crying. Brydus started to feel guilty for not thinking about him all these months. When she awoke and opened her eyes, Jenny was fussing with some dresses and a few pairs of shoes.

"Miss, I found a few dresses for you to try on and some shoes. I think the red dress will fit you the best. Why don't you try it on?"

"For what? Where am I going?"

"Well, I was hoping you would join the others for dinner tonight. Master Joaquin insisted that you join the house, yet you continue to refuse him."

"Master Joaquin, as you call him, doesn't own me." Brydus reminded her.

Jenny hung up the dress. "Well, I guess they're right about you being afraid of Miss Monet… she tells everyone you're afraid of her. And she boasted that if she catches you looking at Master Joaquin, she knows how to put you in your place." Jenny threw that part in, hoping it would get Brydus moving.

Brydus bounced off the bed, "Oh, is that right? Hmm, that's really interesting. What else is she saying?" Brydus asked as Jenny smiled wickedly.

"Well, I really don't want to repeat gossip, but… I heard her bragging about herself and saying that you're so manly…who would look at you, when she is the vision of loveliness, and you're just…"

"And I'm just what… come on, spit it out."

"She said you're a black crow that couldn't get a rise out of a dust storm."

"What? That doesn't even make sense." Brydus looked at Jenny and back toward the tantalizing red dress. "Jenny, tell the chef to set another place for dinner. We'll see who's a black crow."

"If you're sure, I'll run your bath. You get ready, and I'll make sure she has a great view." Jenny laughed all the way to the kitchen. The women were anxiously waiting to hear Brydus' response.

"Did she go for it?" Cassia asked excitedly.

"She went for it. I really didn't want to tell her what Monet actually said about her. If I did, she probably wouldn't wait for dinner to pounce on her."

The dress fit Brydus beautifully, and the strappy black heels enhanced the shape of her legs. When Jenny finished with Brydus' hair and makeup, she looked in the mirror and couldn't believe the difference. "Is that me?" Her skin was radiant. Her hair had a shine that it never had before. She felt like another woman… the makeup gave her a healthy appearance.

"You look radiant, Miss Brydus. Wow! All eyes will be on you tonight. Here, put on these earrings to complete your look."

"Thank you, Jenny, not bad for a black crow," she said proudly. Jenny smiled broadly as Brydus fussed over the low-cut dress.

"Oh… I just enhanced what God gave you, Miss."

"Do you think it's too low in the front? I feel rather naked."

"Believe me, around here, you'll be considered overdressed. It fits you wonderfully."

Joaquin sent Dan to escort Brydus to dinner. He was surprised that she agreed to come this time. Dan waited at the door a few seconds before he knocked. When Brydus opened the door, his eyes almost popped out of his head. "Oh…my…God," he could only stare, and his hands began to sweat as he looked into the eyes of the most beautiful woman he had ever seen. Brydus gave him a curious look.

"I'm here to escort you to dinner," he said, turning red. Her stomach began to grumble. She was so hungry, and the aroma coming from the kitchen was not helping. The dress she wore gave her a sexy sway as she walked. When Dan opened the door to the formal dining room… the room went silent.

"Ah shit," Demi said as he drained his beer mug.

Brydus grabbed Dan's arm for support. Without realizing it, he reached over and patted her hand to let her know that everything was going to be all right.

Joaquin sat at the head of the table and almost fell out of his chair when he saw Brydus walk toward him. Monet saw his reaction and was furious as she sat to his left. Brydus silently prayed that she would be seated with the others instead of Joaquin. She could hear her own heart beating in her ears. There he was, more handsome than ever, with Monet sitting close by. Everyone stared at Brydus. Joaquin felt a twinge in his loins, and his hands began to sweat. Dan walked Brydus to the head table right across from Monet as if he was daring Monet to say anything.

"Damn," Joaquin whispered under his breath… "God, please don't let us be related."

The men were already half-lit before dinner was served. Monet sat right across from Brydus and was already giving her dirty looks, but Brydus shot them right back.

"Please sit. You are our honored guest," Joaquin said, trying not to stare at her and make a fool of himself.

"A toast!" shouted Demi, "A toast to our success!" Everyone agreed, shouting and clinking glasses. Brydus reached for a piece of bread, knowing she could not drink on an empty stomach.

"Have some fruit; dinner will be served any moment now," Joaquin offered. Handing her an apple, however, she would not return his glance. He made her feel uncomfortable. Monet noticed that Joaquin could not keep his eyes off Brydus. The red dress she wore complimented her color, covering her blushing cheeks. She tried not to look at Joaquin and stared down at the table where Demi laughed and cracked jokes. He held up a beer and winked at her. She smiled and shook her head.

"Joaquin, honey, I don't think I'll be able to eat anything." Monet finally blurted out, unable to keep what she was feeling inside anymore.

Joaquin gave her a side glance in disdain. "Are you not feeling well?" he asked with sarcasm in his voice

"No, it's the company…I don't like her. I don't trust her. Please send her away," Monet spoke as if Brydus was not sitting right in front of her.

"What did I tell you? You can leave if you don't like it," he reminded Monet, pointing at the door.

Demi laughed, "This shit's going to be good. I can feel it!" he said, watching for Monet's next move. Joaquin cued Dan, just in case anything happened. Monet never ceased to surprise him.

"Why should I go to my room? She's the stranger." Joaquin gave her a stern look, and she squirmed in her chair. Brydus licked her lips and smiled. When Brydus looked at Joaquin, his mouth went dry. He started to say something to her when Monet shot some cream across the table, hitting Brydus in the face and neck. "Oh, shit, it's on!" Demi cried out ecstatic. Brydus saw red. In a flash, she jumped across the table, dress, heels, and all. Brydus grabbed Monet by the hair, sitting on her lap, with her knife pressed firmly against Monet's neck.

"I will cut you from ear-to-ear, you bitch. I swear on every angel in heaven," Brydus promised.

The room erupted; Joaquin held Brydus' wrist. "Let go of the knife," he said in a low deep voice.

"You must not want your arm…let go of me," she yelled as they struggled with the knife. Monet's wailing cries for help echoed throughout the house.

"I'll let go of you as soon as you let go of her…please," Joaquin begged. Brydus had a handful of Monet's hair with her neck turned to the side. Dan had Brydus by the waist but wouldn't pull her for fear that she would cut the still screaming Monet.

Demi was beside himself with laughter. "Holy shit! Now, this is what I call dinner entertainment!"

Brydus was so angry she pulled away from Joaquin's grasp, but Dan still held her by the waist. "She's not worth it," Dan whispered in her ear.

Demi continued to laugh and carry on. "That's what you get for messing with the wrong people…yes, there is a God; thank you, Lord… payback is a bitch, isn't it? That's what you get, bitch! Yes Lord, hallelujah." He shouted at Monet, who was still crying hysterically.

Brydus pulled away from Dan's tight grip and pushed Monet away from her.

"I'll walk you to your room," Dan offered.

"Don't bother," she continued to ignore him, walking faster.

"Brydus…please stop and talk," Dan yelled, almost chasing her.

"I don't want to talk to you…or any of you for that matter!"

Dan wanted to make peace. "Miss Brydus, I can understand how you can misconstrue our intentions to make you feel welcome," he blocked her way.

"I think you're doing a banged-up job," Brydus said sarcastically. "I just want to get out of this crazy place. Four weeks in this insane asylum is enough punishment. I was better off out there where I know who my enemies are," when she reached her room and tried to close the door, Dan stood in the way. Louis was trailing not too far behind.

"I'm speechless," Louis said, coming up behind Dan, "I bow down to you…I am in your debt."

Brydus was confused, "Let me get this straight…I almost hurt someone, and you're happy about it?"

"Ay, she deserved it – it's about time she got some of what she dishes out around here," Louis added.

"I'm baffled…please leave…I can't deal with this right now."

"But we want to know more about you…we know your name because of the others, but who are you, and where do you come from?" Dan asked with a new sense of enthusiasm.

"Yeah, and where did you learn how to kick ass like that? I have never seen Big Willie go down like he did. That was sheer poetry."

Brydus tried not to laugh, "You people are all crazy," she said, shaking her head in disbelief. Jenny excused herself when she reached Brydus' room.

"Thank God, the only sane person in this house, come right in," Brydus instructed. Jenny opened the door wider for the two servants carrying trays of food and drinks. Brydus could smell the rich food. Her mouth began to water; she was so hungry.

Joaquin followed, instructing the girls where to place the food and how to lay it out. He thanked them and then turned his attention to Dan and Louis. "Gentlemen, if you can excuse us, please, we have a lot to talk about."

"Hey, if there's anything you need, Miss Brydus…you can call on old Louis."

"Out," Joaquin ordered as he closed the door. Turning his attention to her, he said, "Well, I'm glad to see that you can speak more than one word at a time. Please sit…I promise you there will be no more interruptions.”

“So, are you going to arrest me for trying to kill your wife?” Brydus stood before him defiantly.

The word wife hit Joaquin like a ton of bricks. “No, I am not arresting you, and she is not my wife.”

“Sorry to hear that,” Brydus replied.

Joaquin was confused. “Why would you say that?”

“You make a nice couple. Whether you deserve each other or not remains to be seen.”

“Well, I don’t want to comment on that right now…but please sit and eat. I’m sure you’re very hungry.”

Brydus was not shy about eating heartily.

He watched as she tore into the chicken. “Looks like you were hungry.”

“This is delicious. You have some wonderful cooks,” she said, digging into the bread and potatoes.

“Yes,” he said, not wanting to laugh at how she attacked the food. “I’m glad you enjoy the food, but please allow me to apologize once again. We try to treat our guests very well here. So, tell me a little about yourself, Brydus. Many rumors are floating around, seeing that you have been very unsociable. People tend to make up stories about the beautiful, mysterious, brown-eyed woman.”

"What do you want to know?"

"Where do you come from? Who are you?"

For a second, she wondered if Joaquin could be trusted, "My name is… Brydus Moreno. As for where I'm from, we call it The Valley of God. Maybe you've heard of it."

Joaquin's heart sank, "I have. I know of this place. I have something interesting to show you." Joaquin pulled out the picture of his grandmother when she was young. When Brydus saw the picture, she almost choked on the wine that she was drinking.

"Do you know her?"

"Yes…" she replied, as she looked at the picture of the beautiful woman smiling so carefree, "Ahe was the first…Nylaya," she whispered, "She was the first to…"

"Is she your kin?" Joaquin interjected. "Are you related in any way?"

Brydus shook her head no, "Nylaya is my idol, but we are not related."

Joaquin had not realized he had been holding his breath.

"How do you know Nylaya? Is she still alive…she hasn't come to visit in so long."

"Nylaya is well, and she is also my grandmother," Joaquin said proudly.

It was Brydus' turn to be surprised, "I should have seen the resemblance. Nylaya is beyond words. I'm sure you are very proud of her."

"She is also my idol," Joaquin mentioned, "and she is still as strong and beautiful as ever."

"I'm curious. How did you end up here? Did you inherit this beautiful place?"

"Yes, in a sense. Nylaya, as you know, was way ahead of her time. She sensed pending danger and informed everyone that they needed to rely on each other to survive the coming storms. My grandparents prepared for the Dark Days. She kept on saying that something terrible was coming. My mother met my father doing community work. They were involved in rescue missions. I am her first born, and Demi was born three years later. Nylaya used to say we were lucky that we survived the Dark Days. Our families still thank God every day for helping us endure those terrible times. My grandparents had a farm. It had everything needed to sustain our growing family. My grandmother has this sixth sense about things and was very proactive, not leaving anything to chance. I was much too young to understand, but my mother always tried to explain things to me about why we had to live on the farm. I lived there for eighteen years before my parents and grandparents decided it was safe to leave the farm. They wanted to find out exactly what was happening in the surrounding areas. They wanted to find a good settlement. Our parents left us with my aunt Alexandria, Uncle Kyle, and a servant man named Israel for a few months. Later my aunt and uncle left, taking their two daughters, Krystal, and Audrey, leaving us with Mr. Israel. Audrey was the eldest of the two girls and grew up with Demi. They were in love ever since they were children."

"Who is Audrey?"

"She was the love of Demi's life since birth. They loved each other from the beginning. However, she's…she's gone now…she passed away a while ago. Anyway, Mr. Israel took good care of us. He would tell us every day not to lose faith. Demi was driving us crazy because he missed Audrey so much when her parents took her away. A few months later, after my aunt and uncle left, Mr. Israel had a heart attack. Demi and I found ourselves alone and scared. Therefore, we set out blindly to find our parents. After living like wild animals for a few weeks, we found a man almost beaten to death in a cemetery, down by the old church. Man, we were so hungry and dirty from traveling without direction. Demi and I were about to bury him until we found out he was still alive. Under his direction, we brought him here to his home and cared for him the best we could. I found a doctor that helped, but his recovery was slow. Demi and I became his sons, so to speak. He taught us everything he knew about farming and running a ranch. I guess it was in our blood.

This providence started off with a hundred outcasts and refugees. He taught us how to turn it into what it is today."

"Hm, interesting, and your parents, did you ever find them?" Brydus asked curiously.

"Yes, they found us…my grandmother said that blood calls to blood, and they found us eighteen months later. Soon after that, my Aunt Alexandria and Uncle Kyle also came and settled not too far from here. Mr. Romero Santiago was a great man. He lost his whole family and was never the same. He owned six thousand acres, a vast ranch, twenty-four homes, the lumber mill, and the fishing camp. He died three years after we found him. The beating affected him more than we knew. Mr. Romero was just happy to have us here. We became his family, and for a while, he seemed content, but I can only speculate. When he passed, he left everything to Demi and me.

"Loneliness is one hell of a sickness," Brydus said sadly… "Anyway, I'm glad you found your family. I know the feeling… I've been home sick myself."

"So, what's your story…what brings you out into this crazy and dangerous world?"

"Destiny…that's what my grandmother used to say…that's why Nylaya had to leave. She was too valuable to the development of the new world to be kept hidden. Now I understand why she had to leave the valley."

"Well, are you married…ah…engaged?" Joaquin stuttered.

"No, I'm not married yet…I was engaged. Well, that is, before I left, I was… I've been away more than a year now, and he said he'd only wait two years."

Joaquin was taken aback by her comment, "Hm, interesting."

The wine was going straight to her head. Brydus caught herself staring at this gorgeous man's lips and imagined how it would feel to have them pressed against hers. She began to feel uncomfortable with her own feelings. Her face was flushed as she squirmed uncomfortably. *Some girls have all the luck,* she thought…*it must be the wine.* Tomorrow she will wake up and realize it was just the combination of drinks, rich food, and great company. Tomorrow she will realize he has a beautiful woman, no matter how ignorant she is. His woman was flawless. His baritone voice put her in a trance, letting her mind wonder how it would be to be with someone like him.

"Brydus, are you alright?"

"Yes, I'm sorry, it's the wine that makes my head fuzzy," she giggled.

Her smile was infectious as he tried to concentrate on what he was saying, "Well, um, in all my travels, I haven't met anyone like you or my grandmother. Although she did mention that there was another birth. That must have been you. I remember how excited she was when she heard the news. I was too young to understand why she was so happy. This might sound funny, but I used to sit on her lap and ask her why I didn't have eyes like hers. She would laugh and say, "Because I'm me, and you're you. She was smart, sweet, and always had time for us. When Audrey was born, she became the princess of the family. Audrey could brighten anyone's day, and Demi fell in love with her."

Joaquin found himself strangely drawn to Brydus. He loved her spirit and independence. In his eyes, Brydus was a strong woman, beautiful, with a great mind. He imagined taking her in his arms and kissing her until she was giddy. He teased Brydus with his smile, sending chills through her body. She needed to say something that would defuse the sexual tension she felt sitting across from him. "Your settlement is beautiful. I can spend hours just staring at the people coming and going."

"In that case, I want to show you something. I want to take you to my favorite spot. It's heavenly. I'm sure you will agree with me."

I would follow him anywhere, she thought.

Holding her hand, following him through the back hallway and up a spiral staircase, still wearing heels, hoping they didn't get stuck on the stairs.

When Joaquin opened the door, she was speechless. The view from the top was spectacular. "Joaquin, this is beautiful," she said as the breeze ruffled her hair.

"I come here when I want to be alone, and I look out over the estate, thanking God every day for all of this." Brydus could see all the farms and lights of the houses that reminded her of bright stars twinkling in the dark of the night.

"Hey, let me show you something else." He led her onto a small platform with an old coin-operated viewer. "If you look through those two holes, you can see everything closer."

Brydus was so excited that it was making her laugh. Her dress blew softly in the breeze, and Joaquin took his time looking at the beautiful, shapely legs before him. He climbed up next to her to show her how to focus the lenses. Joaquin took in the sweet scent of her hair and body, gently bringing a lock of her hair to his lips while getting as close to her as possible. She felt his closeness and tried not to let him know how his nearness affected her. She wanted to touch him, to feel his hands holding her.

"Where did you find this thing? I love it. I can see the people in town."

"I brought it from the Inner Cities. It was a part of the old Empire State Building before it burned to the ground."

Joaquin was so close to her face that she could feel his breath on her skin.

"Here, let me help you down. It's getting windy up here and a little chilly as well." Joaquin wrapped his arms around her and kissed her. It felt like a bolt of lightning shot through her body, so she pulled away from him.

"I'm sorry, it's just that…you look so beautiful in the moonlight, and I got carried away," he apologized. Brydus was speechless. She stared at his mouth and the lips that sent shock waves through her body.

"I… I think I should go now. Thank you for sharing this with me. It was very nice," Brydus blushed, wanting to stay but remembered who he was.

"You're the only person I ever shared this with, Brydus. You can come up here any time you please; the view is pretty spectacular during the day." Joaquin came closer to her again, backing her up until she felt the cool wall against her back. He reached for her face, forcing her to look at him. When she looked up, he kissed her again. This time she opened her mouth to receive the full effect of his sensuous lips on hers. The intensity made Brydus pull away from him again, fearing that she couldn't resist him. Joaquin reached for her hand and kissed it.

"I'm not sorry for wanting you and kissing you, Brydus. I never meant to disrespect you…please believe me."

Brydus couldn't answer him, feeling guilty for wanting him just as much. He walked her back to her room in silence, but he felt good about making his feelings known to her. The last thing Joaquin wanted was for them to be uncomfortable around each other.

"I was wondering if you would join us tomorrow, we are going to check out the progress on our building projects, and I'd love to show you around."

Her eyes lit up, "Really, I would love to! What time should I be ready?"

"Be at the stables around 8 am."

"I'll be there, and thank you again for taking me to your special place."

Joaquin started to celebrate when he was out of earshot. He was tipsy and feeling great. The only sour note of the evening was when she announced her engagement. But it didn't matter, he felt free and alive again, and the kisses were only a prelude to what was yet to come. As Joaquin entered his room, his whole mood changed. By the smell of the perfume, he knew that Monet was in his room. She turned on the light as he walked in.

"It's been hours…you spent more time with her than me."

"Why are you even in my room? You embarrassed me and my household. You should be ashamed of yourself."

"She tried to kill me! You saw her…and then you have the nerve to go have dinner with her, and heaven knows what else."

"I am tired, Monet…and I've been tired of your tantrums and outbursts for far too long. This isn't for me. I don't like that much drama in my life, day in and day out. I'm sick of it. This isn't the first time you've acted like a fool in front of people…so give it a rest. Go to your own room. I truly don't want to be bothered with you." He turned his back to her, going into the other room.

Monet realized she had gone too far. She needed to get back in his good graces. "Darling, don't treat me like this, please. I'm so sorry. I promise I will apologize first thing tomorrow. I'm truly sorry…I just love you so much," she started to cry uncontrollably. "I will be better. I promise…please let me stay with you tonight."

All Joaquin could think about was the brown-eyed beauty. Her smile haunted him, even as Monet and he came together; his thoughts were not on what he was doing.

The next morning, Monet watched from her window as Joaquin joined his crew. It had taken Monet a long time to get to where she was in her life. From the beginning, she focused all her efforts on Joaquin. He had everything she wanted in a man. He was extremely handsome, young, and, most of all rich. She would not set her sights on anything less. Although she preferred Demi, with his rough exterior, Demi was still mourning the loss of his girlfriend and was untouchable.

Since his parent's visit, things seemed to change for the worse. Monet remembered dreading their arrival. They were a very close-knit family with high family values. From the beginning, she felt so uncomfortable; she never knew what to say or follow their conversations. Nylaya frightened her. She hardly spoke, but when Nylaya looked at her, it was as if she could read her mind and could see right through her. The family went out of their way to be pleasant and cordial to Monet. They expressed interest in her by asking many questions about her plans for the future. All she could do was laugh, not wanting to tell them what she was really thinking.

But now, everything was moving in the wrong direction. She paced nervously around her room, thinking she had too much to lose if Joaquin found out the truth.

Monet tried to forget the look on Jewel's face when she witnessed her striking one of the children with a stick. They got into a huge argument which ended with Monet crying. The last words that they spoke to each other scared her. She panicked, afraid it would get back to Joaquin and ruin all of her plans to marry him. The conversation haunted her for days, and now after this latest blow-up, those words came back to remind her that she needed to be careful. She thought long and hard about that day.

The shriek from the child brought Jewel into the small dining room. Monet was ready to shake the child holding her by her arms when Jewel's voice echoed behind her. "What's going on here?" she questioned intensely.

"Nothing," Monet said, pushing the child back into the kitchen. "She's fine," Monet laughed nervously; "Children, they cry for nothing at all these days."

Jewel glared, "Really? That mark on her face indicates otherwise." There was fear in Monet's eyes. "Is this how you handle your staff?"

"No, never, it was…an accident.

Jewel paused for a few seconds. Her eyes were staring into the frightened Monet, "You're a gorgeous woman, Monet… I can understand my son's attraction to you, but he will never marry you."

Monet was stunned at her blunt comment, "Why in the world would you say such a thing? I adore Joaquin, and he loves me," she forced a smile.

"I know who you are…and I know what you are after…but he has to figure things out on his own. However, I will not stay under the same roof with you any longer… I do not want to cause you any grief… my family and I will leave tomorrow."

"Wait a minute…what do you mean you know me?" Monet blocked her path. "Am I not good enough for your son?"

"You can take it any way you please, but you are not fit to be my son's wife. How can you sleep with one and desire another? Do you think people don't notice?"

"There has never been anything between Demi and me ever!" Monet tried to sound shocked.

"I never mentioned a name, but now that you brought it up, I'm pretty sure you've tried…I am older, and I see things clearer than you think," Jewel said confidently.

"Whatever Demi told you is a lie…he's jealous of what Joaquin and I have."

"You know very little about my sons. They do not envy each other, and they certainly don't have the same taste in women."

Monet became aggravated. Feelings of anger surged through her body. She fought hard to keep it under control. "Things were perfectly fine around here until you came to stir things up. Joaquin is happy. He loves me; I guess you can't stand to see him happy and content," Monet replied.

"On the contrary. If my son was happy and content, he'd be married to you. The fact is that after a year, you still don't have an engagement ring on that pretty little finger of yours. I would be concerned if I were you. My son is very traditional. He wants to get married and have a bunch of children. Something I am sure is not on your agenda."

"Why are you being so cruel and making these accusations about me? I've been nothing but sweet and kind to you since you arrived. What you witnessed between that…that girl and I, it has never happened before."

Jewel smiled, looking around the room, thinking if only the walls could talk, "I have seen the cruelty and contempt in your eyes for others, and the lust you have for my other son. You are not the woman for my Joaquin, and he will not marry you, I assure you."

Monet could not contain her anger anymore. "You listen to me," her eyes blazing with rage. "Joaquin may be your son, but I sleep with him every night, so you can try to talk him out of marrying me, but sex is a powerful tool, and I use it well. So, step aside, old lady. I'm here to stay."

"For now…lust has a way of fading, and I know my son. He wants children and a wife that will stand by him, work with him…and love him." Jewel held up her hand as she walked away, pointing to her left hand's third finger. "Never going to happen."

Monet was having a hard time sleeping after that encounter. His mother was going to be trouble when it came to the marriage. *I will have to insist that we marry right away,* she thought. After a year or two, once she becomes the lady of the estate, she will slowly take control of his organization. "After all, accidents do happen…then maybe Demi's feelings will change, and we can run the estate together." Monet looked at herself in the mirror and laughed… "Darling," Monet called herself, "why shouldn't I enjoy my rise to the top? After all, this is where I belong, and I intend to stay," she smiled wickedly as she crawled back into bed. It was too early to think. After lunch, she would make plans to eliminate that black bitch that was coming in between her and the plan to stay on top.

Chapter 13: The Children

Demi was in a foul mood the next day, and when he found out that Brydus was going to join them to visit the new construction sites, he argued with Joaquin.

"What is she doing here?" he asked when he saw her with the rest of the crew.

"I invited her to come with us. I want to show off the estate. Do you have a problem with that?"

Demi eyed Joaquin, "She's your problem, not mine. I don't care. Whatever you do, just keep her away from me."

"Stop being a puss, and be nice. She is our guest," Joaquin replied sternly.

Demi couldn't stay angry at his brother, "Don't mind me, brother, I had too much to drink last night. I will try harder to be a good host."

"Thank you, I would appreciate it, and so will she. Oh, and by the way, she is no kin of ours," Joaquin grinned mischievously.

"Damnit, I wish that I'd known that before. I would have knocked her on that pretty little ass of hers," he chuckled, "You sure seem happy about that."

"What does that mean?" Joaquin asked with a huge grin on his face.

"I saw how you looked at her yesterday, food falling out of your mouth. You couldn't keep your eyes off of her, could you?" Demi laughed, "Why am I kidding myself? All the men were checking her out as she strolled over to her seat. Yeah…she's smoking hot. I had to ask Audrey to forgive me for looking."

Joaquin burst into laughter, "I was not expecting her to walk in like…like... man, I don't even have words for how she looked. Anyway, you'd better behave. Remember what happened to Monet last night."

Demi roared, "Holy shit, man…that was great! You couldn't make that shit up, high heels and all. The way she swooped over the table and bam… she snatched that bitch's hair and put a knife to her throat all in one move. It was a beautiful thing. I don't think I've ever laughed so hard in my life. She would be my hero right now had she not kicked me in the nuts."

"Are you ever going to get over that? She was defending herself, plus you can sometimes be aggressive with women."

"I may get over it someday. Thinking back to yesterday, don't you wish you had a picture of Monet with her eyes bulging out and that black crap around her eyes from crying? I almost kissed that woman for making my day, but then I thought about my nuts," Demi said as he grabbed his crotch.

"Um, I already did," Joaquin said smiling, "I kissed her for you, little brother."

"You whore! You kissed her, and you're still standing? How'd you manage that?"

"It was an accident. It just happened."

"Yeah, accident my ass, let me guess, you tripped and fell on her lips. Man, you're such a liar. You've been dying to get with her from the moment you saw her. I don't blame you… anything's better than that plastic fake bitch Monet."

"There she is," they watched her mount her beautiful black horse, "be nice. She may be your sister-in-law someday," Joaquin said with a huge grin.

"I'll try, for your sake, but don't expect any miracles."

Brydus looked radiant that morning. She found out how Jenny was bringing her all of those nice clothes. A seamstress lived nearby, and she was charging her clothes to Joaquin's account. She picked out a pair of black fitted pants and a white, very well-fitted shirt with short sleeves and a low-cut neckline.

"Brother…doesn't she know she shouldn't wear those tight clothes? Especially around a bunch of horny men," Demi commented.

"It doesn't matter what she wears. She's going to look… appealing," Joaquin said, staring at Brydus.

"Appealing…my ass, you horny bitch," Demi replied, laughing.

"Good morning, gentlemen. It's a beautiful day, isn't it?" Brydus smiled brightly, nodding towards Demi.

"Swell," Demi said with sarcasm, but she ignored his remark.

"It is a beautiful day for a ride," Joaquin couldn't help but smile as Brydus motioned him to look at her face and not her breasts.

"Touché," he said, smiling.

Brydus was too busy talking with Louis, Big Willie, and Terry to bother with Demi. All Demi did was grunt and make faces every time they said something.

Joaquin loved every minute as he explained what they wanted to achieve and their plans for future projects. Brydus was well educated in farming and even gave some constructive suggestions on growing certain crops.

"Your lands are so beautiful. You have done well," she commented to Joaquin. "The people are healthy and content. It's amazing to see such progress after all that has happened."

"Thank you, we try to keep a balance," Joaquin said proudly. "Demi was the brainchild behind the co-op."

"I didn't do crap…so stop looking at me, woman," Demi said sarcastically.

"Aww…are you still angry with me because I hurt you?" Brydus teased.

"What makes you think you hurt me?" he replied, rolling his eyes.

"I think you hurt his pride more than anything," Louis said, pointing to his crotch, and Joaquin tried hard not to laugh.

"Ok, so what now…you want a piece of me?" she said, teasing him. "Come on, let's do this. I might even let you win."

Demi rolled his eyes again and sighed, "You want to do what? You want to fight me…are you crazy, woman? I'll wipe the ground with your ass."

"Aww, so you're still talking all this shit. Come on, big boy…let's do this, so you can get it out of your system." Brydus jumped off her horse, taunting him.

Demi looked down and shook his head, "Stupid woman, get out of my face."

Everyone laughed at Demi's expense. Joaquin knew he would not intentionally hit Brydus.

They stopped for some lunch at a small diner on their way back through town. They had pork ribs, potato salad, green beans, and sweet tea. Brydus loved all the progress they made and how neat and clean the streets were. Most of the buildings and stores were painted in bright colors. *It is a booming exchange,* Brydus thought as she watched merchants and customers haggle over the price of their products.

Joaquin explained the procedures working for them, and Brydus was very impressed. She was enjoying her day out. Jake was right. There was still a sense of humanity in the world. She was thrilled that Joaquin had asked her to walk with him down to the farmer's market. Being close to him gave her strange feelings she had never experienced with anyone else. Her heart raced every time he reached for her hand.

Halfway through their walk, the emergency siren started wailing in the town square. Everyone dropped what they were doing and ran to see what was happening. Joaquin and Brydus' horses were brought to them, and they headed towards the crowd forming in the middle of the small park that sat near the entrance to the forest. A young woman held on to a couple of rag dolls, clutching them tight against her chest, crying hysterically. "My babies are gone…someone help me find my babies!" she cried.

"What happened?" Joaquin asked as the woman cried uncontrollably.

"I was making lunch. It was such a nice day, so I let them play in the yard. When I called them for lunch, they were gone…the gate was open, and they were gone."

Her husband held her trying to comfort her, "I found their doll babies near the tree line," the husband said, "but I didn't see them anywhere. The woods are too vast to search by myself." Joaquin and his men could hear the fear in his voice.

"That's what we're here for. How long have they been missing?" Joaquin asked.

"At least two hours. It's hard to tell. I tried looking for them myself. I hope I didn't waste valuable time," the father said, wiping the sweat off his brow.

"Big Willie, let's get some men together. Louis, we're going to need some supplies and a map of this area. Damn...it will be dark by the time we're ready," Joaquin expressed frustration.

The forest had packs of wild dogs that had killed at least a dozen people in the last year. They tried for years to capture them, but there were just too many. However, the dogs were contained in a certain area ruled off-limits to everyone. The dogs were territorial and attacked anyone that crossed their path, and the girls were lost right in the middle of their territory.

Within a couple of hours, the community was organized with weapons and supplies. Demi finished assembling the rest of the volunteers. Only those who knew how to track were allowed to join the rescue teams.

"This is going to be dangerous. Thank God for the moonlight. At least that will help a little, but heaven only knows what's roaming around out there at night. Stay with your partners. Signal with flares if you find them, dead or alive. Good luck, men, and God bless you all," Joaquin said. "Let's move out!"

"Demi, I can help," Brydus said, approaching him.

"I prefer that you stay with the women," Joaquin interrupted.

"Another pair of eyes can be helpful," she argued.

"Joaquin is right. Know your place, woman."

Brydus was not surprised by Demi's comment, "Don't be ridiculous. My place is where I'm needed."

"I don't need to be worrying about you too. So, if you want to help, stay with the women. Make coffee, you know, make yourself useful," Joaquin said.

Brydus was speechless, "What a couple of assholes, big and biggest," she pointed to Joaquin, "Make your own damn coffee!" She got on her horse and rode away.

"Pastor, watch these women and pray for the girls' safe return," Joaquin instructed as he tried to see in which direction Brydus rode off. "Damn, woman, always wanting to be in the middle of everything. Pastor, please, make sure no one else enters these woods, got it?"

"I'll do my best, son. We will be praying for your safe return also." The women waved as they watched the men disappear into the woods in pairs.

Brydus returned after a while and watched the missing children's mother rocking back and forth, crying, and holding the tiny rag dolls against her face. The woman ran towards Brydus. "Please help find my babies. I heard what you did for those other people…please, they say you don't fear the night, and you can see in the dark. Please help find them. I'm begging you."

"Miss, I'm not superhuman. Your children's rescue is in good hands."

"Yes, but…you're a woman, so you know what I'm feeling. I can't live without my children," she uttered so sadly it was breaking Brydus' heart.

"I will try to find your babies, but I hope you understand that I can't guarantee anything," She replied, noticing the look of desperation on her face.

"I have a good feeling about you. I think you see things differently than most," the mother's eyes were red from crying.

"The men are very good at what they do. I will go and help… I need rope and a flare gun. Also, would you pack some cheese and bread and fill this cantina with wine? That's all I need. The rest we'll leave for God to decide."

She prepared herself with her flashlight and double-barrel shotgun that she always took wherever she went.

The pastor tried to stop her. "Miss, I can't let you go in there. You heard what Joaquin said. No one else is allowed to enter the woods. Miss, you should stay with the women."

"Pastor, I don't want to disrespect you, but I don't give a rat's ass what Joaquin and his dopey brother said. If you don't want to get hurt, I suggest you move out of my way."

"I truly cannot let you go. It's dangerous," the pastor insisted, blocking her path.

"I'm not asking your permission. Relax, Pastor, I was born in the woods, and I was raised by a pack of wolves." Brydus laughed and continued towards the woods entrance, ignoring the pastor's pleas to return.

She was used to the menacing sound of the night and the movements that go on as the creatures of the night come out to feed. It was a full moon, which helped illuminate her path, but she knew the moonlight could also create a false sense of safety.

Blackie made her aware of the danger that lurked ahead. She could also read Blackie's instincts as they traveled down the dark and desolate pathways along the creek. The light on her headgear allowed her to see far ahead. After about an hour, Brydus began to speculate how the young girls wandered this far into the woods without encountering any dangerous animals. She heard no cries for help, nor did she see any signs of carnage. Then Brydus began to think as a child would. Something must have distracted them. *They must have gotten lost,* she thought.

She continued to ride deeper into the dark forest until she heard several dogs barking in the distance. Brydus urged Blackie to turn around, stopping short when she thought she heard something else besides the furious barking. It sounded like male voices. Slowly, she inched her way towards the sound of the vicious dogs, and then Blackie suddenly stopped. She realized somebody was trapped by the wild dogs, maybe up a tree or in the creek. As she inched her way closer, she came upon a huge ditch. Someone had fallen into it and was yelling at the dogs poised to attack.

She hid in the bushes on the far side of the ditch. She fired a shot into the pack of mangy dogs, listening as they ran away, wounding one or several of them. The two men cried out for help when they heard the shotgun blast. She dropped two glow sticks to see how deep the crevasse was, wondering who was trapped. "Are you alright down there?" Brydus yelled.

"We're hurt, but I'm not sure how bad,' Louis replied, franticly wiping the blood from his face.

Slowly Brydus lowered herself down using a rope that she had tied to a tree. Louis met her at the other end.

"You have no idea how glad I am to see you," he said, hugging her.

"Let me see that," she said, examining the deep gash in his head.

"I'm bleeding a little. I must have hit my head on a rock down here. Other than that, I'm not too bad. Demi is hurt. He's propped up against the side," she shined the light on Demi.

He smiled, trying to keep himself upright against the dirt wall. "You bullheaded woman, thank God you didn't listen," Demi said in agony.

"Where are you hurt?" she asked.

Demi had scrapes and bruises all over his left arm and shoulder. She touched his shoulder, and he saw stars.

"Oh shit," he groaned, almost passing out from the pain.

"I think it's dislocated, but I'm not sure, and I don't want to pull on it," she said. Brydus shined the light back on Louis. "Hey, I'm going up first. Tie this rope around yourself, and keep it away from your head, so it doesn't make things worse. Once I get to the top, I'll use Blackie to pull you up. Do you trust me?" She asked him.

"I do," he tried not to alert her to how badly he was hurt. Once Louis was pulled to safety, Brydus climbed back down for Demi. "Come on, big boy, I'll help you," she guided him towards the rope and slipped his feet into a loop. "Just hold on with your good arm, Blackie will do the rest."

"I love you," he said, making her laugh. Slowly Blackie pulled him out. Demi groaned with every abrupt movement, relieved when he reached the edge. Brydus began to administer first aid with the small kit that she carried.

"I'm sorry, Louis, the is gash the deeper than I thought. I hope this glue holds it shut, so it stops bleeding." Brydus made a sling for Demi. She noticed how pale he was but didn't want to alarm him. Demi closed his eyes; he was in so much pain he could hardly stand.

"Where the hell did she go?" Demi asked as he grimaced in pain.

"She went to find our horses." In the distance, they heard another shot and dogs whimpering while running away. A few minutes later, Brydus startled them when she reappeared from the darkness. "Alright, guys, here are your horses. If you follow this path, it will lead you straight out of the woods."

"No, I'm not leaving. I am staying until someone finds those girls, dead or alive," Demi protested.

"You're hurt. Stop being such a pig-headed fool; you need medical attention," she argued, "what about you, Louis…why don't you start heading back?"

"Demi's right. We have to keep pushing on."

Brydus was frustrated with their macho bullshit. "I have never in my life met such chauvinist fools. Your testosterone levels are off the charts. You would rather suffer than get help, yet you call me bullheaded," she fussed at them.

"We can't let our injuries or a few dogs interfere with finding the girls. We have to move on," Demi argued. "Louis, you can go back if you want. You have a head injury."

"No, I'm staying with you, so save your breath."

Brydus shook her head. She could see that Demi's breathing was a concern and was worried about him.

"Look… I know you're in serious pain. I have something I can give you. It's a natural remedy, my mother's own formula. It may not take the pain away completely, but it will take the edge off so that you can ride."

Demi and Louis were like zombies, following Brydus down a narrow path until they reached a brook. "Do you think they came this way, Brydus?" Louis asked. "We have been traveling for over half an hour now."

"Sometimes, you have to think like a child. What would children do? I remember when I was their age; I used to love to play in the water. If they wandered this far, they probably would have gotten thirsty and may have come this way for something to drink. Keep your eyes open for anything that looks out of place, like a toy or anything that a child would play with."

"How about something red, there, by the bushes," he pointed, "I see something red," Louis said somewhat dazedly.

"Good eyes." She rushed to check out what it was and smiled. It was a piece of what may have been part of a dress. "Smart cookie," Brydus mumbled, "she left us a bread crumb. Hey, if you guys want to rest a little, I'm going to look around." Demi slid off his horse and sat against a log lying on the ground. Brydus used the light on her headgear to take a look around.

"What are you looking for?" Louis asked.

"If you were a child, and it was getting dark, where would you hide?" To the left was a small cliff with bushes and trees growing from it. "Hm, interesting, I'm going to climb up that cliff to see what is beyond the trees," Brydus said, thinking out loud.

"It's too dangerous. I'll go up," Demi said, barely able to get up. Brydus glared at him like he was the town idiot.

"Really, Demi, you can hardly move! Just sit your ass down… I'm just going to check things out…unbelievable," she mumbled, shaking her head. The cliff was not very high, and it had a wide walkway. It was easy to climb. Demi and Louis watched from below.

"She's a bossy ass broad, isn't she," Demi said, annoyed.

"She knows her shit; I've got to hand it to her."

"There's no way those girls came this far," Demi whined.

"They've been gone since early this afternoon, so it's a possibility," Louis argued.

They watched until Brydus' light disappeared behind some bushes. "Brydus, are you alright?" Louis shouted, not wanting to be too loud and alert the dogs to their presence. There was no answer, and Louis started to get nervous.

"Give her a few minutes, bro. She'll yell if there's a problem." A few minutes later, they spotted her light coming from behind the bushes. She was carrying one of the girls, and the older one followed close behind her.

"Demi, look!"

The younger girl started to cry in Brydus' arms.

"We got lost," explained the older one. "I got scared when I heard the dogs, so we climbed up the rock and found a hole to hide in," the little girl said, holding two little puppies in her arms.

"Hallelujah, thank you, Jesus!" Demi cried, "They're alive."

The flare lit up the sky, signaling that the girls were found. The younger one was crying because she was so hungry. When Brydus brought out the cheese and bread, the men looked at each other. They never thought of bringing food for the little girls.

"How did you know they'd be hungry?" Louis asked, surprised.

"I didn't... that was for me. I didn't know how long I would be out here. I've got some wine in my bag. Want some?"

Louis laughed and drank heartily, "I never thought about that either," he added.

"One thing my father taught me is that you have to be prepared for all scenarios, which is ingrained in my head." She was concerned for Demi. Afraid he may have internal injuries. After getting the girls situated, her focus turned toward Demi. Brydus knew he would have a hard time staying on his horse on the trip back.

"Hey, do you need some more pain medication?" He was clammy to the touch.

"Actually, it did help a little. but it numbed my tongue a bit."

"Yeah, it will do that. I'm going to tie you into your saddle so you won't fall off your horse and injure yourself more if you fall asleep or pass out. Sorry, it may be a little uncomfortable for you, alright? I'll have a hold of your horse, so don't worry."

Demi managed a smile, "Thanks, Brydus, you saved my life."

"Don't thank me yet. Thank me when I get you home and seen by a doctor."

The men exited the dense woods two at a time, exhausted but concerned whether the girls had been found alive or dead. A few of the teams were attacked by the wild dogs, but they managed to scare them away.

Joaquin was on the fourth team to exit the woods. When he found out that Brydus had disobeyed him, he was furious, and now he had an extra worry.

"I tried to stop her," the pastor explained, "but she's scary, Joaquin. She looked at me with those big brown eyes of hers, and just the look alone made me panic."

"Women…" Joaquin answered, shaking his head. As teams continued to exit the woods, Joaquin became more agitated as time went by. He paced nervously with the doctors and staff, who were worried about the outcome. As the hours ticked by, they lost all hope that the girls were found alive. Finally, two and a half hours later, the final team emerged from the woods. The girl's father waited anxiously by the entrance praying for a miracle.

"Papa… papa," the older girl cried, running to him. Holly jumped into her father's arms, "We got lost."

"Oh my God, thank you, God!" he said, looking to the heavens with tears rolling down his cheeks. He kissed his little girl's face over and over again. Megan had fallen asleep in Louis' arms. Everyone gathered around to see if the girls were alright. The reunion was a tearful one for all involved. But Brydus was still concerned about Demi, who now had a very high fever. She quickly handed him over to the medical team, which didn't waste time addressing his injuries, and Louis, barely holding on. Brydus waited until the doctors stabilized them both and pushed the gurneys into the ambulance for transport. When Brydus turned around, she bumped into Joaquin's chest. He had been standing right behind her all along. He grabbed her by the arms.

"We need to talk," he said sternly.

She cocked her head to the side and stared at him, "You know what, Joaquin, as much as I would love to stand here and chat with you. I'm really tired, and when I'm tired, I get nasty. So, I suggest if you have anything to say to me, you should hold that thought until after I've had some rest."

"Alright, smart ass, but we will talk. So, have a nice long, restful sleep. Because tomorrow first thing. It's you and me." Brydus ignored him, riding alongside the ambulance that carried Demi and Louis. She headed straight to her room once she arrived at the estate. She was so tired and hungry, having to give away her food to the others that she had packed for herself. To her surprise, Jenny had left some food for her and some refreshments on ice. *Sweet Jenny is always looking out for me,* Brydus thought, scarfing down some food. She washed her face and fell asleep.

She slept so soundly that she didn't even wake up when Jenny closed the blinds and covered her up at three o'clock in the morning. When Brydus awoke, Jenny was filling the gorgeous, oversized tub with hot water and a bubble bath, so she could relax her tired muscles. "Jenny, you're a gem. How can I ever thank you?"

"No thanks needed. You saved those little girls, along with Demi and Louis. It's all over the estate."

"They would have found them. I just got lucky," Brydus said as she leaned back in the tub. "Jenny, you spend so much time here. Are you married or have someone special? A pretty girl like you should have a lot of boyfriends."

Jenny blushed, "Actually, I have a boyfriend. We see each other on the weekends. He works with the construction crew." Jenny was beginning to get emotional. She called her pretty. Jenny always considered herself plain and homely.

Brydus munched on some grapes and cheese that Jenny had brought up earlier. She felt like a queen soaking in the tub. The water felt good against her skin. Then a loud knock on the door interrupted her peace.

"I'm in the bathroom," she yelled. The door opened, and in came Joaquin looking clean-shaven and well-groomed. *God, why does he have to look so good?* she thought to herself. Joaquin lingered at the bathroom door leaning against the frame.

"Did you not hear me say I was in the bathroom?" Brydus yelled.

Joaquin smiled. "Yeah, but the timing is perfect. You can't walk away or hide. It appears that I have your full attention."

"Fabulous," she said sarcastically, "now what is so important that you can't wait until I see you later?"

Joaquin moved a chair closer to the tub and sat down. Brydus sunk down so he couldn't see her naked body. "Hm, I don't think your bubbles will last for longer," he could tell she was uncomfortable.

"Really, Joaquin, is this necessary?"

"Brydus, I need to make something very clear to you. When I tell you something, you need to listen to me. You could have been hurt going in the woods by yourself."

"Can you turn around so I can get out, please? The water is getting cold."

Joaquin turned around reluctantly. He smiled, looking at her through the mirror. She wrapped the thick blue terry cloth robe around her, securing it tightly. "I think you've mistaken me for someone else."

"What does that mean?" Joaquin asked, turning back around. "As long as you're under my roof, you are my responsibility. When I tell you to stay put, I mean it," he was getting angry. She slipped into her soft slippers and returned to her bedroom.

"Look, I am not your ditsy girlfriend or one of the people you govern. I'm a free woman, and I will come and go as I please. I've lived in the woods all my life, and I'm well aware of the dangers."

Joaquin grabbed her by the shoulders, "You're a free woman, huh? What happened to your fiancé, the man you supposedly left back home? When I give an order, I expect everyone, including you, to obey them; do you understand me?" he trapped her against the wall with his arms.

"I think this conversation is over," Brydus replied. His closeness always made her uneasy. She looked down toward the floor, not wanting to look at his face, knowing her eyes would betray her. She could feel his breath against her cheek.

"What you need is a good spanking, and I'm just the man to give it to you," he snapped at her. When she looked up, he held her face gently and kissed her. She felt her knees go weak, and a sudden thrill rushed through her body. Joaquin leaned against her, kissing her again. She didn't struggle this time, welcoming the strange sensations his kisses awakened in her. He let her come up for air. "I've wanted to do that since I first laid eyes on you," he tenderly touched her face and neck. She was frozen in place and didn't want him to stop until she broke the spell by pushing him back and turning away from him.

"Joaquin… please leave. I need to get dressed."

"I'm not going to apologize for how I feel. I understand if you don't feel the same way towards me. I don't expect you to, but I hope you give it some thought." Joaquin touched her hair. "Please join us for dinner tonight. The girls baked you something special for your birthday," Brydus turned around.

"My birthday, I almost forgot my birthday."

He pulled her into his arms and kissed her passionately again.

"Happy birthday, Sweetcheeks. I want you to enjoy yourself. Monet will not be joining us."

It took Brydus a while to recover from his kisses. The guilt was killing her, wanting him so badly. Knowing he was with someone else. Then there was Derrick, who said he would only wait for so long, and that time was almost up. She knew deep in her heart she had no intentions of rushing back to him.

Joaquin awakened something in her that she never knew existed. Now she understood what her mother meant. She couldn't look at him without wanting to wrap her arms around him and kiss him. Brydus wanted Joaquin to touch her. She felt the heat rising inside her, even now, as she thought about him.

"Mami, you raised a tramp. I'm in lust with a man who is taken. I wish you were here, so you could tell me what to do," she whispered while looking in the mirror.

Chapter 14: Happy Birthday

Brydus was still reeling from Joaquin's kisses as she traveled down the hall to visit Demi. She wanted to take her mind off the tingling sensation that Joaquin gave her every time he came near or touched her. From a distance, she could hear Demi griping and complaining to the nurses attending to him.

"Hey," she said, peeking into his bedroom, "why are you giving these nurses such a hard time?"

"There she is, the only woman around here that makes sense. Come in, my love. Why didn't you come to see me sooner? I was beginning to think you didn't love me anymore," Demi grabbed her with his good arm and kissed her cheek. "God, you feel so damn good, woman. Pull up that chair and talk to me, will you."

Brydus pulled her chair up next to his bed, resting her elbows on it, "How are you feeling, bad boy? Your color is back. That ghoulish green color didn't do a thing for you." They laughed.

"Thank you again. This is the second time you have saved my life. I know we didn't get along initially, but I'm glad you didn't hold my pig-headed stupidity against me. I'm in your debt."

"I told you we can duke it out and get it out of your system, but you weren't going for it."

"Girl, you probably would have worn my ass out, and then what? How was I going to save face with my men?" Demi chuckled.

"I would have taken it easy on you, I swear."

"Yeah, like I'm going to believe that one," he stared at her, touching her hair.

"You're so beautiful… you remind me of my Audrey. You would have liked her."

"Joaquin told me a little about her and how much you two loved each other."

"I've never stopped; I will miss my Audrey until the day I die."

"So, tell me about your injuries."

"Well, let's see, I have a partial tear in my shoulder which hurts like hell, it's also dislocated, and that hurts like hell. My ribs are extremely bruised, which hurts like hell, but other than that, I'm great." Their laughter could be heard all the way down the hall.

"I heard that my brother is angry with you. Forgive him. He's just trying to protect you."

"Well…your brother, he walked into the bathroom while I was enjoying a nice relaxing bath. Soothing my own aches and pains, then he started in on me. I wanted to…"

Demi interrupted her, "Throw yourself at him and make love to him," he smiled, knowing he hit a nerve.

Brydus looked at him with pouting lips, "Am I that transparent?"

"Yeah, both of you are…how can you not see it? Baby, he's in love with you. This is real for him. I know my brother, and when he looks at you…I see stars in his eyes and in yours too."

"I do have feelings for him," she looked away shyly, "but I can't let go of the guilt. I don't blame Monet for hating me. She has every right to…"

Demi grabbed her hand, "Let me tell you a story about Monet. She doesn't love my brother. She's a money-hungry bitch. She loves what he has, and you want to know why I know? When she first came here under the pretenses of remodeling some of the rooms, she tried to seduce me many times. It started from the very beginning. Yes…it was tempting, but there was something that I just didn't like about her. When Audrey went missing, my brother was really concerned about my mental state. For years, I kept going downhill. So, he sent me to my uncle in the Inner Cities for therapy. I was suicidal, and I needed help. When I returned four months later, Monet had moved in and was sleeping with Joaquin."

"Did you ever tell him why you disliked her or her intentions?"

"No, but I blame myself for not interfering sooner."

"Does he love her, or did he ever love her?"

Demi kissed her hand gently, "He doesn't love Monet, and he never did. It was just sex, a booty call, if you know what I mean. Brydus, I was a mess for so long. The owner of these lands and properties left everything to Joaquin and me. We found him close to death near one of his children's graves. We nursed him back to health, and it was like we gave him a reason to live. Joaquin was working fourteen to sixteen hours a day and, on top of that, worried about me. So, Monet was just a release for him. Monet played her cards well. When he was exhausted, she was there waiting to make him feel good, at least for a moment. I blame myself; I wasn't here to help. It wasn't until my family came to visit last year that I realized what a burden I had been on him… but he never said anything, never complained when I was falling down drunk or if he had to get up in the middle of the night and get me out of jail. He never once said, "Get over it; it's been years." Not a word. Joaquin just wanted me to feel better about myself, which is his weakness. He's a good man, Brydus. He loves to help everyone, and when it comes to women, he has a soft spot for the helpless ones."

"But Monet seems to really love him now. She's always around him, kissing and rubbing him."

"Brydus, the reason that my family cut their visit short was because of her. Monet was coming on to me every time an opportunity presented itself. In fact, the same day we brought you here, she was all up in my face…I can't stand her. So how much does she love my brother if she's inviting me into her bed? We're not bad people, a little rough around the edges, but I love and respect my brother and know he loves me."

"I knew what kind of people you were when I saw how you cared for the women and children," Brydus said. "I was just angry and afraid for them. I'm sure you were pissed at me," they both laughed.

"Don't remind me," Demi added.

"But when I saw Joaquin for the first time. I felt something in the pit of my stomach, and I really tried hard not to think about him. But I can't help it. Demi, I don't know what love is. I thought I loved Derrick when I was with him, or maybe I was just horny. I mean, I've barely been kissed. I've never had sex," Brydus said as she laid her head on the bed. "Help me, Demi. What should I do?" Demi touched her hair playfully, unaware that Joaquin was watching from the doorway. Joaquin clenched his jaw as he watched the interaction between Brydus and Demi.

Joaquin cleared his throat, alerting them to his presence, "Am I interrupting something? Should I leave and come back later?" he asked sternly.

"Actually…I have to go. The girls brought me a dress to wear to dinner. I should try it on." Brydus said, making an excuse to leave. "I'll see you then, love," she kissed Demi lightly on the lips.

"Happy birthday, sweetheart. I'll talk to you later," Demi said, laughing.

Joaquin felt like someone kicked him in the stomach. Demi waited until she walked out of the room before turning his attention to Joaquin.

"So, what's going on with you two?"

"Well, you know, bro. We just had mad sex right here in this bed. What do you think is going on, stupid?" Demi replied, annoyed.

"I could hear both of you laughing and carrying on…let me know if you're interested in her, and I'll back off."

Demi couldn't stand the look of hurt on his brother's face, "You know when I first saw her. I said to myself, damn, she is hot, but when I got to my room. I looked at Audrey's picture and into her eyes. I felt guilty, then I started to see Brydus as a person instead of a sex object. However, you know what really got to me…is how she looked at my dumbass brother. We were talking about you idiot; she's in love with you."

Joaquin cracked a smile. "Good, because for a minute there, I thought I might have to break your other arm," he said jokingly. "So, what did she say about me?"

Demi started to laugh, "You're so full of shit, Joaquin; she is just confused and a little naïve. The woman's a cherry, bro. I don't think her old boyfriend got to even second base with her."

Joaquin looked surprised, "No, tell me it's not true. He must be a big ass puss. I don't understand it, a fine-looking woman like that? Man, I wouldn't be able to keep my hands off of her. I wonder why this douchebag even let her go off on her own…shit, he must be gay. All I know is…I can't stop thinking about her. Perhaps I should just give her some time."

"I know you're my older brother, but listen to me on this matter. I wish I had all the time back that I wasted being away from Audrey. Don't waste your time, bro. If you love her, and she loves you, to hell with what other people say. Make it happen. Let her know right now. I realized how short and fragile life truly is when I lost Audrey. If I had a chance to do it over…I would have told her father to kiss my ass. Now all I can do is beat myself up because I was too simple-minded to see he was trying to keep us apart."

"I know, Demi. I can tell that losing Audrey still pains you. Maybe you're right… I'll be honest about my feelings and see what happens. What's the worst that can happen? All she can say is get the hell away from me, you pervert. But after stealing kisses this afternoon and not getting kicked in the nuts, I think that's a good sign." They laughed. "You're right about letting her know how I feel," Joaquin said after a moment of thought. "On a funnier note, I'll bet you were wide open when she got your jewels."

"Nope, I walked right into it, and it's not funny, bro. One of them still refuses to come back down," he chuckled.

"Well…I'm glad you guys made up and that you get along with her now."

"What's not to love? She's great…she's honest and real, and I know she is the right woman for you," Demi replied.

"I love everything about her, even her stubbornness. So, I see you're doing better. I have a surprise for you. Our cousin Krystal just arrived, and you know how she loves to take care of you."

Demi rolled his eyes. "Beautiful, that's just what I need," he struggled to make himself comfortable; "You know she's going to drive me crazy."

"You're her favorite. Good luck!" Joaquin said, laughing. "I'll check in on you later."

"Swell." Demi rolled his eyes.

Birthday Celebration

Brydus was mesmerized by the beautiful gold dress that Jenny laid out for her. She held it against her body, and it felt like silk. When Jenny entered the room, Brydus embraced her.

"Jenny, this is way too much. It's so beautiful, and the shoes! I'll look like a princess with them on."

"A very sexy princess," Jenny added. The dress fit Brydus perfectly, and the gold strappy heels made her legs look long and shapely.

"Why don't you let me do your hair? I'm really good at it." Brydus let Jenny take over. She straightened her hair and turned her eyes mysterious with a smokey eye look. When Brydus looked in the mirror, she was amazed at the transformation.

"Is that me, oh my God…? I look so freakin hot!"

"You look fabulous. Mr. Joaquin won't be able to keep his hands off you."

"Oh yeah…and who said I wanted his hands on me?" Brydus teased.

"You did. It's written all over your face. Don't be afraid of love, Ms. Brydus. You may like it."

Brydus was nervous as she hurried down the hallway to the main dining room. She took a deep breath before she opened the door. Everyone was there, including Demi, sitting in a comfortable chair. The room was decorated with flowers and streamers; the food smelled delicious, and the cake was exquisite. When everyone sang happy birthday to her, she fought back the tears.

"You guys, this is amazing, thank you." The music started, and the eating began. She gazed around the room to see if Joaquin was among the crowd, but he wasn't. Troy forced her out onto the dance floor, and for the next hour, Brydus danced with all the guys. Demi was having a blast shouting comments from his chair, laughing, and carrying on. Brydus was dancing with Big Willie when Joaquin cut in.

"Thanks for getting her warmed up for me," he said, holding her so tight she could hardly breathe, and the butterflies in her tummy were working overtime. "You look amazing, Sweetcheeks," Joaquin complimented.

"I didn't think you were coming."

"Why would I miss your birthday? I just had to run an errand, that's all." His lips were so close to her ear that she almost fainted. She could feel his desire pressing against her, but she didn't know what to do.

"Did you eat some cake? It's delicious," she tried to make small talk to defer from how he was making her feel.

"I'll get some later," Joaquin answered. "Dancing with you is where I want to be right now." The more they swayed to the music, the tighter he held her.

"I think I need some air," she said, fanning herself.

"Let's go out on the terrace. Joaquin grabbed two glasses of champagne on their way out. He looked so good in his black pants, accented by his white shirt, and he smelled divine. She couldn't look him in the eyes.

"Brydus, tell me what you're thinking. You're so tense. What's wrong?"

"I don't know... when I'm around you, and you're so close, I can't think straight."

Joaquin tilted her face to look at him, "I want us to be together. I think you are my soul partner, and I hope you realize that by now. Look in my eyes and tell me you don't feel anything for me," he held her chin and kissed her tenderly. "I want to hold you," he tightened his grip around her waist. "I want to kiss those lips until they're swollen," he pressed his lips to her temple. "I want to make love to you until you can't walk the next day," he felt her body tense up.

"Joaquin, what are you saying?" she pushed in his chest to put some distance between them.

"I'm going to tell you the truth about how I feel. I know what women like to hear, those sweet lines of love, but that's not how I feel. I want to kiss you until you can't breathe. I want to touch you in places no man has ever touched, and I want to make love to you until we both drop dead from exhaustion." Brydus tried not to laugh. He was so cute; the way he expressed himself just made her want him more. "Tell me how you feel. I've already expressed my feelings, be honest with me."

Brydus started to get emotional, "It's hard for me to tell you how I feel because…I've never felt this way before. I enjoy your kisses and having your strong arms around me. But you have other concerns, and I don't want to get hurt." Joaquin pulled her closer, tightening his embrace, and whispered in her ear.

"Listen to me, my love. I understand your fears. I would never hurt you intentionally. I love you. Please trust me. I swear on this day that you will be my wife someday." He didn't give her a chance to reply, kissing her sweet lips.

Brydus could feel his longing for her as they continued to dance into the night. The band played some of the most romantic songs ever written as if on cue. He couldn't take his eyes off her, singing some of the words to the music. Brydus didn't care about anything except being in his arms for that evening. She realized her true feelings toward Joaquin and wasn't ashamed about how she felt anymore.

They enjoyed the rest of the evening together. Everyone left them alone as they continued to sit outside under a perfect moon stealing kisses and telling her what he wanted to do to her. She laughed, enjoying the closeness and the magic of the night.

She cried again, thanking everyone for her gifts and for such a lovely time. Afterward, Brydus agreed to give Joaquin time to work things out with Monet.

Jenny helped Brydus carry her gifts to her room, "I feel like Cinderella, and I danced all night with my prince," she told Jenny. "He surprised me at every turn…my God, I don't feel like myself anymore. It's like I've turned into this other person."

"You were always a beautiful woman, but you didn't realize it until he awakened it in you. I told you that Mr. Joaquin couldn't keep his hands off you. So, are you two a couple yet?"

"Yes and no, he needs time to get things straight with Monet. Once he takes care of that issue, maybe we can go on from there."

When they reached her room, there were a dozen red roses on the table, a small box, and a note. When she read the note, she started to cry.

"Oh my God," her hands shook when she opened the box. There was a platinum pear-cut diamond solitaire ring. She closed the box right away, "Is this a joke?"

"What does the note say?" Jenny asked, admiring the ring.

Slowly Brydus opened the note. She couldn't stop her hands from shaking.

"To my future wife: please accept this ring with all my love. Happy Birthday, Sweetcheeks. Love, Joaquin."

Brydus stared into space in disbelief. "I can't accept this," she said as she opened the box and admired the stunning ring once again.

"Why not, do you love him?"

"I think I do…I mean, I know I do…but isn't it a bit too soon?"

"Not when you two belong together."

"I can't…no, not like this; I've got to see him." Brydus raced down to his room, knocking on his door. When he answered, his shirt was off, as he was ready for bed."

"Did you get my gift?" he smiled, and Brydus melted on the spot. "Come in and sit down. Now you know if someone saw you coming to my room, by tomorrow, there'll be a rumor that we are sleeping together." She found it hard not to laugh at him.

"Joaquin, what were you thinking? It's exquisite, but this is an engagement ring."

"So, are you refusing me?"

Brydus shook her head, holding back her tears, "No, but I think it's a little premature. Can you hold it for me until I'm ready to wear it?"

He pulled her into his arms, "I don't care who knows, but I do respect your decision. You come to me when you're ready…I'll be waiting." She kissed him, this time losing herself in his arms.

The night was winding down, and the partiers were staggering back to their rooms or homes. Monet watched as Brydus left Joaquin's room an hour later. The rage that was rising in her was evident. Brydus was in the way of what Monet wanted, and she wasn't having any of it. "It's time to go bye-bye bitch," she said aloud.

Monet was desperate. Everything was crumbling down around her. Ever since his nosey parents came to visit, things had been different between her and Joaquin. It was time to take action. Monet would get her man back, no matter what extreme measures she had to take.

Joaquin couldn't sleep. All he thought about was how good Brydus felt in his arms and when he would see her again. Brydus was like a drug to him. The more time he spent with her, the more he realized that she was the woman his grandmother spoke about. Brydus would be his true love. But he had a dilemma, and that was Monet, who was being very difficult. Joaquin wanted with all his heart to do the right thing. However, he would not let Monet get in the way of his happiness. He loved Brydus, and she would be his, even if he had to be harsh with Monet.

Chapter 15: Lola

Monet knew she needed help to sabotage Joaquin's attraction to Brydus. When the house was asleep, she dressed quickly in her dark clothes. Donning the black cape that she always wore whenever she didn't want to be detected leaving the estate, shielded her perfectly. Over the fence and down the gloomy path she traveled, twisting and turning in the darkness toward a single faded light that seemed to be out of place in the dense forest.

The cottage was located a mile north of the estate. The gate to the cottage opened quickly as she pushed her way up the three shaky and worn-out steps. She threw open the squeaky door leading to the combination living and dining room area. The house smelled of rich herbs and spices. Rows of small bottles and concoctions rested neatly along the shelves of the kitchen walls. All clearly labeled and in alphabetical order. Plants hung upside down in different stages of dryness in preparation for being turned into some sort of potion.

Monet searched the rest of the three-bedroom cottage, slamming doors and calling out for the resident. "Lola, where the hell are you?" she yelled, calling her inside and outside with no answer. Monet looked around the small kitchen, which had not changed in years. Frantically she searched the small bottles for a love potion to help her with

Joaquin. She jumped when the door flew open, and there stood Lola with a rifle pointing straight at Monet. Lola was a tall, thin, regal-looking woman with a solid white streak running through her long hair. The fine lines around her eyes didn't mar the stunning beauty she still was.

"Oh, it's just you," Lola said, dismayed, "It's late. I wasn't expecting any visitors. So, what brings you out on this dark night?"

"Cool it, Lola. I know you keep late hours. Where's your drone? He's usually right behind you."

"Well, thanks for asking. My husband is out setting traps."

"Good, I hate it when he's hanging around here when I visit, looking at me with those condemning eyes like he's some prize."

"He is my prize, and I'd appreciate it if you keep my husband out of this. Now, what do you want? It seems like the only time you come around here is when you're in trouble. So, what is it this time?"

"You act as if I don't pay you well for your services."

"Your tainted silver doesn't help me sleep at night, if that's what you mean. It actually burns with contempt. I get rid of it as soon as I can."

"Well, I'm in great need of your magic potions. The love potion you sold me the last time has worn off, it seems, and I need something stronger this now."

Lola sat at her reading table and shuffled her cards, chanting something under her breath. "Monet, it's been two and a half years. If he hasn't proposed to you yet, he never will."

Monet jumped up from her seat, not wanting to hear what Lola had to say, "Look, I did my part. I submitted to his family and his employees."

"You know I find that hard to believe. You've never submitted to anyone, let alone those you deem beneath you."

"I don't need this shit from you, Lola. What I need is a solution, not your stupid comments." Lola reshuffled the cards, ignoring Monet's outburst. She shook her head as she laid out the cards and crossed them.

"What do you see, witch?" Monet asked.

"Sit down," Lola replied as she took a deep breath. "There's a woman involved… a dark woman. Aww… an extraordinary woman, a natural birth, one of great beauty and strength," she was excited.

"That black bitch is ruining everything for me," Monet said, frustrated.

"Be quiet and sit down; you're breaking my concentration. This dark woman has a strong mojo… hmm, I wish I could meet her."

Lola's comment made Monet furious.

"Whose side are you on, witch!" Monet shouted.

"I'm sorry; it's just that this is extraordinary. Her planet alignments right now are perfect, just like the day she was born. What a blessing to have one in our midst."

Monet was getting angrier by the minute, "How do you know all this? You've never even met her!"

"It's right here in the cards. I've never seen anything like this before," Lola said, intrigued by what the cards told her.

"What about me? I'm paying you for this."

"Alright, according to the cards, you might want to find yourself another sugar daddy. Their destiny is intertwined."

"What do you mean intertwined? Are you telling me the truth, hag?"

"It means that they were born for each other. It is their destiny to be together. Just like Demi. Why do you think it's been so hard for Demi to break that bond with his wife? She was born for him. Do you have any idea how hard that is? Sometimes it takes years to find your soul partner. Sometimes they never meet, and they die unfulfilled."

Monet was perplexed, "Wife…what wife? Demi was never married."

"That's how much you know. He was married to the girl a little more than four months before she disappeared. Demi was lucky to have been with his soulmate from her birth. Now I see the same connection between Joaquin and this woman. The draw between these two is powerful. You need to back off right now."

"Look, witch, I don't live by your cards or your interpretation. All I want to do is rid myself of this black bitch. If I seduced him once, I could do it again. She threatened me once, and that was enough."

"Monet, you're only asking for trouble. Bail out now before it's too late." Monet glared at Lola. She took the cards, swiping them off the table, sending them everywhere.

"That's what I think about your stupid cards and advice. I'm a stunning woman with a body that men would kill for, and that skank hasn't got anything over me."

"Monet, that's what I'm saying. You can find yourself another man willing to give you everything you want and love you."

"I want what I want. Look at me, you old hag. Every day I grow more and more beautiful. No one can match my stunning beauty."

"Where do you think you got your beauty, sweetheart? It wasn't from your father's gene pool, but I know what you did inherit from that bastard... your cold-blooded heart. I tried so hard to bring you up right and give you a sense of morals."

"Had you stayed with my father, I wouldn't have had to endure this life of poverty. Do you know how embarrassing it was to tell people that I lived with nasty, dirty gypsies, and then you go and married one?"

"Had I stayed with your father, we would have been dead. I was raped and beaten within inches of my life by that devil. If it wasn't for Ramon and his family, you wouldn't be alive to curse him right now. Ramon and his family found me bleeding and beaten so bad that they didn't think I would survive. Ramon loves me, and you loved him at one time. That is until you found out about your real father. Why that man had to come looking for you, I still don't understand. But you couldn't see beyond his riches and wealth. I told you he wouldn't give you a damn thing. He is the most hateful man in the world. I don't know how I lived with his cruelty and abuse all those horrific years."

"So, you would rather live like this, in this broken-down shack?" Monet said, disgusted.

Lola smiled, "Oh, my hateful little child, I'd rather live under a rock with Ramon than in a palace with that devil that you now call father. God saw my hurt and pain. So, He gave me Ramon… and you. Then you grew up and turned into your father. His wickedness flows through your veins and into your wretched heart, and just the thought of me giving birth to you…makes me sick inside."

"Stop with the drama. Just because I refuse to live like this, you don't have to start with your shit. I belong in a grand house with servants at my feet, and Joaquin can give me that," Monet said, trying to silence her mother.

"But you don't love him. Don't you have any scruples? How can you sleep with one brother and lust after the other? For heaven's sake, girl, what does that make you, a gold-digger and a whore."

Monet's laugh echoed throughout the house, "It makes me smart. I use what I have to get what I want. I'm good at it, and it's not hard. Joaquin is a handsome man and a great lover, but his brother… there's some badass spirit in him that excites me. Joaquin is… too nice to everyone. He treats his bastard staff like equals. They need to know their place. I know he'll always do the right thing.

On the other hand, Demi is rough, especially when he's unshaven and musty-smelling. It just does something to me. I can just imagine his passion in bed." Monet stared into space, thinking about Demi and how it would feel to have a stormy night of unrelenting sex with him.

Lola watched her daughter amazed, "Wake up, child, Joaquin doesn't love you. The man is using you for sex just like you are using him. His brother can't stand the ground you walk on. Demi is untouchable, and that's why you want him so much. It would be better for you if you let Joaquin be happy. Monet, you're going to lose. Joaquin is deeply in love with this dark woman." Monet went into a fit of rage, shuffling through the kitchen drawers looking for a knife.

"You see this," she pointed the knife at Lola. "I will cut out that bitch's heart and feed it to the pigs." She was screaming so loud that they didn't hear the door slam. Ramon came up behind her and wrestled the knife out of her hand, then grabbed her by the neck. Monet pulled away from him. His piercing blue eyes glared at her. His skin was golden from the days in the sun. His white hair and beard made him stand out among his family.

Ramon threw the knife in the sink, "What the hell is going on here? I can hear you two arguing a mile away," his presence filled Monet with rage.

"This is between her and me, so stay out of it!" she screamed at him.

Ramon was disgusted, "Who the hell do you think you're yelling at? Remember she is still your mother, and in this house, you will respect her, or you don't have to come here anymore."

"I'm reminded every day of who my parents are and are not," Monet's eyes were brazen with hate. "Why didn't you let me die? The life you two gave me was nothing more than torture," her eyes swelled up with tears, "we had nothing. I envied the family that lived across the fence. I watched those kids riding their horses, playing games, and wearing nice clothes, and I had nothing. They would call me gypsy girl – dirty gypsy, and when Howard, the oldest, showed interest in me, I thought it was real. You didn't know that, did you? I was thirteen, and Howard was sixteen when he took my virginity. Well, I should say, when I gave it to him. He would jump the fence almost every night, and we'd make love under the trees," Monet smiled, remembering the good times. "He would chase me around, and we'd laugh; when he'd catch me, he was ready for some more loving. He was only sixteen, but he was built like a man. He said it was our little secret… and I thought he loved me. Every time we had sex, he would say my name over and over…I loved it because I was in control. He'd say how good it felt and how beautiful I was, calling me his very own sex angel.

"Yes, he would bring me little gifts, and I thought he meant it when he said that he loved me," Monet's eyes were tearing up, "until that one day when I went over to see him. His father was close by, and he wouldn't even acknowledge me. I called to him… but he kept walking, ignoring my pleas. I cursed him that day, him and his snooty sister, thinking she's all high and mighty, looking down at me. All the while, she was having sex with the stable boy. She grabbed me by my arm, pulled me behind the barn, and slapped me. She laughed, saying that her brother could never marry a dirty gypsy slut like me. I sunk my teeth into her hand; she screamed, and I cursed them with death. I'm glad the wife and children died in that accident. That's when I learned that men couldn't be trusted. They are only be used and set aside like garbage."

"You're going straight to hell, girl," Ramon said, disgusted with Monet.

"You're pregnant again, aren't you?" Lola asked, not surprised. Like she normally would, Monet didn't answer right away, "well, are you?"

"Well… maybe, it's a strong possibility."

"Is it his, or don't you know? Because you only act this crazy when you're pregnant," Lola questioned.

"It could be, but I'm not sure. I had a few interludes with other men."

Lola shook her head with loathing, "This makes the third time, and what's worse is that you can't even say who the father is."

"You're a whore, a disgusting little whore," Ramon bellowed, hitting the table with his fist.

"Ramon, please, you're not helping," Lola pleaded.

"It's true. She sleeps with all these men and doesn't even bother to protect herself. I'm sick of it. I'm sick of her coming here treating you like shit, getting you all upset, and leaving, until the next time she needs something from you." Ramon slammed the door to his bedroom.

Lola couldn't say anything to defend her daughter, "You know, had you not terminated that first pregnancy, you probably would have been married to Joaquin by now. He always does the right thing, and now you have no clue who this baby's father is. How far along are you?"

"I wasn't sure that first baby was his. He always uses protection and…I realize that I can be a little reckless at times. Anyway, I'm not sure this time either, but I'm not too far along. I'll let you know if I need your famous potion. I'll find a way to get Joaquin back. Maybe this baby will work out to my advantage."

"Monet listens. You can't put this baby on him if you're unsure."

"Lola, when will you learn that I do exactly what I want? I will blame this kid on him, and by the time the brat is born, I will be his wife," she gave Lola a devious smile.

"Yeah, and what about the woman? Do you think he'll let her go that easy? I think you're playing with fire. Let him go…Monet, there are other hearts to conquer."

"But none as delicious as this one. Once I get rid of her, he'll be unhappy for a little while. Then I'll cheer him up with the great announcement that he's going to be a daddy. He'll forget that black bitch in a heartbeat."

Lola couldn't help but laugh, "That's insane, and he's not stupid. He is going to have a paternity test done. What will you do if the test comes back and reveals that it's not his child? Oh, and another thing, you hate children, remember? What are you going to do with the child afterward?"

"I'll just get a nanny. It's simple. Why does everyone make such a big deal out of nothing? All I have to do is push the damn thing out and hand it over to someone else to raise. It will satisfy his yearning for children, and I will be the queen of my own castle. After I am living happily ever after, you will never see my face around this dump ever again."

"I think you're making a mistake." The bitterness was written on her face. "You can't continue to use people like this, Monet."

"Well, I don't really care what you think. Now give me a strong love potion. I need it to at least get him interested in bed again!" Monet shrieked while desperately rummaging through the bottles against the wall.

"I told you, no amount of love potion will separate those two. When are you going to understand that?" Their argument continued to escalate to the point that Ramon came out of the bedroom again.

"Shut up! Every time you're in trouble, you come here getting your mother upset."

"Sweetheart, don't get angry … I'll handle this," Lola said, trying to pacify him.

"Face it, Lola, she's a whore. How many illegal acts will you perform to help this ungrateful slut?" He saw the sadness on his wife's face, "Never mind, I don't even want to hear this," he turned to Monet. "You raise your voice in this house one more time. You're going to be drinking your meals through a straw." Monet sucked her teeth and rolled her eyes. He slammed the door of his bedroom again, this time so hard it caused the pictures on the wall to shake.

"Well, that was special. Now give me what I came for, so I can leave this wretched place from hell," Monet said sarcastically.

"I don't have anymore. You took the last bottle I had."

Monet clenched her teeth, "What the hell? You're no help at all, are you? You're useless to me," Monet's words cut into Lola like a knife. Those were the same words her ex-husband screamed at her daily. Those words would always bring back horrible memories. The hate and venom that came out of his mouth were always accompanied by a punch or kick.

"Get out," Lola said in a harsh but controlled voice, "don't come here again. You're not welcome anymore."

"Fine, that's truly what I expected from you. My father was right. You're a weak and pathetic woman.

"Get out! You demon from hell! Had I known you would turn out like him, I would have crushed your skull as you were being born." A chill engulfed Ramon as he ran out of his room to assist Lola.

Monet laughed as she left the house, leaving the door and gate open along the way. "Losers, you belong together," she yelled as she fled. Her evil laughs resonated throughout the area. Lola fell into Ramon's arms, weeping. He tried to console her, rubbing her back tenderly.

"She does this to you every time she comes around. I know she's your daughter, but you have to face it, sweetheart. She's evil."

"Hold me. Every time she talks like that to me, it brings back such terrible memories of the cruel and inhumane life I lived under his roof."

"Baby, you have two more wonderful children. My love, Emily is a great child, and Lee adores you." Lee was Lola's son's middle name which he preferred to use instead of his first name, a name which he detested.

"Thank God Emily wasn't home this time. The last time Monet came to visit, they almost came to blows. "Lee, my sweet boy, he is always defending me, how I miss him. Unfortunately, Monet is going to learn things the hard way."

"Monet is in for a rude awakening, but I think it's time," Ramon said.

"I know… and I can't help her. I saw it in the cards."

"Look at me," he tipped her face up to look into his eyes, "we have an amazing grandson, and Emily's husband is a great father. Lee is far away from the influence of his father. He's happy. Sadly, all we can do is start praying for Monet and hope that she'll find true happiness someday."

Monet, still conniving, began to assess her options, planning how she would make Brydus pay. Now she had to find another way to seduce Joaquin. If she was pregnant, she wasn't very far along, and Joaquin would be the father whether the child was his or not. Monet laughed as she contemplated a plan to get Brydus away from Joaquin. She climbed over the same fence that separated her from a long-time dream so long ago. All those memories, the hated homemade clothing and homeschooling, the shame she felt, everything came back instantly.

When she was older, she begged Ramon to let her go to public school, where she developed a reputation of being a bully. Most of the girls were afraid of Monet. Since she matured early, the male teachers were an easy target. Monet learned how to use her beauty and sexuality to get what she wanted. She only dated boys from wealthy families, and they would do anything for her. When she finished school, she cried and begged Ramon to let her go to a small art school. The tuition was very small, and to keep her happy, Ramon and Lola made the sacrifice to send her there to study. She majored in interior decorating and was very good at it. For a while, it seemed like she was going places. Until she found out that sometimes the students got the opportunity to get hands-on experience at some of the wealthier estates.

When Joaquin walked into the storeroom, all eyes were on him. The twenty-four young women made any excuse they could to stroll by him. Joaquin needed a few of the rooms redecorated. Even though Monet made several trips, she did not catch his eye. Monet begged her instructor to pick her for the assignment, but he chose a senior. For some mysterious reason, the girl fell violently ill and couldn't take the assignment. The instructor didn't want to go through another unpleasant episode with Monet, so he gave in to her demands. Giving her the assignment that should have lasted only two weeks; however, it turned into more than two years at the Quintanilla Estate.

Monet had an instant attraction to Demi, and at first, they were friends. They would talk about the things they liked. But he was still grieving for his lost love and wouldn't succumb to her advances. When Demi was sent away for mental health reasons, she turned all of her attention towards Joaquin, who worked long hours and came home late and tired. Slowly, she took advantage of the situation, rubbing his shoulders and running his bath, seducing him with wine and sweet temptations.

Once she moved into the house, she began to change. She became demanding and short-tempered with the staff, and her true personality spilled out in the open. Her cruelty was taken out on the weak and timid servants. The young ones ran from her whenever they saw her coming, and she loved it. It made her feel empowered to have the servants fear her.

Monet had only moved into the house six months before she found out she was pregnant the first time and went crying to Lola, wanting the dreadful thing out of her before it ruined her shape. They argued bitterly, but as always, Lola gave in and provided her with the means to flush out the fetus. Even though she became violently ill, she welcomed the pain during the three days it took to abort the baby.

Monet loved the new freedom and power she had wormed her way into. Since Joaquin was hardly around and his brother was away, she fashioned herself the grand lady of the estate. Everyone hated her but feared losing their position at the main estate. Though she was able to control most of the staff, some opposed her. The kitchen staff banded together, complaining to Joaquin about how she treated them. He put a stop to her unruly demands and frequent outbursts.

Life was good for the silver-haired beauty until Demi returned from the Inner Cities. He came back with a different attitude and mindset. He began to change towards Monet, and when she touched him, he would push her away. One stormy night while Joaquin was away, she knocked on Demi's door, frantically crying. Pretending that the lightning was scaring her and she needed company. At first, he was convinced she was terrified of the thunder and lightning. He held her as she cried hysterically in his arms. Demi felt it strange that she would come to him. He tried to soothe her nerves, but when he felt her hands rubbing his back and shoulders, he tried to put distance between them. However, Monet held on tighter until he aggressively pushed her away.

Monet was in a trance; she had dreamt about making love to Demi so many times. Slowly and seductively, she pushed her flimsy gown off her shoulders, letting it fall to the floor. Like a porcelain goddess, she stood before him, her beautiful silver hair flowing down her shoulders. She lifted her arms to him, and he started to laugh. Monet was mortified. He belittled her so severely that she ran out of his room crying. The next morning, she tracked him down and found him outside the stables.

"Demi, I want to apologize for last night. Storms do strange things to me, and I feel neglected lately," she giggled seductively.

Demi looked at her with contempt, "You're afraid I'll tell my brother about your little visit, aren't you?"

"I know it looks pretty bad… You're his brother, but I didn't know what I was doing last night. I was afraid."

"So that's your excuse. You came to my room with one thing on your mind."

"Demi, please try to understand, I…"

He cut her off. "You know, sometimes you amaze me. I honestly don't know who you are. But I do know this…you are not good for my brother. Joaquin deserves better."

Monet felt like someone slapped her in the face, becoming increasingly defensive, "Are you saying that I'm not good enough for your brother? Is it because I don't come from money? Well, I'll let you know that my father is rich, and he has many connections."

"I'm not talking about money or connections. I know your family; they are decent, hard-working folk. Ramon and I have had many conversations in the past."

Monet turned bright red, "Well, he is not my father, and whatever he said about me is a lie," she protested.

"Unfortunately, you never came up in the conversation. It's not always about you, Monet. Believe it or not, there are more important things to talk about besides who you are screwing. But I am curious to know what you expected would happen last night. After all, you were naked."

Her eyes got misty for a minute, "I was lonely. I hadn't seen Joaquin in two weeks. A woman has needs too, and I always liked you. Demi, I know you've been going through a rough patch, and I thought we could comfort each other."

"Oh, so you used my grief to come on to me and do what… make me forget the love of my life? Betray and stab my brother in the back? I would do anything for Joaquin. He is my blood! And we respect one another. Loyalty, that word is not in your vocabulary, is it? You're a taker, and I hate that in a person!" Demi expressed angrily.

"You're wrong about me, Demi. If we were together, you would be my all," she put her hand on his, but he snatched it away. "Your brother would have never known. It would have stayed between us." She moved closer to him.

"I would know. Monet, you disgust me, and I wouldn't soil myself with the likes of you. You're no better than a dog that eats its own shit. Thank God you're just a piece of ass for my brother. Stick this in your brain, woman. You will never be more to him than a quick lay. He will never marry you, and please don't waste your time on me. I know where the whore houses are if I need one. Which I'd rather prefer. It's cleaner than being with you."

Monet swung at Demi, but he caught her hand, "You're a fool. You could have had all of this," she touched her breast, "had you not gone to a mental institution, maybe all of this would have been yours. What I hear in your voice is bitterness. When you returned home, I made sweet hot love to your brother. He is fascinating, a great lover, sweet, kind; maybe you should take a few lessons from him."

Demi chuckled, "You are truly delusional if you believe that I ever wanted to be with you. I'd rather pay a prostitute than lay with someone like you. Don't get comfortable, Monet. You're not staying." He rejected her hand once again, ignoring her presence.

For days Monet was afraid that Demi would tell Joaquin, and her plans would be ruined. That was a year and a half ago, and Monet was no closer to being married now than she was then. Demi's words still sting her to this day. The fact that Demi could see right through her drove her crazy and made her want him even more.

When Monet reached the house, the estate was quiet, returning from Lola's. The guard nodded as she walked in through the back door, the kitchen, and straight upstairs toward her room. She stopped at Joaquin's door to see if she could hear any sounds coming from his room. But there was only silence. Her bed was turned down, and the moonlight flooded the room. She stared out the window, listening to the sounds of the night that sometimes intensified the stillness. Tonight, she felt the room closing in on her more than usual. She took her clothes off and let the moonlight bathe her beautiful, shapely body. Touching her flat belly, wondering what a baby would do to her perfect frame. She touched herself provocatively in the mirror, wishing that Joaquin was there with her and hoping that having this baby would lure him back to her.

She wondered if it was worth the pain of childbirth to gain her permanent status within the estate as the wife of a rich overlord. Monet smiled to herself. *Destiny is what I make it*, she thought. She would surely give Joaquin comfort after Brydus was out of the picture. Insisting that they marry quickly before the child is born. If nothing else, Monet knew that Joaquin would do the right thing for his child.

Chapter 16: Crossing the Line

Brydus couldn't get enough of the history, biography, and reference books she found in the huge library. Some books were ancient, full of dust, but interesting. She found a book of actresses from the twentieth century, 1929 – 1999. The glossy pictures were a little faded, but she was captivated by these women's beauty and outstanding achievements.

Sometimes Brydus would catch Louis going through some of the books, and he would mark certain articles thinking that she would be interested in reading them. Louis was in his fifties and lived through the Dark Days. He was always full of great information, and Brydus loved pumping him for more, "Tell me, Louis, did you know any people like me?"

"I wish, but people lost their color hundreds of years ago. It was gradual, with all the new cosmetic advances; you could look any way you wanted. Change your skin color, your eye color, everything. Then there was a breakthrough when changes could be done genetically before a child was born. Now that's when they started to make big money, and like anything else, they needed victims. That's what I called them because they truly didn't know what they were getting into. So, they offered large amounts of money if you volunteered to be a test patient. Well, when you have families barely making ends meet, what do you expect? People were knocking down the door wanting a piece of the new age of beauty. That's how it started. It wasn't until a few hundred years later that they discovered the damage it had on the balance of the races. And that, my friend, is why you are so important. You are our future and a reminder that we made such an enormous mistake."

"When I was young," Brydus said, remembering, "I felt like I had this terrible disease. I was so different, and my mother cried all the time. It wasn't until I was older that I understood the reason behind all her tears. My trainers sat me down and explained why I was treated differently and how important my survival was. Not only to our community but also to the outside world; I felt so trapped… like this heavy load was weighing down on my shoulders. It wasn't until the twins were born that I began to feel like I wasn't a freak."

"Twins, you mean there are more like you?" he was amazed.

"Yes, beautiful twin girls. I started their training. Louis, if you think I'm bad, you should see these two. They are remarkable, and they're only eight years old."

"Oh my God, could it be possible that nature is finally taking over again? That is wonderful news," Louis said, unable to control his enthusiasm.

"I believe that. So far, there have only been females born like me. We are hoping for a male; that would give us more hope for the future."

"You are so right. I was so thrilled when I first met you… Joaquin's grandmother is held in high esteem by everyone. We are delighted to have such an influential woman in our midst. Nylaya is truly incredible."

"Yes, she is wonderful. We are so lucky to have her too."

"Well, I'm happy you are here. Brydus, these books are important to us to know where we came from and don't make the same mistakes."

"It is important to me to understand who I am and to have my identity attached to my color. It is a big part of me and my people. Nylaya's people were called African Americans. She is also of mixed Latin ancestry. We were called Latin Americans, and our cultures are very similar."

"Yes, you and I are both from the Afro-Latino culture, which I hold dearly."

Brydus was fascinated with their conversations. It took her mind off the many bitter arguments Joaquin had with Monet.

Brydus was so engrossed in her reading that she didn't hear Monet and Krystal open the door to the terrace where she now sat drinking juice. She was fantasizing about the different places she saw in the books, thinking what an exciting era it was to be alive.

"So, this is how you keep yourself occupied when you're not trying to steal someone's man?" Monet said as Krystal followed close behind her, sitting at Brydus' table.

"Can't you find someone else to harass or someplace else to sit? I'm really busy right now," Brydus replied, not looking up from her book.

"You're the only bitch I want to harass," Monet said arrogantly and full of confidence.

Brydus finally looked up from her book and took a deep breath, knowing this would not end nicely. "I'm not even going to ask you why you're here. Just say whatever you're going to say and leave me the hell alone."

Monet laughed, "Oh, I have plenty to say to you, home-wrecker. I know you're screwing him, so don't try to act surprised or high and mighty. I let you get away with that last episode in the dining room, but I'm not afraid of you." She stood close enough to annoy Brydus, waving a finger at her.

Brydus closed her book, "You know. When I got up this morning, I said to myself. What a beautiful day. I think I will enjoy the nice spring air… read a good book, relax, and maybe even get a little sun. But you have ruined my perfect day with your stupidity. Don't blame me if you and Joaquin are not getting along. This isn't something new. Furthermore, if I was screwing your man, he wouldn't be your man anymore, would he? He'd be in my bed."

Krystal's eyes opened wide at Brydus' response, which took Monet by surprise as well. Most women were intimidated by her, but Brydus wasn't moved by Monet's words.

"Look, whore, I want you to leave. Run away and don't look back."

Brydus stood up from her chair, "First, you need to watch what you're calling me. You don't know me. I can be a mean-ass bitch, but you really don't want to go there again. I don't want to hurt you, but don't push me."

"Don't worry," Monet said with a smug little smile, "that won't happen again, but you need to leave."

"Who's going to make me leave? Would that be you and Miss Shithead over here? I'd like to see that. Because the day I let someone like you beat me, I may as well lay down and die."

Monet laughed louder, "You're not so tough. You may have him between your legs now, but… when he gets tired of you, he will come running back to me… you're just an imitation." Monet ripped open her shirt, exposing her breasts. "This is what he likes. He likes an experienced woman who knows how to move in bed and how to play with his tool. I'll have him eating out of my crotch again. You have no idea how to please a man, and I know my man. I know what he likes. So, the next time I see you up in his face, I will kick your ass. Do I make myself clear?"

Brydus squared off to her, closing the distance between them. "First of all, put your saggy breasts away. I'm not impressed. You're damn lucky this isn't my house. Because your ass would be over this wall face down on the lawn. You may scare everyone else around here. You abuse and beat on them, but you've picked the wrong bitch to mess with this time. I'd advise you to turn around and get out of here before I change my mind and hurt you both."

"Come on, Monet, let's get out of here." Krystal urged, pulling her away.

"Well, you know where I am. Just say the word, and we can take care of this," Brydus said without blinking.

Krystal pushed Monet through the doors. Monet was so angry that Brydus was not even the slightest bit bothered by her threats.

Brydus tried to concentrate on her book, and after a few minutes, she was back on track.

The sun was going down when she realized how hungry she was. She had missed dinner again. She tried to avoid any gatherings that included Joaquin. She dreamt about him all the time and couldn't hide her feelings when he was close to her. He always invited her to ride or join him and the others in the recreation room. But she always declined. She couldn't stand looking at his smiling face knowing that she couldn't touch him, and Monet was always nearby.

The kitchen staff was more than happy to make her something to eat. They made her a nice sandwich while she continued to read her book. It was one of those lazy evenings. Brydus had to occupy her time with something that would help her stop thinking of Joaquin, remembering how wonderful it felt when he held her. Those kisses on the night of her birthday still lingered in her heart. There were days that she wanted to knock on his door and smother him with kisses. But she couldn't bring herself to be with him until things were over with Monet. Joaquin promised to give her time, and no matter how long it took, he'd be waiting for the moment when she wanted to be with him.

Joaquin was very busy with his ranch, but he always took the time to send her cute little messages, just to let her know that he was thinking about her.

As Brydus reached her room, she sensed that something was wrong. Placing her ear against the door, she heard someone crying inside. Quickly she opened the door, and there was Jenny in a heap of clothes, all torn to shreds. Her left eye was already turning black and blue. Brydus went to comfort her, "What happened?"

Jenny wiped her eyes, "I'm sorry I couldn't stop them."

Brydus was shocked as she looked around at the disaster in her room. "Who did this, Jenny? Who hit you?"

"I tried to stop them, but Krystal grabbed me by the hair, and Monet punched me in the eye."

Brydus was furious. Her brown eyes smoldered with anger as she marched down the hallway toward the recreation room, where they gathered to play cards and shoot pool.

Jenny tried to stop her, "Please, Miss Brydus, I'm alright. It's not the first time. I can live with it."

Brydus turned to face her, "But I can't. This will end tonight," she said through clenched teeth.

Jenny held her arms, pleading, "I don't want you to go. You're my friend."

"Never again, do you hear me? They will never hurt you again if I have anything to do with it!" she screamed as her voice echoed throughout the hall.

Monet was at her usual table playing cards with Krystal near the pool tables. Joaquin bragged about his skills at the pool table with some of his crew members. The music was playing, and it was Joaquin's turn to shoot. When he saw Brydus coming toward him, he looked up and smiled. Brydus grabbed him, giving him a tongue lashing of a kiss, taking him off guard. He was enjoying her forwardness. The guys started to whistle and clap until she turned toward Monet.

"Now show me what you got, bitch!"

Joaquin knew this was serious when Brydus turned over the table to get to Monet. Monet grabbed a bottle and swung it at her wildly. Big Willie grabbed Brydus from behind, putting her in a bear hug, and Louis grabbed her hands.

"The minute you step outside, you're done," she yelled, pulling away from them. Joaquin tried to handle the situation, but all Monet could do was cry, holding on to him like the innocent little victim. Joaquin sat Monet down and ran after Brydus, who was now arguing with Big Willie in front of her room. He still had a steel grip on her wrists, trying to talk her down. Jenny could only cry, begging them not to hurt her.

Joaquin was shocked when he saw the room. The mattress was cut open, everything on the dressers was tossed on the floor, and all the lotions, shampoos, and liquids were emptied on the floor.

"Big Willie, get off of me! I've got to get out of here before I kill someone," she yelled. When Big Willie let her go, she ran down the hall to the back stairway toward the stables. Big Willie and Louis looked at each other, understanding why Brydus was so angry.

"Joaquin… this is crazy. Monet went too far," Big Willie said, scratching his head.

"Big Willie, Louis, follow Brydus and don't let her out of your sight. I'll get to the bottom of this. Hurry, please." Joaquin couldn't get his mind around the damage in Brydus' room, and poor Jenny was still crying in the corner. Her black eye was throbbing and was now closing.

"Jenny, what happened? Who did this?"

She started to cry louder, "I tried to stop them, but they hurt me. That's why Brydus is so upset. She was defending me." Joaquin put his arm around Jenny as she shook in his arms.

"Please don't send Brydus away, please, I'll do anything," Jenny begged between sobs.

"How can I send the woman I love away for defending someone dear to me? I promise you I will bring her back… ok?" Jenny nodded. "I'm going to bring her back. You go to your room and rest, alright?" She tried to smile. "Alright, no more crying," he said.

By the time Big Willie and Louis reached the stables, Brydus had saddled her horse and was well on her way. The stable boy tried to stop her because it was dark, but she shoved him aside, saddling her own horse.

"Tommy, do you know in which direction she went?" Louis asked.

"She went towards town. She said something about needing a drink before she killed someone," Tommy explained, wondering what happened.

When Joaquin walked back to the rec room, Monet was still crying hysterically. The room was packed, but no one tried to comfort her. She threw herself at him when he walked in. However, she didn't expect him to push her away, sitting her back down.

Joaquin turned to his crew, "I want to apologize to everyone. But if you don't mind, I need to ask everyone to leave, and I'm sorry this happened... please, everyone, except for Troy. Nelly, can you please help clean up around here a little?" Monet tried again to wrap her arms around Joaquin again, and he stopped her.

"I'm done with you. Stop it, and stop your fake crying! I'm so tired of your shit."

"Why are you angry with me? I'm the victim here. You saw what she did. We were playing cards quietly, and she viscously attacked us. Why are you defending her? She threatened us earlier this afternoon, saying that she would throw us off the terrace and beat us down."

"You crossed the line, Monet," he replied

She tried to interrupt. "But I..."

"Don't! Don't try to make up some bullshit story... in fact, I know exactly what she was doing all day long. First thing, she rode her horse, then she worked out. After that, she had some breakfast. Then went for a swim, and guess what? Demi and I were looking out the window when lo and behold, you two came up to her on the terrace… we saw everything. Even when you ripped open your shirt. Both of you are going to clean up that mess. If you try to get anyone to help you, they will be fired." He turned to Nelly, who was standing behind the bar. "Nelly, spread the word; they're done if anyone touches anything in that room."

"Yes, sir."

"I'm ashamed of both of you for acting like animals. God, it makes me sick to my stomach just looking at you both."

"How can you say that about me after all we've been through? I gave you all my love, and now you're turning on me. Why can't you see her for what she is? A manipulator and deceiver! And Jenny is lying. If someone beat her up, it was that black bitch… or she did it to herself. She's always looking for sympathy from you, and who knows… she probably destroyed that room herself to get me in trouble."

"So now you're insulting my intelligence by telling me that you had nothing to do with destroying that room and beating poor Jenny. Do I have stupid written on my forehead, woman? I want that room clean before you two even think about going to bed tonight. And if it's not clean, you both better find another place to stay from now on."

"Joaquin, darling, why are you torturing me with your indifference," Monet started to cry. "Ever since she came here, you've been treating me like shit. Telling me to move when all I want is to love you and make you happy," she sobbed louder.

"I've been asking you to move for over a year. I haven't been happy for a long time, and let's be honest, you don't love me; you just love what I have. Well, it's time to move on because I want to be happy; I want children; I want a woman that I can love and respect. That woman is not you."

Monet became hysterical, throwing herself against him, "How can you say that? When we mean so much to each other. I want children too… please give me a chance to prove that I can be the woman you need."

Joaquin pushed Monet away gently. "We've been through this before. Last year, when my mother left, I told you it wasn't going to work. Don't make this any more difficult than it has to be… I suggest that you get started on cleaning up my room."

"Cousin Joaquin, but that will take us all night," Krystal said in her whining voice.

"Then you should have thought about that before you followed Attila into that room."

"It's not fair!" Monet argued, still insisting it wasn't her.

"You have a choice, clean that room tonight, or find another place to live. Those are your options."

Joaquin slammed the door when he reached his room. He started to throw things in a bag when Demi knocked and let himself in. Joaquin was so angry he couldn't speak at first.

"Hey, I heard the whole thing. Are you alright?"

"Yeah, I'm just tired of this whole drama shit. All I know is that room better be right when I get back."

"Bro, you know Brydus keeps to herself because of those two. That's crazy."

"Demi, she was so angry. She would have killed Monet. The way she threw that table, I got chills. I freaked… I don't want my future wife in jail for murder," he barked, feeling frustrated.

Demi tried not to laugh, "I'm sorry, I don't mean to make light of the situation, but you're a fool if you don't go after that woman."

"I am. That's why I'm packing a bag. Louis just called me; she's at the Blue Moon getting wasted."

"Well… alright, I would go with you, but I'm not feeling well. That pain medication makes me loopy."

"Keep an eye on those two. Make sure they don't leave before the room is clean.

"Don't worry, my brother, I will torture them all night."

"Thanks, bro. I don't mean to burden you with those two."

"Don't even think about it. You go, don't worry about these bitches. I got this."

The Blue Moon

Big Willie had no problem finding Brydus. The men swarmed around her like flies. Big Willie had to push his way through to her at the bar, where she sat. Her eyes were glassy already, and her speech slurred. Big Willie pulled the man next to her off the seat by his collar. He was extremely close. "Sweetheart, how are you?" He looked at the row of glasses in front of her.

"Oh hi, big teddy-bear Willie, I've seen better days," Brydus said sadly.

"How many of those have you had already?"

"Oh, just two…they're sooo good." The bartender held up six fingers.

"Sweetheart, you haven't eaten. It's not good to drink like that on an empty stomach." He turned to Chris, the bartender, "Anything good in the kitchen?"

"The fried chicken is excellent; it's very popular."

"Alright, Chris, I'm going to need two orders of chicken, and can you get me a table? Joaquin will be here to settle the bill."

"No problem, I'll get Amanda to clear you a table, and as far as the tab, everything has been paid for... she's awfully good for business, if you know what I mean."

Big Willie convinced her to sit at the table that Amanda was cleaning for them. "Sweetheart, I ordered something to eat, so please hold off on the drinking," Big Willie begged as Amanda set the table.

"Two more of these, sweet lady," Brydus said, smiling.

Big Willie grabbed her hands, smiling at her, "No more until you eat."

"If I don't get two more of these, I will kill someone."

"Alright then, two more, Amanda, and can you find out what the ETA is on the food? Thanks, honey." Louis joined them at the table. He started to laugh when he saw how wasted Brydus was getting.

"Looks like you've been hitting those drinks pretty hard, doll face."

She grinned at him, "They're sooo good and peachy. These two are mine; you get your own fizzy things." She tore into the chicken when the food came like she hadn't eaten in days.

"Brydus," Louis asked, "Do you like Joaquin? That kiss you laid on him was no joke, sweetheart."

Brydus stared at him, trying to focus. Struggling to find the right words, she just nodded, "That man is perfect, you hear me? He has these big arms, a beautiful chest, and those lips… I dream of them every night. I mean, I dream of him every night, not just his lips. But they're usually kissing mine… you know." Louis and Big Willie were laughing, enjoying the moment.

"So, it's safe to say that you have strong feelings for him," Louis asked, looking over at Big Willie, shaking his head.

"No, I don't like him… I love him," Brydus said in a childlike voice. "I want him to make love to me, but I have a terrible secret." She looked around to see who was close enough to hear. The guys sat patiently, wondering what the big secret was. "Come closer, now, this doesn't leave this table, alright," she put her forefinger to her lips, "I've never been with a man before," she whispered. Louis laughed so hard that he nearly fell out of his chair.

"See, I knew you would laugh. It's so embarrassing," she said, pouting.

Louis held her hands, "No, Mami, that's nothing to be ashamed of. There's nothing wrong with waiting for the right person," he patted her hands.

"He's right, sweetie. You'll know the right time. Hey, there's Joaquin." Big Willie waved him over.

Joaquin sat next to her and smiled at the guys. "So… I got some rooms for the night, and I think my little street fighter here has had enough to drink." Brydus sat quietly, staring at the table, and finished her last shot.

"Ah, you may want to talk to her about L-O-V-E. She's really opened to it," Big Willie said, helping Joaquin with Brydus.

"Pretty lady…one, two more please," she waved at Amanda.

"Oh baby, you're finished," Joaquin said as he held her in his arms.

"Those peachy things are good. Where are they?"

"No more peachy drinks, time to go night, night." She had a hard time walking, allowing Joaquin to throw her over his shoulder when they stepped outside. The Grand Hotel was the newest reconstruction in the area and was only a block away. The hostess helped Joaquin with Brydus. They laughed as she moaned about the room spinning.

"Man is she going have a mean one tomorrow," Louis said, feeling sorry for the hangover that Brydus was going to have in the morning.

"I'll fix her up, but she's going to need clothes. Those bitches ripped up everything, even her underwear."

"Boss, I think there's a small boutique downstairs. We can pick up something temporary in the morning," Big Willie offered.

"That sounds like a plan, and then I'll take her shopping in the afternoon. Thanks a lot, guys. Let me get my baby to bed, so she can sleep it off."

Brydus struggled to get up from the bed and find the bathroom. Joaquin helped her to the door, just happy to be with her. It didn't matter what condition she was in. He turned down the bed, but when Brydus came out of the bathroom, she was wearing nothing but her underwear and bra.

"Ah, baby…um, where did you leave your clothes?"

She spun around, looking at the pile in the bathroom and then back to him.

"I'm going to bed. I don't sleep with clothes on."

"Ah… I know, sweetie, but in this situation… you need your clothes on. Because you see, I'm a man, a really horny one, and I can't sleep with you looking like this."

"Joaquin, I know you've seen naked women before… I'm tired." He helped her into bed.

"You're right; I have seen many naked women, but none more beautiful than you."

She wrapped her arms around his neck, "Kiss me, Joaquin," he held her tenderly in his arms, kissing her sweetly and playfully, "Make love to me," she said in a small child-like voice.

He chuckled, "Sweetcheeks, that's music to my ears, and I would love to… but not tonight. I want you to remember every second of our passion. Your first time should be special," he kissed her again. "I tell you what, next week we'll go to the Inner Cities. I'll get us a nice room for a week," Joaquin said as he kissed her neck. "I promise we won't leave our room for two days. Now try to sleep, my love."

Meanwhile, Monet was beside herself when Joaquin left. She screamed at Krystal almost all night about how she was losing her hold on Joaquin. "What are you going to do? He's with her now," Krystal asked while cleaning the floor in the bathroom.

"I have a few tricks up my sleeves, you see, Krystal; no one helped me get into this house. I used my secret weapon to lure your cousin into my bed. This body of mine is my weapon. I know how to use it, to bend him to my will. My only downfall is your aunt and grandmother. They influenced him, which is why he is turning away from me. I have to find a way to get back in his good graces and lure him back into bed with me so I can work my magic."

"Monet, Brydus is in your way… to be honest, she scares me. Did you see how angry she got? I thought she was going to kill us."

Monet just smiled, "I know, but Joaquin won't allow her to harm us… I know that deep inside, he still wants this. She's just something new, a plaything. In the long run, I know how to satisfy that sexual craving of his."

"I think Demi is paying her a lot of attention, and you know how I feel about him."

Monet gave her a side glance, "You know, I never understood your feelings for him. He's way older than you, a blood relative, and he was your sister's ex-boyfriend. I mean, he is juicy and all but why him?"

"All my life, I came in second to my sister Audrey. I had to fight for everything. My sister had my mother's undying love. Why? She wasn't even her biological daughter, just my father's love child… a child born from his lust. When I came along four years later, I watched how Demi treated my sister… he loved her so much that it was sickening. As a child, he loved her, and she…couldn't stay away from him. Their love was pure, and I hated her for it. I longed for him to look at me the way he looked at her. Sometimes they didn't even have to talk, just a look to know what they were thinking and feeling. I used to spy on them making out, and I pretended it was me he was holding so powerfully and passionately."

"But she's gone, she's dead. It's been years… when will he stop grieving for her and join the living?"

"That kind of love doesn't die, Monet. It just lives on in a spirit that haunts you for the rest of your life," Krystal said with a sigh. "The day Audrey disappeared, I watched my father spying on her through a hole in the wall that led into her bedroom. He didn't see me, but I saw him holding and touching himself, and the look of lust in his eyes nearly killed me.

Audrey had everything, my mother, my father, Demi, and I was always in her shadow. When she was gone, I was so happy. No more second best for me. I was the special one now, and I waited… I waited until I was older and pretty, to see if Demi would look at me the same way he looked at her."

"I didn't know you were so insecure. Use your beauty; it will bring him to you. Use your sexuality to lure him into your arms. You have been with other men, haven't you?"

"Boys my age, who stumble over their own feet… no real passion, not like the kind he had with my sister. Their passion haunted me for so long, those tender words he spoke to her. The moans of love and passion made me cry. It was something to watch, and that's what I want."

"You know Demi's your cousin, and if you have children, they can come out all messed up and everything, aren't you worried?"

"No, that's silly. Only brothers and sisters have children like that. Anyway, I want to make him happy, and if he wants children, I'll have to give him what he wants…right?"

Monet knew how Krystal felt, but she kept her feelings for Demi to herself. She wondered how it would be with him on many occasions. "Does your mother know you have the hots for your cousin?"

"Heavens, no, she would never let me come without her if she knew. She'll be coming for a visit in a few weeks," Krystal giggled, "she already caught me with our next-door neighbor's son."

"Well, well, you naughty girl, I didn't think you had it in you."

"I had to get away for a while… and my poor Demi… When I saw him hurt, I freaked out! You know I hated my sister for years because I loved him. But a girl gets horny just waiting."

"You know that's right. Well, I guess you already know what you want. It doesn't mean you can't have some fun along the way," they laughed.

"Hm, sounds good to me."

"I have great plans for that black bitch. By the time I'm done with her, Joaquin will be totally disgusted with her. I shall welcome him into my loving arms once again, where he belongs."

Hotel Room

Brydus was in the shower bright and early with a raging hangover. Joaquin laughed every time he heard her moan from inside the bathroom. "Sweetcheeks, are you alright in there?"

"I'm dying," she said from the shower. He opened the door to the steamy bathroom.

"Hey, Sweetcheeks, Louis dropped off some clothes, a toothbrush, ah… hairbrush. I also ordered you something to settle your stomach and your headache. So… what if I join you in the shower? I can wash your sexy back."

"How about you don't," she said, moaning. He enjoyed teasing her; he could tell she was in pain when she came out of the bathroom.

"Baby, you look miserable. Here drink this down and take two of these… it works wonders. In an hour, you'll be good as new. I'm going to shave, so you relax, ok?" Brydus couldn't look him in the face. Joaquin paraded around the room in his underwear, and she wondered what happened last night.

"Joaquin, can I ask you something?" He turned to face her with a devilish smile, "… did we do… you know, last night?" He laughed as he watched her drink the last of the concoction, making a sour face.

He pushed her to the bed, pinning her down, lying on top of her with a face full of shaving cream. "You don't remember the hot, monkey sex we had last night?" he rubbed his face against hers. "You screamed for more… I'm surprised no one came to the door complaining about the noise. Don't you remember, baby? Now I'm hurt." He pulled away from her and continued to shave and tease her.

"The last thing I remember is looking down at the floor… oh my God. I'm such a slut. I don't feel any different." She touched herself and looked at the bed for signs of blood.

"Relax, baby, nothing happened last night… you wanted to. You asked me to, but it didn't seem right."

"You're lying; I wouldn't say anything like that!"

"Look, Sweetcheeks, you begged me to make love to you, we kissed a lot, and you took your own clothes off. Now, if you think you're getting out of our date, you're sadly mistaken."

"Date, What date? We made a date?" She asked, confused.

Joaquin pulled her from the bed into his arms, "Yes, we made plans. Next week, we are going to the Inner Cities for seven days. I'm going to get us a really nice suite with a fireplace and Jacuzzi. We're going to have some wine, relax with soft music, and make love for two days." She couldn't resist his kisses. "Your first time should be special."

Brydus pulled away from him, "And I agreed to all this?"

"Yes, and you're not getting out of it because you sealed it with a kiss." She laughed at him. All she could think about was how damn cute he was and the lustful glimmer in his eyes.

"You took advantage of me. I was drunk, for heaven's sake." Now it was her turn to tease him. Joaquin grabbed her by the waist from behind, kissing her neck, sending strange sensations throughout her body.

"No, you see, I could have taken advantage of you last night, but I wanted your first time… our first time together, to be memorable. I want to be able to tell our children that our first time was amazing and romantic."

"Ah, Joaquin, aren't you forgetting something? You're already talking about children. Are you crazy?"

He turned her around to face him as his smile faded, becoming extremely serious, "All I know is that… when I'm near you, I want to hold you and kiss you. My body aches for you." His kiss brought her emotions to the surface.

"We've only known each other a few months. How could you be so sure?"

"When I first saw you with all those leaves in your hair and mud on your face, you were throwing daggers at me with your eyes… I knew then." He kissed her neck and lips, "I wanted to kiss that cute little mole on your lip."

"Joaquin, why am I feeling guilty? I left a fiancé behind. Then there's Monet, who will make our lives miserable."

He sat her down on his lap, getting frustrated, "You know, I thought about your so-called fiancé. What kind of man lets the woman he's supposed to love and want to marry, walk out into the world alone?"

"He wasn't prepared, I told you."

Joaquin interrupted her, "let's cut the shit. I'm putting myself out there. I have strong feelings for you, and I know you do, too. I want to be with you, including having a serious relationship that will lead to marriage. Tell me to my face that you don't want me."

Brydus threw her arms around his neck, "I do care, more than I want to admit." He kissed her arm. She had to admit how she was feeling, "I want you to make love to me and drive me crazy with passion."

"Good…that's all I wanted to know, that you want me just as much as I love you… there I said it…I love you, baby, and want you. We're going to make plans for a life together."

Brydus kissed him, wanting to feel him close to her, "Joaquin… can we keep this quiet? Just for now? If this woman comes at me again, I'm going to punch her in the face."

"Alright, just for a while, but I don't care who knows, do you understand me? Now we're going to eat something, go shopping, and enjoy the rest of this day together."

After a nice breakfast, the couple went on a shopping spree. Brydus was in another world as she went from one store to another trying on clothes, waiting for Joaquin's approval. After a long, exhausting afternoon, they had a fabulous dinner before heading home.

The house was quiet when they marched up to her room to see the damage and what needed to be replaced. Brydus smiled when she noticed that her room was put back together. Jenny had the mattress replaced and all the things that were destroyed. Joaquin pulled her roughly to him and kissed her, throwing her against the wall. She could feel his wanting pressing against her as she lost herself in his kisses and touch.

"I'd better go now and leave you before I ruin our plans," he whispered near her ear. Brydus moaned with delight, responding to his nearness and kisses. "We'll continue this tomorrow. I should leave now before I change my mind." His last kiss left her breathless and tingling all over. She smiled as she began to put some of her new things away when there was a knock at the door.

"Miss Brydus, it's Jenny. May I come in?" Brydus threw open the door and hugged her. Jenny got caught up in her happiness.

"I had the most extraordinary day, but last night is still a blur."

"Mr. Joaquin said he loved you last night before he left to find you. I'm so happy for you. You deserve to be in love. Mr. Joaquin is a wonderful man… but I knew he had eyes for you from the start, I could tell."

"This is the happiest I've been since I left home… but nothing is easy. I feel guilty deep inside because of Monet. You see, I can sympathize with how she feels. His touch and kisses, especially when he whispers in my ear… I can't even remember my old boyfriend's face anymore."

"Miss Brydus, don't feel guilty about her. She had her chance to make him happy, but it was always about her. There's only so much voodoo one can do."

"Voodoo, what do you mean?"

"I found some things in her room with Mr. Joaquin's name and picture, bizarre stuff," Jenny laughed, "but I got some holy water and sprinkled it all over. I guess that neutralized it." They both laughed.

"Can she be that desperate? It's my fault."

"No, that was there long before you came. No one knows this, but the townspeople do talk. When Joaquin is not here, she disappears for days. I think he knows something about her screwing around with other men. I've also witnessed her following Demi sometimes. He despises her, never wanting to be alone with her. I remember one time when she slipped into his room and took one of his shirts. The next day I went into her room to put something away, and I found the shirt hanging in the closet. It had his name attached to it and a red candle. I told Mattie, who has a cousin that is a pastor. We both went into her closet and sprinkled holy water on the shirt and around the area."

"I didn't know that…I would never think that she would do something like that."

"Her mother is married to a gypsy; she only reads cards and sells potions. Ramon's mother puts it together. She doesn't practice the dark arts, but she is a card reader."

"Now you're scaring me."

"Oh, you would never know that they were related. They are really nice people. Her sister favors her in looks, but she is a wonderful person. They attend all the charity events and celebrations. They are part of our community."

"Why is Monet so wicked? I have never encountered anyone like her."

"My father always said that karma is a bitch. It will catch up to you someday. I can't wait for the day it catches up to her."

Chapter 17: Inner Cities

Brydus was happy just to get away. She was done with all the madness at the main estate. Everyone was tired of listening to the violent arguments between Joaquin and Monet almost every night. Monet would throw things and sometimes take them out on one of the staff members. Most of them stayed out of her way, and others stood up to her.

The roads to the Inner Cities were horrendous, and travel was hard at first. They couldn't travel by car because the roads had deep potholes. Some sections were missing, making travel by car almost impossible. The roads were more manageable to travel as they entered the larger providences. When they reached the border between New Jersey, crossing through the Lincoln Tunnel into the Inner Cities, it was like crossing into another world. The citizens of the Inner Cities worked to repair the tunnel damaged by the riots during the Dark Days. They made the mile and a half connection into the Inner Cities a museum. Memories of how New York used to look. It had bright and cheery exhibits with beautiful memorabilia. Joaquin was Brydus' travel guide. And she bombarded him with millions of questions as they passed the beautiful pictures from the past. Her jaw slowly dropped when they reached the other side. "Oh my God, Joaquin… this is incredible. I can't believe this is real, the houses, the railways…"

"They keep the stables on the outskirts of the city… it gives the city kids a chance to make money, so they help keep the stables clean, feed and exercise the horses.

"Have you ever thought of moving up this way? It is amazing!"

"No, I see this as my getaway, vacation spot," Joaquin expressed.

"Well, I can see myself getting away a lot."

Joaquin made arrangements at one of the best hotels in Citizens Square. The place was once known as Time Square before the Purest Movement burnt most buildings and stores down. Anicasio Plaza was one of the first luxury hotels resurrected in the city. All high-end hotels from the past were destroyed by fire and torn down for safety purposes.

However, the city was beginning to come back to life. Four other hotels were being constructed in the surrounding area. Brydus was experiencing as if she was walking into the past. The Inner City was booming with activity, people coming and going, sometimes people came just to stop and enjoy the moment.

Once they took care of their horses, they stepped into the solar-powered transit system. Brydus had only read about this type of transportation in books but never thought she would see one or ride in one herself.

She couldn't keep still as they waited for the train. She closed her eyes as the gentle breeze from the other trains passed, adding extra excitement to the experience. There were vendors selling flowers, coffee, and donuts with colorful signs or balloons.

Joaquin held her hand to keep her still, "Alright, this is the game plan. First, we'll have to go and see my uncle. He's waiting for us. We'll spend a few hours with him, and he'll show you around. Then we'll have dinner with him, maybe his wife Renee will join us. Then it's off to our hotel, where we'll have some wine and cheese waiting for us. Then we'll spend around two days making love."

"Two days, is that possible?" Brydus laughed.

"Baby, anything's possible. We'll come up for air to eat every now and then. We have to keep up our strength. The next day we can go shopping. Visit some of the museums. Then go back to our room, spend a night full of sweet loving, and head home the following day. What do you think?"

"You have a lot of that sweet loving going on."

"Oh, it's on, baby. I waited a long time…you promised. I don't care if you were drunk at the time. A promise is a promise," he teased her.

Brydus put her arms around his neck and kissed him, "Mumm, I hear you got great skills," she whispered.

He laughed loudly, "Oh, I've been known to rock a few worlds. Don't worry; I'll have you calling me big daddy by the end of the night."

"I guess we'll see about that," she said, with a certain gleam in her eyes. "I'll be the judge of that."

"Oh…you're in big trouble, woman," he said, nuzzling her neck.

The train ride was amazing. Brydus glued herself to the window, watching everything that went by, like a five-year-old. She saw all the new construction in the midst of what was left after the Dark Days. The individual homes were perfectly lined up and painted in bright colors. Parks and monumental buildings were under construction. Dig sites were retrieving artifacts from the past.

Inner Cities Main Headquarters

Jesse was excited as he waited for Brydus and Joaquin to arrive at the entrance of his headquarters. There was an instant fondness between the two. "Oh my God, Joaquin, you didn't do her beauty justice. Such a pleasure to meet you, my dear," he kissed her hand.

"Now you know why he runs this place. He's a smooth talker," Joaquin said, proud that his uncle was pleased.

"It is such an honor meeting you. I've heard great things about you," Brydus said, starstruck.

Jesse chuckled, "Oh, and she's smart too! Let me introduce you to my world." Jesse said, taking her by the hand to introduce her to the Inner Cities Command Center operations. She couldn't get enough of all the high-tech operations. Clinging to his every word as he narrated the history of the Inner Cities and explained the concept behind Prison Island.

The theater size screens of Prison Island flashed with red and green lights, indicating who was a guard or a prisoner. Yellow lights indicated that it was a family member or visitor. Cameras kept constant surveillance of the island and passengers who visited or people who worked on the Island.

"What you've done is overwhelming to me," Brydus exclaimed. "The progress is breathtaking. I'm so impressed. But I was under the impression that this technology was lost during the Dark Days."

"We lost so much, but we also have young minds working to put the pieces back together. One of my main goals is to have some of our other satellites up and running by the end of the year. It will improve communication in our country, South America, Europe, and connect to the rest of the world."

Our organizations are trying to restore our constitution. That is our plan for the rest of the nation. That's why we decided to call ourselves the New America. Our plan is to build and make life better for everyone. I guess what I'm trying to say is, not only for our country but for our neighboring countries. It will take time, but we hope not to repeat the same mistakes of the past. Our children deserve better. Their future must be a brighter one. We have some great overlords and tribal communities that make a big difference in many states. Understand things are not perfect… yet." Jesse smiled.

"I admire all the work you've done. Thank you for sharing this with me. I love it! I can't thank you enough for taking time out of your busy schedule to show me around."

"Ah, my dear, it was my pleasure. You are welcome here anytime, and I hope to see you for dinner tonight. My wife, Renee, is excited to meet you." He kissed her hand again.

"I can't wait to meet her."

They met at Jesse's favorite restaurant, Sofito, known for the best Spanish cuisine in the area. Dinner was very eventful. Renee was a very energetic person, which made it enjoyable. Brydus understood why Jesse was attracted to the highly educated, beautiful, and informative woman. Renee invited Brydus to the gift shop, which was located upstairs, leaving the two men alone to catch up.

The waitress refilled their wine glasses as they watched the two women walking away. Jesse gave his nephew one of those looks parents give their children when they want to question them about serious matters. "So, how serious is this relationship?" Jesse asked.

Joaquin smiled wickedly, "It's about to get really serious tonight."

Jesse smiled. "Son, just make sure you treat her with respect. She is extraordinary. When I look into her eyes, I can imagine how my mother looked when she was her age. I see why my father went nuts when he first set eyes on my mother. Brydus is like a sponge, absorbing all kinds of information. I love it. I think my sister would approve of her, but there is another issue. What's going on with Monet? Is she still in the picture? I just can't see her moving aside to let another woman take her place."

"Uncle, the problem is that she never had a place. She moved in under the pretense of staying only a few weeks. Monet only hears what she wants to hear. I never made any promises to her, never even said that I loved her, not even in the heat of passion. In fact, the only times we ever spent together were at dinner or in bed. I tried to invite her to social events, even for a ride, but she refused me. And I know for a fact that she has been sleeping around. The only thing I'm guilty of is having sex with her, and that wasn't too often." Joaquin became solemn. "Since my parents' last visit, I can't stand being around her. I know they couldn't wait to leave my house last year because of her."

"So, you never found out why your mother left in such a rush?"

"I don't know. The only thing she would say is that she couldn't be under the same roof with that *puta* (whore). She wouldn't say anything more."

"Your mother had a violent argument with Monet, and some terrible things were said on both sides. I shall leave it like that. Marry this young woman soon. When I see you both together, it warms my heart. I like her a lot, and as you see, Renee embraced her. That's a great indicator. She's usually a great judge of character. Believe me, son, Renee really tried to like Monet when she met her. But all she could tell me was, there was something about that pretty woman, something sinister."

"I realize that Monet didn't have an ideal life, but her cruelty towards other people is barbaric, and I don't like that. Demi hates her guts, and I don't understand why. He won't be in the same room with her unless he absolutely has to," Joaquin explained Demi's attitude towards Monet.

"There is definitely something there. Well, I hope you enjoy the rest of the week here. Maybe the next time we talk, it will be about your upcoming nuptials."

"Oh…it's going to happen, even if I have to drag her to the church myself." They both laughed.

Brydus was overwhelmed by the beautiful hotel lobby. Things were very simple where she came from. The hotel room was elegant and plush. Brydus felt like a queen in a palace. Joaquin had the staff place roses throughout the room, with two bottles of wine on ice. There was a fireplace and a double Jacuzzi adorned with candles. The room was decorated in beautiful shades of green and gold. The massive bed had an elaborate headboard with a ceiling mirror. Brydus laughed when she saw herself in the mirror.

"What an idea. What purpose does that serve?" Joaquin laughed at her naïveté. He lay next to her and whispered in her ear.

"That's for making love. You can watch yourself while you, well, you know, it's a great turn-on," he chuckled.

She was embarrassed. "Alright, Brydus, that's one for the idiot tree," she said aloud, giggling. He pulled her up off the bed.

"That's alright. I'll show you some impressive moves," he kissed her passionately, feeling his yearning pressing against her.

She pushed him away gently. "Hey, I bought something special. Let me go change."

"Alright," he said, already breathing heavy, "but don't take too long, or I'll have to come and get you." Joaquin wasted no time setting the mood. He lowered the lights and turned on some romantic music. The wine was working its way to his systems, and his clothes were off.

When she appeared at the entrance of the room, he smiled. She walked towards him in sheer pink lingerie, with delicate lace ruffles around the neck and shoulders. The lingerie opened in front with thin pink panties to match. She had applied lip gloss and a hint of perfume to complete her seductive look. Joaquin could only smile as she walked toward him in her high heels.

"Damn, are you sure this is your first time? Woman, you look good enough to eat." Joaquin didn't wait until she reached him as he scooped her into his arms, kissing her so passionately she was breathless. He laid her gently on the oversized bed running his lips from the sexy curve of her neck to her brown nipples. Soft moans escaped from Brydus' lips as his tongue caressed her breasts and flat stomach. Brydus felt herself fall into a pool of sensual bliss when he touched her secret place with his lips. She couldn't hold back the moans of passion. As her breathing became deeper, she felt like her body was on fire, arching herself towards him, surrendering entirely to his will.

"Sweetcheeks, *querida, te amo*," he said as he slowly entered her, holding back his own ardor. Joaquin captured her lips as he pushed into her, unleashing a flood of pleasure and explosions of climatic seizures. Joaquin couldn't hold back any longer. He had to succumb to the rapture of finally being a part of her, holding her in his arms and making her his. Brydus held on to him as she began to understand the intimacy of making love and becoming one with another. Joaquin chuckled as he nuzzled his face in her hair, smelling her essence.

"I can't wait to do it again," Brydus said, still breathing heavily.

"Yeah, and just think we get to do it repeatedly until one of us can't anymore." She laughed at his eagerness to please her. They held each other and talked about what they liked about one another and their future together. Making love in different places, drinking wine, and enjoying their time together. Just as Joaquin planned, they didn't leave the room for two days.

When they finally came up for air, they took time to see some of the museums. Brydus loved browsing the quaint little shops that made up Citizens Square. She spotted a small shop that sold unique jewelry and rare items. She dragged him into a small curious shop that smelled of incense. It had a little bit of everything, cute dolls from different countries, lotions, and potions for just about everything.

Brydus lost herself in the small shop, fascinated by all the trinkets. There was something that caught her eye. She wanted to give Joaquin a ring that signified her affection for him and found a case with male rings. The silver band had a beautifully engraved dragon on it, with a tiny ruby for an eye. One of the store owners had been following Brydus throughout the store. She pulled out the tray for her to examine the rings closer. "May I ask you a question?" asked the mysterious store owner. Brydus smiled and took off her sunglasses. The woman's eyes grew as big as saucers. "Please forgive me for staring."

"I'm used to it," Brydus replied. She picked up the dragon ring to get a better look.

"Miss, can I read your palms? You have fascinating lines," she asked and smiled. The woman wore a beautiful colored scarf hiding her graying red hair. She had green piercing eyes and just enough eye makeup that brought out the gold speckles in them. Brydus didn't know what to say. She just wanted to buy a ring for Joaquin and be on her way. She looked over to where Joaquin was with the other saleswoman looking at earrings.

"Why would you want to read my palms? I don't believe in that stuff."

The woman grabbed Brydus by the hand, and it scared her. "There is danger ahead."

Brydus pulled away.

"I'm sorry, I didn't mean to frighten you." The woman looked over toward Joaquin, who was still busy with her daughter. "Please allow me a minute; I want to see the outcome."

Reluctantly, Brydus let the mystic turn her hand over. After a few minutes, the woman smiled, which made her feel better."

"Everything is well. The outcome is good. Your husband is a fortunate man."

"No, I'm the lucky one... I would like to purchase this ring, please."

The woman looked at it, "It's a beautiful ring. I know the maker. His work is excellent. Do you know his size?" She gave her his size. The woman continued to stare at her strangely, making Brydus uncomfortable. She patted her hand, "I shall give you a special price for a special woman. You have a great future ahead of you...and he will be part of it, but first, there will be a trial that will change your love and commitment to each other. Bonding the two of you together."

"Ah...um...thank you, I guess. Could you add these earrings and bracelets to my purchase if it's not too much? Thank you." She couldn't wait to leave.

"Please come again," the woman added, shouting from across the room as they were leaving.

"That was an interesting shop. I don't believe that I've ever noticed it before," Joaquin mentioned. "The woman read my palm, but I think she just wanted to flirt with me."

"Why wouldn't she? You're a hunk, I would have," Brydus teased playfully.

"Yeah, I'm sure you would have. So, what did you get?"

"Well, I wanted to get the girls some trinkets. Jenny and some of the kitchen staff… really look out for me."

"That's great! It looks like you bought out most of the earrings and bracelets."

"I don't want to leave anyone out."

"Hmm…you bought Jenny a bunch of stuff. She's a great kid. I'm glad you like her and get along so well."

"She's my special friend. I want to let her know how much I appreciate everything she does for me."

The last night was emotionally difficult for Brydus. After sweet, playful lovemaking and heavy kissing session, she cried in his arms. "What's wrong, baby? Did I leave something out? We did everything I promised."

"No, everything was perfect. I just hate going back to all that hostility. I never dreamed of meeting someone like you… I feel so loved and wanted. It's the kind of love that my mother used to talk about. But I can't help feeling guilty, and I had forgotten all about Monet."

He kissed the tip of her nose and lips, "Listen to me, Sweetcheeks. I don't care who knows about us. I love you, and I want you to wear the ring I gave you. I will deal with Monet and her nonsense…you can trust me."

Brydus smiled through her tears, "I do trust you. If I were to die tomorrow. I would leave happily, knowing that you love me, and I love you just as much. This week will live in my heart forever. I want to give you something too." She pulled out a little package containing a purple velvet box." Joaquin laughed when he opened it.

"It's beautiful. Where should I wear it? Which finger?" She placed it on the third finger of his right hand.

"When we get married, I'll switch it and put it on the other hand where it belongs."

He smothered her with kisses, pinning her to the bed, "hum, I'm really going to have to work on how I'm going to top this week. When we have our honeymoon. Sweetcheeks, you have made me so happy. I can't express myself. Everything is going to be alright. I will help Monet find her own place and give her a little money to tie her over until she gets on her feet."

"You know it's not going to be easy," Brydus said, shaking her head.

"I know, she's going to go kicking and screaming, but she needs to move on and find her happiness elsewhere. I've already found mine."

Joaquin tried to make the trip back exciting for Brydus. He could tell that the situation that she was going back to was on her mind. His men could also sense when Brydus was troubled. They understood that getting Monet to leave would not be an easy task. Brydus comforted herself every time she looked at her ring. It was splendid. She cried again when Joaquin took the ring he had for her and got down on one knee, putting the ring on her finger. She only wished her parents were there to see how happy she was and give her their blessing and advice.

It was raining when they arrived at the estate. The late afternoon rain added to Brydus' gloom. Her only comfort was when Jenny came to greet them. She felt a little chilled, longing for a hot bath as Jenny accompanied her to her room, where it was warm and inviting as always. Jenny wanted to jump out of her skin in anticipation of the details she hoped Brydus would tell.

"Brydus, you're killing me! Tell me…how did everything go? I want details! Oh my God, you're wearing your ring!" she screamed, giving her a big hug.

"Everything was perfect. It was just how he planned it. I felt as if I were in a dream."

"Oh, that's wonderful, but get to the good part. Did you two… you know?"

Brydus laughed, "More than I care to divulge," she replied. "It was better than I imagined. I used to hear stories from friends about their first sexual experience and how awful it was…but I was blown away, Jenny. At first, I was a little nervous, but I did what you told me with the lingerie, and it was a big hit. Joaquin is amazing… I'm glad I waited. He was funny, and although I don't have anything to compare it to, he was passionate, thrilling, and sometimes when I think about it, I get emotional."

"You mean like you are now?"

"Yes… I know it's silly, but I miss my family, and I wish I could share my happiness with them, especially my mother. She always talked to me about passion and love. I want to tell her that she was right."

"That's so sweet… it was that way with my mother before she passed," Jenny hugged her again. "Come on, cheer up. Tell me, what your plans are now?"

"Well, the biggest hold-up is going to be Monet. I won't do anything until he has resolved her issues."

"Monet was out of control. Yelling and screaming at everyone. Mr. Demi had to set her straight a few times. Krystal, she's such a bitch. She's beginning to act just like her. I think Demi's ready to send her back to her mother's.

He was so angry with her last night that he had to walk away."

"Well…I'm afraid of what's coming next. I know that when Monet hears about our engagement, she will start trouble. You know I'm ready for her. I'll stay out of her way because I don't want to hurt her. Hopefully, Joaquin can get things straightened out, and they can come to an understanding."

Jenny shook her head, "Unfortunately, things are never that easy with Monet, but stand your ground. I was always afraid of her temper and of losing my position here. Brydus, watch yourself. She doesn't play fair. When she wormed her way into this house and Mr. Joaquin's bed, she planned to marry one of the Quintanilla men."

"I guess we shall see. I love him, and he loves me, the guilt is bothering me, but I'll just have to deal with that."

Brydus took a nap and afterward jumped into a tub of steaming hot water. All she could do was relive all the magnificent moments she had spent with Joaquin. The light knock on the door startled her. She heard the door open and close. When the door swung open, Joaquin poked his head in.

"You scared me," Brydus shouted, throwing a wet washcloth at him.

"I'm just in time," he took his clothes off and joined her in the tub. She felt alive again as he touched her naked body, kissing her with vigor and bruising her lips.

"I missed you… hm, you feel so good. Did you get some rest?"

"Yes, a little, and how about you?" she asked as he held her tenderly.

"There is no rest for the master of the house. I had a pile of forms and correspondences to go over. There were some fires to put out, so to speak. So, I decided to take a break and visit the one person who brings me great joy." She closed her eyes, snuggling up against him, pretending they were the only two in the house.

"I'm sleeping with you tonight. I just wanted to tell you, and I don't care who knows it. We are together now, and this is my house, and you are the woman I love."

"I love you more," Brydus replied softly. "When we are in this room, it's just us. I'm shutting out the whole world."

"Hum…that sounds like a great idea." All Joaquin thought about was making love to her and loving her at the moment.

Chapter 18: Monet Fights Back

Monet was not herself during any of her pregnancies. Her emotions were like a rollercoaster out of control, and she could not control her temper or actions. Monet went to Joaquin's room, slipped into one of his shirts, and waited for him. However, he never returned to his room. She had fallen asleep in his bed, waiting for him. But not before rehearsing what she was going to say. Then in a fit of anger, she forgot all the sweet words and began to break and toss things around the room.

When Joaquin didn't find Monet in her room, he knew where she was. He took a few deep breaths when he witnessed the destruction of his room. A splash of cold water woke her from a deep sleep screaming obscenities. Joaquin stood over her, watching with anger in his eyes. His room was wrecked. Everything was on the floor; his family's clothes, lotions, and even pictures were smashed against the bathroom door. Monet realizing, what she had done, immediately started to cry.

"Joaquin darling, where have you been? I was worried sick about you, especially when you didn't come to bed last night."

He looked around his room. "What are you doing here?" He said in a controlled yet stern voice. "What did you do to my room? Looks like one of your famous tantrums. You are a truly sick woman," he yelled sarcastically.

Monet took off the wet shirt, taking her time changing into her nightgown. "I was waiting for you, my love," she stretched out her arms to him, "come to me, my one and only."

"Monet, first of all, stop your bullshit. Listen one last time to what I'm going to say. Don't come to my room anymore. This room is off-limits to you. Are you awake now?" She stared at him with vacant eyes, "I want you to fully understand what I'm telling you, so there's no misunderstanding. You've crossed every line there is to cross. You treat people like shit, and I do not have it anymore. How dare you strike one of my employees," he exclaimed, trying hard to keep his anger in check. "You have two weeks to find a place to live. No more! I'm tired of you bullying my people. Get out of my bed, get out of my room, and start packing your shit!"

"What about us? We've been together for two years, and now you're just throwing me out for no reason? So, I disciplined a disrespectful servant. I yelled at her to make sure that she knew better than to be disrespectful. Everyone blew it out of proportion and tried to get me in trouble!" She started to cry again.

"Enough! There were witnesses who saw you slap the girl across the face. She has black and blue marks to prove it. How can you stand there and lie to my face, trying to justify your actions!?" He yelled, losing his temper.

"And you take their word over mine? If you were honest, you would tell me that you only want me to leave because you want that black slut. She's wormed her way into your pants. I know you're sleeping with her," she challenged him.

"Well… we're doing a lot more than sleeping together, but that's none of your business."

"You're not even denying it. How could you!" she screamed.

"Come on, Monet, how many different ways do I have to tell you before it sinks in? I don't want to be with you. We have nothing in common. The only thing we ever did was screw, which wasn't even good all the time. I want to be happy!" he yelled. "I want to get married and have children. I want to marry someone who likes the same things I do."

Monet started to cry again. "I can be that woman. I can be anything you want me to be. I want to get married and have a child. You have to give me another chance, please. Just tell me what you want."

"You're not listening…and it's getting on my last nerve. I could never marry you! You lost the respect of my family. I don't know what happened between you and my mother, but I cannot marry someone my family disapproves of. You don't love me, and you never did. You love this!" Joaquin said, pointing around the room and out of the window at the estate grounds. "This life is what you love. I can't and won't deal with you and your bullshit anymore."

Monet threw herself at him. "Please don't say that! I've loved you from the first time that I saw you."

Joaquin pushed her away and laughed, "You are unbelievable. I've tried to do the right thing for you. I'm still willing to set you up in a nice place. Give you enough money for a fresh start, even though I have no loyalty to you. Two weeks, that's your time limit. Now get out of my room and never come in here again. I don't even want to look at you."

He sat on his bed frustrated, wishing he had never gotten involved with her. Monet was so different in the beginning, sweet and kind to everyone. He realized that if he wanted any kind of life with Brydus, he needed to get her out of his house. He noticed how good Brydus was with people. When she was teaching little Eric how to handle a difficult horse, he saw the excitement and happiness on the young boy's face. Brydus would be fantastic, the perfect hands-on mother for their children. Joaquin knew his parents would approve of Brydus, which made him happy.

Earlier that morning, as he looked at himself in the mirror, he saw a lucky man. He felt a new sense of direction when Brydus held him tenderly from behind, kissing his back, hugging him playfully…it was like heaven.

On the other hand, talking to Monet and having to speak to her so harshly didn't set well with him. He hoped that she would be more mature. Every time he brought up the subject of moving, she would go into a crying frenzy. As Brydus lay sleeping in his arms this morning, he realized he had to be more direct and assertive when it came to Monet. When he heard all the things she was up to and how she bruised a young girl's face, it pissed him off. This was not the first time she had brutally hurt one of the children.

One of the young girls, Rosie, hid her face from Joaquin that morning, hiding the five finger marks that were clearly black and blue.

Joaquin headed to his office, contacting a friend to help find a suitable place for Monet. He was tired of her tantrums, and the sooner he could get her out, the better.

Monet knew she had gone too far once again. She didn't even know what made her that angry to strike Rosie so violently. The poor girl had only given her the wrong juice, and she erupted into a rage. Rosie was so scared that she dropped the glass, and Monet slapped her hard across the face, calling her stupid. Some of the kitchen staff witnessed the attack and began yelling at Monet. They weren't afraid of her anymore, and Monet feared losing control over the staff. It wasn't only slapping the girl that triggered the confrontation, but it became pretty violent when she began throwing things at the kitchen staff.

Joaquin had another score to settle, catching up with his brother at the gym. He wanted to make sure that his cousin Krystal wasn't connected to the attack on the kitchen staff.

Demi was sweating as his physical therapist stood by, ensuring that he did all the exercises correctly. "Come on, Demi, five more," The therapist encouraged. Demi struggled to finish the last five reps.

"Sonofabitch, that hurts; are you done torturing me," he whined.

"We're done for the day, but tomorrow you're going to push it a little more if you want to gain mobility in that shoulder."

When he saw his brother, his eyes lit up. "Thank God you're home, brother. What brings you to my dungeon of pain? Sorry that I wasn't available to meet with you yesterday. I was in so much pain that I slept for two days."

"That's alright. I was just catching up and putting out fires. So how are you feeling? Are you ready to go out in the field?"

"I'm ready, bro, but that bastard doctor won't release me," he sighed. "Joaquin, look, I can't take it anymore. Monet and Krystal are causing so much commotion and causing problems everywhere. We have to do something about those two."

"That's what I wanted to talk to you about. What the hell's going on? I heard what happened with the kitchen staff, and I've already ripped Monet a new one. I wanted to be sure about Krystal before I kick her little ass all the way back home."

"Joaquin, if she wasn't our cousin…I would have strangled her by now. It was a battle of food, dishes, and chairs, like in a movie. After Monet hit the girl, Nancy went after her. You know she's a big woman, and then they got into it. Krystal threw food at Nancy, hitting her in the face, which started a bigger fight." Joaquin rolled his eyes in frustration. "Anyway, I calmed everyone down and sent them to their neutral corners. Krystal followed me to my room, bitching at me, demanding I fire Nancy. I wasn't feeling good, and all I wanted was for her to shut up and go away. But no! That little bitch barged into my room, slammed the door, and started ranting about all sorts of nonsense. Then she says the stupidest thing that she could have ever said to me." Demi paused a moment to let himself calm down before he finished. "She asked me when I would forget my dead girlfriend and give her a chance to make me happy. Joaquin, I could feel the steam coming from my ears. I was so pissed."

"Well, there is no mistaking that she's always had a crush on you. She was always jealous of Audrey. Everyone loved Audrey. Even when she was young, it was hard not to fall in love with her. Krystal was always so sneaky and devious," Joaquin reminded his brother.

"Krystal doesn't seem to remember that she is my cousin. But Audrey wasn't a blood relative. When I told her we were married before she disappeared, she flipped out. Saying that Audrey took everything, and now I'm in bed with her ghost. Krystal hated Audrey, and I have lost all respect for her. I will deal with her as a family member, but other than that, she can kiss my ass. Send her home. We need some peace and quiet around here," Demi suggested.

"I'll handle it," Joaquin said. "She's a follower, and that's the problem. Monet has a hold on her, and Krystal looks up to her, which isn't good. Hopefully she will follow Monet right out the door. If not, then I'll have to kick them both out."

"Well, enough about those crazy bitches. How did everything go with you and Brydus?" Demi asked with a smirk on his face. Joaquin stared into space, remembering the wonderful time they had spent together. It seemed more like a dream to him now that they were back in hell.

"Man…Brydus and I had such a great time together. We didn't leave our room for two memorable days. We were so happy. To come back to this shit is driving me crazy. I can understand why Brydus didn't want to come back to this hell."

"Man, I'm sorry," Demi replied, watching his brother stress. "So, I guess Jesse and Renee approved of your new woman."

"They loved her. Renee wanted to take Brydus home with her. Uncle Jesse wants me to marry her as soon as possible. Just so you know, we are officially engaged and will set a date as soon as Monet is gone. I told Monet she has two weeks to find a place," Joaquin emphasized.

"You're too nice, brother. I would have had her clothes packed and sent her on her way long before now. Considering all the things she's done to you and the people around here, you are being far too kind."

"I know, but I can't see myself throwing someone out into the street like that."

"And Brydus is alright with that? I mean, for heaven's sake, Monet was your mistress." Demi challenged.

"I know…but as long as I keep my baby happy, she's okay with everything. Brydus knows that I love her, but if I were to just throw Monet out, she would feel even guiltier than she already does," Joaquin added.

"I guess you're right. Audrey would have made me do the same thing. Just do me a favor and watch your back with Monet. I don't trust her."

"Speaking of trust, I have to visit our foundry in the mountains. The folks up there have been wondering when we have our meeting. So, I would appreciate it if you would keep a keen eye on everything."

"I'm sorry you have to go instead of me. Especially since I know you would much rather stay here in bed," Demi chuckled.

"My job is to be your backup, and I will do my job."

"I will watch the troublemakers. The guys and I will make sure that they don't destroy anything or hurt anyone while you are away."

"I appreciate it, Demi. This is very important, and we're overdue." Joaquin took a deep breath. "Now I have the delightful task of finding Krystal and kicking her in the ass."

"Give her one for me too. Good luck." Demi cheered him on.

Krystal was sunbathing when Joaquin approached her. She was startled when he called her name, choking on her iced tea and spilling some on her legs.

"Cousin, how are you?" she asked, trying to pretend that she didn't know why he was hunting her down.

"I want you to pack your bags. You're going home," Joaquin directed.

Krystal jumped up from her chair. "but why, what did I do?" She questioned, trying to sound innocent.

"You can sit there and act like you haven't done anything, but I know better. Besides, this is my house, and I can do whatever the hell I want." Joaquin said, reminding her of his position.

"But we're family. You can't just kick me out," she cried.

"Family or not, you are out of here. You and that bitch have disrespected my house for the last time."

"Please, Joaquin. Listen to my side of the story before you make any judgments," Krystal pleaded.

"I'll give you five minutes to explain yourself, starting now," he agreed.

"Monet and I were eating breakfast. She asked for apple juice. Well…the girl bought her orange juice instead. I know Monet is upset that you are sleeping with that other woman. She just lost her temper. But she didn't mean it, honestly. Next thing we know, Nancy is flying in from the kitchen, threatening Monet with a wooden spoon. Well… one thing led to another. That's when the food fight started."

"And you think that's acceptable behavior? Throwing food and hitting a poor, innocent child?" Krystal rolled her eyes and twisted her lips in protest. "Sit down!" Joaquin's anger flared up again. "The next time you roll your eyes at me, I will put my foot so far up your ass; you will need surgery to remove it. Now…I don't give a shit if you don't like what I am about to say! Ever since you've become friends with Monet, you've gotten worse. You were a spoiled, rotten child, and now you're a spoiled, rotten young woman. I don't have to put up with your shit. You are not my responsibility, and as for that woman I'm sleeping with, she's going to be my wife. I expect you to treat her with respect until you walk out of these doors. Or you don't have to come here anymore."

Krystal was so stunned that she was in tears, "How can you talk to me this way? Why would I be nice to her when Monet is my friend, and I know she loves you? I can't be nice to the woman stealing my friend's love from her."

"Monet isn't the woman I love, and I never said I loved Monet, and she knows it. I have chosen the woman for me, and not that it is any of your business, but it isn't Monet. Oh…and a piece of advice before I go, stop harassing Demi about Audrey. She is a touchy subject, and if you care anything about him, you'll realize how much it hurts him. Now go pack your bags. You're going home."

"But my mother will be here in a couple of days. Please, Joaquin, I promise I will stay out of trouble," Krystal begged, "I will stay out of everyone's way. I promise."

"Your mother's coming, are you sure?"

"I swear! I decided to come on ahead because we were arguing so much. I thought that maybe we needed to give each other a little space," she sobbed.

"You'd better be telling me the truth. I will contact your mother. Against my better judgment, I'll give you another chance. Stay away from my brother. He's ready to choke you… and stay away from Brydus. It would also do you good to distance yourself from Monet as well. She's a bad influence on you. I'm going away for a couple of days. When I get back, if I hear that you are connected to any drama, I will personally put your clothes out with you right behind them."

"I promise I will behave. You'll see." Joaquin wasn't convinced, but he knew that if his aunt really was coming, Krystal would try to behave.

Monet didn't wait long before she left to hunt down Brydus and confront her. She found Brydus in the kitchen making spices with Nancy and the other cooks. This time, Monet was ready for a fight, wearing stretch pants and a loose shirt.

"So, here's the black bitch that's sleeping with my man," Monet said as she walked into the kitchen.

Brydus turned to face Monet and stopped her from coming any closer with one look.

"Are you referring to Joaquin, my fiancé?" Brydus asked, showing her the ring, "sleeping is the last thing on our minds when we are together."

Nancy giggled, "Oh shit," she said and moved away. "Go ahead, Miss Brydus, you tell her."

Monet crept closer to Brydus, "You shut up. This is between me and this bitch. We're going to settle this today! You will leave now, or I'll make you leave."

Brydus stepped up to her, "You and what army?" she asked curiously. "You may intimidate the people around here, but don't get it twisted. I'm not afraid of you. You or your mini clone Krystal, who is usually up your ass."

"He was my man until you came around shaking your ass at him. He might want you for now but just remember this. He will be running back to me when he's done with you. I know how to handle a man, and I know what he likes. You're nothing but an untalented bimbo! He'll tire of you very soon, and I will be there, waiting for his return," Monet said smugly.

"Well, that's really strange because we set a date last night after having hot steamy sex in the bathtub," Brydus said, not telling the truth. "That doesn't sound like a man who wants to run back into your arms, does it?" she added. Monet felt the anger creeping up inside of her. Brydus and Nancy watched as her face changed from one shade of red to the next; until they thought she was about to burst into flames.

"We'll see about that. Don't hold your breath. I'll just say my goodbyes for now. You'll be walking the unhappy trails when I am done, with your head hung low. Knowing that you messed with the wrong bitch," Monet threatened.

"I can understand your hate towards me. I never set out to fall in love with him. Joaquin insisted there was nothing between you two but sex. He told me that he asked you to leave way before I came into the picture. I'm sorry."

Monet stared into space; her lips curled with malice. "Keep your apology to yourself; it doesn't move me. I will get him back, and that's a hundred percent guarantee."

"Then we have nothing more to say to each other," Brydus replied, watching Monet leave the kitchen laughing out loud.

Joaquin hated to leave Brydus behind, but he assured her that things would change. Monet was quiet all day. Every once in a while, she'd look at Brydus and smile deviously as if she had a big secret. The night before Joaquin was leaving Brydus, he had dinner in her room, away from everyone.

They just wanted to be alone with each other. Jenny and Mattie prepared a special meal for the lovers. After dinner, they spent time in the hot tub, talking about their plans for the future, including the children they would like to have together. Brydus never dreamed something like this could happen to her. She wanted to tell her family about the great man she met and fell madly in love with. She longed to see her family, but she knew she had to obey the law of her culture. The year went by so fast after leaving the valley. She began to heal from the passing of her dear friend Jake, wondering about the women and children who had made this area their home.

"Joaquin, I want to visit Rev. Wilson after you leave. It would keep me occupied and away from here. I miss them and long to see how they are doing." He kissed her neck. She leaned against him as the water soothed the anxious feelings running through her body.

He agreed, "I think it's a great idea. I heard they're doing really well. Rev. Wilson is preaching at one of the smaller churches, and the kids are all in school."

"Really, I can see her doing that. How long will you be gone?" Brydus asked, broken-hearted.

"A few days. It takes half a day to get there on horseback, but it takes longer in a car. The roads are still badly damaged. I have a great crew. Demi usually handles the yearly meeting at the foundry, but the doctor wants him to stay put a few more days."

"I understand. I just think it would be nice to visit my friends and stay out of trouble." She kissed Joaquin, missing him already.

"If you have any problems, Demi will handle it. Just let him know if you're having trouble with anyone," he insisted.

"I will, baby," she promised.

Joaquin held her tight and found it hard to let her go. She completed his life, and he was excited about their future together. Her safety was his number one concern, especially when he was away.

A knot formed in her throat as she waved to Joaquin, watching him leave on his journey. After such a romantic night together, she hated seeing him go and couldn't wait until his return. She had decided to leave the next morning to check in on her friends. It would be easier for her to be away from the house rather than having Monet follow her everywhere she went.

Jenny helped Brydus prepare a package for Rev. Wilson. She hadn't seen her since the day they were separated. Now that she was settled, Brydus wanted to bring her a housewarming gift. She was excited to see her friend again and couldn't wait to fill her in on everything going on in her life. Joaquin wouldn't be back for a few days, and she needed to fill her time with positive energy.

The night was lonely for her. It didn't take her long to get used to Joaquin's bed presence. She didn't think she could miss someone so much. She wore a shirt of his that was too big, tying the front in a knot, not caring that it was too large for her. It was her security blanket. Early next morning, before Brydus left, she wanted to check on Demi. They played cards together the night before, and she wanted to let him know her plans. Demi was his old chipper self, cussing out the physical therapist and giving the nurses a hard time.

"I should return this evening unless I decide to stay. In that case, I'll be back tomorrow morning," she informed Demi.

"I think that's a great idea. Give my regards to everyone," he replied, smiling.

"I will; I can't wait to see how the girls are doing."

"If you are not back by tomorrow evening, I'm coming after you. I understand why you have to get out of here, but you can't leave me with these crazy bitches too long. I'll be alright playing cards all by myself," he replied, pretending to be sad.

She kissed him on the cheek and whispered. "Stop being a baby." He laughed and kissed her hand.

It was early, and most of the people in the house were still asleep. Brydus couldn't find the stable boy. "Johnny?" She called out to him several times with no response. This wasn't like him. He was always up early to feed and water the horses. As she saddled her horse, her mind was on Joaquin praying everything was alright. The roads were still perilous. She looked at her ring, and a sense of happiness flooded over her spirit. She heard a noise behind her thinking it was Johnny, and turned around to see if Johnny had returned but didn't see anyone. She started to load the gifts she packed for Rev. Wilson and the children when everything went black. She only struggled for a moment before blacking out.

Thomas laid her on the floor. Then he tied her hands and feet before putting her into the truck. Gino was shocked as he stared at the dark beauty that was just given to him. It made him nervous right away.

Monet watched with glee as he closed the truck door. "I want you to destroy her. Sell her to the worst brothel you can find. I want her raped and beaten regularly," Monet expressed a sick sense of excitement. The intensity in her voice sent a chill through Gino's soul.

"Why are you so angry with this beautiful woman?" Gino asked in his thick Italian accent.

"She got in my way… nobody screws with Monet and her man. I want her to pay for all the shit she put me through. You should get some big money for this black bitch. Now go, get out of here before the house starts waking up. Take the side exit so you won't be seen, and take her beast of a horse with you. They will think she got lost and couldn't find her way back." Monet laughed, "Remember not to untie her feet. She knows that karate shit."

"Lady, I won't go to jail for you. I'm leaving now; there are guards all over the place." Gino tied Blackie to the back of the truck. As soon as they got a mile away from the estate, he started to act up. Blackie was making too much noise and getting agitated. Thomas tried to calm the horse down, but he was afraid of him. When Thomas loosened the rope, Blackie moved towards him, and in fear, he dropped the rope. Blackie scraped his hooves on the ground as if telling Thomas to beware. Then Blackie ran off before he had a chance to recover him.

"Thomas, get back here!" Gino yelled, afraid someone saw them. "Forget about that damn horse. We have to put some distance between us and this place. God…what has this woman gotten me into?" Gino whipped down the road at a pace he didn't normally travel. Thomas held on like a little child, afraid they would crash.

Thomas was Gino's overgrown son who had a very low IQ. He had the mind of a child but the strength of a bull. Gino had to tell him what to do practically every minute of the day. Sometimes Thomas would cry when he did something wrong.

Gino was a merchant who traveled from Pennsylvania to New Orleans, selling whatever he could get his hands on. His standard merchandise consisted of clothing, shoes, and things that a person would need. He was fortunate enough to have access to some very exclusive estates.

When he ran into Monet on the way to the market, he couldn't help but stop and listen to what she had to say. Monet told him a story about a woman destroying her relationship with her husband. She explained to him that Brydus beat her and tried to kill her on several occasions. Monet told such a compelling story that he agreed to take Brydus away and sell her to a brothel. However, he did not expect such a beautiful, natural woman and regretted helping Monet from the beginning. But now, it was too late to turn back. Besides, Monet had threatened him if he wanted to back out.

Gino didn't normally deal in human trafficking. The fact that he also had three other people besides Brydus was just a coincidence. In Pottstown, PA, Gino picked up a young mother and her child given to him by the young woman's stepfather. The six-year-old child could pass for her stepfather's son. When the mother approached Gino, he understood why she wanted them away from her husband. She had faded black and blue marks on her face and neck. Gino was to deliver them to the sweat mills right outside New Orleans. He would get half of the money upfront and the other half from the sweat mill owner.

It was one of the most horrific places to work. Children and their parents worked side by side. They slept on cots in the two huge gyms that used to be an old high school. One side was for the women and children; the other was for the men.

The food at the mill was worse than prison food. They were allowed to take one bath a week and wash their clothes the same way. Half of their salaries were paid for their room and board. The young mother, Lupe, knew her fate, but there was nothing she could do. It was either going to the sweat mills or dying out in the elements with her son.

Laura was a prostitute who convinced Gino into taking her to one of the brothels. They were hunting for her, to run her out of York, PA, for sleeping with all the married men in her community. Laura would seduce the men with her fake French accent. She was a pretty woman with long red hair and striking blue eyes. She was well-built and very sensual.

Gino was feeling pains of regret as beads of sweat ran down his face. If he were to get caught, Thomas would die. He had never spent a day away from his father, and Thomas didn't handle change well. Thomas had a steel grip on his seat as Gino continued to push his misshapen truck down the bumpy roads."

"Papa… that woman, you know the one with the black hair? What are we going to do with her?" Thomas asked as he hid his eyes in fright.

"I don't know, Thomas. Why, are you afraid?"

"Yes, papa, she scared me a lot."

"Don't worry, son, I'll take care of you," he wanted to sound brave, but he was frightened for his safety and his son's life in his heart.

"You can take care of me, and I'll take care of you. Okay?" Thomas said, reassuring his father.

"That's the way it's always been for us, Thomas. We take care of each other. So don't worry, Papa has to go very fast now. You just relax, alright?"

When Brydus awoke, she had difficulty adjusting to the little bit of light filtering through the truck's roof. She was in chains and started to freak out. Lupe tried to calm her down, being a very gentle and soft-spoken person. "It's okay. You are not harmed," she said in a soothing voice.

Brydus pulled on her chains. "Where am I?"

"Settle down. You're going for a ride," Laura answered in her fake French accent.

"What is this, and where are we going?" Brydus covered her eyes.

"We're in a merchant's truck, on our way to the outskirts of New Orleans," Lupe explained. "I'm not sure, but I believe you were sold to him, just like we were."

"Oh… my… God," Brydus started to cry out of fear and frustration. She remembered what Jake told her about human trafficking. "Did anyone get a look at who did this to me?"

"I heard a lady's voice," the little boy said, sitting next to his mother.

"And what is your name?" she asked. The boy smiled. Brydus smiled back at him, not wanting to scare him.

"My name is Douglas, but they call me Dougie."

"How long have I been here?"

"You were unconscious for a few hours," Lupe replied.

She was confused and started to bang on the back wall of the truck to get the driver's attention.

"What are you doing? Do you want him to get pissed off at us?" Laura argued. Brydus ignored her and continued to bang with her feet. They felt the truck slow down and move off to the side of the road. Brydus was standing by the door when it was opened. Thomas started to scream when he saw her eyes. "Papa, it's the devil. Help me!"

"Get these things off my feet," she demanded. Gino didn't waste any time pulling out his rifle and aiming it at her. Brydus looked him up and down, sending chills down his spine.

"Please stand back, Miss. I don't want to hurt you." She jumped off the back of the truck, dragging the chains with her, grabbing the barrel of his rifle and pulling it to her chest.

"Go ahead, shoot me," she said in a low steady voice.

Beginning to perspire, Gino had to think quickly. "No, I won't shoot you, but..." he said as he pointed his rifle towards Lupe and Dougie. "I will shoot them; would you like their blood on your hands?" Thomas cowered behind his father as Brydus stared him down. Gino fought to keep his rifle steady.

"Okay, mister, I'll play your game, but we're hungry, thirsty, and one of us has to pee." Gino lowered his rifle, breathing a sigh of relief, letting the women relieve themselves. Afterward, he handed them something to eat and drink.

Laura looked at Brydus suspiciously, "Who the hell are you?" Laura asked as her French accent faded in and out. "I mean, have you lost your mind pointing that weapon at your chest?"

"No... but I see you've lost your accent. I knew he wouldn't shoot me. There's no money in a dead person, and he wouldn't have killed them either. However, I'm in the middle of nowhere without transportation or a weapon. I have to wait until we're closer to civilization… before I make my move."

"You're escaping?" Dougie asked, wide-eyed and curious. "Take us with you! I don't want to go to a sweat mill," his lips trembled as he started to cry.

Lupe tried to soothe her son, "He's afraid; we've heard horror stories about these places."

"You should be afraid. These places are horrendous. Why would you want to go there?"

"My stepfather got tired of us. He said he couldn't take care of us anymore. So, he sold us to the mill," Lupe said sadly, still trying to comfort her son.

Brydus felt bad for the young boy. His face was thin and fragile, and when he looked at his mother, it broke her heart. Lupe was in the same physical condition. Her droopy shoulders and the circles under her eyes told her story. Little Dougie played with a small toy boat, which he never let go of. He called it Clipper Joe.

Brydus engaged him in small talk and played a word game with him, taking his focus off their situation. He laughed when she tickled him for getting a word correct. After a while, the three were laughing as if they had no worries in the world. Laura complained about noise and laughter, especially when Brydus tickled Dougie.

"What the hell is wrong with you people?" Laura whined. "You two will be dead in a month working in that sweat mill… and here you are laughing as if you're going to a party. You dumb bitches."

Brydus wanted to strangle Laura. Everything that came out of her mouth was negative. "You're scaring the boy… if you don't have anything nice to say, keep your damn mouth shut!"

Laura twisted her lips, turning her face away from Brydus, who annoyed her with angry looks.

"It's okay, Miss Brydus. We're used to it," Lupe said, looking defeated.

"No, it's not alright. Everyone needs to have hope, and she's a miserable bitch. Brydus looked at Dougie, who buried his face in his mother's lap. "Hey Dougie, look at me. How would you like to live in a really nice place?" He looked at her bewildered. "Where I live, there are many young boys and girls like you… and you know what? They go to school to learn how to read and write, they play in nice parks, and some of them ride their own horses."

His eyes grew larger than normal, "Mommy, can we go there, please? I want to go to school to learn and ride horses?"

"Oh, and your Mommy can work and make good money so that you can buy nice things," she added.

Laura let out a loud chuckle, "Why would you fill their heads with such nonsense? Even if you did escape, how do you plan to get them to this mythical place?"

Brydus flashed the diamond ring on her finger. "This should bring me more than enough money to get them to a place where they can start a good life."

"But that's an engagement ring. I would never allow you to sell it!" Lupe cried.

Brydus looked at the ring and started to get emotional. "I'm sure Joaquin won't mind… he'd want me to use it," she kissed it, remembering the sweet words he said as he placed it on her finger.

"Your fiancé must be a good man," Lupe added.

"Joaquin is the love of my life. He's handsome and kind, but strong… he is a good man. Many good people there will help you. I can introduce you to my friend, Rev. Wilson. She'll take you under her wing."

"Look… why are you two listening to this wild woman? She'll dump you just like your stepfather did. Ain't nobody nice around here, and who's to say your man wants you to bring some skinny ass woman and a snotty kid into his house?"

"Woman, if you don't shut the hell up! Joaquin Quintanilla is a powerful and generous man. He's an overlord of a huge community and is building homes for his people." Laura shrugged her shoulders at Brydus, "You are so miserable, keep your comments to yourself and leave us alone."

"Could it be true? Is there such a place? We've never been anywhere until now," Lupe asked, full of hope.

"Yes, it's a beautiful place where Dougie can go to school and have friends his age," Brydus confirmed.

"It sounds like a dream, like some of the books that I used to read." Lupe sighed.

"Well, it's not a dream, and when I get out of here, I will not leave you behind, I promise."

Quintanilla Estate

Joaquin was happy with the outcome of his meetings and was able to wrap things up early. A strange feeling had been haunting him ever since he started out. When he arrived at his estate, he found it odd that Brydus wasn't around to greet him. He went to her room, and when he didn't find her there, he proceeded toward his brother's room. Demi wasn't there either. Joaquin stopped some of his staff, but they didn't recall seeing her all day. He started to feel uneasy. No one had seen Brydus since the day before. Finally, he ran into Jenny, whose face was as white as a sheet.

"Mr. Joaquin, thank God you're home early… it's Brydus. She's missing," Jenny explained as she broke down into tears.

"What do you mean missing? Where's my brother?"

"He's in the stables. The stable boy found the package that Miss Brydus was supposed to take with her. It was hidden in one of the horse's stalls."

He raced all the way to the stables with Jenny close behind him. Demi and Louis were searching for clues.

"Joaquin, damn, I'm glad you're back!" Demi rubbed his head. "It doesn't look good. I called the authorities, and they should be here any minute."

Joaquin stared at her horse, "The horse is saddled. Who saddled her horse?" he asked the stable manager, who stood beside his young son.

"No, sir, we overslept, both of us. I felt like I was drugged. I couldn't wake up. Johnny found Blackie outside, by the fence. She always takes excellent care of her horse. We knew something happened. So, we contacted Mr. Demi."

Joaquin looked at the scene. "Jenny, are you sure she was supposed to take this package? Blackie was saddled, which means she didn't leave here on her own. She's cautious with her horse." His mind went to the only conclusion he could think of. "Demi… someone has taken her," he shook his head, trying not to overreact.

"But she's a fighter. She would have fought. There's no sign of a struggle," Demi argued.

Louis was confused as he traced the tire marks. No one ever used that side gate. "Boss, look at the tire marks. They came in this way and left the same way, out through the side gate. Someone let them in. That gate is always locked," he explained.

The investigators arrived in record time. Robert Longfellow was the lead investigator. He was the one to find the cloth with chloroform. "She didn't have a chance to struggle. They must have known that she wouldn't be easy to capture."

Joaquin tried to remain calm, but his insides were tearing him apart. Demi watched his brother closely. He knew that feeling of dread all too well. Joaquin called on some of his crew, and there was no hesitation. They came to his aid immediately. He picked thirteen of his trusted men and a young doctor in case of any illness or accidents as they prepared to follow whoever it was that took Brydus.

Joaquin was impressed by all the information they were able to gather in such a short time. After conferring with his men, they had some clues about what happened to Brydus.

"All the merchants who came into town were questioned except one named Gino. Who travels with his son from Pennsylvania to New Orleans. All merchants must get a special pass if they want to do business in the area. One of the vendors saw him in the square the day before yesterday, but no one has seen him since," Robert Longfellow, the investigator, explained, taking notes for himself.

"So, it's safe to say that New Orleans is where he's headed," Joaquin asked. Thankful that they had learned in which direction he was going.

"That's your man. We searched and questioned everyone. They say he left early yesterday morning."

Demi tried to keep Joaquin encouraged, but he shut down. He hardly spoke two words to anyone. Joaquin sat on the edge of her bed. Everything was as she left it. Demi knew the look all too well, seeing his own face in the mirror a thousand times after Audrey went missing.

"How do you do it? I can't even think straight. How do you keep on going?" Joaquin asked sadly, holding on to the nightgown she wore the night before he left. Demi hugged his brother's neck. He knew how Joaquin was feeling. Tears threatened his eyes.

"It's not easy… but I must say there is a big difference between Brydus and Audrey's disappearance. Brydus was taught how to survive. She can fight and is highly resourceful. I was supposed to protect Audrey, and I wasn't there for her. But now that we know which direction he's headed, we can go find her and bring her home. One day at a time, brother. I'm here for you."

"Thanks, right now I have to focus. I called Uncle Jesse, and he gave me a great contact in New Orleans." Joaquin watched his men preparing for the trip. They only needed one more piece of information. The merchant's map. Without that, it would be impossible to find her. The merchants use certain roads that afford them easy travel.

Demi knew there was something else on his brother's mind. "Joaquin, I know that look. What else is going on?"

Joaquin turned around and faced his brother, "Why do I have this strange feeling that Monet had something to do with this. Could she be that devious?"

"There are a lot of things you don't know about Monet, but I believe your instincts are correct. Who else would want Brydus gone? Everyone loved her, except for you know who."

"I contacted Michael Blankenship. I want this matter investigated thoroughly. If Monet is behind this, she's going to jail," Joaquin clenched his jaw in anger.

"All I know is that someone let them in the side door. Not too many people know about that side entrance."

"You're right, and she's been living here long enough to know this information. Right now, I need to concentrate on finding Brydus. Thanks for coming with me. I really need you to keep my focus."

"I'm with you all the way, brother."

"I understand. I just think it would be nice to visit my friends and stay out of trouble." She kissed Joaquin, missing him already.

"If you have any problems, Demi will handle it. Just let him know if you're having trouble with anyone," he insisted.

"I will, baby," she promised.

Joaquin held her tight and found it hard to let her go. She completed his life, and he was excited about their future together. Her safety was his number one concern, especially when he was away.

A knot formed in her throat as she waved to Joaquin, watching him leave on his journey. After such a romantic night together, she hated seeing him go and couldn't wait until his return. She had decided to leave the next morning to check in on her friends. It would be easier for her to be away from the house rather than having Monet follow her everywhere she went.

Jenny helped Brydus prepare a package for Rev. Wilson. She hadn't seen her since the day they were separated. Now that she was settled, Brydus wanted to bring her a housewarming gift. She was excited to see her friend again and couldn't wait to fill her in on everything going on in her life. Joaquin wouldn't be back for a few days, and she needed to fill her time with positive energy.

The night was lonely for her. It didn't take her long to get used to Joaquin's bed presence. She didn't think she could miss someone so much. She wore a shirt of his that was too big, tying the front in a knot, not caring that it was too large for her. It was her security blanket. Early next morning, before Brydus left, she wanted to check on Demi. They played cards together the night before, and she wanted to let him know her plans. Demi was his old chipper self, cussing out the physical therapist and giving the nurses a hard time.

"I should return this evening unless I decide to stay. In that case, I'll be back tomorrow morning," she informed Demi.

"I think that's a great idea. Give my regards to everyone," he replied, smiling.

"I will; I can't wait to see how the girls are doing."

"If you are not back by tomorrow evening, I'm coming after you. I understand why you have to get out of here, but you can't leave me with these crazy bitches too long. I'll be alright playing cards all by myself," he replied, pretending to be sad.

She kissed him on the cheek and whispered. "Stop being a baby." He laughed and kissed her hand.

It was early, and most of the people in the house were still asleep. Brydus couldn't find the stable boy. "Johnny?" She called out to him several times with no response. This wasn't like him. He was always up early to feed and water the horses. As she saddled her horse, her mind was on Joaquin praying everything was alright. The roads were still perilous. She looked at her ring, and a sense of happiness flooded over her spirit. She heard a noise behind her thinking it was Johnny, and turned around to see if Johnny had returned but didn't see anyone. She started to load the gifts she packed for Rev. Wilson and the children when everything went black. She only struggled for a moment before blacking out.

Thomas laid her on the floor. Then he tied her hands and feet before putting her into the truck. Gino was shocked as he stared at the dark beauty that was just given to him. It made him nervous right away.

Monet watched with glee as he closed the truck door. "I want you to destroy her. Sell her to the worst brothel you can find. I want her raped and beaten regularly," Monet expressed a sick sense of excitement. The intensity in her voice sent a chill through Gino's soul.

"Why are you so angry with this beautiful woman?" Gino asked in his thick Italian accent.

"She got in my way... nobody screws with Monet and her man. I want her to pay for all the shit she put me through. You should get some big money for this black bitch. Now go, get out of here before the house starts waking up. Take the side exit so you won't be seen, and take her beast of a horse with you. They will think she got lost and couldn't find her way back." Monet laughed, "Remember not to untie her feet. She knows that karate shit."

"Lady, I won't go to jail for you. I'm leaving now; there are guards all over the place." Gino tied Blackie to the back of the truck. As soon as they got a mile away from the estate, he started to act up. Blackie was making too much noise and getting agitated. Thomas tried to calm the horse down, but he was afraid of him. When Thomas loosened the rope, Blackie moved towards him, and in fear, he dropped the rope. Blackie scraped his hooves on the ground as if telling Thomas to beware. Then Blackie ran off before he had a chance to recover him.

"Thomas, get back here!" Gino yelled, afraid someone saw them. "Forget about that damn horse. We have to put some distance between us and this place. God...what has this woman gotten me into?" Gino whipped down the road at a pace he didn't normally travel. Thomas held on like a little child, afraid they would crash.

Thomas was Gino's overgrown son who had a very low IQ. He had the mind of a child but the strength of a bull. Gino had to tell him what to do practically every minute of the day. Sometimes Thomas would cry when he did something wrong.

Gino was a merchant who traveled from Pennsylvania to New Orleans, selling whatever he could get his hands on. His standard merchandise consisted of clothing, shoes, and things that a person would need. He was fortunate enough to have access to some very exclusive estates.

When he ran into Monet on the way to the market, he couldn't help but stop and listen to what she had to say. Monet told him a story about a woman destroying her relationship with her husband. She explained to him that Brydus beat her and tried to kill her on several occasions. Monet told such a compelling story that he agreed to take Brydus away and sell her to a brothel. However, he did not expect such a beautiful, natural woman and regretted helping Monet from the beginning. But now, it was too late to turn back. Besides, Monet had threatened him if he wanted to back out.

Gino didn't normally deal in human trafficking. The fact that he also had three other people besides Brydus was just a coincidence. In Pottstown, PA, Gino picked up a young mother and her child given to him by the young woman's stepfather. The six-year-old child could pass for her stepfather's son. When the mother approached Gino, he understood why she wanted them away from her husband. She had faded black and blue marks on her face and neck. Gino was to deliver them to the sweat mills right outside New Orleans. He would get half of the money upfront and the other half from the sweat mill owner.

It was one of the most horrific places to work. Children and their parents worked side by side. They slept on cots in the two huge gyms that used to be an old high school. One side was for the women and children; the other was for the men.

The food at the mill was worse than prison food. They were allowed to take one bath a week and wash their clothes the same way. Half of their salaries were paid for their room and board. The young mother, Lupe, knew her fate, but there was nothing she could do. It was either going to the sweat mills or dying out in the elements with her son.

Laura was a prostitute who convinced Gino into taking her to one of the brothels. They were hunting for her, to run her out of York, PA, for sleeping with all the married men in her community. Laura would seduce the men with her fake French accent. She was a pretty woman with long red hair and striking blue eyes. She was well-built and very sensual.

Gino was feeling pains of regret as beads of sweat ran down his face. If he were to get caught, Thomas would die. He had never spent a day away from his father, and Thomas didn't handle change well. Thomas had a steel grip on his seat as Gino continued to push his misshapen truck down the bumpy roads."

"Papa… that woman, you know the one with the black hair? What are we going to do with her?" Thomas asked as he hid his eyes in fright.

"I don't know, Thomas. Why, are you afraid?"

"Yes, papa, she scared me a lot."

"Don't worry, son, I'll take care of you," he wanted to sound brave, but he was frightened for his safety and his son's life in his heart.

"You can take care of me, and I'll take care of you. Okay?" Thomas said, reassuring his father.

"That's the way it's always been for us, Thomas. We take care of each other. So don't worry, Papa has to go very fast now. You just relax, alright?"

When Brydus awoke, she had difficulty adjusting to the little bit of light filtering through the truck's roof. She was in chains and started to freak out. Lupe tried to calm her down, being a very gentle and soft-spoken person. "It's okay. You are not harmed," she said in a soothing voice.

Brydus pulled on her chains. "Where am I?"

"Settle down. You're going for a ride," Laura answered in her fake French accent.

"What is this, and where are we going?" Brydus covered her eyes.

"We're in a merchant's truck, on our way to the outskirts of New Orleans," Lupe explained. "I'm not sure, but I believe you were sold to him, just like we were."

"Oh… my… God," Brydus started to cry out of fear and frustration. She remembered what Jake told her about human trafficking. "Did anyone get a look at who did this to me?"

"I heard a lady's voice," the little boy said, sitting next to his mother.

"And what is your name?" she asked. The boy smiled. Brydus smiled back at him, not wanting to scare him.

"My name is Douglas, but they call me Dougie."

"How long have I been here?"

"You were unconscious for a few hours," Lupe replied.

She was confused and started to bang on the back wall of the truck to get the driver's attention.

"What are you doing? Do you want him to get pissed off at us?" Laura argued. Brydus ignored her and continued to bang with her feet. They felt the truck slow down and move off to the side of the road. Brydus was standing by the door when it was opened. Thomas started to scream when he saw her eyes. "Papa, it's the devil. Help me!"

"Get these things off my feet," she demanded. Gino didn't waste any time pulling out his rifle and aiming it at her. Brydus looked him up and down, sending chills down his spine.

"Please stand back, Miss. I don't want to hurt you." She jumped off the back of the truck, dragging the chains with her, grabbing the barrel of his rifle and pulling it to her chest.

"Go ahead, shoot me," she said in a low steady voice.

Beginning to perspire, Gino had to think quickly. "No, I won't shoot you, but…" he said as he pointed his rifle towards Lupe and Dougie. "I will shoot them; would you like their blood on your hands?" Thomas cowered behind his father as Brydus stared him down. Gino fought to keep his rifle steady.

"Okay, mister, I'll play your game, but we're hungry, thirsty, and one of us has to pee." Gino lowered his rifle, breathing a sigh of relief, letting the women relieve themselves. Afterward, he handed them something to eat and drink.

Laura looked at Brydus suspiciously, "Who the hell are you?" Laura asked as her French accent faded in and out. "I mean, have you lost your mind pointing that weapon at your chest?"

"No… but I see you've lost your accent. I knew he wouldn't shoot me. There's no money in a dead person, and he wouldn't have killed them either. However, I'm in the middle of nowhere without transportation or a weapon. I have to wait until we're closer to civilization… before I make my move."

"You're escaping?" Dougie asked, wide-eyed and curious. "Take us with you! I don't want to go to a sweat mill," his lips trembled as he started to cry.

Lupe tried to soothe her son, "He's afraid; we've heard horror stories about these places."

"You should be afraid. These places are horrendous. Why would you want to go there?"

"My stepfather got tired of us. He said he couldn't take care of us anymore. So, he sold us to the mill," Lupe said sadly, still trying to comfort her son.

Brydus felt bad for the young boy. His face was thin and fragile, and when he looked at his mother, it broke her heart. Lupe was in the same physical condition. Her droopy shoulders and the circles under her eyes told her story. Little Dougie played with a small toy boat, which he never let go of. He called it Clipper Joe.

Brydus engaged him in small talk and played a word game with him, taking his focus off their situation. He laughed when she tickled him for getting a word correct. After a while, the three were laughing as if they had no worries in the world. Laura complained about noise and laughter, especially when Brydus tickled Dougie.

"What the hell is wrong with you people?" Laura whined. "You two will be dead in a month working in that sweat mill… and here you are laughing as if you're going to a party. You dumb bitches."

Brydus wanted to strangle Laura. Everything that came out of her mouth was negative. "You're scaring the boy… if you don't have anything nice to say, keep your damn mouth shut!"

Laura twisted her lips, turning her face away from Brydus, who annoyed her with angry looks.

"It's okay, Miss Brydus. We're used to it," Lupe said, looking defeated.

"No, it's not alright. Everyone needs to have hope, and she's a miserable bitch. Brydus looked at Dougie, who buried his face in his mother's lap. "Hey Dougie, look at me. How would you like to live in a really nice place?" He looked at her bewildered. "Where I live, there are many young boys and girls like you… and you know what? They go to school to learn how to read and write, they play in nice parks, and some of them ride their own horses."

His eyes grew larger than normal, "Mommy, can we go there, please? I want to go to school to learn and ride horses?"

"Oh, and your Mommy can work and make good money so that you can buy nice things," she added.

Laura let out a loud chuckle, "Why would you fill their heads with such nonsense? Even if you did escape, how do you plan to get them to this mythical place?"

Brydus flashed the diamond ring on her finger. "This should bring me more than enough money to get them to a place where they can start a good life."

"But that's an engagement ring. I would never allow you to sell it!" Lupe cried.

Brydus looked at the ring and started to get emotional. "I'm sure Joaquin won't mind… he'd want me to use it," she kissed it, remembering the sweet words he said as he placed it on her finger.

"Your fiancé must be a good man," Lupe added.

"Joaquin is the love of my life. He's handsome and kind, but strong… he is a good man. Many good people there will help you. I can introduce you to my friend, Rev. Wilson. She'll take you under her wing."

"Look… why are you two listening to this wild woman? She'll dump you just like your stepfather did. Ain't nobody nice around here, and who's to say your man wants you to bring some skinny ass woman and a snotty kid into his house?"

"Woman, if you don't shut the hell up! Joaquin Quintanilla is a powerful and generous man. He's an overlord of a huge community and is building homes for his people." Laura shrugged her shoulders at Brydus, "You are so miserable, keep your comments to yourself and leave us alone."

"Could it be true? Is there such a place? We've never been anywhere until now," Lupe asked, full of hope.

"Yes, it's a beautiful place where Dougie can go to school and have friends his age," Brydus confirmed.

"It sounds like a dream, like some of the books that I used to read." Lupe sighed.

"Well, it's not a dream, and when I get out of here, I will not leave you behind, I promise."

Quintanilla Estate

Joaquin was happy with the outcome of his meetings and was able to wrap things up early. A strange feeling had been haunting him ever since he started out. When he arrived at his estate, he found it odd that Brydus wasn't around to greet him. He went to her room, and when he didn't find her there, he proceeded toward his brother's room. Demi wasn't there either. Joaquin stopped some of his staff, but they didn't recall seeing her all day. He started to feel uneasy. No one had seen Brydus since the day before. Finally, he ran into Jenny, whose face was as white as a sheet.

"Mr. Joaquin, thank God you're home early... it's Brydus. She's missing," Jenny explained as she broke down into tears.

"What do you mean missing? Where's my brother?"

"He's in the stables. The stable boy found the package that Miss Brydus was supposed to take with her. It was hidden in one of the horse's stalls."

He raced all the way to the stables with Jenny close behind him. Demi and Louis were searching for clues.

"Joaquin, damn, I'm glad you're back!" Demi rubbed his head. "It doesn't look good. I called the authorities, and they should be here any minute."

Joaquin stared at her horse, "The horse is saddled. Who saddled her horse?" he asked the stable manager, who stood beside his young son.

"No, sir, we overslept, both of us. I felt like I was drugged. I couldn't wake up. Johnny found Blackie outside, by the fence. She always takes excellent care of her horse. We knew something happened. So, we contacted Mr. Demi."

Joaquin looked at the scene. "Jenny, are you sure she was supposed to take this package? Blackie was saddled, which means she didn't leave here on her own. She's cautious with her horse." His mind went to the only conclusion he could think of. "Demi... someone has taken her," he shook his head, trying not to overreact.

"But she's a fighter. She would have fought. There's no sign of a struggle," Demi argued.

Louis was confused as he traced the tire marks. No one ever used that side gate. "Boss, look at the tire marks. They came in this way and left the same way, through the side gate. Someone let them in. That gate is always locked," he explained.

The investigators arrived in record time. Robert Longfellow was the lead investigator. He was the one to find the cloth with chloroform. "She didn't have a chance to struggle. They must have known that she wouldn't be easy to capture."

Joaquin tried to remain calm, but his insides were tearing him apart. Demi watched his brother closely. He knew that feeling of dread all too well. Joaquin called on some of his crew, and there was no hesitation. They came to his aid immediately. He picked thirteen of his trusted men and a young doctor in case of any illness or accidents as they prepared to follow whoever it was that took Brydus.

Joaquin was impressed by all the information they could gather in such a short time. After conferring with his men, they had some clues about what happened to Brydus.

"All the merchants who came into town were questioned except Gino, who travels with his son from Pennsylvania to New Orleans. All merchants must get a special pass if they want to do business in the area. One of the vendors saw him in the square the day before yesterday, but no one has seen him since," Robert Longfellow, the investigator, explained, taking notes for himself.

"So, it's safe to say that New Orleans is where he's headed," Joaquin asked. Thankful that they had learned in which direction he was going.

"That's your man. We searched and questioned everyone. They say he left early yesterday morning."

Demi tried to keep Joaquin encouraged, but he shut down. He hardly spoke two words to anyone. Joaquin sat on the edge of her bed. Everything was as she left it. Demi knew the look all too well, seeing his own face in the mirror a thousand times after Audrey went missing.

"How do you do it? I can't even think straight. How do you keep on going?" Joaquin asked sadly, holding on to the nightgown she wore the night before he left. Demi hugged his brother's neck. He knew how Joaquin was feeling. Tears threatened his eyes.

"It's not easy… but I must say there is a big difference between Brydus and Audrey's disappearance. Brydus was taught how to survive. She can fight and is highly resourceful. I was supposed to protect Audrey, and I wasn't there for her. But now that we know which direction he's headed, we can go find her and bring her home. One day at a time, brother. I'm here for you."

"Thanks, right now I have to focus. I called Uncle Jesse, and he gave me a great contact in New Orleans." Joaquin watched his men preparing for the trip. They only needed one more piece of information. The merchant's map. Without that, it would be impossible to find her. The merchants use certain roads that afford them easy travel.

Demi knew there was something else on his brother's mind. "Joaquin, I know that look. What else is going on?"

Joaquin turned around and faced his brother, "Why do I have this strange feeling that Monet had something to do with this. Could she be that devious?"

"There are a lot of things you don't know about Monet, but I believe your instincts are correct. Who else would want Brydus gone? Everyone loved her, except for you know who."

"I contacted Michael Blankenship. I want this matter investigated thoroughly. If Monet is behind this, she's going to jail," Joaquin clenched his jaw in anger.

"All I know is that someone let them in the side door. Not too many people know about that side entrance."

"You're right, and she's been living here long enough to know this information. Right now, I need to concentrate on finding Brydus. Thanks for coming with me. I really need you to keep my focus."

"I'm with you all the way, brother."

Chapter 19: The Rescue

Joaquin now had all the necessary information to leave and the provisions for the dangerous quest. When Monet found out that Joaquin was going after Brydus, she freaked out, throwing a tantrum, trying to stop him. "Are you crazy? Running after her, not knowing where she is? Is it impossible to believe that she left you? Maybe she was scared and ran away. It happens all the time," Monet hollered.

He pushed her aside, "Brydus did not run away. She would never leave her horse or me. So, get the hell out of my way. I'm going to find her, and I swear to God! If I find out that you had anything to do with this, you're done! Do you understand me?" he yelled with such intensity that Monet had to take a few steps backward.

"Joaquin, forget about her. I'm here for you. I've always loved you. How can you just toss me aside, as if I meant nothing to you! She doesn't love you like I do, Joaquin!" she yelled hysterically, running after him as he walked away from her. "Joaquin, come back!" she screamed, watching Joaquin ride away, ignoring her cries. "You'll be back… you can't treat me like shit, pushing me aside like nothing… I will be your wife and the mistress of this estate! You can't get rid of me that easy!" Monet ran back into the house, through the kitchen, where most of the kitchen staff just stood listening to her ranting. They knew that she was going to be difficult. Her eye makeup was streaming down her perfect face, looking like she had a meltdown. When she stormed into the kitchen and saw the staff, it provoked another set of emotions.

"What the hell are all you looking at? This is your fault… all of you filling Joaquin's head with lies about me! Don't think I don't know how you all go behind my back, talking about me. Jealous of what I have! You're all a bunch of losers… fat and ugly. When I become the mistress of this estate, you're all going to hell! I will make it a point to kick you all out on your fat, ugly asses." Monet raved on for a few more minutes until she saw Jenny hiding behind Cassia. She pulled Jenny out by her arm. Jenny struggled to get away as Cassia tried to separate them.

"You little bitch! You're the main cause of my misery. You've been sneaking around, filling his head with lies about me!" Monet pulled a knife from the butcher block and lunged at poor Jenny, who started to scream, running away from her.

Cassia wrestled with her trying to get the knife away, but Monet's anger strengthened her. She nicked Cassia on the shoulder. "I'll kill you bitch, and dance on your grave."

Samuel, the head butler, caught her wrist before she had a second chance to plunge the knife deeper. When Monet tried to pull away, she cut herself on the arm. There was blood everywhere. "Get away from me, all of you! You're all trying to hurt me because I'm beautiful! I'm perfect! I will make you all pay. I swear!" Her face was red with rage. When she walked away, Monet slipped on the bloody floor. But no one moved a muscle to help her. They stared at her with pity.

Jenny ran into Cassia's arms, crying uncontrollably, hoping that her injuries weren't as bad as they looked. "There, there, now everything's alright, my dear. We won't let that woman hurt you, I promise."

"She hates me! I know she's going to kill me someday. Miss Brydus isn't here to stop her." Jenny was shaking. Frightened that Monet would come back for her.

"Sweetheart, Monet hates everyone. She knows you are terrified of her, so she comes after you, but don't worry. We have all decided to band together and fight that crazy-ass woman. Even if we all lose our jobs. However, I don't see that happening. So please stop crying, honey. You can work here in the kitchen with us until Master Joaquin brings back your Brydus." Jenny wiped her eyes with her apron. She looked at Cassia as if she needed to hear those words again.

"Do you think he'll ever find her?"

"Honey, true love is hard to stop. He's in love with her, and you told us he gave her an engagement ring. I heard them talking, and I could hear the emotion in his voice. He will not come home without his beloved."

"That is so romantic. Oh Cassia, I can't wait for the day that bitch is out of here. Then we can walk down these halls without fear," Jenny said proudly, with tears of hope for their future and for her friend.

***

Monet needed stitches. As the doctor worked on her, she cried hysterically.

"Listen to me. You shouldn't be feeling anything. Why are you crying?"

"He abandoned me. I think I'm pregnant, and he ran after her leaving me behind, carrying his child." The doctor's jaw dropped, knowing she was about to drop a bomb on the Quintanilla Estate, and it wasn't going to be pretty. The doctor was skeptical. Knowing Joaquin is a man of honor and would do the right thing. He was worried about what would happen when he returned with Brydus and found out that Monet was pregnant, naming him the father.

"Are you sure?" The doctor questioned, hoping it was just talk, "How long have you known?"

"I'm not positive, but I think I am. I've been under a lot of stress lately."

"Monet, I think you need to take a pregnancy test, just to make sure." It only took a few minutes for the test to reveal the results. She was pregnant, and soon trouble would result from this unpleasant news. Monet smiled triumphantly as word spread throughout the estate that she was expecting a child, and it was Joaquin's.

Meanwhile, Joaquin and his crew didn't know what was ahead of them. The roads to New Orleans were treacherous, and every time they thought they were making headway, the road presented a new challenge. Joaquin was frustrated by the fact that they were running into a different obstacle every few miles. They questioned some of the other travelers, and they too seemed lost and dismayed. Demi looked at the map they had. It was so old that every turn they made took them further away from their destination.

How do these merchants get around? There has to be another route, Demi thought. Cisco continued to work with the radio. An hour later, they finally connected with someone that they could understand.

"This is Joaquin Quintanilla calling for Pastor Ricardo Lecanto." The radio hummed for a few seconds before a faint voice came through.

"Thank God, this is Pastor Ricardo. I've been trying to reach you all day. I've been in contact with your uncle. How can we assist you?"

"Pastor, we are looking for a route that is not a dead-end. Is there another road that merchants use? We are not getting anywhere following this old map." The frustration and inability to continue were getting to Joaquin.

"Where are you right now?"

"We are on old Route 77, outside of what used to be Galax. We came down Route 95, but the roads are destroyed," Joaquin replied, praying they didn't' lose the signal.

"Okay, I know where the problem is. There is a merchant's route, but first, you will have to turn around and find a small settlement called Wytheville. The road is tough to see. It used to be the main highway at one time. The road is Route 81 now. I'm going to talk fast because our signal is not the best. That is the merchant's route, it looks bad, but it will get better as you travel further south. Joaquin, this is very important. You will come against a roadblock. The merchants pay them off to get through. Don't let them bully you. Take the roadblock by force if you must. I hope you're packing. Show off your strength, and they will back down. If not, they will demand all your supplies and try to scare you. Call me when you get on the other side. Our communication will improve then."

"Thank you, I owe you one. We are locked and loaded. Thanks for the information. We know what to do, and I will be in contact with you soon. Over and out," Joaquin said, feeling more confident. "Demi, let me see that map. Okay…

we must go back about 20 miles and go through Wytheville. We're looking for Route 81."

It appeared that the more they traveled, the worst the roads became. But once they crossed onto Route 81, the roads began to clear, and travel was easier on the horses. It was almost dark when they reached the roadblock. There were long lines of people trying to gain passage through the small entranceway. The roadblock was made of old rusty cars piled high on both sides. It had a smaller door inside of a huge one. They used ropes and pulleys to open the smaller entrance. Most merchants made deals with them and were not detained.

Joaquin and Demi were highly disturbed by the setup. "How long have you been waiting around?" he asked an older man and his wife, pulling a small wagon containing all of their belongings.

"We've been waiting since this morning. My wife almost passed out from the heat. But some people have been waiting for a day or so," he replied, tired and weak from waiting in the hot sun.

"What's the hold-up?" Joaquin asked, annoyed.

"They open up when they want to. That way, they can charge us more."

"If you don't have the money to pay, what happens?" Demi asked, grinding his teeth.

"They take your things," the man's wife answered, "even if they can't use them," she said, shrugging her shoulders, feeling defeated.

Sometimes they just beat you up and then send you on your way," the elderly man added sadly.

"Has anyone tried to go around?" Cisco asked, feeling sorry for the couple.

"I have heard stories of people who have tried. But there is barbwire on both sides, and sometimes you can't see it until you're tangled in it and bleeding. Plus, most of us don't have the energy to travel that far off the road. Not to mention, finding the way back when you fail."

Joaquin was furious, and the more he spoke to the travelers, the angrier he became. Gathering his men, he told them to arm themselves. He had a plan to take over the roadblock and do away with it for good.

Demi and Big Willie stood in front of the small door and called the leader out in good faith. After a few minutes with no response, they unloaded a few rounds into the door. When the smoke cleared, a man named Hawkeye shouted to them that he would open the door and asked them not to shoot. Hawkeye was in his mid-forties, with tattoos all over his body. He carried a rifle in his hand. "What's with all the shooting? All you had to do was knock," he said, smiling, but Demi and Big Willie were not amused. Demi pointed the shotgun directly at his chest.

"Who gave you the authority to block this road?" Demi asked.

Hawkeye laughed, opening the door wider. He had four crew members pointing rifles at them, "The ones with the bigger guns." Hawkeye said as he and his crew laughed. The others were of the same age, tattooed and in dirty, gang-style jackets. All were packing rifles, both men and women. Hawkeye lit a cigarette and continued to laugh. "I do believe we outnumber you two fine gentlemen. Now, if you want to come through, you'll have to pay the price, and we decide what that is." They had all sorts of things piled high everywhere, getting rusty.

"I'm not impressed," Demi replied, annoyed when an explosion caught their attention. Ten of Joaquin's men came from the billowing smoke, all with high-powered rifles. "Now, who has the bigger guns bitch?" Demi pulled Hawkeye by his jacket, shoving the shotgun up under his chin.

"Hey man, I was only playing," Hawkeye said, putting his hands up, "You can take a joke, can't you?" He laughed nervously. Joaquin's men had the rest of the gang on their knees with their hands behind their heads. The women tried to talk themselves out of the situation, stating they were forced to do what the men said.

Joaquin made his way into one of the broken-down trailers. They lived like animals in filth. He went from room to room and found three more people hiding behind fake walls. Joaquin and his crew gathered them all together after going through the trailers. He pressed the barrel of his rifle against Hawkeye's head.

"Who's in charge?" Joaquin asked. They all looked at Hawkeye, who confessed that the roadblock was his brainchild.

"Hey, we're just trying to make ends meet," he laughed nervously, "Everyone needs to make a living. If you guys want in on the action, I can make it happen. Hell, we were ready to up the price… you know, inflation," he laughed. Big Willie picked Hawkeye up by his jacket and slammed him into a nearby heap of trash.

"How about working like decent people," Big Willie said, not amused by his comment.

"As of right now, this operation of yours is over!" Joaquin commanded, "Demi, let's blow the shit out of this hell hole. We're living in the New America bitch, and, we say, no one has the right to own these roads. They belong to the people." He addressed the group of miscreants. "You guys have about twenty seconds to get on your piece of shit bikes and get the hell out of here. I suggest you don't stop until you hit the ocean."

"Kiss my ass, man! We ain't leaving until we get our stuff," Hawkeye tried to sound brave.

Joaquin cocked his weapon and smiled at him. "One… two… three, I'm counting." They stumbled over each other, trying to get to their bikes. They doubled up in a rush to get away, roaring off into the darkness.

"Get these people back. Let's blow this bitch!" Demi yelled. It took a few sticks of dynamite to topple the roadblock. People began to cheer and clap as they watched the roadblock go up in flames. That night, hundreds of people gathered together around a huge bonfire. They dusted off their instruments, guitars, fiddles, drums, and harmonicas. Everyone danced and shared a little bit of food, rejoicing. Joaquin smiled at the celebration, wondering why everyone made such a big deal about the situation. But after talking to some of the couples, he found out that people have been beaten down for so long. They just needed a reason to celebrate. This victory gave them that reason. They said this act of kindness gave them hope for their future.

Joaquin sat back, watching everyone celebrate. He realized how much more needed to be done. Society had come a long way since the Dark Days, but it still had a long way to go. He understood why his Uncle Jesse worked so hard to make changes. So that this country could rise up out of the ashes and again be the great nation it once was.

He thought about Brydus as he rubbed the charm he had made for her but didn't get a chance to give it to her. Never knowing he could love someone so deeply. He looked up at the open sky, hoping that he would hold Brydus again in his arms. He thought about the great life they could have together and the children that would make his life complete.

Joaquin watched Demi dancing with a pretty young lady, swinging her around and around. He could hear her giggling. However, deep inside, he felt much sadness for his brother. He always wondered why Demi couldn't move on after Audrey. Now he understood him more than ever. Now he understood the pain his brother experienced after losing the love of his life. Realizing that Audrey would always be part of Demi, just as Brydus would always be a part of him.

***

While Gino had a three-day head start, each day brought him more and more stress dealing with Brydus. She refused to go peacefully. Brydus demanded more each day, and Gino was sick of her by the fourth day. During supper, she picked his brain to see where he was taking her and who was behind her kidnapping.

They sat by the campfire, "So, do you really think you'll sell me to a brothel?" Brydus asked.

Gino looked at her with tired eyes. He couldn't even enjoy his coffee. "My dear, you would not do well in a brothel. Customers go there to be loved, not beaten to a pulp. However, I do have an idea of what to do with you. What you do from there is up to you. I don't care. I just want to get away from you, far, far away."

Brydus laughed, "You know, you're not so bad, Gino, but this isn't over. I feel that big-chested bimbo is behind this, and she will pay dearly."

Gino swallowed hard. Brydus had a way of inciting fear in people, and he did not want to be caught in the middle of her wrath. He had deep regrets about his involvement with the kidnapping. He would have never agreed to take her if it had not been for the money. *I will drop her off as soon as we reach New Orleans,* he thought. Then disappear for a while until everything cooled down.

Quintanilla Estate

Alex took charge the minute she arrived. Her nephew had sent her a message about what was going on. She immediately wrapped things up and traveled to the estate. The staff filled her in on all the details. Right away, she knew that Monet had something to do with the young woman's disappearance. She drilled Krystal for hours to ensure that she had nothing to do with the kidnapping. Alex would not let up on her until she was satisfied and relieved that Krystal was not involved. However, this newly formed attachment she had to Monet did not sit well with her.

Monet was furious when Alex took over the running of the house. However, Monet would never try to manipulate Alex, feeling uncomfortable around her. Alex was always one step ahead of her, and it made Monet uneasy knowing that she knew why Joaquin's parents left. She had Joaquin's ear, being the nearest living relative to the estate, they were very close. Now that Alex was in the house, Monet needed to portray the victim, and she played the part very well.

The staff was ecstatic when Alex took control of the household's management. She asked Monet to step aside, letting her know that she was the grand mistress of the house until her nephews returned. Monet backed down and didn't argue the point.

The news of Monet's pregnancy did not move Alexandria at all. However, her daughter Krystal made it sound like Monet was giving birth to royalty.

"Mom, why are you not happy? Don't you see what this means? Monet will soon be the mistress of the estate. After all this time, she will get her true reward."

Alex looked at Krystal unemotionally. She took a deep breath and shook her head, "There is nothing to be happy about when there is no love in the relationship. Monet may want to be the mistress of this estate, but Joaquin will not let it happen."

Krystal was surprised by her mother's comment, "How can you say that, Mother? He loves her. This other woman is just a plaything. I am sure he will do the right thing and marry Monet. You always said that he's an honorable man."

"Krystal, you are such a silly young woman. He will never go against his parents, even if a dozen children were involved. Think about it, honey. Why would he ask her to leave if he loved her so much? He is willing to put her up in a nice house and pay for expenses until she can get on her feet. This didn't just happen. Joaquin has been asking her to leave for over a year."

"He's a grown man. What does the family have to do with his choice of a wife?"

Alex knew her daughter was naïve. Krystal wanted desperately to believe that Monet was good, so she only saw that side of her. She didn't really know what family honor meant, nor did she know that a child doesn't always save a bad relationship. Alex knew that from experience.

She put her arm around her daughter. "Krystal, a man like your cousin, is the kind of man that loves deeply. My father was the same way. Look at Demi. His love for Audrey will forever live in his heart."

The mention of her dead sister's name always infuriated her, especially when it was used in the same sentence with Demi. "To Joaquin, family means everything, and he wants to make sure that the woman he chooses will fit in with the rest of the family."

Krystal rolled her eyes in frustration, "Mother, you never liked Monet, and you're such a snob. You don't know her as I do. She is sweet, kind, and the most beautiful woman around. I know Joaquin will come to his senses once he finds out that a baby is involved. That horrible woman has turned him against Monet."

"Really, child, you're so young and naive. Things are not always black and white. There is a lot to this relationship. You know the sweet side of Monet, but there is another side of her. One day you will see it for yourself."

"Well, she's my friend and needs me. I don't care what the others say about her. They envy her position here, making life impossible for her. She is the victim of all this mess. These people need to recognize that she's in charge."

"These people, as you call them, are loyal to the Quintanilla family. They are paid staff, and they don't have to put up with her nonsense. I know she's your friend, and I commend you for sticking with her. But don't let Monet bring you down with her. She's a destroyer."

Everyone that came in contact with Monet was put in their place. She was not letting anyone forget that she was carrying Joaquin's child, parading around the estate with a smile, confident that Joaquin would marry her once he found out that she was carrying his baby.

The staff was always Monet's target for cruelty, especially the kitchen help. Monet's feeling of superiority made her think they were hers to command and push around. But Cassia and some of the old kitchen staff made it clear they didn't work for her, which angered her even more.

Her greatest triumph came when Alex arrived. It was her way of spreading the news to the rest of the family, letting them know she would soon be one of them. Monet put a small pillow under her shirt, making her look farther along in her pregnancy.

"So, what do you think, Alexandria? How do I look with a little belly?" she asked, turning sideways in front of the mirror. "I already ordered some adorable clothes and a wedding dress that will allow me to hide my belly."

Alex was not enthused, "Tell me something dear, what you will do when Joaquin comes back with the other woman. Who do you think he is going to choose?"

Monet turned toward Alexandria abruptly, "Well, you sure have a way of taking the fun out of things. Do you really think I planned this? Believe me, this is the last thing on my mind. You know babies mess up your body, and I love my shape. Plus…" she became quiet and started smiling maliciously. "Joaquin will never find her. This country is too big. She is lost forever. If he does, it will be too late. She will be worthless. That's if he finds her at all. When Joaquin comes back all destroyed and depressed. I'll be waiting for him to run back into my arms. Especially when he sees my swollen belly."

"Really… for your sake, I hope you're not involved with this kidnapping. I think you underestimate my nephew. He is no fool. He is a good man, but you will have to prove to him that this is his child."

"Joaquin is the only man I've been intimate with," she protested, "why is everyone questioning paternity? We've been together for two years and are very sexually active."

"He may have his doubts, so make sure your facts are correct. There's been much talk about your… secret late-night engagements. However, I shall give you the benefit of the doubt. If you need anything, let me know," Alex said snidely.

"Hm," Monet was scared, but as long as Brydus was out of the picture, she could entice Joaquin back to her bed. Monet considered the fact that he wanted a child. She counted on his emotions to take over, seeing this baby born, and believed it was his child the whole time. She believed he would decide to care for the baby because of his desire to have children.

"People have always envied me. They wish that I wasn't here. But they are all sadly mistaken. Joaquin and I will get back together. I know who the father is. Joaquin is the only man I have ever loved," she stated proudly, trying to convince everyone.

Alex didn't want to laugh in front of her, so she turned away. Krystal walked into the room, wondering why Monet's face was flushed. "What's so funny, Mrs. Alexandra? Don't you believe that I love Joaquin?" Monet asked, raising her voice.

"Mother, this is serious. Monet loves Joaquin. She's proving it by having his child. I think it's romantic." Krystal always felt like she had to come to Monet's defense.

Alex continued to laugh, shaking her head. "Monet, you forget that I know why my family preferred shortening their visit. Coming to my place for the rest of their visit. I know the ugly truth, which I'm sure you haven't shared with my daughter. Maybe you want to share that with her now? But then again, I think you really don't want Krystal to see the real you…. or your feelings for Joaquin.

The color drained from her face. Krystal was the only friend and ally she had. If Krystal knew the truth, Monet would lose the only person that even resembled a friend or, at best, someone who idolized her.

"I don't know what you're talking about. But whatever lies they're spreading about me. I would prefer that you keep it to yourself." She ran out of the room, leaving Krystal wondering what was happening. Monet tried not to cry, but the tears began to spill when she reached her room. Her emotions were unbalanced, and she hated it. One minute she was happy, the next minute, she would rage out of control.

That night Monet broke into Demi's room and lay in his bed. She saw the pretty picture of Audrey smiling from within the frame. She held it in her hands, "You lucky bitch, you have a hold on him even in death," she said. It pissed her off so much that she wanted to smash it in anger. Why didn't he love her like he loved Audrey? She thought, wanting him so desperately. Monet would dream of Demi holding her in his arms, making her scream in ecstasy. Now that she was pregnant and found it harder to keep her feelings for him a secret. Every time she was around him, she felt the need to lash out at him simply because he didn't want her. Now she was, stuck with the dragon lady breathing down her neck. Watching her every move. Monet put on one of Demi's shirts and splashed some cologne on it, falling fast asleep. She dreamt that he was on his knees, begging her to run off with him.

The Outskirts of New Orleans

Brydus had long conversations with Dougie along the way. He was a sweet boy with dreams of being a veterinarian. He loved animals but was never allowed to keep any. She wanted to keep his mind off the dreadful place they were going to. Her heart went out to him and his mother. She knew that they wouldn't survive long in those mills.

It was the night before they were to reach New Orleans. Everyone went to sleep except for Brydus and Gino. The night was warm, and Gino had them sleeping outside, which was cooler.

Brydus sat next to Gino by the campfire, "Gino, I need you to do the right thing for once," she pleaded. "I need to know which mill you're taking them to," he looked at her sadly.

He threw more twigs into the fire and sighed, "There's nothing you can do; save yourself and forget about them. It's very dangerous."

"Don't tell me what I can or can't do. You know damn well they won't survive the mills. Please, if you have any human decency, tell me. Let me worry about the rest."

Gino smiled for the first time since the start of this nightmarish journey, "I know what you must think of me." He sighed. "This is my first and last dealings with human trafficking. I can't deal with the stress. I was instructed to take them to Randall Yeakey's Mill. He owns one of the largest, unfortunately, the worst mill in the area. Apparently, her stepfather made a deal with the devil."

"Why Gino, why would he sell that sweet woman and child? Was he that desperate for money?"

He stared at the fire, remembering that first time he meant Lupe's parents. He had concluded then but didn't vocalize it was a family issue, "That well runs deep," sigh, "I'm afraid. I believe it was more out of shame than anything else. They lived in a modest home. The wife was a beaten and broken woman, looking older than she was from years of mistreatment and abuse. If I'm not mistaken, the boy belongs to the stepfather, and she could be with the child again, I'm not sure. I heard that she would sleep with the stepfather to stop him from beating her mother. She was raped repeatedly from the age of fourteen and had her first child at sixteen. She lost one other from a severe beating that he gave her. You can't make me feel worse than I already do."

"I believe the stepfather sent them to die. He had to know those mills are a death trap."

Gino went into his backpack and pulled out a paper. "Here's a map of the area. It's easier if you know where you're going. Also, I've decided to sell you to Jim Mostowski. I know that sounds terrible, but if I just give you over to him, he'll get suspicious. He owns an import-export business, which was just a front for other stuff. He works out of an old police substation right outside the city limits. It's only him, his son, and two other employees, so there's not a lot of security."

"Thanks, I appreciate the information," she laughed.

"One last thing, Jim Mostowski is a conniving pig. Falu, the overlord, is getting ready to close down his operations. He's just waiting for word from the Inner Cities to make his move."

"How do you know that?"

"Falu is a very powerful and a feared man. He's young, strong, and extremely intelligent. He has over a hundred thousand men in his service. I'm one of the few merchants he permits on his property, and the gossip train runs deep."

"Thank you, Gino. I will get them out of there. I have my methods, and I will use all of them even if it kills me. I'll save them from that fate," Brydus assured him.

Gino laughed, "I'm sure you will, my dear, I'm sure you will."

Brydus put her hand over his, "Sometimes, we get caught up in shit that is out of our control. But I know you have a good heart. I can tell this isn't easy for you."

His eyes misted, turning away from her, "It's the hardest thing I've ever had to do, and I will regret it until my dying day."

Morning came, and they continued their arduous journey. Dougie loved to hear Brydus talk about the Quintanilla Estate and the ranch. Her words gave him hope for a better future. "Miss Brydus, tell me again about the boys and girls where you live." Dougie cuddled close to her.

"Better yet, let me tell you about one of my favorite shops. It's called Emma's Delights. Ms. Emma and her daughter Tracy make all kinds of candy there..." She described all the different stores. Dougie listened to Brydus until he fell fast asleep in his mother's lap.

"Lupe, I want you to promise me something. Promise me that you will hold on until I come for you. I don't know how long it's going to take. Please believe me that I will come for you and Dougie."

Lupe felt such a warm feeling in her heart. Life had not been good to young Lupe, "You have been a Godsend, Brydus. If not for you, we would be starving right now, and this trip would have been unbearable. I know it's not where you want to be, but I'm glad you are here."

Brydus put her hand over Lupe's, squeezing it tight, "They say things happen for a reason. I'm glad we met."

Laura was restless, the trip was long, and she didn't like the company, "Oh God… you two are making me sick. I can't wait to get away from the both of you," Laura said with disgust.

"Why don't you come with us?" Brydus suggested.

"No thanks, my mission in life is to work my way into Falu's estate. They say he keeps women for his pleasure, and I intend to be one of them."

"Do you really enjoy sleeping with different men like that? I mean, why would you want to be somebody's whore?" Brydus asked, confused.

"A girl has to do what she has to do. Not everyone is born with your looks and talent to scare the shit out of people. You would probably do well at his estate. I hear he treats his women very well, and when he's finished with them, he sets them up with their own place and business. So, if I have to be his whore for a while, then so be it."

"I'm sorry if I came off judgmental. I don't know what people's circumstances are. I had a very sheltered life with loving parents. I understand you have to use what you have to make life better for yourself. I wish you luck."

"Well…you're not as bad as I thought you were. If you change your mind, I hear he's extremely handsome, strong, and wealthy," she giggled.

Brydus found Laura amusing, "I think I'll stick with my man… he's big and strong too."

It was night when Gino finally arrived at Jim Mostowski's place. Jim always kept late hours because of his line of work. A light was still shining in his window. Gino peeked through the filthy glass. Jim was in the middle of eating when he answered the door, wiping his hands on a dirty rag.

"Witan! (Welcome) my friend. It's been a long time. Where have you been?"

"Oh… I've been up north roaming the usual routes I travel during the spring and summer months."

"So, what do you have for me? Something interesting, I hope?" Jim asked with his assistant Calvin next to him.

"I have a very unique fighter. I came into possession of her because she got into some trouble, and her owner didn't want to deal with her anymore." Gino didn't want to elaborate. Jim rubbed his balding head, giving Gino a curious look. The only thing Jim ever understood was money.

"Since when do you deal in human trafficking? I thought you loathe that type of business?"

"Oh, believe me, it's just a one-time deal. I don't have the stomach for it, but the money was too good to pass up."

Jim and Calvin laughed. They knew what money does to people, especially in these times.

"I hear you. Let's take a look at him and bring him in."

"Ahh, it's a female," Gino corrected. "You have never seen anything like her in your life. I'll bring her right in but beware. She has a mouth on her."

Gino opened the back of his truck to let Brydus out, "Remember what I said," Gino whispered, "he's a sucker for pretty women, so he'll be drooling over you. Be very aggressive, and he'll stay away from you. I know you'll figure out how to get away from him. Oh… and get a horse. He has many. Good luck, Brydus."

"Thank you for all of your help," she smiled at him. This was the first time since he took her that Gino didn't feel guilty. He walked Brydus to the old substation, pretending to struggle with her. Jim and Calvin's eyes almost popped out when Gino pulled Brydus into their office. She stood tall, proud, and arrogant.

"Holy shit, man…what the hell? She's beautiful. Who would throw away a perfectly beautiful woman like this? Those eyes, and hair, are they real? Hm, amazing!" Jim exclaimed, examining her.

"A jealous wife," Gino explained, "Are you interested or not? I can take her elsewhere."

"No, no, no, I'm really interested." Jim turned to Brydus. "So you're a fighter, huh?"

Her eyes pierced him, "I can whip your fat ass," she answered defiantly.

"Oh my, what fury," he looked at her from head to toe. "Yes, very passionate indeed. Calvin, take this lovely woman to her new suite." Calvin was frozen in place. He couldn't keep his eyes off her. "Calvin! Did you hear me...idiot," Jim yelled, bringing him back to reality?

Jim was beside himself. When Brydus was out of hearing range, he started to jump up and down with his chubby self.

"Gino, she's as good as gold. What kind of fighter is she?"

"I think she's a... street fighter. Yeah, a street fighter, that's what her owner said."

"Talk to me, how much? Now you know I'm just a small businessman, so be reasonable."

"Honestly, I just want to get her off my hands because she's a pain in the ass, and Thomas is afraid of her." Gino wrote a number on paper and passed it to him. Jim's eyes lit up like flashlights.

"Deal... now you can't come back later and ask for more money. She's going to make me rich!" He stroked his beard whenever he thought of profits.

Brydus looked around the small jail cell. It had an old cot, a filthy sink, and smelled like pee. Calvin was star-struck and couldn't take his eyes off her. He stuck his face between the bars, grinning, showing off his nearly toothless smile.

"Do you want to keep those eyes, fool?" she scowled at him.

"Gee, you're one scary bitch," he whispered. "I like that in a woman."

She walked closer to the bars, "Why don't you come over here, and I'll show you just how scary I can be?" she smirked. The gleam in her eyes sparkled, causing Calvin to take a few steps backward, bumping into Jim.

"She's scaring me, Jim."

Jim had money signs in his eyes as he looked at Brydus, salivating, "Well, my pet, what can I do to make you comfortable?"

"This place is a pigsty; do you really expect me to sleep on that nasty cot? Are you crazy or just stupid?" She yelled. "This place isn't fit for animals."

"Calm down, my pet. I'll send Donny in with clean linens and some food. You see, I'm not such a difficult person to get along with. We're going to be good friends, you'll see…trust me."

"Hm, I really doubt that," Brydus said, glaring at them.

"Well, my pet, we'll talk more tomorrow when you feel rested. Donny will take good care of you."

A few minutes later, Donny came in carrying a bunch of faded flower print linens. He was a tall skinny young man with acne and didn't smile much because of his crooked teeth. But he was soft-spoken, and she felt sorry for him.

"Donny," she beckoned. He looked at her, surprised. "I need a shower. I haven't had one in a week."

Donny looked around. He was alone and wouldn't know what to do if she'd tried to escape. "I can take you to the showers. We've got plenty of hot water, and I know where I can get you some soap. Unfortunately, I can't get you any clean clothes... we're locked in for the night."

She smiled at him to put him at ease, "I understand," she said kindly, and he relaxed a little more.

After a nice hot shower, she sat down to enjoy some food. It wasn't the best, but she was hungry. When she returned to her cell, Donny had cleaned up. She had to look around to ensure it was the same place.

"I hope you're comfortable. If you need anything, just holler; I sleep in the back. You have a good night."

Brydus found it hard to fall asleep. The thought of Lupe and little Dougie living in that awful place was heavy on her spirit, and aching for Joaquin was breaking her heart. She wondered what he was thinking and if he wanted her back.

She had to focus on a plan to escape. Then find Lupe and Dougie. It was not going to be easy. Brydus said a prayer for her new friends and Joaquin, praying that he wouldn't forget her so soon.

At the same time, Joaquin stared up at the stars. He couldn't help but wonder where Brydus was at that moment. He thought of what she must be going through in such a dangerous place. The news coming from this area gave him chills. "Hold on, my love," he whispered to himself, "I'll find you."

Joaquin and his men would be twenty miles away from New Orleans the following afternoon. The information he received from his contact was invaluable. Pastor Roberto had not only guided them through the merchant passages. He had also alerted them to hazards along the way, stopping them from making mistakes and losing valuable time.

In the morning, Joaquin was in better spirits. He had not been able to sleep well since the kidnapping. Poor Demi had run out of things to say, trying to keep Joaquin's mind occupied. Especially when Joaquin would fall into a deep depression, where he only responded in short sentences. But that morning, he was into everyone's conversations. The weather was hot. By mid-day, it was already steaming outside, slowing them down. They found themselves watering the horses more often and letting them rest.

Brydus was up early, starting trouble when Jim arrived at the station. He had already attended two business meetings at the arena with fight promoters. His eyes twinkled as they stood transfixed, drooling at the prospect of making a lot of money.

Brydus had a cool gleam in her eyes. She was playing his game, waiting for the right moment to wring his neck.

Jim was proud of his new fighter, "You are exquisite. I have never seen anyone like you before." His eyes began to dance, from her face to her breasts, thighs, and legs. "I can surely make your stay here very pleasurable. I have contacts that can get you anything you want… for… well, you know."

"You're a pig! A slob! I would rather slice my wrist than let you touch me."

Jim turned red at the intensity of her contempt, "Well, you're in a great mood this morning. I had no idea I disgusted you so much. But maybe after a good beat down, you'll be more amiable towards me. After Sheba beats you senseless, your disposition should be… shall we say, more enlightened."

She heard a gasp come from Donny. "But Sheba's three times her size and weight," Donny explained with a worried look.

"Well, maybe she should have thought about that before she started calling me names, hurting my feelings."

"I'm not afraid of you or this Sheba. Bring it on, fatty," she taunted.

Jim's eyes lit up with excitement, "I hope you can fight my pet. Sheba is a very worthy opponent."

"I'll have no problem kicking your fat ass. Is that good enough?"

"Oh, my pet, I hope you can do better than that. Calvin will be in to take some publicity shots. I want to get you in the arena this Saturday. It will be great exposure when I take you on tour." Donny followed Jim into the outer office, arguing with him about the fight. However, Jim was not backing down. He wanted to get Brydus into the arena before it got closed down for good. Donny ran back to Brydus, who was not concerned about the match.

"Donny, why are you so upset… you don't think I can take on Sheba?"

"Miss Sheba is a big woman. She has crushed many of her opponents… you're too pretty to get hurt like that," he hung his head.

Her heart began to swell when she saw the concern in his eyes, "Listen to me, Donny; you have to help me escape from here. If you don't, the man I am to marry will rain hell down on this place. He is the nephew of a mighty man. If and when he finds out that Jim has me captive, he may send him to Prison Island if he doesn't kill him first."

Donny was lost for words. He looked down at the floor and then around the place that had been his only home, "What should I do? I can leave the door open, and you can get out."

"Tell me the truth, what will happen to you if you leave the door open, and I escape?"

Donny put his head down again, "I would be severely beaten and probably kicked out into the streets."

"I don't want to put you in that predicament, but I have a plan."

Publicity shots were taken and distributed throughout the city. The buzz was everywhere about the new female street fighter. The pictures they took primarily focused on her eyes, and she gave them a look that expressed her feelings. She wore very little in the photos and posed in fighting stances, with her muscles flexed, stomach taut, and hands balled up into tight fists.

That night she laid out her plan with Donny, who was so nervous, but he surprised Brydus with the courage to go through with the plan.

Jim was out promoting the fight, showing off the rest of the taken pictures. Other promoters didn't trust Jim. They thought he was trying to scam them like he had done in the past. The other managers couldn't wait to see the newly dubbed 'Raven Queen' in action.

Eric Medina had dealings with him before and knew that Jim was a con artist. He was surprised that Jim sat confidently and comfortably in his office. Eric motioned to one of his guards to stand by the door. Jim proudly laid out the pictures of Brydus on his desk.

"You have a lot of nerve Jim… altering those pictures. Do you want us to believe you have a creature this beautiful in your possession? Man please… what kind of scam are you running now?" Eric Medina stared at the pictures trying to see if he could tell how they had been altered.

Jim laughed, "I know that I have not been honest with you at times. I have also promoted less than desirable candidates in this arena. But I swear she is all you see and a fighter to boot. Look, you have Ben in the first bout with Harry. To make the deal even more attractive. I'll let her fight the winner of that match."

"You're pitting a man against a woman. Are you nuts?" Eric questioned.

"Hey, it would make a great show…besides, I believe she can beat your man. However, if you're scared…then find me someone else for her to fight."

Eric blew cigar smoke in Jim's face, "Alright, I'll bite, but I want her if she's as good as you say. I'll take her on the road and promote her myself. If she's not, I will kick your fat ass and blackball you from all events. Are we clear?"

"You'll see. I promise you won't be disappointed. I have a feeling she's as good as she is beautiful."

"You better be right. Falu is on my ass, and I have to take advantage of the fact that he's out of town. That bastard's ruining things for everyone," Eric whined.

"So, we have a deal," Jim said, full of excitement, knowing that Brydus could bring him the riches he desired. He had always wanted to live in a fancy mansion, with servants at his beck and call.

"We have a deal for now… we'll see what you bring," Eric replied, still suspicious of Jim.

"Okay, tomorrow night, but be prepared to be blown away," Jim said, smiling as he walked out of Eric Medina's office.

Meanwhile, the transmissions between Joaquin and Pastor Roberto were terrible. The closer they got to the city, the worse the received transmissions. Once they reached the twenty-mile mark, they seemed to pick up more momentum. However, the mid-afternoon rains started again, slowing them down and making the ground slippery and treacherous. When the rain stopped, the heat returned. They could see the steam rising from the broken road. Joaquin's men were used to traveling in all types of weather, but they didn't do well in the extreme heat.

Ronald Peterson began to feel sick. He was throwing up, and his temperature had spiked, yet he had not told anyone, thinking he could continue. He fell from his horse and was injured. The young doctor tried to stop the deep gash in his head from bleeding, but his fever was another concern. Ronald was pale and unable to stand up. "I can't help him out in the open. We'll have to find some kind of shelter," the doctor urged.

Demi pulled out the old map and began to pinpoint where they were in conjunction with the city. "Joaquin – look here, that sign, H is for a hospital. According to this map, we're only three miles away."

"Sweet... Doc, we'll go on ahead and alert them that we're coming. Please get him stabilized enough to be moved. Let's get him in a more comfortable position," Joaquin ordered. "Louis, I need you, Cisco, and Big Willie to come with us. The rest of you, please help Doc keep Peterson as comfortable as possible.

The hospital was not easy to find. They rode back and forth until they realized it was right in front of them, hidden by overgrown bushes and trees. Cisco and Louis climbed through the dense brush to find the main driveway leading to the hospital. Demi cut his way using his machete to clear a path. He hit one of the directional signs, which pointed to the emergency entrance. "Urgent Care Center...beautiful, hey guys, the ER is this way." For an hour, they hacked through the tangled jungle that engulfed the hospital until they found the main entrance, but without electricity, they could not open the doors.

Louis edged himself around the building, to the back where they usually kept the generators, followed by Cisco. Cisco helped Louis open the door to the power terminal, and with small flashlights, they made their way through the compartments. Cisco started to flip switches until he found the main switch. Everything lit up like a Christmas tree. They slapped each other fives, excited that something was finally going their way. They continued to flip switches, and after a few minutes, the whole place was lit up like a Hollywood theme park. Demi found a backhoe that they could use to clear the road that led to the main entrance. He was like a little boy playing with a new toy. Back and forth he went until he cleared the passageway.

The hospital was a satellite urgent care center. The grand opening was set for three weeks after the Dark Days struck. The facility's construction continued when the world fell apart and chaos began. The hospital was equipped with the latest medical technology, equipment, and medical devices. However, it was never opened to the public. No one had ever opened the doors or turned on the power. The solar panels were still collecting energy all those years. The men cheered when the water faucets started sputtering out the first streams of water in years.

Joaquin found the emergency response vehicles, but the batteries had to be charged. In the garage, they found new batteries, still in original packaging. "Wow, look at all this shit," Joaquin said, pointing to the brand-new equipment sitting on dusty shelves.

Demi pulled a battery off the shelf, "let's hook it up to the charger." Thirty minutes later, the battery was fully charged, and they were on their way back, hoping to reach Peterson in time.

It was getting dark, and they knew the roads were not in the best condition. With caution, Cisco drove the ambulance, trying not to get stuck in the hundreds of potholes and deep crevices along the way. Joaquin and Demi rode ahead to prepare their injured crew member. They waited impatiently with their wounded man for Cisco to arrive. Then they realized that they would have to carry him and meet up with the ambulance.

The Doctor felt he had struck gold when he saw the hospital and all the new equipment. He was so excited that he forgot the patient outside. Big Willie and Cisco carried Ronald into the ER and laid him down. He was pale and beginning to go into convulsions. The young doctor worked on him, wishing that he had a nurse to assist him.

Joaquin knew that hospitals had communication rooms. They started a search throughout the building. Demi found it on the upper level just off the main corridor. It took them nearly an hour to figure out how to work the equipment. When Pastor Roberto's voice came in crystal clear, everyone cheered, excited they had arrived.

"Pastor Roberto, we are in a hospital somewhere north of the city. How far are we from you?" Joaquin asked.

"I'm not sure, my friends. I didn't even know there was a hospital in that area," the Pastor walked towards the back window, "Oh my God, I'm looking out of my window… I can see the aerial lights of the towers above the hospital. Wow... you're right on the outskirts of the city."

"The doc is working on one of our friends. He looks pretty bad, but I'm hoping he will be alright now that we have shelter. So, when can we meet, and where?" Joaquin asked anxiously.

"Something must be going on in the arena. There is so much traffic, and the crowd is going crazy. These events tend to bring out the bad elements, the criminals, prostitutes, and the youth who want to be thugs. How about if we come to you tomorrow, let's say around nine in the morning, and we can get started with our search? I'll have some of my people out in the field to start looking for anyone that fits her description."

"That sounds great. We'll be ready. We're exhausted and probably not thinking clearly anyway."

Pastor Roberto could hear the anxiety in his voice, "Don't worry, Joaquin, we'll find her. If she's here, I don't think there's a place to hide her. Flash a little gold or silver, and people will sell their own mother."

"That's what I'm counting on, hey… thank you. We would have never made it without your help."

"My pleasure, friend, your uncle saved our lives, and we can now see a great future for all of us because of him.

"We owe you," Joaquin said. "I'll see you tomorrow. Oh, by the way, do you know a good nurse? Doc could use some help with our friend."

"Actually, I do. I'll bring her with me tomorrow. Stay alert, over and out."

Joaquin was drained from all that happened during their journey south. He was grateful for his brother and his men's support. "Hey bro, ten pieces of gold say that you'll be making sweet love to your woman by tomorrow night," Demi said, trying to reassure Joaquin. "If I know my girl, she's probably kicking somebody's ass right now trying to get away."

"You know I will rip this city apart to find her," Joaquin replied, running both hands through his hair, praying that Brydus was alright and found safe.

Chapter 20: The Fight

Bataille de Sang Arena

The roars from the crowd were deafening. Brydus began to get energized – all those years of sacrificing and training were going to finally pay off.

She had never fought in an arena of this magnitude. There were cameras on her face that projected onto a huge screen in the center of the massive stadium. The arena was packed. Brydus knew she was not the favorite. They labeled her the villain, so she decided to put on a show. When the media came towards her to get a statement, she pushed them away. Brydus scowled at everyone, and before she went into her locker room, she flipped everyone the bird. The crowd squealed with excitement as they watched her fussing at the camera crews.

Jim was in heaven watching people pour into the arena wanting to see the fight between the two Queens. Queen Sheba was the champion, and the newcomer Raven Queen was not disappointing the crowd with her pre-fight antics.

Eric Medina was waiting in Brydus' locker room, trying to throw his weight around. He lit his cigar, waiting for her to arrive to make his move. Donny stayed out of his way because Eric was a bully. He watched closely, wondering what he might do to Brydus. Everyone in the fighting realm knows Eric's reputation for abusing his female fighters. If they were pretty, he would demand sexual favors in exchange for his connections in the fight circuit. He was the one man who could catapult a fighter into the spotlight or destroy their careers if he didn't get what he wanted.

Eric wanted to speak to Brydus to ensure she was under his influence, ready to bully her the minute she walked in. Letting her know he was the boss. He dropped his cigar when he came face to face with the look of death. "Who the hell are you, and what are you doing here?" she asked with venom. Eric swallowed hard, surprised. He was not expecting such an attitude from her.

"I'm sorry, I-" he stuttered. "I just came to wish you good luck. I'm a promoter," he put out his hand to shake hers, but she ignored it. "I wanted to meet you… your pictures don't do you justice."

Brydus taped her hands, still ignoring him, "You know what? I don't give a rat's ass who you are. But if I were you, I'd leave before you get hurt, dick face."

It took him a few seconds before he found his voice, "Ah, um, well, I just wanted to let you know that I am responsible for making many women fighters successful. If you do what I say, I can do the same for you."

She turned abruptly towards him. Her eyebrows rose with such anger that he decided it would be safer to stay close to the door. "Listen closely, douche face, I don't need a damn thing from your sorry ass," Brydus closed the distance between them. "I hope you understand what I just said."

"Well… in that case. I hope you know that the fighter who wins the first match will be fighting the winner. That means you will be fighting that champion," he backed away from her, "I hope you are prepared," Eric added, smiling. Donny watched from the corner, hoping that she would let him have it.

"I hope he likes dirt," she replied in a menacing tone. "Because he's going to be spending a lot of time, face down in it," she continued to wrap her hands.

"It's a man. You do understand that. Aren't you at all concerned? I can assure you that they are both great fighters."

Brydus stopped what she was doing and moved closer to him, adjusting his collar. Her proximity was making him nervous. "Look here, mister. I don't care who you are. You're stinking up my air with your shitty cigars and stupid talk. I just want to beat the shit out of someone and get out of this piss-hole. You can say bye-bye now." She led him toward the door, pushing him out, and slamming it behind him. Eric recovered quickly, hoping no one saw how frightened he was. He composed himself, embarrassed but thrilled. She stirred something in him. He rushed to find Jim watching the massive crowd still flowing into the stadium. Jim saw dollar signs. People were still trying to pay to watch the fight. "Jim!" Eric shouted above the noise. "We need to talk. Come to my office." Jim followed him down the stairs to his window office, where he could see the action without being in the middle of the crowd.

"What the hell… I was this close to her," Eric said, holding up two fingers with a small gap between them, "and she dissed me like I was shit. That bitch has balls. I thought you were shitting me. But she is the real deal. I mean… everything about her: her hair, eyes, and that body, damn. Oh, and the best part is her attitude. Man, all I saw was dollar signs… so how much do you want for her contract?" Eric was prepared to pay big money for Brydus.

Jim wasn't surprised, "Why would I want to sell her? She's a money magnet. I just want you to help me promote her. I finally have a great fighter," he said. "She's going to the top. Maybe overseas. Now that's where the real money is."

"Promote her… I want to get down and dirty with her, man. I still have a boner. What I wouldn't do for one night with that bitch."

"You and I both man, but neither of us has a shot in hell with her. Unless she all of a sudden gets really horny." They laughed.

Eric lit another cigar, "I have a good feeling about tonight."

"Well, the place is filled to capacity, and people are still trying to get in. This is truly a money night." Jim said, wiping his mouth.

"I think I'm going to change my bet right now. I was going to bet against her, but I believed that would lose me a lot of money. She is definitely a winner."

"Oh, I put my money on that bitch the minute I met her. She's angry, and the look in her eyes says she is ready to fight," Jim admitted.

Brydus looked at the costumes they laid out for her to choose from. They were no more than high-cut bikinis, made from black leather. She chose the one that fit her best, but it didn't cover much. She looked at herself in the mirror and rolled her eyes. She felt naked, but it would have to do. She had to test what she was wearing by moving around, getting warmed up, flipping, and throwing kicks, hoping the little bit of leather didn't fall off while she was fighting.

"God, I hope Joaquin never sees me in this. He'd have a fit," she said to herself. Her boots were calf length and form-fitting. Brydus continued warming up by stretching and hitting the heavy bag. Afterward, she braided her hair back tight and tied it off with a piece of rawhide. She could hear the cheers from the crowd as they introduced the opening fighters. The commentator announced that the winner would fight the new queen.

Brydus smiled, knowing she had to put on a good show so Jim wouldn't suspect anything and would be at ease with her. The rumbling from the crowd sounded like thunder. The two fighters came out and went through their ritual, revving up the people in the stands. Donny was back to help finish taping her hands, locking the door behind him, and pushing the camera crew back. They were trying to get a shot of the dark beauty.

"I've never seen a crowd this big. They all came to see you, Miss Brydus." Donny said with a terrified look on his face. "I spoke to Sheba, and she's on board with everything."

"That's great news, Donny, because I really don't want to hurt her."

Donny gave her a peculiar look, "Can you really beat Sheba? She's three times your size."

"I could easily kill her. It's not hard," she said casually.

His mouth went dry, "Have you killed before?" his voice shook slightly.

She put her hands on his shoulders. "Yes, in self-defense, and it's a terrible thing… you never really get over the act. I've been training since I was old enough to walk… size means nothing in a fight… it's the skills of the fighter that you need to watch out for."

"I'll be waiting for you when you're finished. Please be careful," he said with sincerity in his voice.

They could hear the groans from the crowd as Samuel and Harry slammed each other around the ring. Donny was afraid for Brydus, knowing she had to fight a man. He watched her with concern as she continued to warm up, not looking a bit apprehensive about what was to come.

"I've watched these two men fight before… they're really strong. Have you fought a man before?"

She started to laugh, "Relax, Donny. You're more nervous than I am. I've fought against many men before, more than one at a time."

A loud thunderous roar signaled that the fight was over. Samuel was the victor. He was strutting around the ring, pounding his chest, listening to the crowd's cheers. One of the announcers put a mic in his face. "So, how does it feel having to fight a woman?"

"I'll show that black bitch where she belongs. Her place is in the kitchen or on my shit," he answered, holding his crotch. "By the time I'm done with her, she'll be begging me to ride her!" He screamed into the mic, and the crowd went wild. "Send that bitch out! I'll teach her who's boss." Donny looked at Brydus, hoping she would change her mind.

"Trust me, Donny, I'll be fine." She walked out slowly through her entrance, with two guards in front making sure that the crowd didn't try to throw something or jump from their seats to touch her. They booed Brydus as she entered the ring with great confidence. She raised her arms towards the crowd. When she dropped her robe, the whole atmosphere in the arena ignited. Both men and women began to whistle and scream crude remarks. It took the Master of Ceremonies almost five minutes to calm them down. Brydus did her best to remain confident and intimidating. The announcer tried to shove a mic in her face, but she pushed it away. "Get that shit out of my face, asshole!" she yelled.

"You're mine, bitch. I'll have you bent over, screwing you from behind," Samuel taunted her.

"With what, that shriveled up thing you call a dick? Please, I've seen bigger ones on rats," she calmly teased, waiting for his ego to snap. It made him angry enough to come at her before the bell rang. Brydus saw it coming and skillfully blocked his blow.

"You say that now, bitch, but when I'm finished with you, you'll be begging for some of this," he grabbed his crotch again.

"Right," she muttered under her breath.

The referee pushed him back to his side of the ring. Samuel was pissed and told Brydus he would break her in two. She showed him her middle finger with an innocent-looking smile. He came at her when the bell rang, charging like a bull, low and steady. Her foot went easily to his face with a sidestep, and then, adding insult to injury, she came down with a well-placed blow to the back of his exposed neck. The crowd groaned, cursing and booing.

It took him a moment to stand up while the referee was counting. Brydus waited with her arms crossed. When he stood up and staggered backward, she continued the assault, kicking and punching him repeatedly, trying to tire him out. Samuel started getting dizzy from blows to his head and kidneys. The crowd booed her more as they tried to encourage their champion, "Get her!" they shouted over and over. Samuel tired quickly. His punches did not connect with their target but instead hit only air where she once stood. He was a slugger; that's how he fought. Brydus' continuous kicks to his kidneys, stomach, neck, and chest weakened him. His only chance to recover was between rounds. His trainer tried to motivate him. Samuel sat in his corner, breathing hard. "Sammy, she's kicking your ass out there. You haven't landed a single punch to slow her down," his coach said, trying to stop the bleeding from the bridge of his nose.

"She's too fast. She has either been trained very well or has to fight to stay alive. Either way, when I throw a punch, she blocks it, or she's just not there. That bitch is wearing me out."

"Well, if you don't do something, those kidney blows will have you pissing blood, now get out there and kick her ass!" he yelled in his face.

Eric and Jim sat in the front, drooling over the money machine they stumbled onto.

"God, she's beautiful. The way she looks will make any man grab his junk," Eric said, crossing his fingers, hoping she wouldn't get hurt during the match.

Donny was smiling as he rubbed Brydus' shoulders. "I don't know what to say. I've never had this much fun in my life."

"I hope he gives up soon, I'm holding back as much as I can, but it's not easy."

"Holding back?" Donny said, baffled by her comment.

"Yeah, he's just a brawler. All he knows how to do is throw punches."

The bell rang, and Brydus saw that Samuel was tired and barely moving. He swung and constantly missed, staggering into the ropes more often than standing up straight. After another punch from Brydus to his kidneys, he fell on his face bleeding from his nose. The crowd booed and cheered simultaneously as Brydus was announced the winner of the match. She shook her fist in the air at the crowd, and they got riled up again.

"The winner!" the announcer shouted as he held up her arm.

Brydus was ushered back to her room by guards and bouncers. Some of the people from the crowd jumped from their seats, trying to get at her. Donny was excited, hugging and putting his arm around her to protect her from the crowd.

"That was amazing! Where did you learn how to fight like that? Oh my God, I wish I could move that fast." Excited, he barely took a breath between words. Brydus smiled, listening to him, as she went behind the screen to change into another outfit, which was just as provocative as the first.

Brydus looked at herself in the mirror and smiled. She had remembered all the training Master Lu Jung and Mistress Chong had given her. Focusing all of her pent-up anger and concentrating on her fighting skills. All her pent-up anger was being directed into every punch or kick that she threw. Brydus realized she would be able to fight and hold her own as long as she stayed focused. It wasn't her fighting style, but she did what had to be done without killing him, and she was pleased.

Eric's face was pale, looking at Jim, who couldn't sit still. "What's wrong with you?" Jim asked. "Aren't you seeing dollar signs? She kicked the shit out of him, which means big money."

But Eric was more concerned about who she was. "Jim, she fights like she was trained as a professional. Who is she? Where did she learn to fight so well that she could kick the crap out of a man twice her size? She barely broke a sweat."

"Who cares where she learned. Wherever, whatever, or whoever, this bitch will bring in the money? People will follow a circuit all over the world that has a fighter like her. Think about it. We can take this overseas where the big money is!" he salivated over the idea.

"Jim, you asshole, training like that is expensive; if someone can afford that kind of training for her, someone is probably looking for her," Eric tried to explain.

"Calm down. You're such a prick. Why do you always think there's something wrong. You've talked to her; did she say anything to you?"

"There's always something with you, and I don't want to be caught up in this mess. Things just seem too perfect. She's due back in thirty minutes. I think I'll go talk to her," Eric said, getting up to leave.

"Please do. You're worrying about nothing," he waved him off. "Asshole," Jim mumbled under his breath, annoyed.

Eric walked towards Brydus' locker room, throwing away his cigar before he knocked on her door. She was wrapping her hands when Eric let himself in. He couldn't help but stare at her in her skimpy outfit. Her skin shimmered with sweat from the fight. "What do you want?" she growled.

"Whoa, calm down. I just came in to say that it was an awesome fight. Who knew you had all those skills?" Eric laughed nervously.

"So, what are you saying, a woman can't fight?" She frowned.

"Oh, hell no, I'm saying that you fight like a professional. Have you had professional training?" he asked.

She stared at him, making him uncomfortable. "My father taught me the arts so I could defend myself when assholes like you screw with me. If you know what I mean. Get to the point, shithead. I have another fight in thirty minutes. I don't have time to waste on your stupid questions."

"I am just curious. You are a pleasant surprise, a breath of fresh air, so to speak. I have great plans for your career. You will love them," he boasted, walking out and turning back to her. "I promise."

"Don't count on it." She said, pushing him out the door and slamming the door in his face while he was still talking. Donny laughed once he knew that Eric couldn't hear him. Donny hated him, and now Eric was getting back what he had dished out for all those years.

Sheba was a close contact fighter, grabbing and squeezing her opponents. When she punched, she put the entire weight of her body behind it. Which meant someone was going to get hurt. Sheba was the favorite in most of her fights. The crowd loved her.

Brydus sat on the bench thinking about Joaquin and wondered if he missed her as much as she missed him. She held back her tears, telling herself not to cry or it would ruin her studio makeup. She became a totally different person in the ring, making her feel strange internally. In truth, she didn't like to hurt people. But in the ring… and a crowd wanting blood, the monster appeared… that killer instinct deep inside she kept hidden. Never did she think she'd be in a place like this. Never in her life, she thought, would a crowd react to her in such a way. Riling her up, making her feel like she wanted to show off her skills.

There were two lesser fights before her match with Sheba, which went by quickly. The next thing she knew, the fights were over, and she could hear her name being announced.

"This is it, Donny. I'll see you tonight. And don't worry, I won't hurt Sheba," she smiled.

"I trust you," he replied, still excited.

Calvin knocked on the door to let Brydus know it was time. She could hear the crowd cheering as Queen Sheba raised her arms to her fans. As the favorite, Sheba paraded around the ring, breaking things with her hands and over her knee. The crowd chanted her name, cheering for their champion. Sheba knew how to put on a show. This was her life, and she earned the title of Queen Sheba.

When Brydus walked out, the crowd began to throw things at her from their seats. They booed her and chanted, "Sheba, knock her out!" over and over. Brydus stood on the ropes, then saluted the crowd by flipping them her middle finger with both hands. The reporter put the mic in her face. "Raven Queen, do you have a few words for the audience?" She grabbed the mic, "Eat shit and die!" she shouted. The energy from the crowd was overwhelming. Brydus could feel energized once again.

She stood across from Sheba, knowing she would be a force to be reckoned with. When Brydus disrobed, the whistling and vulgar remarks started again by the men in the crowd. She moved with grace and style, flexing her muscles with every move.

Sheba paced back and forth, waiting for the announcer to start the match. Brydus leaned on the ropes, stretching and lifting her legs high. The men went crazy. Finally, the announcer settled the crowd, giving Sheba the props she was entitled to as an undefeated champion.

The match started, and as any good competitors would do, they began to feel each other out, pacing around, taking shots at each other, checking for weaknesses. Sheba charged, but Brydus was faster and able to escape her grasp. Sheba tried to push her around the ring as she had done with most of her opponents. However, Brydus flipped and moved around too much.

The crowd booed Brydus when she managed to get away from Sheba's grip and punches. Twenty minutes went by, and Sheba finally got Brydus locked into one of her holds and then began to squeeze her. Brydus struggled to get away and landed a blow that caused Sheba to loosen her grip on her enabling her to pull away. They were both exhausted, but Sheba's fatigue was showing, slowing her down in the ring. Sheba's jabs were coming less frequently. That motivated Brydus to go full steam ahead, with one final kick to the stomach that brought Sheba down, letting out one final grunt. Brydus pinned Sheba to the ground, then yanked the rawhide strap from her hair, noosing it around Sheba's neck, pulling it tightly until the referee called the fight.

The crowd booed Brydus, calling her a dirty fighter and shouting obscenities. Brydus stayed in character as she stood on the ropes cursing at them. Jim's face turned bright red with laughter. This was better than he could have ever expected. Jim and Eric watched the crowd's reactions, knowing they were finally on their way to the big times, and

Brydus would take them there. Eric jumped into the ring to raise Brydus' arm, proclaiming her the winner. The booing continued as the crowd threw trash in protest. Sheba's crew helped her up and out of the ring as the shouting continued from the fanatical crowd watching their favorite champion taken away.

When the referee declared Brydus the winner, the crowd went crazy again, shouting "cheater," swearing, and the threats worsened.

The guards escorted Brydus back to her locker room again. Cameras followed her, trying to get a statement to transmit to the crowd. But Donny locked the door behind them, not letting anyone else in. Donny was overwhelmed with excitement, "How can you move like that?"

"Many years of back-breaking practice with my father. He started my training when I was only four, and other trainers that were just as brutal. I learned to fight, so I didn't get whipped whenever I wasn't paying attention."

"You mean they whipped you, like a beating whipping?" He asked, shocked.

"No; more like a, you'd better focus whipping. Anyway, they taught me many fighting styles, and then one day, I beat one of my trainers, and that's when they began to respect me. Before I left home, we trained for another year together, but that's another story," she added.

"The car is outside. We have to go now. There are two more matches scheduled for tonight. It will take forever to get out of here if we wait any longer," Donny advised, putting a robe over her. They peeked outside the door and the hallway to make sure no one was roaming outside her locker room. "The area is clear. Follow me. I know a quicker way out," he said, feeling important for the first time in his life. He took her hand, leading her through a few unoccupied rooms and hallways. Brydus felt the cool air against her cheeks, taking a deep breath. The car was right where Donny had parked it. There were no guards as he drove it out of the private parking space. The streets were empty. All they could hear was the thunderous sound of the crowd coming from the arena.

"Well, everything is set. Jim probably won't be back until he is finished counting all the winnings and settles all the bets. I know that he bet heavily on you, so he made a lot of money tonight. I'm sure that will make him very happy. I have everything packed for you, and the horse is ready. I gave you my saddle and the best horse that we have. You'll like Baloo; she's just like you, strong and dangerous," he explained while smiling at Brydus, knowing he was doing the right thing. Deep inside, he was going to miss her.

"Why would you give me your saddle? What are you going to use?" she asked, surprised.

He looked down to the floor with his shoulders hunched over, "I have no need for it anymore… one of Jim's beatings hurt my back, and the doctor said that I shouldn't ride anymore because it will make it worse."

Brydus was heartbroken for the boy, understanding his pain, tearing up for her new friend she would never forget. She put her hands on his shoulders, comforting him. "Why don't you come with me? I promise you, I will take good care of you, and no one will ever beat you again."

"I can't leave," he said sadly, "this is the only place I've ever known. He beats me, but he is still my father. Besides, who will take care of him when he's sick?" Brydus was shocked that his own father would beat him in such a way and treat him like a slave instead of a son.

"Donny, I'm afraid to ask, but what about your mother?"

He shrugged his shoulders again, "Jim told me she was a whore who ran away soon after my birth. But old man Riley who used to work here, told me a different story. Riley was an old rancher who looked like he was about a hundred years old," Donny smiled, remembering his old friend. "Riley told me she wasn't a whore, and that she was kind and loving, but Jim mistreated and abused her. Riley said she died giving birth to my brother, who died soon afterward. Old man Riley took me to her gravesite, but Jim doesn't know that. Deep inside, he blamed himself for her death, so he made up a story that she abandoned us."

"Listen to me, Donny, you are a good person. If you ever need to get away, look for me. Just remember the Quintanilla settlement up North in Pennsylvania. Do you understand? I promise you, I will care for you, find you employment, and a nice place to live. Promise me that you will come when you decide you have had enough. Just know that you have a safe place to go."

"I promise," Donny replied softly.

Brydus got herself together so she would be ready for him when Jim arrived. She put on a very tight, alluring shirt and shorts that fit her the same way. She tied her hair up and applied some lip gloss, making sure that her lips were wet and sexy.

Shortly before daylight, Jim came stumbling in with three bags of money, winnings from the fight, and his cut from the ticket sales. "Where is my prizefighter?" he bellowed, putting his money on the desk. "You have made me very happy, my pet. I hope you slept well," he said, smiling at his money machine.

Brydus stood seductively by the bars of her cell, "I've been waiting for you. After a fight, I get very hot, if you know what I mean," she blew him a kiss.

Jim nearly fell trying to get to her, "Oh, my pet, I knew you would come to your senses. I can give you anything you want, you only have to whisper it, and it's yours. All I want is to be in your arms, my sweet angel."

"That's exactly where I want to be, come on in, and let me whisper to you what I want." Brydus walked over to the bed and invited him to come to her. Jim couldn't take his eyes off her tantalizing breasts, the shirt she wore was revealing everything, and her long legs were so beautifully shaped, teasing him. She blew him another kiss, then laughed seductively, teasing him with her lips, watching him fumble with the keys trying to open the cell door. "Come to me, my sweet hunk of a man, let me help you relax. I know you've had a busy night." Jim sat on the cot as Brydus came behind him, pressing her breasts against his back.

"Oh my… I'm really enjoying your touch, my lovely pet," he moaned. As he melted under her touch, she began to massage his back, "Oh, that feels so good, my pet. People have no idea how hard I work. Do you realize how rich we are going to be because of you? You can have whatever you want, a house, clothes, you will want for nothing. You just keep fighting like you do, and there is no stopping us." Jim continued to talk about his plans as Brydus positioned herself, preparing to knock him out.

"My, my, my…you have this knot right here at the base of your neck. I'm going to work it out for you. Now close your eyes. I wouldn't want that little old knot to ruin the good time we're about to have."

"Anything you say, my lovely," he said, almost asleep. Gently, she massaged his neck, and then in one quick move, Brydus put him in a sleeper hold. Jim went down quickly. While she hogged-tied him, Donny waited nearby and left, locking the cell door behind her.

"He's not dead, is he?" Donny asked, concerned for his father.

"No, he's very much alive. He'll sleep for a little, but when he wakes up, he will have a real nasty headache."

"Everything is ready. The horse is outside. This map will lead you to the mill where your friends are. Be careful, Ms. Brydus. Those mills are dangerous. Oh… here, take this; it's a hat and a pair of glasses that Sheba wanted you to have."

"Thank you so much. The glasses help. I hate when people stare at me."

"What will you do for money?"

Brydus reached for one of the money bags on the desk and smiled, "I'd say this is enough to cover my share of the winnings."

"You deserve it. You will always be my champion," Donny said, grinning, "There's a gun dealer on bourbon street… the place is called ah…Gun Nuts, yeah, that's it, Gun Nuts. I think you can trust the owner. He won't rip you off like some of the others."

When Brydus gave Donny a kiss, he blushed, turning bright red. "I'll tie you up loosely so that you can free yourself later, and then I'll be on my way."

The sun was bright as she stopped by Sheba's to say goodbye. "Hey girl, I thought we made one hell of a team. Thanks for not killing me," Sheba said, hanging outside her window.

"Why don't you come with me, Sheba? Is this what you want to do for the rest of your life?" Brydus asked.

Sheba looked away with misty eyes, "This is all I've known, Brydus… here, I'm somebody. I have fans that love me. Out there…I'm just a fat lady. I'll be alright. I'll get another match, beat the shit out of them, and regain my title. You go marry that man of yours."

"You know where I'll be if you change your mind." Brydus nodded, turning her horse towards the city. She made plans to rescue her friends from the mills and find her way back to the man she loved.

Chapter 21: New Orleans

As promised, Pastor Roberto and his crew reached the hospital entrance early the following day.

"This is amazing! A fully functional hospital was right in our backyard," Doctor Janis cried with excitement, leaving the rest behind. It was the most remarkable find for both medical staff and those who needed medical treatment. She had to make sure Falu was informed when he returned from the Inner Cities conference. Janis touched the walls just to make sure it was real.

"It's beautiful." The automatic doors opened as she strode in, looking back at the rest of the crew, amazed at their find. Pastor Roberto and the others laughed at her, feeling the same way.

Pastor Roberto called out to anyone who would hear him, "Hello! Hello, is anyone here?" he yelled, walking down the hall toward the ER. Doctor Anderson was running some test when he looked up, surprised that he had an audience.

"You must be Doctor Anderson. I'm Pastor Roberto."

"Doctor Anderson, at your service," he replied, thrilled when he found out that two nurses and another doctor were with him.

"You have no idea how happy I am to see you. For a minute, I thought that I was the only doctor around."

"This is a miracle of grand proportions. We've been working out of the main hospital, but it was heavily damaged during the Dark Days. The other two hospitals were burnt down. We still have many problems with so few resources," Pastor Roberto stated, holding his hands in a prayer-like position.

Dr. Janis touched her cheeks, "Oh my God, this is amazing."

"Well, let me see if I can round up the others." Doctor Anderson said. "They're exploring the hospital. We've already found so many wonderful surprises. Everything is brand new from what I can gather. It was scheduled to open three weeks after the Dark Days, but as you know, everything happened so quickly. It's likely no one really knew that this place was here, and those that did probably died during the catastrophe."

Dr. Anderson turned on the intercom, alerting the others that Pastor Roberto and his crew had arrived. Within minutes, they gathered together, exchanging pleasantries and stories over coffee. They sat down to discuss their strategy on how and where they would start searching for Brydus.

"Sorry about last night. It was crazy. When they have events like that, it's better to stay put. Trouble hits the streets. The overlord in this region is trying his best to end the corruption. He's not doing a bad job. Falu is tough, and he wants to do it legally. Now, do you have a picture of her? I'll get some of my men to scout out the area, hitting some of the brothels where women just seem to disappear. Can we make copies and hand them out?" The pastor asked.

Joaquin handed him a picture taken when they went to visit the Inner Cities. He stared at the picture of him and Brydus. She was smiling at Joaquin, sitting on his lap.

"Damn… sorry, I cursed. She is stunning. I can't believe she's here. She is really a natural birth, with no alterations, and her eyes are brown? Hm, interesting," the pastor said, holding the picture.

"Natural birth, no alteration. What you see is what she is," Joaquin replied.

"Wild and dangerous too," Demi added.

"Wow… um, she shouldn't be hard to find. We do have women with black hair, but they have different color roots."

"What do you think our chances are of finding her today?" Joaquin asked, hoping for a positive answer.

The pastor scratched his head. "The good news is that she will be easy to spot. The bad news is… she's worth millions on the black market. They may be hiding her somewhere or have already smuggled her out of the city."

That wasn't what Joaquin wanted to hear. He sprung from his chair, pacing in front of the window. "I won't leave here without her. I swear to God, I'll die looking for her." He banged his fist on the table.

Demi hated watching his brother getting so stressed out. "Joaquin, we're here for you. We didn't travel this far for nothing." Demi was interrupted by Cisco and Dan, who had been out shopping for supplies.

"We got here as fast as we could. We found her," Cisco blurted, out of breath, holding up a poster of Brydus in a very revealing outfit, her eyes glaring at them.

"That's our girl, The Raven Queen?" Joaquin said as he read the poster, excited that they had a lead, "Where did you find this?" He asked, with hope in his voice.

"They're all over. Apparently, she was the headliner last night. Everyone's talking about her," Dan added.

"Thank you, this is great news, guys. At least now we know where to start."

"Look down here. It's sponsored by Jim Mostowski." The pastor said. "Gentlemen, we have our first lead. Let's get cracking; his place is not that far from here."

***

Meanwhile, Brydus waited patiently for the gun shop to open. She put on her sunglasses and pulled the hat down lower before entering. There was only one clerk in the vast store. She examined some of the shotguns but was looking for something different. Brydus wanted something special, something in the line of an automatic shotgun with a long-range barrel.

The clerk watched her closely with cameras he had placed all over the store. After a few minutes of wandering from one display to another, not liking the quality and style of the weapons, Brydus walked over to the counter where the clerk stood just staring at her.

"Do you have anything modified, something that I don't see out here?" He continued to stare at her. "Hello? Do you, or don't you?" she questioned more forcefully.

"You're her aren't you, the fighter from last night?" he asked.

She took off her glasses and scowled at him. "Do you have what I'm looking for or not?" she demanded. His jaw dropped. He scooted backward and flipped a hidden switch, which opened a panel behind him.

Her eyes lit up. "Now that's more like it," Brydus pointed to one that caught her eye, and he handed it to her. It was an extended barrel long-range shotgun straight from the UK. She smiled as she handled the weapon.

"It's rare and light. One of the best on the market," the clerk smiled, expecting a sale.

She flipped it around in her hands. "I love it. How much?"

He got caught up in her excitement, "This is from my personal collection. I'll give you a great price if you sign my poster of you," he asked.

"I can do that, but I also want these two guns and the ammo. Do we have a deal?" she smiled happily.

"You have no idea how honored I am that you walked into my shop. You don't mind if I take a picture with you holding them? I'd like to brag. It's good for business."

"Mister, I don't care how many pictures you take, as long as I walk out of here with these three babies and enough ammo to blow the shit out of a particular place."

"Awesome, let me get my camera."

***

The pastor pointed to the building that Jim worked out of. When Joaquin caught Jim trying to run out the back door, he dragged him back by the collar, throwing him on top of his desk. Joaquin cocked his gun, pressing it against his forehead. "Where is she? What have you done to her?"

Jim was sweating from every pore of his body, begging for mercy, "I swear to you, she knocked me out and left this morning. She stole my money. I swear, please don't kill me!" he pleaded.

Demi whispered something in his ear, "Joaquin, there's a young man who wishes to speak to you outside. I'll take over here." Demi pulled Jim up to a sitting position.

Jim closed his eyes; beads of sweat were running down his face, "I swear… I didn't know she was a free woman. Please don't kill me," he cried, begging Demi not to hurt him.

Donny pleaded with Joaquin, "I… I helped her escape. I can tell you where she's heading… please don't hurt my father. He didn't harm her in any way. He was kind of scared of her."

"Where is she, son? Talk to me before I lose my temper."

"Yes, sir… she went into town a few hours ago. She needed to purchase a weapon to rescue some friends and take them back home with her… she promised them that her fiancé would help them."

Joaquin chuckled; even in trouble she's thinking about others, "So she spoke about me?"

"Yes, sir, all the time, she said you would bring this house down around us when you came for her. She's my friend. Brydus is the only person who treated me like somebody. Please don't bring our home down, sir."

Joaquin sighed, "Son, I don't want to hurt you or your father. Just tell me where to find her."

"She went straight down Bourbon Street to a gun shop called Gun Nuts. I told her that the owner was fair and would give her a good deal. You can't miss her. Miss Brydus has our best horse, Baloo. Baloo is wearing a red saddle with the initials DW on it."

"Thanks for your help, son. I only want to take her home, that's all."

Donny smiled timidly, "I understand completely, sir."

***

Meanwhile, Brydus studied the map, tracing the miles to the mills. She was hungry and wanted to stop at one of the many coffee shops along the strip. It was hard for her to travel through all the poverty, with homeless people huddled together to share what little they had. Children played in the dirty lots with rusted cars and rotting furniture. However, she had seen worse. Some of the buildings were being renovated. Brydus could see that some store owners wanted to make their business inviting and cheerful.

She tied Baloo near a vendor who was selling colored candles. The elderly vendor had a teenage son helping, who looked like he could use a good meal. He smiled at her and nodded as she walked toward him.

"Hey, would you like to make some extra money?" she asked.

His eyes widened. "Yes, ma'am. What can I do for such a beautiful lady?"

"It's easy. All you have to do is watch Baloo until I get back. I'm going to get something to eat… I'll give you two

461

gold coins now and another two later," she placed the gold coins in his hand. The boy grinned, looking over at his mother, who was shocked that someone was being so generous.

"I will guard her with my life," he promised. That was more money than they had seen in years. "Gold, mother, real gold, can you believe it?"

Brydus went across the street to get something to eat. The young girl brought her some coffee, and she ordered a sandwich. It was a beautiful day, and she enjoyed watching the marketplace come alive. Amid all the sadness and despair, people still pushed forward to make ends meet and carry on with their lives. A few minutes later, there was a loud explosion. A few buildings down from where the vendor stood. It shook everything. When Brydus looked, flames were coming from the roof of an old theater. Dark smoke billowed through the roof. Within a few minutes, a crowd had gathered. People ran out of the burning building, coughing and rubbing their eyes. Brydus joined everyone else who was watching. Falu's men were trying to push back the crowd that was forming. A young woman dropped her bag, pushing her way through the crowd. She let out a chilling scream right next to Brydus. "Oh my God, my children are still in there!" she screamed, then tried to push her way past the guards that were not letting anyone get close.

"Please, please, please, I'm begging you. My little girls are in there!" she cried franticly.

"I'm sorry, miss, I can't let you go in there," the guard said. The woman began to cry louder.

Brydus became angry, "Look, asshole, her children are in there. If you won't let her go in and get them, you go and save them," the man looked at the woman, then at the building.

"Oh my God!" she screamed.

Brydus argued with the guard, who ignored the woman's cries for help, making her frustrated. "Where are your girls? Tell me!" Brydus asked, demanding a quick answer.

"They're in the back on the second-floor balcony, three girls, my poor babies. Save them, please, I'm begging." Brydus pushed through the guards and ran inside the building. Most of the fire was located on the top two floors, but it was spreading fast. Brydus worked her way toward the back of the theater. The smoke had not reached the auditorium, but there was a lot of commotion. She ran up the stairs, searching for the little ones. Then she heard crying coming from a closet.

Joaquin and his men heard the explosion and hurried to see what was happening. They stopped close to the theater with the rest of the crowd. People were still running out of the burning building, gagging and collapsing from the smoke.

Demi elbowed Joaquin in the gut, "Brother, didn't that boy say that Brydus was riding a horse with a red saddle and…"

Joaquin looked at his brother and shook his head, "Shit… Oh shit, please tell me she's not in there. Whose horse is this?" Joaquin asked the young man who was holding on to its reins.

"Some beautiful lady is paying me to watch it. She ran inside the building."

Joaquin looked at Demi, and they pushed themselves toward the front of the blockade. The woman was still crying and screaming about her daughters. "You jerks should be in there helping her!" The woman shouted at the guards. "Please go help her find my children!" The big fellow held on to her, stopping her from running into the inferno.

"Who is she talking about?" Joaquin asked.

"Some crazy chick with long black hair ran inside looking for this woman's kids. Somewhere in the main auditorium, second-floor balcony, I believe."

"Demi, take the guys and go to the back. There has to be a back door. Start clearing a way. I'll find Brydus and bring them out that way." The guard started to stop Joaquin but changed his mind when he saw how determined he was. He covered his mouth and nose from the smoke, fighting his way toward the auditorium through the hazy front lobby. Dark smoke was beginning to pour into the theater, making it hard to see.

The back door was blocked by trash and all kinds of furniture. The guys worked hard clearing the rubbish away, trying to get to the door. Other people joined in. The door was bolted shut. "Take cover, guys. I'm going to have to blow this bitch." Demi ordered, shooting the hinges off the door, but it seemed to be rusted shut.

Brydus lowered the oldest girl first so that she could help with the younger ones. Some of the stairs were missing, and it was hard to see in the dark. Brydus heard her name being called and thought her mind was playing tricks on her. She was lowering the second girl when she heard her name again. Then she looked over the balcony. She thought she saw a man standing next to the girl. Slowly, she lowered the crying child and quickly tied the rope around the other. The smoke made it difficult to see when she finally realized it was Joaquin standing with the girls. Brydus almost dropped the crying child when she heard his voice.

"Drop her, baby. I'll catch her," he called up to her. Brydus started crying herself. She let her go and then descended the rope, falling into his arms. "Are you okay, baby?" He touched her, making sure that she was unharmed. They kissed passionately as the girls clung to their legs.

"Let's get out of here, baby." They each carried one of the girls, and Brydus pulled the older one behind her. Smoke filled up the auditorium quickly as they felt their way towards the back door. They made a path to the back, where they found people trying to get out the same way. The door was bolted from the inside and locked.

"Get back…" Joaquin yelled so that he could blow off the lock. Once the lock was gone, he was able to unbolt it. They pushed on the door desperately while Demi and Big Willie pulled from the outside. The door finally burst open, and everyone escaped the fire that was getting dangerously close. Joaquin picked up Brydus and carried her toward a clearing. She cried, burying her face against his chest.

"I can't believe you're here. You found me," she said between sobs. He fought to hold back his own tears. His voice was hoarse from the smoke, and emotions almost consumed him. Joaquin kissed her so passionately that it took her breath away.

"Thank God you're safe," he whispered.

She couldn't stop crying, "I love you so much. How did you find me?"

Demi picked Brydus up and squeezed her tight "My girl, thank God, we found you."

"I can't believe you're all here." Tears began to flow again.

"Hey, you're one of us now. Like it or not, you're stuck," Demi said, teasing her.

"We had our bloodhound Cisco on your trail," Big Willie said.

"Thank you so much! I love you all." Joaquin held her tight, not wanting to let her go. Pastor Roberto caught up with them, happy that everyone was safe and unharmed. The fire engines managed to get through the crowd. Ambulances from the new hospital driven by the pastor's people sounded their sirens as they approached. Pastor Roberto's people did all they could, assisting those who needed help.

Big Willie returned the girls to a very grateful mother. They were taken to the hospital to make sure they were alright.

There was much to celebrate back at the hospital. The Pastor and his crew marveled about the new hospital, and they all celebrated Brydus' safe return. She cried in Joaquin's arms as they stood in the shower. He held her as she recounted the whole ordeal and how much she missed him, not knowing if she would ever get back to him.

"How did you find me? Everything was so crazy."

He kissed her tenderly as they lay in each other's arms. "We had a lot of help, and the merchant left many clues, but

Cisco and Dan found your poster. So, who did you beat up this time?"

"Some guy, and a nice woman, it was just a smokescreen to get away. Joaquin, I just wanted you there to hold me. There were days when I thought I'd ever see you again."

"That was not happening. I would have searched forever until I found you," covering her mouth with lingering kisses, teasing her with his tongue, making her respond to him.

"Joaquin," she whispered, coming up for air, "baby, I didn't know if you wanted me back," she said softly, burying her face in his chest, thrilled to be in his arms again.

"Sweetcheeks, I told you that I loved you and never want to be without you," He reminded her, kissing her neck and nipples, tasting each one, feeling her silky skin with his rough hands. His fingers played with her body, making her open to him as he explored her sweetness. She moaned, letting the sensations take over.

"I want you to marry me, here and now, as soon as possible," Joaquin whispered between kisses. Brydus cried. When he entered her, pushing himself deeper inside of her, she was overwhelmed by his tenderness as he whispered sweet words of love. All she could think of was how much she wanted him and missed his touch.

"Yes... I'll marry you, right here, right now, if you want me," feeling her release and his eagerness. They held on to each other tightly, prolonging the moment. "Te Amo (I love you)," he whispered over and over in her ear. Tears of happiness escaped her as Joaquin captured her lips again until he had his fill.

"Sweetcheeks, I know a woman wants a big wedding with her family and friends, but I can't take another chance of losing you. This was torture for me, not knowing what danger you were in. We'll have a big celebration when we get home and then go on a nice honeymoon. How does that sound?"

"It sounds heavenly," she snuggled closer and started to cry again. All the stress from the last week was taking a toll on her, and she released all the tension in his arms.

By morning, everything seemed to calm down. Two more doctors came to the hospital to assist with patients. They welcomed each other as if they were family that found each other after a long separation. As the doctors and nurses joined forces, all the patients were treated by midnight.

The smell of coffee and fresh-baked bread had everyone following the aroma to the cafeteria. It was Elba showing her gratitude for the rescue of her little girls. They had no place to go, so Doctor Anderson allowed them to stay in one of the rooms.

Everyone met in the cafeteria to plan their trip back home, but Brydus argued back and forth with Pastor Roberto about rescuing Lupe and her son.

"I promised! I gave my word to a little boy! I told him that I would come for them. Joaquin, I couldn't go on living knowing they're in that hell hole," she confessed loudly.

"The man that owns the mill is dangerous. Trust me, there is no way we can get in and out," the pastor argued.

"I'm not asking anyone to endanger their lives. I will find a way. I have a map to his mill and a layout of his operation," she stressed.

Demi studied the map and then handed it over to Joaquin. "We can do this," Demi stated, unmoved by the danger. "This isn't impossible. What do you think, Joaquin?"

"I say… let's go rescue them. We have the manpower and weapons," Joaquin acknowledged, knowing Brydus wouldn't leave without them. The pastor gave up, outnumbered and frustrated. His own men wanted to join the rescue party.

Brydus challenged the pastor, "I'm going with or without you. Just thinking about them suffering is making me sick to my stomach."

"Okay, but let me talk to him first when we get there. Maybe I can make a deal for the mother and her son. He knows me, and I might be able to save them without gunfire and bloodshed." Pastor Roberto tried to convince everyone and himself.

"Fine, but if he disagrees, we are going in packing. Brydus made a promise to them, and I will burn in hell before I allow her to break that promise to a young boy," Joaquin cocked his gun.

The pastor agreed reluctantly.

Joaquin and Demi came up with a plan. The pastor took them to an old warehouse filled with trucks of all sizes and models. "These trucks are still in good shape. My brother Carlos and his crew can bring them back to life. They are experts in auto repairs; I can guarantee you they can fix anything, even cars, and trucks dating back to the twentieth century."

Joaquin examined all the trucks, hoping to find a specific model. "An armored truck," Joaquin said, smiling at his brother and nodding.

"Perfect, it's bulletproof," Demi replied.

"Hey, Brother Carlos, can you get this one running for me?" Joaquin shouted to Carlos, who was on the other side of the building. Carlos and his crew of seven walked over and examined the truck.

"Piece of cake. We can have this ready in about five hours, give or take."

"Let's make it happen then. Can we get fuel for it?" Joaquin asked, high-fiving Carlos.

"It takes diesel, so yes, we have enough to get you there and back. Who knows, we might even have enough time to make some modifications," he winked.

"What kind of modifications?" Joaquin asked curiously.

"That, my friend, is a surprise," Carlos said, laughing along with his crew.

The five hours passed quickly for Joaquin as they went over the plan on how they would rescue her friends. When it was time to go, the pastor insisted on driving the truck. He would not admit to anyone just how scared he was driving the ten miles of dangerous roads. The road has wicked twists and turns around swamps full of hungry alligators.

Not many tried to escape through the swamp without directions, and those who managed to escape the mills were never heard of again.

The guards were surprised when they saw the strange truck pulling up to the gate. The curious guards walked up to the driver's side to speak to Pastor Roberto. He recognized him from the health center in town.

"What brings you out these dangerous parts, Padre? And what the hell are you driving?"

The pastor tried to control his nervousness, wiping the sweat from his face, "Oh, this is just something my brother

Carlos has been working on. A special kind of truck made for driving through dangerous terrain. We want to speak with your boss about a business proposition. Still, we can always take our ideas to another mill if he's unavailable. I think he would be interested in this deal. I feel he may be upset with you for stopping us and losing out."

The guard nodded to the other, signaling him to open the gate. "It's early; he should be in his office now. It's the third building on the right."

"Thank you, gentlemen. You have a good day," Carlos said, waving at the guards. He held on tight to the weapon he was carrying on his lap, super excited he was part of the plan. When they arrived, they stationed themselves outside the third building. The pastor ordered his brother to take the wheel.

"You remember the plan?" Joaquin asked him. The pastor was shaking. "No matter what, we're coming in after you. So, if your way doesn't work, we're coming in blasting, you hear me?" The pastor nodded.

Pastor Roberto took a deep breath and went up the wooden steps leading to the building. He looked back at the others for support. The man who owned the mill was very dangerous and enjoyed the misery of others. Randall was not stupid and could sniff out if someone was conning him. He was always trying to stay clear of the law as much as possible. The overlord, Falu, had threatened to close down all the mills if he heard any more complaints, so he guarded his operations closely.

Pastor Roberto walked down the narrow hallway towards the door with the plaque that read, *Boss Man.* He knocked on the door but didn't wait for a response, taking a chance by walking in.

Randall drew his gun, aiming at him, "I don't recall asking you to come in, Padre, but come in and have a seat since you seem to have some balls." Pastor Roberto sat down nervously. "What brings you to my neck of the woods? I hope you're not looking for a donation… because you came to the wrong place," he chuckled, "I'm not into charity work. Money is my calling."

Pastor Roberto laughed nervously. "No, actually, I'm looking for family members who were delivered to the wrong place. I'm told that they were brought here rather than to me. I didn't find out about the mix-up until yesterday. I can pay for their release and your inconvenience."

Randall walked around his desk, scrutinizing him. The Pastor's hands shook as he held out a money bag. Randall snatched it from him, bouncing it in his hands to test the weight, and then threw it behind him on his desk. The Pastor was sweating profusely. He pulled his handkerchief from his pocket to wipe his face.

"So, what are the names of these unfortunate people who were delivered to me by mistake?" he grinned, knowing something was up.

"It's a mother and son, Lupe and Douglas Handover. They were delivered a few days ago." he smiled, wanting to create trust.

"Yes, I remember the pair, young sweet looking woman… thinner than I normally like them, but I can fatten her up for my needs, and the boy… very spirited. He keeps on saying that someone would bust them out of here and take them far away to some dreamland. Children have the wildest imagination, don't you think? But he's really just a pain in my ass."

"Dougie is very bright, and I'm sure that he thinks my home is a dreamland after all that he's been through. Do we have a deal? They will be no use to you. As you've said, she is thin and fragile, and the boy could be a lot of trouble for you."

Randall pushed the pastor's chair back, almost knocking him off. He grabbed him by the shirt pulling him out of the chair violently. "Are you trying to pull one over on me, Padre? You know I hate liars. I can smell the bull shit coming out of your pores."

Brydus' anxiety level was growing as they secretly watched Pastor Roberto struggle to keep his composure. She could see the fear written on his face.

"We have to go in and help him," she said, heading towards the stairs. Joaquin grabbed her by the arm.

"Have you lost your mind? I'm not going to risk losing you again," he snapped.

"Look, I can distract him. If I barge in through the door, you and Demi can come in through that back door," she begged, "We can't leave him there. His way is not working. Now it has to be done our way."

Joaquin looked at the rest of the crew, who were all in agreement." Alright, let's get him out of there."

Randall towered over the pastor, "How about if I keep them and take this money in return for your life. What do you think about that?" he asked, pushing the pastor down. "You made a big mistake, Padre. I'll have your sorry ass thrown off my property, and guess what…you can walk all the way back. That will teach you not to screw with me."

When Brydus kicked in the door wielding her weapon, Randall was startled, "Get away from the pastor, you prick!" she demanded.

He panicked for a second before he pulled out his gun. "I'll shoot him, I swear," Randall said, pointing his gun at the petrified pastor.

Brydus smiled wickedly. "You do…, and I will blow your balls off, go ahead, try me."

"You're the fighter from last night," he grinned, "Now why do you women always go straight for the balls? They ain't never done nothing to you, sweetheart. However, I can sure show you a really sweet time. Why don't we just sit down and talk this over calmly? You put your weapon down, and so will I. I'm sure we can come to some kind of agreement. Come on, sweetheart, you can trust me. Let's talk and work something out."

"I don't make deals with the devil. Now, back the hell away from him. Pastor Roberto, it's your time to leave. I've got this."

"I'll shoot him, I swear,"

Pastor Roberto was looking straight into Randall's gun.

"I'm only going to say this one more time, drop your damn gun before I start shooting," Brydus replied as she tightened her grip on the trigger. "Don't piss me off. I'm itching to blow your ass away." She pointed her weapon at his crotch.

"Aw, come on, baby. Point that thing elsewhere. You're making me nervous. You don't want to ruin a good thing, do you? Shit, I have a room in the back, you know. Let's work this out."

"Move it, fool. I can do this shit all day," Brydus did not waver. Randall took a few steps backward until he felt something hard against the back of his head. Slowly, he turned around. Now it was his turn to have a gun pointed between his eyes.

"I guess you have a hearing problem, asshole," Joaquin pulled him behind the desk and forced him to sit down. Randall dropped his gun and put his hands behind his head. His men were all in the mill getting the workers ready for the day ahead. He knew that none of his men would be back any time soon to help him.

Randall was confused. He didn't recognize any of the people now surrounding him, "What do you want? Money? I've got plenty of money. Please… don't kill me," he begged, glancing at the back door, where Demi stood smiling and winking, as he guarded the back entrance, heavily armed.

"We don't want your filthy ass blood money," Brydus said, keeping her weapon pointed at him.

Joaquin bent down to speak to him, positioning himself next to Randall's left ear. "Now, you listen to me very closely, or you're going to be missing something that you might need later," he said, sticking his pistol close to Randall's crotch. "You're going to get on the intercom and have the woman and her son brought here, right now! Nice and easy, one stupid move, and you're maggot food," he added, now pushing the barrel of his gun into Randall's temple.

"Who are you, people?" he managed to say. Randall could always talk his way out of situations but couldn't think straight. His nerves took over. "Did Falu send you?"

"I don't know who Falu is, but I know you're pissing me off."

"Alright, alright, they're not worth all this aggravation."

"You should have taken the pastor's deal," Joaquin said, winking at Brydus, pushing the mic towards Randall. "Now, get them up here." Joaquin shook him again when Randall didn't key up the mic right away. "Lupe and Douglas Handover, I didn't stutter, did I? Now don't make another mistake because I have enough men and firepower to bring this shithole operation down around you." Joaquin threatened, pressing his gun harder against Randall's temple.

"Alright," he blew into the mic, clearing his throat. "Richard, bring me those two maggots that came in last week, the young mother and her son, and bring them now!" He ordered, trying to sound normal.

Brydus backed out of the door, "Where are you going?" Joaquin asked, wondering what she was doing.

"Trust me, baby," she winked and disappeared behind the door.

"That woman is going to be the death of me." Joaquin sighed. "Pastor, please go out the back way, this may get ugly, and we want you out of the way." He did not hesitate to leave the room.

Randall was shaking as he waited for Richard to bring Lupe and her son. It was the longest five minutes of his life. He prayed Richard would hurry up and wouldn't ask questions. Richard finally pushed open the door shoving Lupe and Dougie into the room, causing them to fall to the floor. He immediately drew his gun and aimed it at Joaquin.

"What the hell's going on here?" he yelled, wondering who was standing behind his boss. When Randall didn't respond, he knew it was trouble. He pointed his weapon at Lupe, who was still on the floor. Richard watched her eyes move behind him. Then he heard the unmistakable click of a shotgun next to his ear.

"Brydus, you're here! I knew you would come for us!" Dougie shouted, seeing her standing behind Richard. He started to run towards her, but Richard grabbed him and held him by his neck, making his face turn red.

"Drop your gun, or I'll break his little neck," he commanded, watching Randall sweat and wondering who these people were. Dougie wiggled away from his grasp. Richard turned his gaze for a moment to see where Dougie went as Brydus sprung towards him using the butt of her weapon to smash him in the head, knocking him out cold.

"I don't think so, asshole."

Dougie ran into her arms. "I knew you'd come," he said, wrapping her arms around her." Demi helped Lupe to her feet after he made sure that Richard was not getting up any time soon. Lupe was only there a few days, and already she had lost weight.

"Bro, take them to the truck and tell Carlos to start it up," Joaquin said, securing Randall to his chair. Richard was on the floor, still dazed and bleeding from the back of his head. Brydus pulled him by the hair to tie him to another chair. Joaquin pressed his pistol to Randall's head once again.

"Just so we are clear. If I find out that you retaliated against the pastor or if he or any of his people even feel threatened, I will come after you. Remember this name, Quintanilla. That's right, fool, you know the name. I can destroy you and everything in your shitty little world. My reach is limitless, and I assure you that you will lose everything. You will spend the rest of your miserable and pathetic life on Prison Island, locked up with worse men than you could ever imagine. Nod if you understand what I just said." Randall nodded, teeth clenched and glaring at Joaquin, "That goes for your men too." Joaquin hit him over the head with his weapon. "That was for hitting on my wife."

Joaquin rode shotgun on the truck's passenger side as Carlos sped toward the main gate. Demi rode on top, lying on his belly, ready to shoot anything that might come after them. Just in case Randall and Richard freed themselves quickly and chose not to heed Joaquin's warning. One of the guards began to shoot at the armored truck. Joaquin took him out, shooting him in the leg as he jumped out of the way of the speeding truck. They made no attempt to stop or slow down. The truck plowed through the steel gate as if it were nothing. "What the hell did you do to this truck?" Joaquin asked, excited.

"Just a few modifications here and there, nothing major, just a little tinkering." Carlos smiled, flying down the tight roads, trying to put plenty of distance between the mill and themselves. Pastor Roberto was petrified. He was sandwiched between a crazy driver and a man who had just shot someone. Dougie was star struck, sitting next to the other men in the truck who were heavily armed, wide eyes taking in the adventure.

Lupe cried in Brydus' arms, "It was worse than I imagined. People lived like animals, and when the food came out, we had to fight for it. The younger ones would do anything to get something to eat."

"You're safe now, Lupe, and if Joaquin has anything to say about it, Randall's place will be shut down for good, and soon." Brydus tried to comfort her.

"Dougie said that you would come. He kept me going. Telling me over and over, don't worry, Mama, Brydus will come for us." Lupe smiled at Dougie, who was enjoying every moment.

Pastor Roberto literally got out of the truck and kissed the ground when they finally reached his place. "Are you alright?" Demi laughed, helping the pastor up.

"That was the most terrifying and exhilarating thing that I have ever done! I don't know whether to laugh or throw up. I won't be able to sleep for a month!" The pastor exclaimed. "Lord, forgive my language, but I thought that Randall would shit in his pants when Brydus rushed in, toting her weapon."

"Are you kidding me, brother? I thought you were going to have a heart attack." Carlos said, laughing at him. "You were quivering so bad the truck was shaking when it wasn't even moving." They all took turns teasing the pastor.

"He won't bother you. I promise you." Joaquin assured the pastor, "I put the fear of Jesse Quintanilla in him."

"Oh, I'm not worried about that. I'll send word to Falu. When he gets back, he'll handle the situation. Randall is afraid of him," the pastor conceded. He walked away, taking in deep breaths, enjoying being home and knowing that things would change because of what they had accomplished.

Carlos turned to Joaquin, "Brother, you have one hell of a woman there, beautiful and dangerous. She can come and rescue me anytime."

"Oh, she's special, alright, in more ways than one." He agreed, winking at Brydus. "And I think it's time for me to go shopping. I have to buy my future wife a wedding ring. Hey, Pastor, would you do me the honor of marrying us tomorrow? I'm not leaving here without making her my wife." Brydus ran into his arms, smiling. Joaquin laughed, slapping her on the hinny. "How can I resist this gun-slinging woman?"

"I love you too," Brydus said, smiling. "But if I am getting married tomorrow, I guess I will need a dress. Come on Lupe, we're going shopping. Dougie, do you mind hanging out with the guys while we are gone?" She knew it wouldn't be a problem for him, as he was in awe of the men.

Joaquin insisted Big Willie go with the women, but Brydus fussed and argued against his terms. She didn't want a bodyguard, knowing she was capable of defending herself. However, he wasn't going to risk their safety. "There is no way that you are going to step out these doors without one of the men. I know that you can take care of yourself, but I don't care. I'm not taking any chances. You either let Big Willie go with you, or you will be getting married naked tomorrow. These are my terms, so what's it going to be."

After seeing the passion in his eyes and hearing it in his voice, she relented. "Alright, you win, baby. Lupe, you don't mind Big Willie tagging along with us, do you?" Lupe was shy. She just shrugged her shoulders.

This was all new to Lupe. She never had the opportunity to go shopping. She always wore other people's hand-me-downs. A wonderful neighbor passed down her daughter's clothes and went around the neighborhood collecting clothes for Dougie. Lupe was hardly allowed outside of the house unless it was to do some work outdoors.

When Dougie was born, her situation became worse. Her stepfather was angry that she got pregnant like it was her fault. Before she married, her mother was a teacher and taught her how to read and write. Lupe was always a little embarrassed about the ratty dresses and shoes she had to wear. She dreamt of having pretty outfits and underclothes like some of the other girls her mother tutored. Never in her life would she have thought of walking into a store to buy a new dress or shoes. They stopped at one of the decorative boutiques that caught Brydus' eye. "Come on, Lupe, we both need a makeover," she grabbed Lupe's hand, pulling her into the charming store. Lupe panicked at first, looking down at the tattered rags she was wearing.

"Welcome, ladies. My name is Cindy, and I'm at your service today. What can we do for you lovely ladies?" Cindy asked, smiling at them.

"Well Cindy, this is my friend Lupe, and she's going to need everything, pretty dresses, and riding clothes, fancy undergarments, oh and shoes to match… can you throw in some perfume and make-up as well, please? Don't worry about the money. I have plenty," Brydus informed the young woman.

Lupe was surprised. "I can't let you do that," she said, blushing.

"I can do whatever I want with my money, Lupe. You are my friend, and you deserve to feel and look pretty, just like every other woman. Cindy, please make sure that she gets everything I've mentioned while I go and look at the gowns." Brydus ended Lupe's objection.

Big Willie nodded at Lupe, who was following Cindy to the dressing room in the back of the boutique. "You did a nice thing for her," he said to Brydus.

"It's what she deserves. I don't want her to want for anything. She's had such an awful life, and I think it's time that her life changes for the better, don't you think?" Brydus said sadly, "Sometimes we forget the sufferings of others. I want her new life to start off with a bang."

"She's really pretty, and that boy of hers is great. All she needs is a little tender love and care." Big Willie smiled.

"Hm, sounds like you may be interested," Brydus teased.

"Maybe… that is if she'll have me," he laughingly admitted.

"What woman in her right mind wouldn't want you, Big Willie? You're the sweetest man in the world."

"You sure know how to make a man blush."

Big Willie had fun following the girls. In one shop and out the other they went. They made him carry most of the packages, which he did happily. When he returned to the hospital, he was exhausted but happy. Lupe and Big Willie hit it off so well that he asked her to be his date for the wedding, and she bashfully agreed.

Demi was the best man, and Lupe was a beautiful maid of honor. Dougie was given the honor of ring bearer. When Joaquin saw Brydus walking down the aisle with Cisco, he smiled, seeing what she was wearing. Brydus found an off-white silk dress that she could use as her wedding dress and a pair of heeled boots that made her shapely legs sexier than ever. She found a small veil and a florist who was more than happy to make her a bouquet.

The wedding was performed in the hospital's cafeteria, but to Brydus, it was a grand ballroom. All she could see was the most handsome man in the world, the man of her dreams. The only people that were missing were her family.

The ceremony was short as the two recited their own wedding vows. Joaquin made everyone misty-eyed as he proclaimed his love for Brydus. She held back her tears, and then he reached out and kissed her. The pastor tried to stop him, but it was to no avail. After Brydus recited her vows, she too gave him a kiss. As the pastor stood by waiting, he jokingly asked them, "Is this the marriage ceremony or the honeymoon?" Everyone was caught in the moment. When Brydus threw her bouquet, the timid Lupe surprisingly fought the other five women for it.

The honeymoon, so to speak, took place in one of the doctor's suites. Their new friends decorated the place and had wine on ice for them to enjoy. Joaquin insisted on carrying Brydus over the threshold. He gently laid her on the bed and nuzzled her neck, sending chills throughout her body.

"Doctor, I'm very hot. What do you prescribe?" Brydus giggled.

"Yes, you are extremely hot," Joaquin agreed, smiling, "I think the only remedy is to give you this very large injection I have. It is guaranteed to cool you down."

She played along, "Oh, Doctor Pleasure, you're my hero." They enjoyed each other, making sure they satisfied one another with unbridled passion. They forgot about the troubles that lingered back home for those precious hours. At that moment, no one else existed outside of their room when they were in the heat of passion. They planned their future and the children they wanted to have. They also made plans to make a trip to see her family. Brydus couldn't wait to show off her husband to her family and the world.

"I love you, Brydus. You make my whole existence complete. I promise that I will spend the rest of my life making you happy."

Chapter 22: The Honeymoon

Lupe gained a little weight in the short time she was with her newfound family. A fondness was forming between her and Big Willie. Dougie clung to Big Willie, following him everywhere he went. He worshipped his friend and enjoyed a freedom that he never had when he lived at home with his grandparents.

Brydus and Joaquin couldn't keep their hands off each other and dreaded the day that they had to leave and return home. Neither one of them brought up the subject of Monet, and neither wanted to intrude on the other's peace of mind.

It was a tearful day when they said goodbye to Pastor Roberto, Carlos, and the rest of the hospital staff. Brydus tried her best to stay positive, especially when she spoke to Lupe, who was afraid of traveling by horse. Big Willie became her protector and wouldn't allow her to fall behind. When they finally reached the area where the roadblock once stood, they were surprised to find that some wandering travelers had cleaned up the abandoned trailers and were now living in them. They made a diner out of the larger one and sold low-cost meals, coffee, soups, and water to weary travelers. Joaquin and Demi were excited about what they saw and gave the new settlers money for supplies to build a welcome center or a place of rest for weary travelers.

Brydus became more anxious the closer they were to the estate, knowing what she was returning to and the fight she had on her hands. When they finally stopped to water the horses and rest, Joaquin took her in his arms. "Baby, I know what you're thinking. I promise I will find a place for Monet as soon as possible and get her out of our home. I love you, baby. I want to make you happy." Brydus smiled, trying to assure him that she was alright, but deep down, she knew that Monet would not be happy and would go kicking and screaming all the way.

When Brydus saw Jenny waiting at the door, she couldn't help but smile at her welcoming face, even at that hour of the night. She didn't recognize the other woman who stood by the door. She was an older woman, very elegant, with striking features, tall and slim. Jenny was so happy to see Brydus that she ran to embrace her.

"I'm so thankful that you're alright, and I'm glad you're finally home."

"I wish that I could say the same, my friend. I'm afraid your face is the only one that brings me joy at this moment. But right now, I'd give anything for a warm bed."

"Perfect, we have prepared a suite for you and your new husband. We have great accommodations for Lupe and Douglas as well." Jenny added cheerfully.

"Who's the lady at the door waving?" Brydus asked curiously.

"Come, I'll introduce you. She is Ms. Alexandra Quintanilla, Joaquin's aunt."

"Oh, and I look a mess," Brydus replied despairingly.

"You look wonderful. Come, she's everything good in the world. You're going to love her," Jenny assured her.

Alex could feel a chill through the thin nightgown she wore, waiting anxiously for her nephews to arrive. Some of Joaquin's men had decided to cut their trip short and return early. They alerted the marriage staff to prepare them for the coming changes. Joaquin and some of his crew stayed behind for his crewmember to recover enough to travel.

Alex was happy everyone was home safely, "Oh my dear, my beautiful girl, let me look at you." Alex said, pulling Brydus close to her. Joaquin and Demi joined the women in the warm kitchen. "My boys, oh how I have missed you! And Joaquin, let me be the first to congratulate you on your marriage! She's stunning. Oh dear, you remind me so much of my mother."

Thank you, Aunt Alex. I'm so glad that you approve. It means the world to me. Let me kiss my tired bride so that she can go to bed. I don't want a grumpy wife in the morning."

"It is such a pleasure meeting you," Brydus added, happy she approved of her. "Please forgive me for not staying up and visiting with you. I'm afraid that I wouldn't be much of a conversationalist," she apologized.

"Oh, my darling girl, I understand. We have plenty of time to get to know each other. You go and rest, sweetheart," Alex kissed her cheek. After Joaquin kissed her goodnight, she disappeared upstairs, with Lupe and Dougie following close behind.

Once all the pleasantries were over, Alex sat her very tired nephews down to discuss the state of the house. "I have never been so happy to see you both safe at home. That woman will be the death of us all." Alex recounted all the events that transpired during their absence. Joaquin had expected trouble from Monet, but not to this extent.

"So now she's pregnant? Who's the father?" Joaquin asked curiously.

"Joaquin, I spoke with the doctor, and he confirmed that Monet is pregnant… and she is naming you as the father," Alex said, verifying what the doctor revealed.

Joaquin was not surprised. "I am not the father. I've always used protection with her. I'm not the only man she has sex with. I can promise you that."

"She claims that one night when you were drunk… you and her…well, as she put it, you both had reckless sex."

"She's lying," Joaquin was steaming as he marched towards Monet's bedroom. She jumped out of bed, surprised when he slammed the door behind him.

"Oh darling, sweetheart, you're finally home," Monet recuperated quickly and tried to throw her arms around Joaquin.

"Get your hands off me! I want you to sit down, shut up, and listen carefully to what I'm about to say," he yelled. The veins in his neck were strained with anger.

Monet pretended to appear shocked. "What is it, darling? Why are you angry with me?"

"Darling my ass, you can drop your act, pretending that you care about me."

"But sweetie…"

He cut her off, "Let me enlighten you. Brydus is my wife," he stated bluntly.

Monet was more dumbfounded that he found her than she was about the marriage. "You're married! How could you marry her, you just met her? I'm having your baby; it's me you should have wed."

"You need to stop spreading lies, telling everyone that I'm the father of your child. You and I both know that's bullshit. I've never had unprotected sex with you, sober or drunk. You have a week to find a place to live," Joaquin roared with rage.

Monet started to cry uncontrollably, "How much cruelty must you inflict on me? I'm pregnant, and still, you treat me like dirt. I thought you would do the right thing. Now our child will be a bastard. Can you live with that?"

Joaquin threw up his hands, "You never cease to amaze me. You're living in a fantasy world. Come back to reality, woman…this is not my child. So, I'd advise you to find the real father or some other chump to blame it on. Oh, and just so you know, there is an ongoing investigation. I'm looking into the crime committed against my wife, and if you are involved, you're going to jail." Joaquin turned around and left her room before Monet could utter a word.

Monet was stunned. Her plan had failed, and her mother was not speaking to her, refusing to make the concoction to flush out the fetus. She paced around her room, wondering what to do next. Her heart was racing with this new revelation, and anger began to overtake the situation she found herself in. Monet felt the walls closing in on her again. She was distraught, taking her pillow and muffling the screams she wanted so badly to vocalize. But was afraid, believing the others would think she was out of control and going crazy. She stood in front of her mirror staring at herself for a long time, wondering about her life, then ripped off her flimsy nightgown, "Why don't you want me…Demi," she murmured. Tears streaming down her face, collapsing to the floor.

The closer it came to the week's deadline, the more desperation consumed her. But Monet vowed not to go down without a fight. She had to think quickly. *That black bitch was not moving her out that easily*, she thought. Monet complained about her morning sickness, becoming helpless, unable to do anything for herself. She found something wrong with every place that Alex took her to see. Monet tried to convince Alex that she did nothing wrong, that her love for Joaquin was real. Crying to her that she had nothing to do with Brydus' kidnapping. Alex didn't want to hear her lies, knowing the kind of woman she was. Monet would cry and whine about everything as Alex continued to ignore her.

Sadly enough, Monet's only faithful friend was Krystal, who became her lackey. Krystal was unhappy that Joaquin married Brydus, leaving Monet to have this baby alone, and felt terrible about her state of mind. She criticized her mother for not doing more to help Monet's situation. "Mother, why is he so mean to her? She's terrified of raising this baby alone, and now he's throwing her into the street. Joaquin wasn't like this until Brydus came. She's putting ideas in his head," she argued.

"Sweetheart, Joaquin wants to do the right thing, get a suitable Monet house, and pay for everything. Krystal, you have to understand the situation between them. You only know her side of the story."

"Well, I can't abandon her now. It seems like I'm the only one who cares what happens to her." Krystal didn't mind doing everything for Monet. She thought it was unfair how everyone was treating her. Joaquin and most of the staff ignored Monet as she stayed pretty much out of sight. Krystal brought her a food tray and arranged it nicely for Monet, who looked extremely pale and sickly.

"Monet, you need to eat something. You look so pale… try the soup," Krystal suggested.

Monet made a face. "It's probably poisoned. Those bitches in the kitchen hate me."

"Well, I don't think that my mother has the heart to poison anyone, and she made the soup," Krystal informed her.

Monet attacked the food as if she hadn't eaten in weeks. When she finished stuffing her face, she ran to the bathroom and threw up.

Krystal knelt next to her, "Listen to me. You can't keep doing that. It's not good for you or the baby," she scolded.

Monet looked at her like she had lost her mind, "Do you really think that I care about this… this thing I have growing inside of me? I feel as if I'm being eaten from the inside out! My breasts hurt, my back hurts, and most of all. It didn't bring Joaquin back to me. All I want is to find a way to get rid of it."

Krystal was shocked, "Monet, that thing is a baby. It is part of you. How can you feel that way, don't you care?" She said almost in tears, and Monet expanded on that weakness, using it to her advantage.

"Krystal, you are my only friend," she conjured fake tears. "Please don't turn on me too. I'm frightened and alone. The man I thought would marry me… ran off and married some unnatural thing and put me out on the street. I don't know what I'm going to do with a baby. This… thing will damage my beautiful body, leave ugly marks all over me, and make it so that no man will ever want me." Monet sobbed on her bed while Krystal sat next to her feeling her pain of abandonment.

"I'm sorry, Monet. I should have looked at things from your point of view. If there is anything I can do, just let me know," Krystal rubbed her back, trying to cheer her up.

Monet grabbed Krystal's hand and placed it against her cheek, "I knew I could count on you. You are my one and only trusted friend. If I ask you to do something for me, even if you think it's crazy, I need to know if I can count on you. It may be a matter of life or death."

"Of course, you know I'd do anything for you," Krystal replied, seeing the desperation on her face.

"Promise me." Monet said in between tears, "Say the words. Say that you promise me."

"I promise, as long as it doesn't get me in trouble," Krystal amended. "I will do my best to help and defend you."

Krystal was concerned about Monet's mental well-being. When she tried to talk to Joaquin about Monet, he refused to listen to her and walked away. Krystal had to find someone she could voice her concerns with, and she knew just whom she could go to. She knocked on his door and waited a few minutes before he answered.

"What is it?" Demi asked, rubbing the sleep from his eyes.

"I have to talk to you. It's very important, please," Krystal found it hard not to look at his muscular chest.

"Sure, come in," he sighed. "What's so important that you found it necessary to wake me?" He asked as he lay back on his bed face down. Krystal sat on the edge of his bed, wanting to touch him. She wanted to feel his strong arms around her and his lips pressed against hers. "Ah, um, I'm concerned about Monet." Demi rolled his eyes and let out a deep sigh as he turned to face her. "Now, before you say anything, please hear me out." She didn't want him to kick her out before she had a chance to say what she wanted.

"What… what can you possibly tell me about that woman that would interest me?"

"Look, I know that Joaquin is your brother, and you have a loyalty to him, but Monet is having his baby. When are people going to understand that?"

Demi sat up on the edge of his bed, watching her curiously. "Why are you so gullible? Why are you the only one who can't see through her evil intentions?" Demi asked, taking her by surprise with his question. Krystal loved Demi so much. She tried to act like a grown-up around him so that he would see her as the woman who had adored him for years.

"I thought you would be a little more understanding. Monet is a helpless woman who is pregnant and hated so much that everyone wants her thrown out into the streets." Krystal was getting upset that Demi wasn't seeing the other side of Monet's situation.

"She is not being thrown out into the street. She is being offered a new place with everything she needs and wants. She's just being the miserable bitch she's always been. Why do you care anyway?" He questioned.

"I care because I know how it feels to love someone who doesn't return that love! It hurts every single day. The pain never stops," Krystal explained.

"Oh… so we're back to this shit again. It's the same old song, isn't it?" he growled.

"I've never stopped loving you, Demi… I can't help feeling the way I do. I will do whatever it takes. Commit whatever sin to be with you. I only wish you would see me as a woman," she said as she knelt at his feet.

Demi felt sorry for Krystal. She was a lovely young woman wasting her life pining after him.

"Krystal, I see you as a woman. You're beautiful and have matured over the last year, but we are blood. First cousins. I don't love you that way. Please try to understand that."

Krystal stood up and began to pace around the room. "I don't care! The heart doesn't know blood; it only knows what it feels. Why can't you see that?" She cried.

Demi started to get heated. "You little shit! Don't tell me about love… I know how it is to love and have it been snatched away from you! Every day I wish that I could rip this pain from my heart. I lost the only woman I will ever love…the one I gave my heart to as a child. If you think that you're the only one suffering, yearning for love, you're sadly mistaken!" Demi said, unable to hold back the tears anymore. "I know how it feels to have her in my arms… kiss her lips and make love to her. At times I wish that I knew where Audrey was buried so that I could be buried alive next to her. I would gladly wait in the ground until death took me just so I could be with her again," Krystal began to shake, crying from being rejected in such a brutal way. She looked at the picture on the night table next to his bed. The picture was taken a week before Audrey disappeared.

"Look at her laughing at both of us. She laughs at you because you can't seem to forget a corpse, and she laughs at me because of our family ties… so either way, she wins. In life, she had you, and even in death, she still has her claws in you."

"Audrey was your half-sister. I don't understand why you hate her so much."

"Ha… you have no idea what it's like living in the shadows of your dead sister. She was prettier, smarter, and everyone loved her more than me,"

"You're so full of shit. You were spoiled rotten. You did whatever you wanted, and your father catered to your every whim. So don't try that bullshit with me, Krystal. The bottom line is this. I still love Audrey, and if I were to be with another woman, Audrey would always be first in my heart. So, I prefer to stay alone because that wouldn't be fair to anyone else."

"I don't mind being second, as long as I can be with you," Krystal said, sitting next to him. "Feel your arms around me and have you kiss me like you used to kiss her." She put his hand against her breast. "Please love me, Demi, or pretend that I'm Audrey and make love to me."

He stood up. "Get the hell out of my room Krystal!" He yelled, pulling away from her. "You could never be my Audrey. Get the hell out of here and find someone who wants you. I am not going to give you what you want. I don't have feelings for you other than that of a family member. You are my cousin. I don't love you that way, and I don't desire you. So, get out of my room!" he opened the door, insisting she left. "And if you are too stupid to see that Monet is a manipulative piece of shit, I wouldn't want you, even if you weren't related to me."

"You don't know what you're missing. Wasting away, longing for a dead woman. When you could get all the love and sex you want from me," Krystal yelled in anger.

"I had the best. If I need to get laid, I know where to get all the meaningless sex that I want. Now go find yourself a nice young man, have a lot of sex and make some babies. Don't darken my door anymore with your nonsense." He slammed the door behind her.

Krystal ran to her room and threw herself on her bed. Crying for a love that she would never have with Demi. She had to share her feelings with the only person who would understand how she felt. Monet was surprised when Krystal came to her bawling about her encounter with Demi. Thinking of the many times, it happened to her. Crying her heart out over Demi. However, Monet always found comfort with Joaquin. He was a strong lover and could always make her forget her heartache. In some delusional way, Monet found joy in knowing that if she couldn't have Demi, no other woman could fill that void in his heart.

"Don't worry, sweetheart. He's not the only man in this sea of studs. You are young and beautiful. Many gorgeous men would love to have a beauty like you in their arms. You have to make Demi jealous, my sweet. The good thing is that you've never been with him sexually," Monet added.

"I wish… but when he was with my sister, I would watch them having sex, and I wished it were me he was holding. I could hear her moaning, and when they came together, she would always call his name. They would do it over and over."

"You watched? Why, you little devil," Monet smiled.

"He would sneak into her room at night. Sometimes I would hide in the connected closet we shared and watch them. He would silence her moans with his lips. I also caught them down by the river once. They went there a lot. I followed and watched as they took off their clothes and jumped in the water. They would have sex on a blanket when they came out," Krystal remembered sadly.

Monet tried to hold back her anger, "Well, that must have been very painful for you to watch," she said, pretending to be sympathetic.

"Painful… it was torture. When Audrey disappeared, I was so happy. Is that terrible?"

Monet touched her face tenderly, "Well, aren't we a pair, crying over these men. Now just what can we do about it?"

"I don't know what to do… I give up," Krystal replied. Monet was smiling on the inside as she watched Krystal weep over Demi's rejection of her. If Krystal only knew that Monet would not hesitate to kill her had she gotten anywhere with Demi.

Alex insisted on a party to celebrate Joaquin and Brydus' marriage. Brydus was trying to stay positive about the living arrangements. She wanted to kick Monet out, but she promised to give Joaquin time to find her a decent place as far away as possible from the estate.

Joaquin and Demi were working like madmen during the day, so Brydus was thankful that Alex was around to keep her mind off Monet. It was the evenings when Brydus could finally rest in Joaquin's arms; those were the times she lived for. No matter how tired he was, he always made her feel special, and his sexual appetite seemed to increase. Brydus always welcomed him with open and loving arms. She felt alive when he held her, and when Joaquin kissed her with such hunger, it took her breath away. Their lovemaking became deeper and more passionate than ever. Joaquin knew exactly where to touch her to make her lose her mind in ecstasy, bringing her to the height of her climax. They lay exhausted in each other's arms, offering tender kisses and words of love until they fell asleep.

In the darkness of her room, Monet plotted her revenge. If she had to leave, she would make it as difficult as possible. She placed her hand on her stomach, cursing the child growing inside her.

Monet tried to convince her mother to help her get rid of the baby again, begging her to help, but Ramon put his foot down, and Lola would not go against his wishes. That morning Monet sealed her disastrous relationship with her family by spitting in Ramon's face as he wrestled to get her out of his home. Ramon threatened her not to come back and disrupt the family, especially Lola, who suffered every time she came with demands. Monet became violent as she picked herself off the ground, throwing rocks at the windows and doors. Her rage was consuming her, and she couldn't control herself. Every little thing bothered her, and as her deceitful plans crumbled around her, she became bitter.

Monet screamed about her unborn child while standing in the mirror, "You will not ruin my body. If I have to cut you out myself, I will have my revenge."

The only bright spot in her life now was how she managed to get Krystal on her side. Without Krystal's help, she may not be able to pull off the treachery she had in mind.

The preparation for the event was more like a grand gala, to say the least. Alex went out of her way to ensure that all the details were to her satisfaction. She took pride in herself for creating the beautiful flower arrangements that adorned the entryway leading into the large living room. Everyone was in place, from the cooks to the waiters.

Brydus insisted that Jenny come as her special guest. Lupe cried when Alex bought her a lovely dress for the occasion, making her feel like a princess.

The lovely music from the trio playing classical music echoed into Brydus' room, from her window, where she could see as the guests arrived. Besides the trio, Alex engaged a band that played various music for dancing and entertainment. The rooms and terraces were transformed into a romantic wonderland, decorated in silver and scarlet. Brydus had not seen Joaquin since earlier that morning. As always, Jenny was there to help her put herself together. She slipped into her short silver sequined dress with spaghetti straps that enhanced her beautiful figure and showed off her shapely legs. Jenny brushed Brydus' hair until it shined, cascading naturally down her back. Then Jenny applied her make-up like a professional artist. When Brydus looked in the full-length mirror, she was amazed.

Joaquin waited nervously for his wife. Most guests had arrived and couldn't wait to meet the new Mrs. Quintanilla. Demi was honored when asked to escort Brydus to the party.

When she saw him in his tuxedo, she almost cried, "Oh my God, Demi, you look so handsome," they laughed.

"Brydus, you look out of this world. My brother is the luckiest sonofabitch on this planet. Take my arm; Joaquin can't wait to present you to everyone as his wife." Brydus held on to Demi as if she would fall off the stilettos she was wearing. When they reached the top of the stairs and saw all the people below, she stopped. "Come on, baby, you're already married. Hold on to me. I won't let you fall."

The musicians played a sweet and soothing version of Here Comes the Bride. She could hear the whispers from some of the guests about how lovely she looked. When she finally saw Joaquin waiting for her on the stage, her heart started to race. She thought he was the most beautiful man in the room, and he was all hers. He looked extraordinary in his tuxedo with a red rose affixed to his lapel. At that moment, everything seemed to be in slow motion as their eyes met. No one else mattered, nor did they care who witnessed their love for each other. When Demi placed her hand in Joaquin's, he couldn't help but kiss her passionately. The guests roared with excitement for the lovely couple as they, too, were caught up in their romance. It was Demi who quieted the guests and bought orders back for the celebration.

"Okay, folks, I think we need to move this along before these two sneaks off. I want to be the first to congratulate my brother on his marriage to one hell of a woman! Joaquin, my brother, I'm truly happy for you speaking from my heart. You deserve all the happiness that this world can offer. I love you, man," he expressed with great emotion and sincerity.

As the night progressed, Brydus forgot about Monet and all the trouble she was bringing upon her new family. Rev. Wilson and the other friends she rescued were invited to the celebration. Brydus wept when they came to congratulate her. She had not even recognized their transformation. Helen and Amy were engaged to wonderful men, and Tenisha introduced Brydus and Joaquin to her boyfriend. She was thrilled to see them finally happy and settled.

While the happy couple celebrated, Monet waited for the right moment to make her presence known among the guests. Monet placed so much pressure and guilt on Krystal that it caused Krystal to change her mind about going to the party. Alex was furious. She refused to even speak to her daughter.

It was after midnight as Monet watched some of the guests leaving. With Krystal's help, she put on a wedding gown and made her way to the top of the stairs to see some of the guests dancing and drinking. "Listen to me, good people," she yelled from the top of the stairs. "This marriage is a sham. I am carrying this man's child, and now he is throwing me out into the streets," Monet spouted for ten minutes, turning different shades of red as she spoke. The guests looked at her, wondering who this crazed woman was, shouting from the top of the stairs. Monet asked Krystal to help her down the stairs. She was without shoes, wearing a dress meant to be worn with high heels.

Demi was outside when he heard the commotion and rushed back into the room just in time to see Monet take a bad tumble down the stairs landing at the bottom. Everyone rushed to her side as they waited for the doctor to assist her. The party was over. She had managed to interrupt the celebration with another of her crazy stunts. With great care, they could move Monet back to her room so that the doctor could examine her thoroughly. Monet suffered two bruised ribs, a fractured leg, and other injuries.

The next afternoon, Demi and Alex waited for her to awaken from her deep slumber. A side effect of the drugs the doctor had given her the night before. Alex pulled open the curtains to let in the sunlight, making her jolt. Monet sheltered her eyes from the sun.

"Wake up! It's time to face the music, my dear." Alex said. Monet could barely move. She was bandaged pretty much all over her body. She looked around to see if Joaquin was with them. "Where is Joaquin?" She asked, disappointed that he wasn't in her room.

"He's with his wife, making love to her. If I know my brother, that's what he's doing," Demi said with much venom in his voice.

Alex moved a chair close to the bed, "You see, my dear, we sent them on a much-needed honeymoon. Far away from here. Demi and I knew you would try something, don't think we didn't know what you were up to. So, we gifted them an exceptional getaway. Jenny and I packed their bags, and they were more than enthusiastic about getting away, especially from you. You really pulled one of the dumbest moves I ever witnessed from you. I'm glad they were gone when you decided to take a leap down the stairs."

They have to come home sometime." Monet murmured at them.

"You tried to kill your baby because you know it's not my nephew's child. How can you be so cruel? Have you any morals."

"You don't know anything about me. People like you, born with privilege, could never understand how it feels to be an outsider. You and your fancy homes and your family traditions… What do you know about hardship? Why should I be ashamed for wanting what you have? So, I tried to abort this thing. Joaquin doesn't want his child, and yes, it is his, so he can deny it all he wants. The truth will come out if I carry it to term." She turned to look away so they could not see the deceit on her face.

Demi wanted to shake her. He was so angry, "We worked hard for our wealth. My brother and I brought this dying estate back to life with back-breaking demanding work. We didn't sit on our asses, treating everyone like shit and expecting people to like us. My family knows hardship, but we don't dwell on our circumstances. Instead, we rise above it."

"This estate was given to you. I knew the stuck-up owner and his family that lived here before you," Monet cried.

"Like I said, this land had fallen into ruins. We worked the land and this estate with our hands to make it what it is now," Demi knelt down closer to her. "Listen to me, Monet; I know you are hell-bent on making my brother miserable. But they love each other deeply. So deeply that even your scheme to have Brydus kidnapped couldn't keep them apart...so give up, you're not going to win." She turned away from him once again. "I know that it was you behind it, and Joaquin knows. Monet, you're not that important. Trust me; you'll get what you deserve... people like you always do."

"You can't prove anything. I'm innocent. You just want me to look bad in Joaquin's eyes, blaming me for her stupidity. Silly woman, she got herself kidnapped just to get Joaquin to feel sorry for her. So, I say, prove it if you can," Monet replied, smiling.

"Just knowing that your scheme failed gives me a lot of satisfaction. Just like my relationship with my Audrey, their love and marriage are meant to be," Demi said, knowing that it bothered her whenever he mentioned Audrey's name.

"And unfortunately, my dear," Alex interjected, "as hard as you tried to abort that baby, by the time your ribs heal enough for you to get up and move around, it will be too late for you to have an abortion. So go ahead and try to move if you can. I'm sure that the pain will keep you in bed for a while. I'm also sure that Joaquin with deal with your stupidity when he returns."

"You know what, Aunt Alex, I'm in charge," Demi said, turning to Monet, "so from now on. all of your meals will have to be bought to your room. You won't be able to move much. And guess who will be caring for you? Mrs. Grayson has volunteered to assist you. The nurse will be in to see you every morning to help with the medication and monitor the baby's progress."

"Mrs. Grayson hates me! Get me someone else; I don't want her near me," Monet protested.

"Sorry, no one else would take the job, so you're stuck with her," Demi smiled wickedly.

"Well, we'll see about that," Monet bit her lip. "Won't we? When Joaquin returns, I demand to see him right away. He'll find me a more suitable person."

Alex straightened out the covers on her bed and tried to make her comfortable. "I'm truly sorry, my dear, but Joaquin will be very busy with his new wife. I think they're trying for a baby or at least having a lot of fun practicing. Now you just relax here in this room. We'll send in the doctor so that he can give you something for the pain. I believe the medication he gave you last night should be wearing off soon. I'll send in Mrs. Grayson to assist you."

Monet was furious. She wanted to pick up something to throw at them, but she couldn't move. "I hate you all! Just you wait!" she yelled as they closed the door behind them.

Alex looked at Demi and sighed, "I wish it were that easy… just shut the door, and the problem will be solved," Alex said sadly, praying for her beloved nephew and the love of his life, who desperately wanted peace in their home.

"She's like the plague, destroying everything in her path," Demi said, "I will make it my mission to keep her from hurting my family again."

"You are so right. All we can do is run interference until she is ready to be moved. I will continue to look for a suitable place for her to move into as soon as the doctor gives the order."

"Thanks for all your help. The party was wonderful, and thank God they were already gone when she decided to dive down the stairs." Demi hugged his aunt, "I love having you around."

"I'm glad to be here. It feels good to be needed. Krystal is all grown up now, and all we do is fight. What can I say?" Alex sighed.

Demi stopped his aunt. He had something on his mind for some time but was afraid to ask her. "Aunt Alex… there is something I have been meaning to ask you, but I'm not sure if you know the answer. Do you have any idea what happened between Monet and my mother during her last visit?"

"Oh dear," Alex touched his face tenderly, "let me order some tea. How about if we sit outside? I love the view from the living room patio." Demi followed his aunt, really dreading the answer to his question. Alex sipped her tea and took a deep breath. "Your mother tried very hard to like Monet. Jewel wanted so badly to find something good about her. However, the harder she tried, the more disgusted she became. Nylaya also noticed certain things but kept quiet. She took it all in stride. You know how your grandmother feels about you boys. Nylaya wanted Joaquin to be happy, and if Monet made him happy, who was she to stand in the way, or so she thought.

However, with her keen senses, your mother knew that pretty, angelic-looking woman was far from what she appeared to be. She caught her looking at you with lustful eyes… at first, she thought maybe it was just her imagination. But she found out soon enough that it wasn't. So, tell me, honey, has Monet ever made a pass at you, or you toward her?"

Demi turned his face away from Alex. She could always read his facial expressions and his body language. "She would flirt with me, you know, harmless flirtation at first. I went to the Inner Cities for help with my depression. When I returned a few months later, she had positioned herself in the house. Monet changed from a sweet and kind woman to this monster in that short time. There were times when she touched me in a certain manner that I thought was odd, but then I thought that she was just being friendly in her own way. I didn't think much of it, but one night, when Joaquin was away, she tried something. She came to my room, telling me that she was afraid of the thunder. However, she intended to seduce me… she made me want to puke. I was so disgusted and repulsed I threw her out of my room. She tried on many occasions to throw herself at me."

"Have you ever mentioned this to Joaquin?"

"No, Auntie, I wanted to, but when I asked him how he felt about her, he said she was allowed to move in because she came bawling her eyes out one night. She told Joaquin that she had a huge fight with her mother and stepfather. Supposedly they threw her out, and she had nowhere to go. It was only supposed to be for a few weeks. He said that she sees other men and that things were never that serious. So, I just let it go."

"Well, your mother saw how dreamy her eyes became for you, which set it off. You know your mother. She doesn't hold anything back. She cried bitterly to your father, but she wouldn't say anything to Joaquin. Knowing that he was already upset about them leaving early."

"Apparently, Jewel knew Monet's mother from before and heard that she was into the dark arts, which made your mother very uncomfortable. Just the thought that she might try to put some kind of mojo on her son made her uneasy. Anyway, I spoke to her and let her know that Lola would never do anything to harm Joaquin. She really likes him."

Alex smiled, witnessing the joy on his face when he saw his wife coming down the stairs. "Now my Joaquin is happily married to a wonderful woman, and they're on their way to Africa for a month. I'm pretty sure that your mother, and the rest of the family, will love Brydus."

"Yeah, I wish that I could be there to see the surprised look on the family's faces when they finally meet Brydus. They love each other, and they will be happy for them."

Alex noticed the sadness in Demi's eyes. She reached out and held his hand. "I miss her too, son," she touched his face. His eyes misted as always when he thought of Audrey.

"Sometimes I can feel her so close to me, and I pray that she is still out there and that someday she will find her way back to me. I will always love her… always."

"I know… that's another reason I had to get away. The house is too big, and I sometimes catch myself staring at the door. Wishing that she would rush through it, telling me she was sorry for being away so long. But then the hours pass and that door never opens… I try to push back the depression that follows those moments. The pain never stops when you lose a child. I will forever blame Kyle for chasing her away, that bastard."

"I guess she'll always stay alive in our hearts," Demi said, trying to comfort his aunt and himself.

Alex kissed Demi's cheek, "It hurts me to see you in so much pain. A love like the one you two shared comes but once in a lifetime."

"Yeah…I knew it from the beginning,"

"I met someone myself… God, how he takes my breath away. Me, after all these years and heartaches. I finally found someone. He treats me the way that I deserve to be treated, and truth be told, it scares the hell out of me."

"Oh really, is that what the glow on your face is all about? So, I guess what they say is true, it's never too late for true love, but it will take me a very long time before I can move on."

"Take your time, son. When you find that special person, your heart will tell you. But right now, we will have to double team Monet. She is not going to be easy to deal with."

"Hey, we make one hell of a team."

"We sure do, sweetheart... we sure do."

Chapter 23: Back to Reality

Alex and Demi met the happy couple at the docks when they returned. Alex felt guilty looking at the newlyweds, so refreshed and extremely happy. Demi rented some rooms for the day, planning on staying at the hotel for the night to start their journey home early the next morning. Once they were both settled in their room, Alex had the unfortunate task of informing them about Monet. Brydus was so upset she locked herself in the bathroom.

"I'm sorry, son, we didn't want you to get home and find her still there without telling you first."

"So, when can she be moved?" Joaquin asked, concerned for his wife.

"The doctor said maybe in a month or so, he's afraid that she will lose the baby if we rush her. The injuries were far worse than the doctor anticipated."

"I need her out! I can't have her living with us any longer. I think Brydus has been more than patient. Don't you think?"

"I hear you, bro. We have Monet confined to her room with Mrs. Grayson attending to her."

"Oh, I'm sure she's thrilled about that."

"Very, but… oh well, she did this to herself."

When Brydus finally came out of the bathroom, everyone waited for her reaction. Joaquin went to her. "I'm alright. I just needed to think for a minute… and I've decided that she wasn't going to ruin my happiness. I love you, baby," she said, trying to understand their predicament with Monet.

Joaquin held her for a long time, "As soon as the doctor says she can be moved, I promise, she's gone," Joaquin tried to kiss away her tears. Let's enjoy this evening and take things one day at a time. Why don't we all meet for dinner?"

"By all means. You two freshen up, and we'll see you later," Alex replied, feeling terrible about the whole situation.

Brydus tried to enjoy herself and convince Joaquin that she was alright, but she was burning up with anger inside. All she truly wanted to focus on was her life with her husband. She tried to stay positive, remembering that they had just returned from a magnificent honeymoon. *It was more like a dream,* she thought. Brydus couldn't wait to send word home to her family and tell them they were now related to a famous woman they all knew. And inform them that the one and only president of the Inner Cities and Eastern Region was now a relative.

Ceuta Village Africa

Brydus and Joaquin were treated like royalty in Africa. When her mother-in-law laid eyes on her, she cried tears of joy and relief. When Jewel first received the news that her son had gotten married abruptly, she shook in her shoes. She thought to herself that Monet must have gotten pregnant, and knowing her son, she figured that he did the right thing and married her. It was the worst possible scenario she could imagine. Right away, she had an anxiety attack.

Nylaya was concerned about her daughter. She was always so open-minded about everything and everyone. Jewel was a very compassionate person. That was why she decided to leave her home in New America and move to Africa with her husband, a great humanitarian. They joined her parents, who were helping communities of children living without adult supervision. The four of them took doctors, teachers, and everyone they could find to join them in this endeavor. It turned out to be a huge success. Jewel and Nylaya were comfortable leaving their boys behind, attending to the estate. The now young men were old enough to make their own decisions, and they were so proud of what Joaquin and Demi had accomplished.

Now Jewel stood on the dock waiting to eat her words. She promised herself and the others that she would try her best to welcome Monet into the family. The whole family held their breath as they watched passengers walk off the ramp. The first person they saw was Joaquin waving at them, pulling a very beautiful dark-haired woman behind him. Before they reached the bottom of the ramp, Jewel had to get a closer look, meeting them halfway. She embraced Brydus, clinging to her, not wanting to let go.

"See, I told you that my mother would love you, and you were worried," Joaquin said, reassuring Brydus, "mother, let me introduce you to my wife, Brydus."

Jewel hugged her again, just as intensely as before, "Thank you for marrying my son," she cried.

The rest of the family was astonished. They did not expect such a marvelous surprise. Nylaya looked at her husband and smiled. "I know her family. What a perfect match." Nylaya held Brydus in a strong embrace. "When I left, you were just a young girl, and look at you now, a beautiful woman and a Quintanilla," she exclaimed cheerfully. "We must celebrate this wonderful union."

When they arrived at their home, they were greeted by the staff. The small, dilapidated community had changed. It grew from just dirt floors and broken-down shacks to beautiful, picturesque homes with paved streets. There was a hospital, school, library, and a few cute shops. The community had taken a huge turn for the better, transforming into a self-sufficient prospering village.

Quintanilla Estate

Brydus had a bad feeling as she entered her own home. The staff was excited to welcome the couple back from their well-deserved honeymoon. But she couldn't stop thinking about Monet's presence in and around her home. No one mentioned the woman upstairs or all the trouble she was causing. They didn't want to spoil the moment. Brydus was quiet when she retired to her room. It was a long trip from the docks back to the estate. All along, Brydus knew that she would have to confront Monet and let her know that her little show the night of the reception did not affect her marriage.

The following morning, when Joaquin went to his office to sort through the mountain of mail and work he had on his desk. Brydus dressed sharply and walked towards the room where Monet was sleeping. She opened the door and pulled open the drapes letting in the sunlight.

"What the hell," Monet whined. When she saw who it was, she turned up her nose, "Oh, it's you."

"Yeah, bitch, it's me, Mrs. Joaquin Quintanilla, catchy name, hm?"

"What do you want?" Monet said, pulling the blanket up to her chin.

"Oh, I just came to chat… I think we are about due for a little tête-à-tête. You know, I just want to make this loud and clear." Her intense stare scared the helpless Monet, "A week after you have this baby, I will kick your ass."

"Are you threatening me?" Monet yelled to see if anyone would come to her rescue.

"Oh, honey, it's not a threat. It's a promise! Your ass is mine, and no one is going to save you from this beatdown."

"You don't scare me. Besides, Joaquin won't let you hurt me."

"Who do you think suggested the ass whipping?"

Monet went pale, "You're lying! He would never…"

"Ask him. It's either that or going to jail. I know that you paid Gino to kidnap me. You see, we became really good friends during our long trip to New Orleans."

Monet turned her face away, "You know nothing," looking anxiously at the door to see if anyone would come to her aid. Krystal walked in with a tray of food for Monet. She looked at Brydus, who stood near Monet with anger locked in her eyes.

"Is everything okay here?" Krystal stared nervously at Brydus, who towered over Monet.

"Peachy… everything's peachy," Brydus leaned toward Monet. "You know, I had a long conversation with my new mother-in-law, and she told me something very intriguing about the reason…she had to leave when she came to visit. I wonder if your friend here would be bringing you breakfast in bed if she knew the truth." Monet couldn't look at Brydus. "Watch yourself; months can seem like years when you are all alone and have no one to speak to."

"I don't think you should be in here, Brydus. You're upsetting Monet," Krystal said, putting the tray down on the table.

"It's Mrs. Quintanilla to you. Do you understand me? This is my house! And you're just a visitor. If I were you, I would pick a better-quality friend? But I guess you can't see that far since your nose is so far up her ass," Brydus slammed the door behind her, wishing she were a fly on the wall to hear what kind of lies Monet was drumming up to tell Krystal.

"You have to talk to Joaquin for me. He won't listen to me, but you can corner him. You see what I have to deal with… she will kill me in this bed, and no one cares." Monet's tears were sincere. She needed Krystal, and she truly believed that Krystal cared for her. If she found out about Monet's feelings for Demi, she knew that it would be the end of her, and her life would be even worse than it was now.

"Alright, I will speak to him, but first, you need to eat something. Mother made this for you. The doctor wants you to gain some weight. He said that when you deliver the baby, you could lose blood, and that will compromise your health,"

The salad looked really tempting, now that she missed breakfast. "I promise, I will eat every bite," Monet said as Krystal helped her find a comfortable position.

"I will go and see if I can find my cousin. Now eat. I'll be back to help you change and comb your pretty hair."

"Krystal, try to convince him to come and see me. It would make me so happy."

"I'll try. I'll be back in a few minutes."

Joaquin was in the middle of a meeting with Cisco when Krystal knocked on the door. She smiled when she opened and peeked in. "May I come in?"

"I'll get those numbers to you, boss. It shouldn't take long," Cisco closed the door behind him as he left.

"So, what's going on, cousin? I have a lot of work to do."

"Yeah, I know… ah, I'm sorry to take up your time… I know that she's not your favorite person right now, but… I really need to mention that I caught Brydus threatening Monet."

Joaquin stopped what he was doing, "You know, I've had a change of heart about you. You have matured. Even though your loyalty is misguided. You are a true friend, as far as Brydus hurting Monet is concerned… I know that my wife wouldn't hurt a bedridden woman."

"Well, I'm only telling you what she said; I'm just the messenger. I also want to inform you that Monet is not eating because she thinks everyone is out to poison her. Now I know it's just her imagination and mental state right now, but still, if you could speak to Monet and let her know that not everyone is trying to kill her, it may help. The doctor says that not eating is starting to jeopardize her health and the baby."

"Alright, I'll see her briefly, but she better not be expecting much from me," Joaquin said, not really wanting another confrontation with her.

"Thank you, cousin, you're a good person. Well, I'll let you go. I know you're busy." Krystal smiled as she left Joaquin's office. She never thought that Joaquin would see her as a mature woman. Now, if only Demi would, it would make her happy.

Brydus tried not to become bitter, but the longer Monet was under her roof, the angrier she became. The arguments started gradually and escalated more and more to the point that Brydus would break down into tears. Joaquin worked long hours and tried his best to comfort and understand his wife and how she was feeling. But the more he tried to assure her that Monet would soon be out of their home, the more Brydus would shut down.

She took to riding early in the morning. Sometimes gone for hours, and it drove Joaquin crazy. She would visit her friends and come home late at times, missing dinner.

Demi saw the friction between them and wanted so much to fix what was driving them apart. "How many damn times did I tell her not to ride alone? Damnit, Demi, if something happens to her…" he said, frustrated.

"Look, I understand her anger. I'll ride with her in the morning. Maybe I can get to the bottom of what's bothering her."

"I can't ask you to do that. You have your own work to do," he threw a pencil across the room, breaking it against the wall, "I love her so much, and I can't stand to look in her eyes and see all the pain."

"Joaquin, I will make time for her… Brydus is my sister now, and I know that bitch Monet has a way of making people crazy."

"I have a conference in two weeks. Uncle Jesse is counting on me to get things wrapped up."

"You were there for me when I needed you. Let me do the same for you," Demi tried to explain. "Brydus is crazy about you. But she's a proud woman. Right now, she has this… this thing in her house that she can't get rid of. The important thing to remember is that Monet won't stay pregnant forever. The bitch has to pop sometime, right?" Demi chuckled.

Joaquin laughed, "I guess you're right. I just wish I could move her ass out of here so that my baby can feel like she's the woman of the house. You know what I mean?"

"Yeah, I understand. Tomorrow I will be at the stables when Brydus gets there, and we will take a ride together and get to the bottom of things."

"Thanks. I've planned a romantic dinner tonight to see if I can pull her out of this funk. I want her to be present, you know, at the moment when we make love."

Early the next morning, Brydus woke up and attacked Joaquin in bed. He was happy to see that she was still eager for him. He always enjoyed an early lovemaking session to start the day. After they showered together, they set a time to meet for lunch. Brydus headed for the stables, where she found Demi waiting on his horse and grinning at her.

"So, where are you going this early in the morning?" Brydus was happy to see him.

"I thought that we could enjoy the warm morning's sun. It's going to be getting cold soon. So where are we going?"

"Just riding, nowhere in particular, sometimes I just need to get away… before I burst."

"Oh… I hear you." They followed the small trails that led through the back of the estate. Not even a mile away. Demi tried to lighten her mood by making jokes and talking about some of his drunken escapades. When they turned near a small patch of trees, they came upon a breathtaking colonial-style house.

"Who lives there?' She pointed to the house with beautiful and mature Weeping Willows and Sycamore trees surrounding it and a small pond on the side.

"It's my house," Demi replied. "I built it for Audrey and me."

Brydus was instantly sorrowful. She knew he still loved Audrey, "It's absolutely beautiful," Brydus added.

"Hey, do you want to go in? Come on, I'll show you around."

"Oh, I couldn't do that. I don't want to stir up any painful memories for you."

"We never lived in it… so there are no memories floating around. Come on, it will be fun. I haven't been in it since it was finished." Demi ushered her up the stairs onto the front porch. When he opened the door, it was warm and inviting. Brydus felt as if she were back in her family's home. The house was cozy and peaceful. It was fully furnished, with curtains on the windows and pictures on the walls.

"I love it… I could see myself living here, cooking and cleaning," she became disheartened.

"Brydus, what's wrong? Why are you so unhappy all of a sudden?" She started to cry, "Come on, honey; don't cry. Talk to me. You know you can tell me anything."

"Demi, you're going to think I'm stupid. I'm married to the most wonderful man in the world. But when I enter those doors, I feel like I don't belong… I feel like I'm a guest in my own home."

"Who makes you feel like that? Is somebody upsetting you intentionally or what?"

"Demi, how would you feel if your wife had her ex-lover living under the same roof with you? Would you like that? And to make things worse, this woman could be pregnant from Joaquin?"

He tried not to smile, "That wouldn't be happening, not in my house. I mean… I couldn't do it… I'd kill him."

"So now you know how I feel, and it's getting worse since we came back from our honeymoon… I feel like going into Monet's room and beating the shit out of her."

"You know this is killing Joaquin too, don't you?"

"Yeah, I know. I love him so much, but sometimes I have this darkness that falls on me, and I just want to lash out. He just happens to be the one who is closest to me."

"What can I do, Brydus?" Demi asked sincerely. "What will give you peace of mind until she can be moved out of your house and your life?"

Brydus looked around the living room. "Rent me your house, if you can bear it. It will be just him and me. At least I'll know that I am in charge here."

He hated to see Brydus so upset, "Say no more. It's yours, whatever it takes. Brydus, I just want to see that smile back on your pretty face."

"Thanks for caring about me, Demi. Had I known that we would be so close when I first met you, I would have been nicer to you."

He laughed at her. "I think it was great. The only thing that I would change is the kick in the nuts, but other than that. I laugh every time I think about it."

"I'm so sorry, Demi," Brydus said as they laughed together.

Joaquin was not happy. When she proposed to move into the other house, he was infuriated, "This is our house, dammit! How is it going to look if my wife is living somewhere else? Tell me, just how do you think that will look?"

"I don't feel like this is my home. At least not as long as Monet is still living here! I can't stand it anymore, Joaquin. I feel like the biggest fool in the world."

"I have to leave in a few days, Brydus. How am I supposed to concentrate knowing that you are somewhere else, instead of here under the protection of my people, in this house?"

"I can take care of myself, Joaquin…" he interrupted her.

"I don't care. You are my wife! If you leave, Monet wins, can't you see that?" Brydus had never seen Joaquin so angry.

"If I don't leave, she will still win because there won't be an us anymore."

The veins on the side of Joaquin's neck were pulsing with anger, "What does that mean?"

"I'm going home," Brydus answered in tears.

"You're not going anywhere! Remember who wears the damn pants around here! You are mine. Mine, do you understand me?" He left her sitting alone, crying on the patio. Demi watched the exchange from his window. He wanted to jump in the middle and fix things between them.

Krystal smiled as she walked by, listening to the argument. Everyone knew that the young couple's arguments were over Monet and the unborn baby.

"I see trouble in paradise," Krystal snickered, passing Demi in the hallway.

"Watch yourself, Krystal, or you'll find yourself walking back home with my footprint on your ass."

Demi tracked his brother down in the foremen's quarters, giving his men instructions. "Joaquin, what's going on?"

"I'm not in the mood, bro. She's killing me!"

Demi blocked his pathway, "You're going to listen to me… I know you're the older brother, but you'll listen to me if you don't want to lose your wife." Joaquin sighed deeply,

irritated with the whole situation. "She's hurting Joaquin…
you have your ex-mistress who says she is pregnant with
your baby and a brand-new wife living under the same roof.
This woman tried to kill Brydus, and she's supposed to turn
the other cheek? If it was her lover, like she put it to me, turn
the tables around and see how it feels."

"She is my wife. This is her home. How is it going to
look if she moves out? I feel like I'm losing my mind,
Demi."

"Who gives a shit how it looks. To hell with what people
say or think about it… please Joaquin, give it a chance? I
promise you. I will be there. If I have to sleep on the front
porch every night, I will. You do whatever you want,
Joaquin, but do what you can to save your marriage and to
hell with everything else."

"I don't want to argue anymore, Demi. I'm sick of it. I
just want to get back to how we were before we came home
and found Monet confined to a bed."

"Just think about it. The house is close by; it would solve
this problem until we can get that beast moved."

That night, when Joaquin went to his room, Brydus was
already in bed. She had cried herself to sleep. When he tried
to touch her, she turned away from him. He forced her to
face him, laying on top of her as she wiggled beneath him.
The smell of liquor was on his breath. Joaquin kissed her

vigorously, pinning her wrists above her head. Brydus tried to no avail to move him, but he was like dead weight on her. He made love to her forcefully without the usual tenderness that she was used to. Joaquin pulled Brydus toward him when he finished, holding her in a locked embrace."

"You belong to me… all of you, don't ever forget that." He whispered in her ear before he fell asleep. Tears dripped from her eyes. Brydus loved him so much but wished that he understood her agony. For the next few days, she avoided him, but he was not taking no for an answer at night. Joaquin was leaving the next day and didn't want to leave their situation unresolved.

"Brydus, we need to talk…" she didn't answer him, "You won. I can't live like this anymore. Whenever I want to make love, I have to fight with you just to touch you. I want peace in my house and in my bed."

It was Brydus' turn to feel guilty, "This was not meant to be a war. Please, let's just forget the whole thing."

"No, if you are not happy here…then we'll go someplace where you will be. I love you, Sweetcheeks. Do you think I want to see you so damn miserable, day in and day out?"

She put her arms around his neck. "I have never loved anyone as much as I love you, Joaquin. I'm sorry I've been such a bitch… please don't hate me," he pulled her tightly in his arms and kissed her fiercely.

"How can I hate you when you breathe life into me each day?" Brydus crawled into his lap and began to unbutton his shirt. It didn't take much encouragement for him to throw her on the bed and finish taking off his clothes. They made wild, passionate love to each other, remembering what made them so eager to be together. Joaquin and Brydus spent the whole day in bed, satisfying each other's lust, committing themselves once again to each other and their future together.

Chapter 24: Everyone Has a Story

It took Brydus no time to move into the four-bedroom colonial house with huge trees already displaying autumn's beautiful colors. The house and area made her feel as if she was home, back in the Valley of God. Even though Joaquin wasn't happy about staying in the small house, he would do whatever it took to keep Brydus happy. But his decision did not come without strings attached. A guard would pass by often to check on her, and Jenny agreed to stay with Brydus during the week. Alex volunteered to keep her company during the weekend when Jenny went home.

Brydus enjoyed Alex's company immensely. She always had some great stories about Joaquin and Demi when they were young. Brydus could only imagine what it was like having those two running around as crazy kids. She needed someone she could talk to, someone with wisdom, with life experience that could offer her advice.

The weather was still warm during the day, but at night it cooled down as the days were getting shorter. It was certain that winter was coming. The birds left their homes for the warm southern weather, leaving stillness and silence in the air.

Alex and Brydus loved taking long walks together. She needed to get her mind off the woman making her life miserable. Alex knew so much about the area's history, which was fascinating to Brydus.

"Did you know that Demi built this place for Audrey?" Alex asked as they sat outside on the porch, enjoying the morning sunshine. "He designed and drew the plans for this house all by himself. I remember when he first showed it to Audrey. Lord, I remember how she came running to me with this huge smile. Look, Mama, she said, this is the house that Demi and I plan to live in when we get married. She was so happy. Those two lived for each other."

"What happened to her? I mean, she must have been a wonderful person to steal his heart. That is if it's not too painful for you to talk about. Demi can't talk about Audrey without getting emotional, and I hate to see him that way."

"Oh, my dear, you must understand the bond between those two to better understand the intensity of their young love," Alex explained. "I used to say they were born for each other, just like I know that you and Joaquin are meant to be together.

Audrey was such a happy baby and child. She lit up the room wherever she went. Audrey wasn't my biological daughter, and Nylaya isn't my biological mother. My mother died in a bombing along with my older brother when I was ten months old. My father married Nylaya when I was about two years old. She is the only mother I've ever known. I was such a needy child, I clung to her, and she never let me go. Mother was pregnant with my brother Jesse before they were married, and when he was born, I promised myself that I would be the best sister in the world.

Before the Dark Days, my parents moved us to a farm up in the mountains. My father's aunt had a beautiful farm. However, she was getting too old to manage anymore. I loved my Auntie Ziza. She was sweet and loving. We would spend our summers as children on her farm. Jesse and I couldn't wait until we came around that bend on that old winding road to see Auntie Ziza's fruit and vegetable stand. We were ready to get into trouble," Alex laughed.

"When Ziza died, father inherited the farm. My parents put a lot of money into it, upgrading everything. They fenced in the whole farm and putting up that six-foot fence around the property took a lot.

I was already married before we all moved to the farm. Jesse was married to Renee. My sister Jewel and Ramiro married early, right out of high school.

Mother urged us to come to the farm because trouble was coming, and she was worried. However, my husband Kyle refused to come right away. He said that Mother just wanted to control us. But she was only concerned about us being caught in the middle of everything."

Brydus was curious, "What kind of trouble? How did she know a threat was coming?"

"I don't really know. She just had a way of sensing when danger was near. Kyle never liked taking advice from my parents, especially Nylaya, who was brutally honest regarding her children's safety. Kyle was afraid of her, and when she ordered him to bring me to the farm, he refused. When the shit hit the fan, he had no clue what to do. We didn't know what was going on. People were dying all around us. It was horrible, just horrible. We hid in an abandoned warehouse with two other couples, terrified of what was happening outside.

My family was very uneasy about Kyle's decision to wait it out. So, my father and brother, with a few friends, made plans, risking their lives to find us. In the middle of all that chaos, they had to set out to rescue us from the madness. I was never so scared in my life," Alex continued. "Everyone was going crazy. People were hijacking cars, trucks, or anything they could find in a feeble attempt to escape. We barely made it out of New York alive. When I saw Father with weapons, it took me to another place. We had to shoot our way out of New York City. Oh my God, when I think back, I knew then that my mother's prayers were following us.

We all gathered together at the farm to try to stay alive. My parents made all the preparations at my mother's insistence. We had everything we needed; food, water, and animals…each of us had our own space. The farm was huge, with ample space for everyone.

We also brought along Tim Berry, a dear friend, and household employee; Angela Melendez was a lifesaver to us. Angela had a very pretty teenage daughter named Maria. Maria was a little slow or simple-minded, as some might say, but still very beautiful. Her mother had complications during the delivery, and Maria was deprived of oxygen for too long. But she was the sweetest person in the world. After a few years, Angela started dating a man from one of the neighboring farms, and they married as well. He was from El Salvador and wanted to return Angela and Maria to his homeland. The problem was that Angela was afraid Maria could not make the trip. It was just too dangerous at that time. Mother promised that we would take care of Maria. We were her family. Even years after the Dark Days, things were still not stable, and the world was still in turmoil.

"Did you have children?"

"No. Not that we weren't trying. I was in my mid-thirties with no children. I knew that Kyle wanted children badly. It made him angry every time I got my monthly. He felt like a failure and started to change toward me, and the family was not happy.

"When Maria became pregnant, we had no idea she was having sex. We visited a few farmers in the area from time to time. So, we assumed it was one of the young men since she never said anything. Maria was such a beautiful girl, with auburn hair, a beautiful face, and a killer smile. She was so innocent…but she was still family to us.

Maria didn't understand what was going on with her body. The poor girl would just stay in her room and cry. I tried to explain to her that she would be a mother, but she just looked at me with a blank, innocent expression on her face.

"I went looking for Maria one afternoon to give her some baby clothes that our neighbor dropped off when I heard her crying in the barn. Kyle had the poor girl pinned against the wall trying to pull up her skirt… I can still remember that poor girl crying. That's when I found out that Kyle had raped Maria and fathered her baby."

Brydus' eyes grew in shock, "Oh my God, what did you do?"

"I nearly lost my mind," Alex replied. "She could never really tell us how long it had been going on or how many times he had forced himself on her."

"So, she didn't even know she was having a baby?"

"Hard to tell. She never said a word about it. My family was furious. My brother beat Kyle within an inch of his life. It was terrible for me as well, because… I thought, looking back, that I still loved him. I was so heartbroken. Kyle took off for a while and then returned, begging my family and me to forgive him. He blamed it on depression. Which I'm sure was a bullshit excuse, but like a fool, I took him back. I was afraid of being alone and confused about the whole thing. This young woman, who couldn't even put a sentence together, was pregnant because of my husband. It was my turn to sink into depression. Kyle and I argued all the time. Mother tried her best to soothe my pain. I begged my mother to send that poor girl away. I didn't think I could stand looking at my husband's love child. But Maria had the mind of a child. It took me a while, but I finally realized that I couldn't blame her for what happened. She was a victim."

Brydus listened as Alex continued. "When Maria went into labor, she didn't know what was happening. She screamed and screamed for hours, and when the baby finally came, Maria looked at the baby as if she was an alien, confused. She wanted nothing to do with her beautiful baby girl. Brydus, I was so scared, but when my mother put her into my arms, I couldn't help myself. I named the baby Audrey, and without trying, I fell in love with her. I put her against my chest, listening to her tiny heartbeat. My heart swelled up with love. I was her Mama, and she was my daughter. Maria ran away as soon as she was able. We felt so bad because we promised her mother we would take care of her. We found out years later that she was living with a really nice family just a few miles away.

"Little Demi would stand next to her bassinet, just staring at her. He would play with her hands. When can she come out and play? He would ask. Demi insisted on letting him feed her. I had to let him hold her, or he would nag me for hours. If little Audrey was sick, Demi wouldn't leave her side. One day when she was eighteen months old, Audrey had this terrible cold. The poor thing was miserable. The next morning when we looked for Demi, we couldn't find him. We looked everywhere. Joaquin found him in her crib. He was holding her. That sweet image will stay in my heart forever. As we watched them holding each other. We realized he was protecting Audrey and willing her to get better."

"Demi couldn't wait until Audrey woke up in the morning. He would feed her and talk to her as if she could understand him. Audrey stole the hearts of everyone who came in contact with her.

Demi taught her how to walk and ride a bike, and he was the one that helped her with schoolwork. She followed him everywhere, but he didn't mind. They played together, and sometimes we would find her in bed with him. He would read her stories, and they would fall asleep together, holding each other's hands. Demi also taught her how to ride a horse. Those two grew up as one, right before our eyes.

Audrey was such a great baby and child," Alex sighed, saying. "She was such a joy to be around, and she had a heart of gold, always wanting to help. She was only five when I got pregnant with Krystal. My God," Alex shook her head. "From the beginning, Krystal was the most demanding child I had ever seen. Kyle spoiled her rotten, and she could do no wrong in his eyes. She made Audrey's life miserable. Krystal always cried and blamed poor Audrey for her discomfort, and Kyle always took her side. By this time, my brother Jesse and his wife Renee had moved back to New York. He was a brilliant young man for his age, a visionary. It was Jesse who began to organize others to start rebuilding the Inner Cities, aka New York City.

We moved away when Audrey was about ten. Kyle wanted to get away from my family, and now that we had two little girls, we were our own family, so he figured the time was right. Things were beginning to settle down in the world, and after much discussion and so many tears, we left the protection of the farm. Audrey was inconsolable. No matter what we did, she couldn't get Demi out of her thoughts. Every summer, we'd let the girls go back to the farm so that they could experience what we did as children. Kyle hated it, but my mother did not ask for his permission.

He faithfully took them the three months of vacation for the following four years.

Our family began to separate. After living on the farm for almost twenty years, joining society again was safe. The world was so different. Mother wanted to settle somewhere safe. Ramiro and Jewel did not want to bring the boys with them until they found a safe place, leaving them with a trusted friend to look after them.

The boys, now seventeen and nineteen, made their way here. That's where they met the original owner who left them this estate. The family found the boys a year later and moved in for a while. Most of my family was involved in all the Inner Cities rebuilding, along with my brother Jesse. So, they traveled back and forth a lot.

Jewel and Ramiro stayed, helped the boys with the estate, and were doing great. On the other hand, we were having many problems. Everything that Kyle tried, failed." Alex stated somewhat remorsefully as she drew in a deep breath. "So, I left him and took the girls. I rented a small apartment, but Krystal kept getting in trouble everywhere we went. One day when we came home, all our things were sitting outside on the sidewalk. We had to live in the streets for a while until my father came for us. I was so afraid. I had two young girls, and Audrey was already looking like a woman. The men would make sexual remarks about her. Brydus, I wanted to die."

"So, Audrey and Demi were apart for a few years?" Brydus wondered.

"Not really. They kept in touch. Demi would stay with us for a while, and Audrey would go to the farm. Demi was always arguing with Kyle about Audrey. Kyle didn't want Demi in the picture. He said that Demi was too possessive of Audrey.

I did what I thought was best and came back home. I was tired of being afraid, and I feared for the safety of my children. Things were hard, and I wasn't able to make ends meet. Demi was in heaven when those two were back together again. It was like magic. That was when he made plans for this house. Audrey picked the area, and they drew up the design for the house."

"I wasn't stupid or blind to it. They were in love. She even told me when she lost her virginity. I didn't know what to say. She said it was all her doing and that Demi didn't pressure her at all. Audrey was fifteen going on sixteen, and Demi was nineteen. He asked me for her hand in marriage. How could I refuse? They would have run away and gotten married anyway. As long as Jewel didn't object, it was fine with me. Everyone loved Audrey. She was the sunshine on a rainy day. And when she was with Demi, it was like a summer's day in the middle of a winter blizzard."

"I can tell it still hurts you to talk about her," Brydus said with concern for Alex.

"I did not give birth to her, but I gave her my love and my heart. You have to understand that Audrey was always a comfort to me. She would rub my feet whenever I came home tired from work. I felt terrible leaving her alone with Krystal, who simply refused to behave. My poor Audrey would kill herself cleaning and cooking so I wouldn't have to. We would fall asleep just talking, and when Kyle acted up, she would step in the middle," Alex explained as she fought back the tears.

"Maybe that's why Krystal feels so insecure," Brydus interjected.

"Krystal was daddy's girl. I tried to have a relationship with her like Audrey and I had, but she would push me away. Krystal became bitter toward us, and it hurt me to the core that she rejected my love.

Kyle followed us back here, claiming that his girls needed him. By that time, I had no love for him whatsoever. But he had nowhere else to go. So, he continued working on some of the many projects the boys had."

"What happened to him?"

Alex looked down at her hands, fighting tears, "You never get over losing a child. Kyle came back, wanting to make amends for everything that happened. I really didn't care if he stayed or left, but Krystal cried and blamed me for everything. She blamed me for her father leaving us and blamed Audrey for everything else that was going wrong in her life. It wasn't until Audrey was presumed dead that Krystal told me she was glad Audrey was gone. What kind of person would say such a thing? She told me during one of her tantrums that she was happy that her sister was dead. Now Demi would love her. I slapped her so hard across her face that I thought I broke her neck. Then in a shouting match, she told me what happened the night Audrey disappeared. It was not easy for me to hear. I was in shock for days.

My parents and the boys were with Jesse. They had just elected my brother to run the Inner Cities. There was a huge celebration. Audrey was supposed to go, but she was so sick that she couldn't make the trip, and little Miss Krystal was being punished for her behavior as usual.

Kyle agreed to stay with the girls while Jewel and I went to the orphanage. There was a chicken pox epidemic, and they needed help tending to the children."

Alex was silent for a moment, remembering that dreadful day, "I remember it was storming that night. It was horrible.

The roads were flooding, and the lightning lit up the sky. Krystal said that her father went into Audrey's room to see how she was doing, and a few minutes later, she heard them yelling at each other. Apparently, Kyle tried to kiss her, and she slapped him. Kyle grabbed her and told her that she would never be with Demi. They struggled, and Audrey disappeared into the night. She was never seen or heard from again."

"I'm sorry; not knowing what happened to her has to be the worse feeling in the world. What happened to your husband?" Brydus asked, engulfed in the story.

"I threw him out. I blamed him for my daughter's death. That bastard was going after his own flesh and blood. I always wondered what it was that I saw in him. I mean, he was an extremely handsome man, and in the beginning, I knew he loved me. But later on, I learned that deep inside, Kyle hated my family. Jesse had this insane good luck on his side, and everything he touched turned golden. Aside from the fact that Jewel was just like Jesse, they were geniuses, and people respected them."

"Demi and Joaquin are so damn handsome, so I can understand why Monet was drawn to them," She said, smiling at the thought of her new husband. "But if she's so in love with Demi, why was she trying to hold on to Joaquin? She claims she still loves him."

"I believe she does love Joaquin in her own sick way. She also knows that by being his wife, she would be the mistress of a grand estate, and she'd be socially accepted. However, my poor misguided Krystal…well, that's another story. You have no idea how often I have talked and tried to reason with that child. The family ties to Demi are close, and he will never cross that line. She doesn't realize that even though they don't look alike, she still reminds him of the love he lost."

"I don't understand why Krystal is so fixated on him when there are so many single young men that would kill to be with her?"

"She can't let go of him because he was the only thing she couldn't take from Audrey."

"Wow, is she in for a lot of heartaches. When she finds out that Monet has been lusting after Demi all along, she will feel like a real fool."

"Sweetheart, some people have to learn things the hard way. As much as I love Krystal, she will fall really hard."

"I guess you're right." Brydus loved their talks; it allowed her to understand the family and the man that she married.

"How about if we go inside and have some coffee. It's getting a little chilly," Alex advised feeling a cool breeze blow through, causing the trees to rustle, indicating that winter would be upon them soon.

Brydus smiled, feeling the peace in her life, "Sure, why not? I'll help you make some sandwiches and turn on the fireplace."

"You're such a dear. I love spending this time with you, Brydus. It makes me feel needed."

Demi came around every day to see what had to be done or just went riding with Brydus. Demi would fill her in on what was happening at the main house. She was lonely and longed for Joaquin, who was detained another week.

On the weekends, they would play cards. Demi would start drinking, and by the end of the night, he was crying on his Aunt Alex's lap. She tried to comfort him the best she could, but sometimes she would join him in his sorrow. Brydus always got caught up in their emotional heartache. But when all of the tears were wiped away, they would feel better. Knowing they had each other to hold on to and remember the person who brought so much joy to their lives.

The weeks seemed longer now that the weather was changing, and the nights seemed cold and lonely. Brydus was very emotional and cried easily. Demi was always there with his big broad shoulders for her to cry on as he comforted her.

By the end of the third week, Brydus woke up earlier than usual, knowing Joaquin would be coming home. She prayed that no messenger would arrive with the news that Joaquin needed to stay longer. She took a shower and ensured that her hair was just how he liked it. She put on a cute little dress and her boots. Demi and Jenny were already eating breakfast when Brydus ran downstairs, full of smiles and looking refreshed.

Demi couldn't wait to tease her, "Whoa…and where are you going, pretty lady, and what's with all the makeup and hair?"

She rolled her eyes at him, "You know damn well that my husband is due back today, and I want to look nice for him… you know, pretty."

"I don't think you'll ever have an ugly day, Brydus. I'm sure he's just as anxious to come home as you are to see him," Jenny added, happy to see Brydus smiling again.

"It is getting cold, and we need firewood for the fireplace," Demi said, looking at the rack where they kept the firewood.

"Demi, I know you have to get to work. I'm sure we can do with what we have. For now, you've been such a great help."

"Yeah, and if I know you, you'll go out and do it yourself the minute I leave. No way. I will chop some wood before I leave."

"And I have to go shopping. Will you be alright here alone for a while?" Jenny asked.

"Sure, I'll be alright. I enjoy my solitude. You two go about your day. I'll be fine."

Demi was chopping wood when he saw a lone rider coming from the direction of the main house. He smiled, "Hey Brydus, come and greet your husband!" He watched as Brydus came running out of the house without a jacket to meet Joaquin, who swooped her up in his arms.

"You crazy woman, what's wrong with you coming out here without a jacket. It's cold out here," Joaquin said, happy to see her.

"You can warm me up," she teased.

"Shut up and kiss me," Joaquin held her tight as they kissed. "I've missed you so much, Sweet Cheeks."

"You have a lot to make up for."

Demi waited for his brother at the door and handed him the ax. They embraced. Demi was glad to see him safe at home. "Here, you do this shit. Welcome home, brother."

"Thanks for holding things down around here. I know you had your own work to do as well."

"Hey, we had fun, didn't we, Brydus? She was cussing your ass out for staying an extra week."

"I was not planning on it, but we got a lot of work done, and I'm proud to say that we are doing fantastic. Now as much as I love you, bro, please leave. I have a lot of catching up to do with my wife," Joaquin winked at him.

"I hear you; I'm leaving. I'll come back later to catch you up on our progress."

Jenny took a few minutes to pack her things and headed home. She could tell they wanted to be alone by the way they were kissing and touching each other. Joaquin picked Brydus up, carrying her upstairs, and they fell into bed together.

He pulled her close to him after they made love. He played with her hair, "I've missed you so much; it was hard for me to concentrate. All I could think about was your sweet cheeks."

Brydus slapped him playfully, "Is that all I am to you, some sex thing?" She pushed him away.

"Well yeah, my sex thing," he kissed her breast, playing with her nipples.

"Stop it. That hurts,"

"Since when?" He teased.

"I don't know. I must be getting my period or something. My breasts are sensitive, and I'm always so tired."

"Baby, when was the last time you had a period?" Joaquin asked.

She leaned against his arm. "I don't remember… hum…maybe? No!" she popped up in bed.

"Since before you were being mean to me, right?" he asked, teasing her.

"Joaquin, I wasn't being mean to you!" she raised her eyebrows at him.

"Yes, you were," he laughed "you were mean and bitchy, and it's all because I knocked you up!"

"Oh my God, Joaquin, you are such a dick…could I be pregnant?" she touched her belly tenderly.

"It's not like we haven't been going at it every time we're together. Get back in bed. I'll show you how it's done." She pushed him away again and ran to the full-length mirror. "Baby, please, come back to bed. I need you," Joaquin pleaded as she examined her still flat belly.

"How can you think about sex at a time like this?"

"Sweetcheeks, I have a confession to make… I think about sex all the time. Come to me. Daddy needs you."

She jumped happily into his arms, "We're going to have a baby, and it's going to be a boy."

"How do you know that?"

"I'm a man. I know these things," he laughed.

She pulled his hair playfully, "Make love to me you… you horny father."

"I thought you'd never ask," Joaquin was happier than he'd ever been.

***

That evening when Demi stopped over to update Joaquin on their progress reports, Joaquin told him exactly what he had already suspected.

"I knew something was up! Brydus, you were moody as hell, crying all the time over silly stuff. So, I'm going to be an uncle! Damn it, I'm happy for both of you." Demi said, looking at Brydus.

"Well… we were hoping you would honor us by being the baby's godfather? I know that if anything would happen to us, you are the only other person I would want to raise my child," Joaquin added.

Demi lowered his head, "Wow, I don't know what to say. I would be honored to be your first child's godfather. I'm excited, bro. Awesome news."

"We want to keep it between us for now. I haven't seen the doctor yet, but I have a feeling this is a honeymoon baby," Brydus bragged.

Joaquin kissed her cheek, "So keep this under the radar, for now, bro. You know how incorrect information gets around here."

"I'll try, but I'm more excited than both of you put together. Man, this is the shit!"

Brydus and Joaquin tried to keep the news about the baby a secret for a while. But the nurse couldn't keep her mouth shut, and the gossip train reached Monet, who was now six months into her pregnancy. Monet was beside herself, demanding to be waited on hand and foot.

The baby was making Brydus overly emotional, and Joaquin made everyone aware that she was also missing her family, especially her mother, Christina. He cut his workload in half to spend more time with her. Joaquin wanted to be involved in everything that concerned his baby.

He tried to be very supportive, though he hated that Brydus refused to return to the main house until Monet was settled in her own place. But he was happy with the intimacy that the smaller house provided. During the day, Joaquin worked in his office and was glad that he now came home to a happy wife, who met him at the door with kisses and hugs.

Brydus felt like a housewife. She and Jenny would spend hours in the kitchen, experimenting with different recipes. Sometimes Alex would come over and lend a hand, offering her years of experience in the kitchen. Demi was the taste connoisseur. He loved the closeness they shared and spent many evenings with the couple. On the weekends, Demi and

Alex would come over, and they would all play cards or games.

Meanwhile, Monet was in rare form. She was miserable. According to the information that she gave the doctor, she was overdue. However, the baby was in no way ready to be born, and Monet knew they would soon be asking questions. She argued with the doctor about her due date, but he felt she was lying, so he kept his thoughts to himself. Monet still had difficulty walking and needed her only friend's assistance. One afternoon, Krystal found Monet in the bathroom frazzled.

"Oh my God, Monet, are you alright?" She helped her off the floor.

"I need your help… you are the only one I can trust."

"What is it? What can I do?"

"This baby has to come out now."

"You are overdue, but your belly is so small, I don't understand?"

"Look, Krystal, the reason that my belly is so small is because it is not Joaquin's baby."

Krystal was shocked, "But you swore it was his?"

"Krystal you are so naïve. I had to try to keep the man I love." Monet knew that the fake tears would bring Krystal around. "When Joaquin went to the Inner Cities with, ugh! You know who? I was crushed… he left me for her. Do you know how hurtful that is?" She cried harder. "I knew I was losing him, so I tried to get him back in bed with me, but he refused. I knew they had been intimate. He made it clear to me that they were together." Monet cried on Krystal's shoulder, "Oh Krystal, my life is a mess," she sobbed.

Krystal put her arms around her, "I understand, but didn't you think that he would have found out anyway?"

"I didn't know what to do. I was heartbroken. I went out and met up with some friends, and one of my so-called male friends took advantage of me. I had way too much to drink and felt sorry for myself. I can't really tell you who it was. When I woke up the next day, I was naked, and two men and one woman were sleeping next to me. I got dressed and ran as fast as I could, and then a month later, I found out that I was pregnant," on cue, Monet produced more tears, and Krystal bought her story. "I know you probably think I'm a horrible person, but I know that Joaquin is a loving and caring man. He would have loved this baby, and he would have been a great father. Now because of this bitch stealing my man, I'll be on the streets with my child."

"Monet, I understand that you are scared. You were treated terribly by my cousin … but I doubt very much that he'll kick you out on the street with a newborn."

"Oh, Krystal, you still don't understand… I have nothing. The man that I love is married to someone else. He has turned his back on me totally and this baby. Whether it was his or not, I had to try anything to keep him."

"But you're lying to him."

Monet was starting to get frustrated, "That is why you will never get your man. As much as Demi drinks, you should have had him in front of a judge by now. You will never get him by just hoping and dreaming. Sometimes you just have to take matters into your own hands. You've had sex before."

"Well…yes, but it doesn't matter if he won't come to me."

Monet turned her nose, "It doesn't matter; you could have still claimed you were a virgin. Demi never had to know that. You are young and could have cried rape and claimed both physical and emotional damages. Afterward, sit back and claim your prize. Demi could have been yours long ago. I'm sure the judge would see your side, considering Demi's drinking patterns."

"I had never thought about that. I'd do anything to have one night of love and passion with him." Monet knew she could play on Krystal's desire for him, "I guess I have a lot to learn. You are such a great teacher," she complimented as she hugged Monet, "So tell me, how I can help you now."

"You have to go pick something up for me. You must follow my directions. I need you to pick something up from this… this woman. All you have to do is give her this note, and she'll do the rest."

"Alright, I'll do it." Krystal followed Monet's directions, but she was not used to wandering alone in the woods. She was afraid; it was getting late and darker by the minute. Krystal was worried that she would be unable to find her way back to the house in the dark. Just as she was ready to turn around, she saw the cottage. She knocked on the door and waited for a moment. When Lola answered, Krystal was shocked by how much Monet resembled the woman. "Hi, my name is Krystal. I have a note from Monet. She asked me to hand this to you personally."

Lola read the note and laughed. "And how is Monet?" She asked.

"She is better now. She had a really bad fall and is having problems with the baby… she had some pretty bad injuries."

"Well, that doesn't surprise me. Wait here." Lola was alone. Had Ramon been at home, they would have had an argument about helping Monet once again, especially after all the things she did and said when she came to visit the last time.

She handed Krystal a package. "Tell her to make sure she takes it with a lot of water. It should start to work by tomorrow."

"Thank you so much. I'm sure she appreciates your help," she said, turning to leave.

"Krystal, please be careful. My daughter likes to use people."

"Your daughter, you're Monet's mother?" Krystal asked, shocked. Monet always said that her family had money.

"By the look on your face, I guess she never mentioned us. Well, the less you know, the better. Just be careful, my dear. You seem like a nice person."

Krystal fled from the cottage, running wildly through the woods, hoping that she could find her way back. When she saw the fence that surrounded the property, she was relieved. As quickly as she could, Krystal rushed up to Monet's room, where she found her waiting anxiously. Monet grabbed the package and smiled. "Thank you, I will have this baby by tomorrow night."

"It won't hurt the baby, will it?" Krystal asked, hoping Monet would show more concern about the baby's wellbeing.

"It shouldn't harm the baby, but don't expect me to be excited about what happens to it.

"Monet, the woman at the cottage, she mentioned that she was your mother. I thought you said your family came from money?"

Monet looked dismayed, "Well, I guess you know my dirty little secret now. Krystal, I never mentioned that side of my family because I was… embarrassed. My mother had an affair with one of her servants, a dirty gypsy landscaper. They ran away together, not knowing she was pregnant by my father. My father is a rich man, a very rich man. My mother used him for his money and turned my brother against my dear, sweet father. He suffered terribly. Anyway, I didn't know about my real father until he came looking for me. You have no idea how happy I was. He was so kind and loving. I was very angry with my mother for keeping the truth from me. He asked me to move in with him. That's when he told me the truth about my mother and her lover. I lived in poverty for years! That is why I've never mentioned her to you. I didn't want you to think less of me," Monet's eyes once again swelled with fake tears.

"I'm so sorry. I didn't know, but I do understand about family. I loved my father, but he did some terrible things too. Things that I don't like to associate with."

"You have no idea how hard it's been. I've had to live with this fear inside of me for so long. Hoping and praying that no one would find out about my dreaded family ties to them."

"Oh, Monet, you can trust me. I will never divulge anything you say to me, but why didn't you stay with your father?" Krystal asked curiously.

"He had a new wife by then, and she thought I was taking my father's affections away from her. My father adores me, so I did the right thing and left. He and his wife were trying for a son. Then this opportunity with Joaquin came up. I was an interior decorator, and he had some rooms that needed to be redone. So, I knocked on Joaquin's door, and the rest is history."

"I know all too well how a father's affection can be misinterpreted, so I totally understand."

"Thank you, Krystal, from the bottom of my heart," Monet said sincerely.

It was freezing and still dark out when the messenger made his way toward the house where Joaquin and Brydus were staying. Howard banged on the door, waking Joaquin from a sound sleep. He hit his foot running down the stairs, concerned that something was wrong. Howard was shaking by the time Joaquin answered the door.

"Come in, Howard. What's wrong?"

"Master Joaquin, the lady is in labor and is calling for you."

Joaquin didn't understand him at first. "What are we talking about, Howard?"

"Miss Monet is having her baby and wanted me to alert you."

Joaquin could feel the heat rising inside of him. "You woke me up from a sound sleep to tell me this?" Joaquin was extremely angry, and Howard could read it on his face.

"I'm sorry, sir, but the lady was most adamant about someone coming to get you. I tried to call but got no answer."

"Howard, I'm not angry with you. I know that you only do what is asked of you. I don't care if Monet's in labor, call the doctor and leave my wife and me alone. Please don't bother me about this matter again."

"Yes, sir, I understand. The doctor has been called, and I will make sure that I relay the message."

Monet's screams were heard throughout the house. She cursed the baby and everyone around her. The doctor was tired of her insane yelling, so he sent in a midwife to assist her. For hours, Monet struggled with the labor pains. The midwife tried to get her to relax, knowing this would help her labor progress. By midafternoon, Monet finally delivered a very small baby girl. Krystal cried when she held the sweet infant in her arms. She was so small and fragile, barely weighing five pounds. The midwife put her in a warming crib because Monet refused to see or hold the baby.

She blamed the tiny infant for ruining her perfect body and for keeping her a prisoner in her room for so long.

Brydus needed to see the baby and see if it resembled Joaquin. The warming crib was in the middle of the room with a light shining on her because the baby was jaundiced. Walking slowly towards the lonely crib, Brydus held her breath. She was flooded with emotions as she watched the tiny baby lying peacefully. "Poor sweet baby," she whispered. *Thank God she is unaware that her mother wanted nothing to do with her*, she thought. Brydus rubbed her back tenderly. The baby was absolutely beautiful. She had rosy cheeks and a small patch of bright red hair.

Joaquin watched Brydus from the door. He could tell by the way she touched the baby that she cared and would make a wonderful mother.

"She's beautiful, isn't she?" Joaquin commented. Brydus didn't even turn around. She felt sorry for the newborn and wanted to pick her up and tell her that everything would be alright.

"She is perfect. What mother wouldn't want such a beautiful baby?"

"Unfortunately, we've found one that doesn't." Joaquin put his arms around Brydus' shoulders and gently rubbed her belly.

"Is she yours…? I wouldn't mind if she were."

"Neither would I, but she's not... the DNA test disqualified me."

"What's going to happen to her? She's so tiny."

"We've contacted her grandmother. She'll be alright with her and Ramon. They're good people. In fact, they should be here soon." Brydus touched her own belly and wondered if her baby would be just as perfect. She would never turn away from her baby, no matter what, she thought.

Lola was ready when Howard appeared at the door. He informed Ramon, who was not shocked as he put his arms around his wife. "It's a girl, and it's not Joaquin's child. However, he is willing to raise her since Monet hates the baby. His wife is on board as well. Mr. Joaquin said that Monet refuses to look at or touch her."

Ramon kissed Lola, "It's our granddaughter, our blood, and we will raise her."

When they arrived at the mansion, Ramon refused to speak to Monet. He stayed downstairs, talking to Joaquin, who was always a gracious host. "I'm sorry that she put you through this. The baby is our responsibility. Thank you for all your help."

"I am more than willing to help financially as well. I don't want this baby to be a burden on you and Lola."

"Well, Emily and her husband are going to take her. We will be there for her with anything that they need. Our little grandson will welcome the new addition to their family."

Meanwhile, Lola tried to make Monet understand that she was a mother now and that the baby needed her, "Monet, for heaven sakes, this is your baby. She came from your body. She is absolutely perfect, just take her into your arms and see how much she needs you," Lola begged.

Monet rolled her eyes, "That thing is a parasite. It has lived off me long enough. I don't care what you do with it. I don't want it or give a damn what happens to it. Put it on someone's doorstep or take it to the church. I'm sure they'll find it a home."

Tears rolled down Lola's cheeks, "How could I have raised such an ungrateful child? You are evil, just like that monster who fathered you."

Brydus and Alex could hear the shouting from the other side of the house. They couldn't believe the foul language that was spouting from Monet. Brydus looked over at Alex, sitting quietly, knitting something for her baby. She was concerned that the argument may get physical. "Is the baby going to be alright with her mother? They seem to have the same temperament." Alex put her knitting down and closed the door to the sitting room.

"Don't worry, my dear. Lola is a wonderful woman. How she gave birth to that monster, nobody knows. She has a great support system. They will look after the child and give her all the love she needs."

"What a way to come into the world. I'm glad she'll be with her family. I hear Monet resembles Lola. Is Lola her true name?"

"She was born Lucia Ivory, a beautiful, lovely woman, and then became a Stockett. That's her married name. She married the very wealthy Larson Stockett, who chased after her for a few years. After they married, he became the most miserable man to ever walk this earth."

Brydus was surprised that Alex knew Monet's family so well, "How do you know her?"

"Oh, my love, hers is a very sad story. They were the first people we met when we searched for Demi and Joaquin. Lola married Mr. Stockett because of a family obligation. Her father was Larson's business partner. That horrible man always had his eye on the beautiful Lola. Her parents were older when Lola was born, and her father didn't want his beautiful daughter and wife to be homeless if he died first. You see, he was in debt to Mr. Stockett. Mr. Stockett was obsessed with Lola. She was young, fresh, and exciting, but he thought every man wanted his wife. A year into their marriage, Lola's father died of a mysterious illness, and like any good daughter, she brought her mother to live with them. Her mother was very fragile and never got over losing her husband. Lola's father wasn't yet cold in his grave when the abuse began. Mr. Stockett knew Lola didn't love him, which infuriated him.

She made plans to leave so many times, but with an ailing mother and, by that time pregnant, the poor dear was trapped. Stockett was happy with her for a while, knowing she would give him a child. When their son was born, she thought he would be satisfied now that he had an heir. But instead, he became very jealous, accusing her of having other lovers, and he would beat her mercilessly."

"But she gave him a son. Why would he be so mean to someone so lovely and kind?"

"Because he was a wicked, mean man, a sadist that loved to inflict pain on helpless people around him."

"So, you knew him?"

"I met him. My brother used to have dealings with him. That was until he found out what kind of a person Stockett was. I met him once at a conference at the Inner Cities. He left me with a bad taste in my mouth with his fake courtesy. Ugh, you can't hide evil; it shows up in different ways.

Poor Lola never went out. She was either inside the house or in her garden, where she went to escape his anger. Larson Jr. turned out to be just like his mother, a sweet child with her good looks. She told me once that her son was her only comfort in those days.

She felt a little freer when her mother died but still sad. Lola wished she could have given her mother a better life…a life away from the cruelty. She told me that she and Larson Jr. talked about escaping and living in the faraway woods where Stockett couldn't find them. They had made plans in their own little world. However, a great blessing came when Mr. Stockett decided to send his son away to a very expensive school abroad. At first, Larson Jr. refused and begged to stay. He didn't want to leave his mother alone with the beast… that's what he called him. I don't blame him. So, Lola convinced her son to leave. Afterward, she would figure out how to get away so that they could meet up later.

Her only solace was her garden, where she met Ramon. He worked on the grounds and would watch her every day. Lola would wave at the handsome Ramon, and he would smile and wave back to her. But one day, while she was reading a book in her usual garden, Mr. Stockett came out of the house in a rage. He slapped her down to the ground because she had miscarried again. Then he rushed back into the house, leaving poor Lola on the ground crying. She felt a gentle hand on her shoulder. When she turned around, she gazed into the most beautiful gray eyes and sweetest smile that she had ever seen, she said to me. Lola panicked. Had Mr. Stockett seen her, he would surely have killed her."

She begged him to leave or Larson would kill him. Lola pleaded with Ramon, touching her pretty face where the five fingers marked her. He replied that he wasn't afraid of him. Had I been closer, he would have never hurt her. Ramon was secretly in love with her."

"Her savior, how sweet," Brydus smiled.

"So that's how their romance began. They met every day in a secluded place in the garden and made plans to escape together. Lola said that the night they left together, she felt a wave of freedom come over her that she had never felt in her life. When they finally arrived at a safe house, they made love for the first time. The emotions took her on a rollercoaster ride of highs and lows. They were together for two years and were very happy. Ramon's family loved her. That's when she changed her name to Lola, not wanting to remember anything about her past.

Her son kept her whereabouts a secret. Larson Lee Jr. was a senior in High School when Mr. Stockett discovered her whereabouts. He found a letter from Lola and tracked her down. Ramon was out at the Tribal Trading Post at the time, and he ran around the house like a madman looking for his beloved and found her almost dead. She had been beaten and raped by Mr. Stockett. Ramon went crazy. His friends rushed to get the gypsy healers. When they arrived, they found him crying, holding her in his arms, with her blood all over him.

The gypsy healers worked on Lola for days until she was stable. In the meantime, Ramon tracked down Mr. Stockett and beat him bloody; believe me, he deserved it. Ramon threatened and warned him that he would kill him if he ever came near Lola again.

Poor Lola was afraid to stay alone, and Ramon needed to make a living, so they moved into the gypsy camp. That's where Monet was born. Lola was pregnant and didn't know whose child it was until Monet was born. They knew immediately that she was Mr. Stockett's baby, but Ramon didn't care. He loved Monet and raised her as his own. Two years later, they had another girl, the spitting image of Lola but with Ramon's gray eyes."

"So, what happened to Monet? Was she always this evil?" Brydus asked out of curiosity.

"Lola said she was a difficult child, always wanting more and more. She noticed the evil in her early on, but she was her daughter, and they did whatever they could to keep her happy."

"Well, apparently, it wasn't enough. She's a very miserable person."

"Who's to say… had she married Joaquin, maybe she would have been happy. But the ugly truth is, I think she loves making others miserable too," Alex confided. Those were her feelings for a long time.

"I can't get over how she speaks to her mother."

"I believe things became worse when she finally met her real father. And figured out that she wasn't a poor little gypsy girl but instead the daughter of a rich merchant. That's when she started to call her mother Lola instead of 'Mom' and kicked poor Ramon to the curb. He was crushed. She was disrespectful towards the man who raised her and did more for her than for his own child."

"So that's how the monster was born," Brydus said, understanding where Monet's evil came from and the terrible way she was conceived.

"There's no stopping her now." They were interrupted by a knock. When Alex opened the door, Lola was standing there with tears in her eyes and very apologetic.

"How are you, Lola?"

"I'm sorry for my daughter's behavior. I beg your forgiveness," Lola said as she looked past Alex to where Brydus stood with her little belly. "You must be Brydus," she extended her hand to her. "I've heard so many wonderful things about you." The first thing Brydus noticed was her eyes. They were so kind and caring. She stared at Brydus and then at her stomach, "It's a boy. I'm sure Joaquin is going to be very proud of his son. Again, I want to apologize for all the grief that my daughter has caused this family. She'll be leaving with us this very minute. I have someone packing her things."

"What about the baby?" Brydus asked, sad that she might be leaving with them.

"My daughter and her husband are going to raise her… she's a sweet baby."

"Lola, if you need anything, you know you can always come to us. Joaquin and I, we are very fond of you and your family. I'm sorry things didn't work out between Joaquin and her." Alex offered, attempting to ease Lola's burden.

"I saw it in the cards," Lola said, turning back toward Brydus, "you were meant to be together. Your destiny was intertwined with his, and your future will be bright once the baby is born but be careful where you step. Now, I have a beautiful granddaughter to spoil with love."

"I'm glad she'll have someone to give her hugs and kisses," Brydus expressed.

"We named her Isaura. It's a strong name. Thank you again for your patience."

"It's a beautiful name. I wish her much luck," Brydus replied, glad she had met Lola.

Monet left, kicking, and screaming. She went to live in an apartment Joaquin had secured for her, one she had refused at first but now has no choice. It was fashionably decorated and had everything that she needed. Alex had arranged to have someone come in every day to help her until she could do it for herself.

Brydus missed the intimacy of the smaller house, but Joaquin was so happy to be back in his home and have Monet out of the way.

Peace returned to the estate. Alex went home and left the couple to continue with their life together. She assured Brydus she would return when she was closer to her due date.

The next three months were full of anticipation for the birth of their baby. Alex returned with so many gifts even though Krystal had a smile. Krystal insisted on helping decorate the nursery, wanting to be part of the big event. Alex had to be there to hold her nephew's hand when it came time to meet his baby.

Brydus was now in her 36th week of pregnancy, and even though she had not gained much weight, she was forbidden to do certain things. Doctor Mason suggested she not go horseback riding anymore. Taking away something gave her so much pleasure, even on the frosty mornings. Brydus was angry when Joaquin ordered the stable staff not to let her come near the stables. So instead, she took long walks and fed the birds by the creek behind the estate.

The morning air was crisp and clear, and Brydus enjoyed the solitude. It allowed her to think and reflect on motherhood and her wonderful life with Joaquin. Her baby was playing kickball in her belly. The strong kicking gave her peace of mind, letting her know it was alright.

Joaquin made an effort to spend more time with her, especially now when she missed her family so much. He loved to play with her round belly. He would rub it until the baby kicked back. He stared at her, loving how she looked when they took baths together. He took pictures of her naked and would whisper to her belly, complaining to their baby whenever Brydus was annoyed with him. "Your Mama is being mean to your Papa," Joaquin would say, making her giggle. At night they would make love and talk about how they would raise their child. "Sweetcheeks," Joaquin kissed her belly, "what are we going to name our baby?"

"Well, I hate all those horrible names you suggested."

"Oh really; if it's a boy, I want him to have a strong masculine name, grrr," he growled like a lion.

"You would, but I want to name him or her after my sister, if it's a girl, Nicole, and if it's a boy, Nicolas, what do you think about that?" Joaquin pursed his lips up for a moment, but when he saw the sad look in her eyes, he knew Brydus was missing the family she loved so much.

"I think it's a great name. I like it," her eyes lit up.

Brydus threw her arms around his neck, hugging him tightly, "I can't wait until you meet my sister, Nicole…she's a special kid. I used to call her my little witch. She has this uncanny way of knowing things before they actually happened."

Joaquin held her sweetly in his arms, listening to how lovingly she spoke about her family, "I know you miss them, baby. I promise, come spring, and when the baby is old enough to travel, we'll go visit your family." Brydus smiled, and it made him happy to put a smile on her beautiful face.

"It's been more than two years since I've seen them. I can't wait to see my friend Ciara so I can show off our baby. If I had to pick a godmother for our child, it would be her. Did I ever tell you that there are twins back home that are just like me? My friend Ciara is the mother of those two beautiful girls."

"Yeah, uh, I think I remember you mentioning the girls. You said their names are Tressa and Yadira, right?"

"I can't wait until you meet them. They are quite a pair," Brydus laughed, remembering everything they did to her when she was trying to teach them new fighting techniques.

"Your community must be blessed. First, there was my grandmother, then the sexiest woman in the world, and now twins. There must be something in the water."

"You're so silly," she said, kissing him playfully.

"I know, baby, but that's why you love me."

"I do love you. Just think, in three more weeks, you'll be holding our baby in your arms."

"I'll be holding both of my babies," he kissed her hands, "I can't tell you how happy you have made me… Te amo, mi amor," he held her tenderly in his arms, knowing he was the luckiest man in the world.

The following morning, after a hearty breakfast, Brydus bundled herself up for her usual morning walk, taking breadcrumbs to feed the birds by the creek. Demi and Mattie walked along the same path discussing the menu for the baby shower. Brydus caught up to them. "Where are you off to, sweetie?" Demi asked.

"Oh, just taking my usual morning walk. I go down to the creek. I enjoy feeding the birds. Where are you two going?"

"We're going to the meat warehouse," Demi said, looking guilty, "Mattie wants to make something special for the baby shower."

"There's nothing too good for our Mistress," Mattie said, smiling. Brydus was moved by her kind words. They parted ways when they reached the stone steps that led down to the small creek. There were icy patches from all the snow and wet weather that had been falling over the past few weeks. Demi turned to remind Brydus to be careful when he saw Brydus fly into the air down the steps. By the time Demi reached her, she was lying at the bottom of the steps in an abnormal position. Mattie screamed and followed him down the stairs, slipping, coming down one by one on her backside.

Demi flew into action, bracing her neck at once as Mattie ran back to the house screaming for help. They had Brydus on a stretcher wearing a neck brace within a few minutes. Demi was almost in tears as he watched the team carry her motionless body into the house, up the stairs, and laid her on the bed.

The doctor and nurse pushed Demi out of the room so they could work on Brydus. Then he realized that Joaquin had gone into town early that morning and wasn't expected back until evening. Alex took control of the situation right away. Demi froze at the door, fearing the worst.

"Aunt Alex, it happened so fast. One minute she was at the top of the stairs, the next thing I saw was her flying in the air and down those stone steps."

"Don't worry, son. I've sent a messenger to find Joaquin, but the phones are out again. Thank God you were there to get her help."

With frustration, Demi hit the wall with his fist, "There must be something slippery on those stairs because Mattie also fell. She came down on her behind." They took turns pacing back and forth until Joaquin came rushing through the double doors into the room where Brydus lay motionless, with all types of machines hooked up to her. He fought the knot that was forming in his throat. He stared at the monitor attached to her belly, displaying a steady beep, which monitored the baby's heartbeat. When Doctor Anderson approached Joaquin, he saw the concern on his face, which scared him.

"Let's talk outside," he asked. Joaquin couldn't speak. He was petrified and didn't know what to expect. The three surrounded the doctor waiting for information. He could see the extreme anxiety on their faces. "She is truly lucky…there should have been some broken bones or some kind of major internal damage. We've checked everything. There's no head trauma. All we saw were bruises."

"What about the baby… is the baby in trouble?" Joaquin asked, holding his breath.

"That's why we have the monitors on her. The baby's heartbeat is strong and steady," Doctor Anderson took a deep breath, "I won't lie to you, Joaquin… she may deliver tonight. There is a little bleeding. The placenta may be separating, and if that happens, the baby is in trouble."

He covered his eyes in frustration. "If she loses the baby, she'll never be the same."

"Joaquin, so far, the baby is doing well. The baby is big enough to survive this delivery, and we are keeping a close eye on her. If we sense any type of complications, we are ready to operate. Right now, I think you should be with her when she wakes up."

Joaquin had been fighting back his tears, but he could no longer hold them back, especially when he saw an ugly scratch along the right side of her face. Tears began falling as he sat beside Brydus, kissing her hand tenderly. "Hey, Sweetcheeks, baby, I'm here, honey… baby, I love you, please be alright."

Alex tried to help attempt to keep her comfortable. Demi sat next to his brother, trying to keep him focused and ensuring he believed they were both going to be all right. Joaquin turned to his brother. "I'm so glad you were there to get her the help she needed so quickly. I don't know how I can ever repay you for all you've done for us."

"You're my brother, and I'd do anything for you. I wish it were me lying there instead of her."

For an hour, they sat in silence, listening to the beat of the baby's heart monitor, until there was a disturbance outside the door. Alex looked at Demi. They went to see what the commotion was when they saw a guard holding Krystal, who was crying hysterically. When she saw her mother, she hugged her. "Mama, I'm so sorry… I tried to stop her, but she had this crazy look on her face. She pushed me into the shed," Krystal babbled on.

"Child, what are you talking about? Who did you try to stop?"

"Monet, I saw her this morning with a jar of grease in her hand. When I asked her what she was doing with it, she told me… well, it was more like yelling. She said that Brydus took all that belonged to her, and she was going to take what was dear to her, her baby. She knew that Brydus walked down those steps to feed the birds every morning. Monet had been watching her for a few days. I tried to reason with her that she needed to leave Brydus alone. That's when she punched me and called me a traitor. We started to wrestle; she hit me hard in the stomach. Monet is strong. She pulled me by the hair, dragged me into the shed, and locked me in. The stable boy heard me banging on the door and let me out."

"Oh my God, she's gone crazy," Alex exclaimed, "are you all right, dear?"

"Mama, I tried to yell at Brydus to go back, but she didn't hear me. I'm so sorry, Mama. I wanted to stop her from falling," she cried uncontrollably.

Demi put his arm around her, "Thanks for telling us the truth and not covering up for Monet," Demi added, noticing the black eye and scratches around her neck. Krystal was shaking.

"My poor baby, I'm going to inform Joaquin. You stay with her, Demi. Maybe the nurse should look at your eye?"

Demi walked the sobbing Krystal to a sitting area, "Demi, I've never seen her like this. The hate in her eyes… I was scared."

"Monet knows how to manipulate people. I thought she was nice when I first met her until she came into my room naked a few nights."

Krystal pushed away from him. "What…When?"

"Don't tell me you didn't know. She'd been trying to get with me for a long time. Why do you think the family left to go to your place?"

"No, Demi, you're wrong. She couldn't stop talking about Joaquin and how much she loved him."

"She came onto me whenever she had a chance, and when I told Joaquin, she lied and started crying. Anyway, all she ever was to him was a booty call. Joaquin never intended to marry her, even if he hadn't met Brydus."

"Oh my God, what a fool I've been. To think that I waited on her hand and foot. I felt sorry for her. All the things she told me about her life and everyone were all lies."

"That's what she is, a beautiful lying bitch, and now she's gone, thank God… but this time Monet will go to jail for her actions."

Chapter 25: Happy at Last

Alex tried to keep Brydus as comfortable as possible. She was still in and out of consciousness. Every time she moved or moaned a little, Joaquin jumped. Every now and then, she would cry out for her mother in her sleep. "Mami… Mami, help me," she tossed and turned restlessly, making Joaquin nervous.

"Honey, I'm here, baby. It's Joaquin," she continued to cry out for her mother and move restlessly.

"What's wrong with her, Doc? Is she in pain?"

"Let me see what's going on with the baby."

When the doctor was finished examining Brydus, there was blood on his glove, and Joaquin freaked out, "What the hell is that?"

"Her water broke. She's in labor… I had a feeling this was going to happen, but the baby was big enough to survive. You have a choice, Joaquin, stay by her side and help her or go outside and let us work."

Joaquin didn't even blink, "I'm staying with my wife," he looked over at Alex, who was already on the other side of the bed.

"Good because this baby is coming quickly."

Brydus finally woke up, aware that she was in bed and in pain. She looked over at Joaquin, who was smiling at her.

"What happened, baby? Why am I in bed?" she asked as she squeezed his hand during a contraction.

"You slipped and fell, sweetheart. You're in labor now."

She grasped him franticly, "Is the baby alright?"

Joaquin laid her back down, "Sweetcheeks, everything is going to be alright."

It's alright, honey; the baby's heartbeat is strong and steady. Now all you have to do is push when the doctor tells you to," Alex said, reassuring her.

"I'm so glad you're here," Brydus tried to bear the pain as much as she could, refusing pain medication. Afraid it would harm the baby's progress. After an hour of horrendous pain, the doctor urged her to push, and Brydus pushed with each contraction.

"Come on, honey, the baby's head is crowning… one more push. It won't be long now," coached Dr. Anderson. Brydus held on to Joaquin, pushing as hard as her body could. "The baby's head is showing," he said and then ordered her to go one more time for the rest of the baby's body, and as if on cue, the baby started to cry.

When he saw his child, Joaquin was emotional, kissing Brydus over and over.

"Dad, come and meet your new son," Dr. Anderson held the screaming baby, so Joaquin could cut the umbilical cord.

Tears were rolling down his face as Dr. Anderson handed him his baby, crying along with his son.

"He is so beautiful," he sobbed.

They wrapped him up and brought him to Brydus' waiting arms. She started to laugh and cry at the same time. Alex joined in the couple's happiness, shedding a few tears of her own. Joaquin held Brydus when the nurse took the baby to weigh and measure him. He was relieved Brydus was alright and the baby didn't suffer from the fall.

Dr. Anderson was happy with the results and gave Brydus a clean bill of health. She was in great shape except for a few scrapes and bruises from her tumble down the stairs. Brydus could hear Demi outside yelling, "It's a boy! It's a boy!" He sounded just as happy as his brother.

After the baby was examined, he was handed back to Brydus, "HI, little Nicolas, it's Mami," she said, speaking the first words to her new son as she kissed him on the head, "We did really well, he's perfect."

"Yes, we did, Sweetcheeks. He's perfect like his mama. I love you, baby. You gave me a piece of heaven."

"Stop it before I start crying again," she teased.

Joaquin smiled down at Brydus and his newborn son, who was resting peacefully in her arms. "I can't help it. A year and a half ago, I would have never imagined falling in love with such a beautiful woman and having such a handsome son. I now realize that life happens really fast, and you have to grab happiness while you can."

When Demi held Nicolas, he was overwhelmed with joy, "You are my nephew, and I am your godfather, which means we will be hanging out, looking for some honeys. I'll teach you everything I know," Demi said to the baby as he slept in his arms, "he's beautiful, man. However, I think he will take after his uncle Demi, you know, rough and tough."

"Yeah, right, you mean he's going to take after his Papi. I can't wait until the family meets him," Joaquin saw the look of sadness in his wife's eyes. "I promised you, baby, as soon as he's old enough to travel, we're visiting your family."

"I know. I just wish that my family were here to enjoy this too."

Brydus only suffered minor cuts and bruises. Her face would heal, and she couldn't wait to show off her precious son to her family.

***

Krystal cooperated fully with the authorities. The investigators reported that the steps had indeed been tampered with, and with Krystal as an eyewitness, they had a strong case against Monet. However, when they finally arrived with a warrant for her arrest, she fled with the baby's father. He left his wife and another child behind, leaving them destitute. They later found out that Monet had been seeing this man whenever Joaquin was away.

Baby Nicholas was baptized in church when he was two months old. Already a round little butter ball, who cooed in the arms of his godparents, Demi and Alex. Demi took his position as uncle and godfather seriously. Whenever Brydus looked for her baby, he was either in his father's arms or Demi's.

***

Spring was coming, and Brydus was anxious to introduce her new baby to his grandparents. When the brothers were summoned to an Inner City emergency meeting, Brydus was upset that she would have to postpone her trip. She became extremely depressed when Joaquin left, knowing that he would be gone for at least two weeks.

"Mattie, both you and Jenny are in charge. I sent word to Alex, so she will be arriving within the next few days," Brydus announced, leaving without Joaquin.

"Is it safe for you to leave, Mistress? What if your husband comes home first? He'll be awfully angry," Mattie said, hoping she'd change her mind.

"I should be back before he comes home, but if not, give him this note. I have to see my family. I can't wait any longer. They probably think I'm dead."

The Valley of God

The flowers bloomed, and the air was fresh and crisp as Nicole pressed her nose against the living room window. "Darling, you've been staring out that window for two days. Why don't you go visit your best friend, Kim? It's such a beautiful morning. Get some fresh air," Christina suggested, worried.

"Normally I would, Mami, but I don't want to miss my sister. I dreamt about her this morning; she was so happy, Mami... I saw her smiling." Every time Nicole mentioned Brydus, it was like a stab in the heart. She'd been gone for over two years, and Christina didn't know if her daughter was dead or alive, but every night she lifted Brydus up to God in prayer for protection.

Alfonso smiled at his younger daughter as he helped his wife pack the groceries.

"Mami, set two more plates for dinner. We have company tonight," Nicole instructed before running up the stairs and disappearing into her bedroom.

Christina looked at her husband, concerned, "What is going on with her? She's been acting strange all week. I hope she won't wake up screaming and crying in the middle of the night again."

"Well, that was three months ago, and she seems to be alright now. But if I were you, I'd make some extra food and set out those plates. This wouldn't be the first time she was right about company coming to visit," Alfonso explained.

"Oh, wouldn't it be wonderful if Brydus did… come walking through those doors," Christina sighed sadly.

"I know you miss her, honey. Whenever someone asks me about her, I get this knot in my stomach, and sometimes I just want to puke."

"Same here… Alfonso. What if…" Christina paused and started to tear up.

"Baby, don't…don't think the worse. Brydus is strong and smart. I have faith in her survival ability, but… I've been thinking about this for a while. I will find her if she doesn't come home by the summer."

"And I won't stop you if it means bringing my baby home," she responded, pleased with Alfonso's gesture. "In the meantime, let me take something out for dinner and set two more places at the table. Your mother always said that Nicole had something special."

"Yeah. Something about a third eye… anyway, I'll help you get supper ready. It will keep me busy, and I can keep an eye on Nicole."

"Sure, honey, why don't you make a nice salad?" Christina smiled.

"Alright, a salad it is."

Nicole showered and pulled out her best dress. With great care, she flat ironed her long curly red hair. Normally, she let it go wild, refusing to tame her thick locks. When Nicole looked at herself in the mirror, she smiled and was satisfied with her look. "Okay, how about a little make-up." Nicole went back to her place by the window, watching every movement. When her father saw her, he did a doubletake from behind his newspaper to see if she was the same child that went upstairs earlier. Nicole was a tomboy. She hated to wear dresses and comb her hair most of the time.

Christina nearly dropped the dishes in her hands when she saw her tomboy daughter looking like a beautiful teenage young lady. Nicole checked the time in the kitchen once again, wearing a strange look on her face, afterward returning back to the living-room window waiting. Christina gave her husband a worried look, "What's up? Is that my Nicole?" Alfonso just shrugged his shoulders as if he wasn't sure.

"You'd better help me set this table. I have chills running up and down my spine right now," Christina said, handing the dishes to Alfonso, who was just as confused.

"I know one thing; I'm not waiting until eight o'clock to eat dinner. Come six, I'm eating. Whether whoever she thinks is coming shows up or not," Alfonso fussed.

Nicole rushed toward the kitchen door, "She's home… my sister's home!" She cried, slamming the door behind her. Christina and Alfonso froze for a second and then heard a voice they had longed to hear. They watched in disbelief as Brydus tied her horse to the post outside with a strange man.

Christina let out a scream, "Oh my God, it's my baby!" They rushed to the gate to embrace her. With tears of happiness falling mixed with kisses and hugs.

Nicole held her big sister tight, "I knew you were coming home today. I've missed you so much."

Brydus kissed her sister's tearful face, "I've missed you too, my little witch," she said as she squeezed her again.

"How are you, my baby? You look wonderful," Christina laughed and couldn't stop crying as she tried to speak. Al was speechless, putting his arms around his girls, huddled in a strong, lasting embrace.

Brydus was caught up in the moment, "Oh my God, I have a surprise for you." They watched as she went to the stranger, still on his horse, smiling at the exchange of affection. Little Nicolas lay quietly in Big Willie's arms when he opened his coat. "Let me introduce you to my son Nicholas. I named him after you, Nicole… these are your grandparents and your auntie."

Christina almost fainted as Alfonso reached for their beautiful grandson. Christina was overwhelmed with happiness, "Are you married?" She asked, still in shock from the sight of her grandson.

"Yes, Mami, I'm married to a wonderful man." Christina looked toward Big Willie, who was tying his horse to the post. "Oh no, Mami, this is Big Willie, my bodyguard."

Brydus explained everything to her family in full detail as they ate dinner. Christina couldn't contain herself when she discovered that Brydus had married Nylaya's grandson, the nephew of the famous Jesse Quintanilla.

Nicole couldn't put the baby down. Every time he made a noise, she was at his side. After supper, Big Willie fell asleep on the living room sofa as they retreated to the dining room, catching up on the Valley gossip. Brydus wasn't surprised to hear that Derrick had to marry Brenda and that they had a baby six months later.

"You were right, Mami. I wasn't ready to marry Derrick or anyone. I grew a lot in the past two years that I've been away. I met the most remarkable man. I went to Africa to meet his parents and Nylaya. I can't tell you how happy she was to meet me. Mami, I know it was hard to see me go, but… when I look back, had I never left, I know I wouldn't be as happy as I am now. I can't wait until you meet Joaquin."

Alfonso rocked his chubby grandson on his lap. Everyone could tell something was bothering him. "I hope to meet him very soon," he said, looking up from the baby. "I haven't discussed this with your mother yet. But now that we have a grandson…I don't want to miss him growing up. So, we're leaving with you." Brydus was shocked that her parents would agree to leave the safety of the Valley. She looked over at her mother, who was crying once again.

"I agree. I wouldn't have it any other way." Alfonso squeezed Christina's hand.

"Does Nicole know?" Brydus asked.

"She knew that you were coming. I'm pretty sure she knows something… anyway, the way she's attached to the baby, I doubt if we can pack fast enough for her," Christina added. "I'm still in awe that you're here, with the most beautiful baby in the world. Now I can sleep again," she joked.

Alfonso was thrilled. His head was swirling with plans, "I'll leave with you, honey, and secure a place for us, and then I will come back to move our things."

"Papi, I live in a mansion with tons of rooms. Joaquin would be offended if you weren't comfortable staying with us."

"Then it's settled when you leave, I will accompany you and my blessed grandchild while your mother and sister stay behind and pack."

"Alfonso, this is going to be such a fantastic move. I'm so excited! Unlike your father, I've never been outside of the Valley. I can't wait to explore the world."

"Oh my God, Mami, everything is new and exciting. I can't wait to show you how beautiful the land is."

They talked for hours, making plans for the move and about what they wanted to do when everyone was back together.

The next day was spent with family and friends that dropped by to see Brydus and the baby. They had a million questions about the outside world. When Ciara found out Brydus was home and with a baby, she couldn't wait to see her and meet her new husband. Nicole ushered her and the twins to where little Nicky lay, cooing and making baby noises.

Ciara tried to fight the urge to pick him up and rock him in her arms. "Oh, how wonderful, he is so beautiful... I remember when you two were little," Ciara said to her twins. "How I loved to just hold you girls," she remembered how she felt when she had the girls.

Ciara watched as her girls followed Nicole outside. Alfonso grinned like any grandfather would when people raved about their grandchildren.

"He's a strong little guy, isn't he?"

"Oh, he's gorgeous, Mr. Alfonso," Nicolas began to fuss. "I guess you want your grandfather back, little one." Ciara handed him back to his grandfather. "Where's Brydus? I can't wait to see her," she exclaimed.

"She'll be right down. She's in the shower," Christina said, coming down the stairs, "I see you've met our little man," she kissed him while he lay in Alfonso's arms.

"He is absolutely gorgeous, just like his mama."

"I hear his papa is not bad looking either," Christina giggled.

"No doubt, I'm sure. Brydus was always a man magnet."

"Look who's talking. You have men lining up around the block with marriage proposals," Christina teased.

"I know, but something stops me. I can't even let a man kiss me. It's really strange… I may never marry."

"Who is this I hear, Ciara?" Brydus cried, running down the stairs to hug her friend.

"Brydus, you look wonderful! Look at you… you're a beautiful, sexy woman."

"What about you? Why aren't you married yet? Who are you saving yourself for?" Brydus teased. Christina took the baby after he fell asleep in the comfort of his grandfather's arms. Ciara started to answer, suddenly stopping talking in the middle of her sentence. Her eyes went blank, staring at the necklace around Brydus' neck with the Quintanilla seal on it.

"Oh my God," Ciara said in a loud whisper. They watched as her eyes rolled back, and Ciara fainted. Alfonso caught her before she hit the floor. When she finally came to, everyone was standing over her, worried. They called her doctor, who administered the smelling salt.

"Ciara, are you alright? How are you feeling?" he interrogated her.

Ciara stared strangely at Doctor Hernandez, "Doc, why are you here?"

"You fainted," he said, checking her pulse.

"I remember that I was looking at Brydus' necklace, and then this pain went surging through my head," she started to sob. "Oh God, I remember… God help me. I remember everything."

"Ciara, what's wrong? That's a good thing, isn't it? That's what you wanted?" Brydus encouraged as Ciara hugged her neck.

"Tell me, Brydus; please tell me… which of the brothers did you marry?"

Brydus pulled away from her. "You're her… you're Audrey, aren't you, Demi's Audrey, right?" Ciara could only nod her head yes. The flow of tears kept coming as if a

fountain of both joy and sorrow, not yet knowing Brydus'
answer.

"Joaquin is my husband. Demi is still waiting for you."
Everyone was confused as they listened to this strange
conversation. "He's never stopped waiting for you, and your
mother is healthy and alive."

Audrey looked around, searching for her girls, who were
still outside playing with Nicole. "I have to go to him,
Brydus... thank you, thank you for waking me," she hugged
her neck tightly.

Brydus rubbed Audrey's back softly, knowing how
much she was missing her own husband, "Boy is he going to
be surprised when he finds out that he's a daddy, but he'll be
happy." She comforted her longtime friend.

"Something was holding me back all these years,"
Audrey said. I knew there had to be a reason why I couldn't
love anyone else. How is he, Brydus? Please tell me
everything," she couldn't stop crying as memory after
memory came rushing back to her.

"He cries every time your birthday comes around. I hear
that he keeps your picture by his bedside. Had I seen that
picture, you two would have been reunited already."

"Everything happens for a reason," Audrey said softly.

"You two are still married," Brydus stated.

"Yes, I remember now. I didn't wear my ring because we hadn't told my father I was married. That night when I ran out into that terrible storm, I knew I was pregnant. I left my rings in my jewelry box. I remember it now."

"Well, you'd better pack. Demi has been waiting a long time for you," Brydus hugged her again.

They made plans to leave in two days, but little Nicolas fell ill with a mysterious fever, so Brydus sent Audrey ahead with Big Willie. She would follow in a few days with her father.

Quintanilla Estate

Joaquin was furious when he found out that Brydus had left with the baby. Demi laughed at him as he witnessed him getting angrier by the minute. "I'll kill her; I swear to God I'm going to kick her pretty ass the minute she steps through those doors."

"Stop fronting… the minute she arrives, you'll be kissing her ass is more like it, you horny bastard. You haven't seen her in two weeks."

"That's beside the point. She should have never left without me," he whined.

"I couldn't stop her, Joaquin. She was so depressed and missed her family terribly. Here, she left a note for you… read it out loud so we can all laugh," Alex said as he ripped it open.

"Dear sexiest man in the world,

Please don't be angry if I am not home before you arrive, but I just couldn't wait any longer to see my family. I realized just how important they are to me, and they must be worried. They haven't heard from me in over two years, as required by our law for someone like me. I am taking Big Willie with me, so don't worry. You know how he is. When I get back, I will be my old self again, ready for action… that's if you're up for the challenge. I love you, baby. You and my little man are my world; I should be back on Saturday, so keep your buns warm for me.

I love you forever.

Your wife, Brydus."

Joaquin pretended to be angry. "According to this letter, she should be here today or tomorrow," he tried not to laugh. "I love her so much, but I'm still going to kick her ass."

"Yeah, bro, you can huff and puff all you want… but we know who has the power. All she has to do is smile, and you melt. I know I've been there… Audrey had me by the nose." Alex and Joaquin laughed, agreeing with Demi.

"I'm still going to give her a piece of my mind and spank that sexy ass of hers."

"Really, Joaquin?" Alex interrupted.

"Sorry, Auntie, I would never hit her too hard. She may like it."

"Yeah, yeah, I hear you," Demi chuckled. "I can't wait to see my little guy."

Things were beginning to look familiar to Audrey as she and Big Willie crossed into the Quintanilla territory. Even though they were tired, Big Willie pressed on, encouraging Audrey to do the same. "Big Willie, what should I say to him? He must have a million questions."

"Miss Audrey, you don't have to say a word. Just remember, he's been waiting for this day for ten years. Take it moment by moment."

They finally arrived in the late afternoon. The minute she came through the gate, she was flooded with emotions. She noticed some new buildings, and the grounds were a deeper, richer color. Audrey remembered how she and Demi used to sneak around, looking for a place where they would not be discovered by her parents or his. Demi was good at finding just the right spot. They would spend countless hours just holding each other and talking about the future. It was quiet when she reached the back entrance to the kitchen.

When Audrey opened the kitchen door, she came face to face with Mattie, who let out a scream, accompanied by a loud crash from the dishes she was holding, "Oh my God,

Miss Audrey… is that you, are you back from the dead?" she exclaimed.

"It's me, Mattie. I'm alive." Mattie screamed again and rushed toward her, putting her in a huge bear hug. "I'm home, Mattie."

The household was in an uproar when the older staff who knew her came running to see if the miracle was true.

"It's a miracle!" Mattie cried as she held on to Audrey.

"What the hell is that racket? Demi yelled, annoyed by the commotion.

"It's probably some girls fighting over you again. You'd better go and handle your women," Joaquin said, teasing his younger brother.

"Not again. I'm going to fire both of them, I swear to God," Demi headed toward the kitchen where the loud sobs and cheers were coming from.

"I've got to see this. You know your brother. He sees a woman crying, and he turns to mush." Alex said as she followed Demi toward the kitchen.

"You're right." Joaquin laughed, following her.

Demi turned the corner and heard a voice he could never forget. As he entered the kitchen, the staff fell silent and began to open a path. When he saw Audrey standing there smiling at him, his heart started to pound in his chest. His feet felt like lead, dragging and weighing him down as he struggled to take another step. She held out her arms toward him

"Audrey… is that you, Audrey?" Demi felt like he was looking down a tunnel, and Audrey was the only thing he could see.

"It's me, baby… I'm home."

He ran toward her and scooped her up in his arms as he started to sob. "Tell me it's not a dream… please!" He squeezed his eyes tight.

"It's me, baby. I'm back. I'm home…" they kissed passionately, not caring who was watching. Everyone in the kitchen was in tears as they witnessed the two lovers kiss and whisper intimate words in each other's ears. When Alex came around the corner, all she saw was a crowd of people in the kitchen crying.

When they parted, she saw Demi, holding someone, down on his knees, crying. When she looked closer, she had to be held by one of the staff. Holding her hand to her chest, "Audrey, my baby!" she screamed, watching the smile on the face of her lovely daughter.

"I'm home, Mama. I was lost for so long."

Demi held her by the waist, holding her tight. The three wept tears of happiness, thanking God that their beloved Audrey was alive and home.

It took Demi almost half an hour before he let go of Audrey, kissing her repeatedly. "I can't let go, my love. I'm afraid that you might disappear again," he whispered.

"No, my love, never again will I leave you, never, I promise," she held his face tenderly in between her hands. He kissed her hands. She could see the pain in his eyes. The reunion was overwhelming for all involved. Even those who didn't know Audrey felt the emotion of a lost loved one returning home.

"God, Audrey, you look wonderful," Joaquin said once he could speak. She explained briefly what happened and where she was all those years. Audrey explained how Brydus' visit and the charm that she was wearing brought her memory back.

"Speaking of my wife and son, where are they?"

"Joaquin, you lucky bastard, she'll be home in a couple of days. The baby had a fever, so she decided to wait. Her father is escorting her home. So be prepared to meet your in-laws. He's a super nice guy. Oh my God," she turned back to Demi, who was still holding her. "Come with me. I have a surprise for you." Everyone followed them outside. There, Audrey pointed. Still on their horses next to Big Willie were his identical twin daughters, with long black hair and almond-colored eyes looking just like his grandmother.

"Tressa, Yadira, meet your father." Demi's jaw dropped as the girls ran to embrace their father. "I was pregnant when I went out looking for you that night."

Demi touched them as if they weren't real. They held on to him as the tears began to overwhelm him once again. "God, I must have done something right. Thank you, God."

It took Demi a few hours to calm down. The whole house was in celebration. Alex attached herself to her granddaughters as she led them around the huge estate and finally put them down to sleep for the night.

Audrey and Demi locked themselves in his room and made love for hours, getting to know each other again. It was Audrey's turn to cry as she recounted the story of that night when she set out to look for him. "Please don't be angry, my love," Audrey pleaded.

"How can I be angry when this is the happiest day of my life?"

Audrey hesitated a few moments, choosing her words carefully, "I wanted so much to go with you that night, but I was so sick. I was throwing up, and I had a fever. Krystal was laughing at me because I kept running to the bathroom. We argued, and I threw her out of my room. I was so angry with her. She tried to blackmail me, saying that she would tell father about us making love in the stable loft. I remember yelling at her to get out of my room. I told her I loved you and didn't care who knew."

"We were married by then, and your mother knew."

"Yes, but remember we asked her not to say anything until you spoke to my father? He started to act like a jerk, saying terrible things. So, we put it off until you came back from the Inner Cities.

Afterward, throwing up dinner that night, I took a shower and put on jeans and a sweatshirt. By then, I was positive I was pregnant, and I was afraid. I plan to tell you when you returned and let everyone deal with it. I fell asleep, and when I woke up, the room was dark. I jumped out of bed when I realized my father was sitting in the chair across from my bed. He had been drinking a lot that evening. All I saw were his red eyes glaring at me, and that's when he asked me, 'You're pregnant from that bastard, aren't you?' He asked. I replied, 'If you're referring to Demi, then yes, he's my husband.' He… he started to hit me with his belt saying that he was going to kill the little bastard growing inside of me. Then he threw the belt away, and… he started touching me… oh God Demi, my own father. I began to scream over and over for him to get off me. He must have come to his senses because he fell to his knees crying. He said… 'I'm sorry, Audrey, I'm sorry, forgive me…please forgive me. I didn't mean it'." She could feel Demi stiffen up next to her.

"I got up, grabbed my boots, and put them on, and then he grabbed my foot, dragging me to the floor. He kept trying to kiss me."

Audrey was in tears as she recounted that horrible evening. "I slapped him really hard and told him that I hated him. Then I ran out of the room. I ran out of the house toward the stables. Krystal was right behind me. She must have been by the door, probably witnessed everything."

"Krystal never said a word. All she ever said was that you were sick. She said she went to sleep, and they found out in the morning that you were gone," Demi said, angry.

"She followed me to the stables, laughing. She asked where I was going. 'It's storming out here,' she said, all the while she was laughing. 'Yeah, maybe you'd better go,' she screamed at me, 'before Demi comes back… I'll tell him the truth about his precious Audrey and her father,' she said, laughing. I slapped her so hard and told her to go to hell. I knew you would never believe her lying ass. I threw on my hood and rode my horse into the dark night. The storm got bad about a mile out. I was so angry and scared that I kept riding faster and faster. It was hours before I realized that I was lost. I remember the wind blowing fiercely, and all that I was wearing was my hooded coat. I cried out to God for help and continued riding fast up one mountain and down another. I saw no one, just the rain hitting me in the face, and then something hit me hard in the head. The next thing I remember was waking up in a warm bed, burning up with fever."

"I was so sick that they didn't know if I would survive. That's how I ended up in the Valley of God. Allen, a very kind and gentle man, found me; his wife Debra nursed me back to health. They saved my life. I had lost my memory and fought to regain my past for years. It wasn't until I saw the charm around Brydus' neck that everything came back to me. You gave me the same charm for my fourteenth birthday." Audrey smiled, remembering that day. Then Brydus told me you were still waiting for me after all this time. I couldn't wait to be back in your arms again." She snuggled close to Demi, and he kissed her tenderly.

"We've both suffered, but it's over now... we're together, and I have two beautiful daughters. You have no idea how happy I am... and my love, if you ain't pregnant by the end of this month... I will be very surprised because now that I have you back in my arms, I will not even let you come up for air."

Demi kissed her shoulders. "I'm glad you haven't lost your sense of humor. That's one of the things I loved about you."

"Oh really, I thought it was... you know," he chuckled, teasing her.

She smiled and rolled her eyes, "That too, and now that you're older, hopefully, you know what to do with it," she teased him.

"I guess you're right. We were both two horny kids, but I made twins, right?"

"Shut up and make love to me again."

"I thought you'd never ask." Demi pulled Audrey back down on the bed, pinning her under him, "I love you, Audrey." She returned his kisses, remembering how wonderful it felt being in his embrace.

"I'm so sorry I put you through hell. If I hadn't left… we wouldn't have wasted all those years, and I can only imagine how much you were hurting because when I finally awakened, I thought you and Brydus were married. My heart ached so bad that I wanted to die."

"Never again will I let you out of my sight," Demi told Audrey as he moved her hair away from her face. Feeling the heat rise in him, kissing those places that made her moan with pleasure, she opened herself, guiding him inside her. It was more than a reunion of two lovers. It was a reunion of two souls that were incomplete without one another, and they finally found each other again.

The Valley of God

Brydus was helping her mother pack, and little Nicholas was resting quietly when someone rang the doorbell. Brydus peeked out the window only to see Derrick waiting on the steps.

"Mami, I don't want to see him."

"He's married, honey. He probably just wants to say hello."

Brydus took a deep breath and opened the door. They're stood Derrick, looking as perfect as always. He grabbed her and tried to kiss her on the lips. However, Brydus turned her face, and he ended up kissing her on the cheek instead. "Brydus, you look fabulous! Look at you! Wow! I always thought you were the most beautiful girl in town... but damn. I didn't think it was possible, but you got better looking. How are you?" Derrick asked.

"I'm well and happy, Derrick. You look... great too."

He waved at Christina as she walked past, but she just rolled her eyes, trying to ignore him. "Hey, I have a million questions to ask you. Walk with me to the park."

She thought for a moment, "Mami, I'll be back soon. Keep an eye on the baby for me?" Together they walked toward the park where they used to meet. It was a beautiful afternoon as they walked down the familiar path toward the small group of benches that sat in front of the water fountain.

"Do you remember this place, Brydus? When it was too hot, we used to jump into the fountain to cool off."

She crossed her arms, "No, Derrick, I would jump into the fountain to cool off. You would scream at me and call me crazy."

"Yeah, you're right. That's what I did. My mother would have freaked out if I ruined my clothes, but that was then. I heard you got married. I can't tell you how hurt I was to hear that."

"Are you kidding me? I heard that you got married two months after I left and that your wife was pregnant then," she spouted.

"Brydus, I'm not going to lie. I've made some mistakes. We all make mistakes, but that doesn't mean things can't be set right again. I've never stopped thinking about you, Brydus. I still love you."

"Oh…is that right? Did you still love me, Derrick, when you were screwing Brenda? While I was still here. Brydus, the big fool, no wonder everyone was laughing at me."

"Oh please… it's not what you think… the thing between Brenda and me… it was just sex. She knew that I was in love with you." Derrick looked so pathetic trying to plead his case. Brydus wanted to slap him. She tried not to compare him to Joaquin, but in her eyes, all she saw was the same old mama's boy.

"I think we should stop right here," Brydus said, trying not to sound angry. "I am happily married, and I heard you have a beautiful son. Derrick, it was never meant for us to be together. Let's leave the past where it belongs and just be friends," she added, trying to smile.

"I wish I could say the same about my marriage. I'm miserable, Brydus, the only thing that brings me happiness is my son, but this marriage was a big mistake. Before you left, all I did was drink, and well… she was there, so things happened. You are my one and only love, Brydus. Let's make this right again like it should have been. We can both right the mistakes that we've made."

Brydus now realized that it was a mistake coming without Joaquin. "Derrick, I don't want to hurt your feelings, but I love my husband. I didn't make a mistake. When I'm in his arms, I tremble with pleasure. When we make love, I cry out his name in ecstasy. He is the first breath that I take each day. He brought me to life, Derrick. I've never felt that way with you and never would. So please stop this nonsense about us being together. Go back to your wife." Brydus could see the anger in his eyes.

"How can you say that after all that we were to each other? We were meant to be together. Your son should have come from me, not from some other jerk."

"What we had for each other was just puppy love bullshit. I married a man who knows how to make me happy. He satisfies all my needs."

Derrick interrupted her, "But I'm not happy. Brenda is a pig. She's dirty, lazy, and a terrible mother. Things would have been so different if you had stayed, and we'd gotten married like we were supposed to."

"Not my problem. I'm in love with a wonderful man, and I have his son. I'm sorry you haven't found the right woman, but I'm not the one, Derrick. Now, I have some packing to do. I'm sorry that we couldn't be friends." Brydus turned to leave, but he pulled her arm and swung her around toward him, trying to kiss her.

"You belong to me, Brydus! It should have been you and me… the perfect couple!" Derrick shouted as his eyes got big and dark, filled with anger.

"Let go of me, asshole! Derrick, I don't want to hurt you. Now let me go!" Brydus pulled free and continued to walk toward her house, but Derrick followed her, pleading for her to stop and talk with him.

"Brydus, please, let's try again. I can't live like this knowing you're with someone else." Derrick grabbed her again, still wanting to kiss her, but she blocked his kiss with her hand.

She again pulled away, "what part of I don't want you, don't you understand? Now leave me alone!"

"Brydus, please, don't leave me again. Love takes time. I'm begging you," he pleaded.

Christina opened the door, her face red with anger. "Go home to your wife and son, Derrick." Brydus yelled. "I never want to see you ever again!"

Christina was watching him as he came up behind Brydus and tried to grab her by the arm. Brydus fought him off as he tried to kiss her yet again. As if kissing him would make her love him.

"Let go of my daughter Derrick… before I tell Alfonso. You know he'll come to your house looking for you and put a foot on your pathetic neck."

He let go of Brydus, frustrated, "She would have been mine if you hadn't sent her away! The nightmare that I go home to every night is your fault, Christina, you and Alfonso, who didn't have enough balls to keep her home where she belonged."

Christina glanced at him, her eyes large and angry, "Brydus was always too good for you. She is more woman than you could handle. She needed a real man, not a puss ass mama's boy. Now go home to the nightmare that you created."

"You will regret this. I swear you will," Derrick yelled, disappearing down the street.

"Spineless bastard, he has a lot of nerve showing his face around here," Christina erupted. "Thank God your father wasn't at home. He would have beaten that poor boy to death."

"What did he think that I was going to do? Just jump into his arms. I was such a fool!" Brydus exclaimed.

"No, my love, you were young and afraid, that's all," Christina held her daughter by her shoulders, "this is his mistake, not yours. As much as it hurt me to see you go… it was the best thing we've ever done. It allowed you to find yourself. I see it now," Christina said, comforting her.

"I was terrified, but I wouldn't change a thing, not even losing my dear friend Jake. Derrick is a loser. No wonder he was in such a hurry to marry me. God… when I think about it, it makes me sick to my stomach."

"The whole thing was very scandalous. It was something that even his family couldn't cover-up. Derrick's father forced him to do the right thing. You have no idea how relieved we were that you were spared from that mess."

Nicholas' fever subsided, and the family made arrangements to leave. Alfonso carried his grandson proudly, not regretting their decision. However, it was strange for them to leave the security of the only home they had ever known. Nicole was thrilled to be on the road, seeing new things. She never once complained about the long hours on her horse. The trip was a learning experience for the young teen. When they stopped at an inn, she got to meet and listen to the stories of other people who were traveling.

"Brydus, I can't wait to meet your husband and see your house. Ciara, I mean Audrey said it was huge," Nicole babbled happily.

"It's pretty big, monkey. We have many horses, a swimming pool, and a ranch with all kinds of animals. You'll see tomorrow. We should be there by midafternoon," Brydus guessed.

Quintanilla Estate

Joaquin looked out of his window, excited to see riders approaching. He called out to Demi and rushed to the stables for his horse. He rode out as fast as his horse could travel. When they were close enough, Brydus jumped down from her horse and ran into his arms.

"Baby, you're home!" Joaquin shouted. They kissed passionately and then reluctantly pulled apart when they heard the sound of someone clearing their throat behind them.

Brydus giggled, "Joaquin, I want you to meet my parents, Alfonso and Christina. My parents just couldn't let little Nicolas grow up without knowing his grandparents," she added, smiling at Joaquin.

"A pleasure to meet you both. You raised one hell of a daughter." They embraced.

Epilogue

The families gathered and blended like they had known each other all of their lives. Brydus now had all that she ever wanted. She had a wonderful husband, an adorable son, and her family. Her parents settled into their own home, not far from where Demi and Audrey lived.

Lupe married Big Willie a year after meeting and gave him a son. Krystal never got over losing Demi to her sister again and left New America, living in France with friends.

Monet was never seen or heard from again. However, there were rumors that she married a much older and very wealthy man who gave her everything she desired, but it was in exchange for her freedom. She would spend the rest of her days living like a caged bird.

Monet's daughter Isaura and Nicolas grew and became playmates. Isaura was a sweet, beautiful girl who adored her grandparents and her gypsy family.

Demi and Audrey moved closer to Alex. She wanted her girls to know their grandmother as well, and just as Demi predicted, Audrey gave birth to a son nine months after they found each other again.

Joaquin's family left Africa and returned home, excited to take their places as grandparents and great grandparents watching over their family as it grew. They relished in the life of their children and grandchildren. Guiding the next generation to become the best they could be, uniting the old with the new.

Brydus and Joaquin's lives became golden when they added two more beautiful children to complete their family. All the ugliness of that first year was forgotten, and the name of Monet was never mentioned, becoming a distant memory. Disappearing like a whisper in the wind.

So Begins The Chronicles of The Dark Days